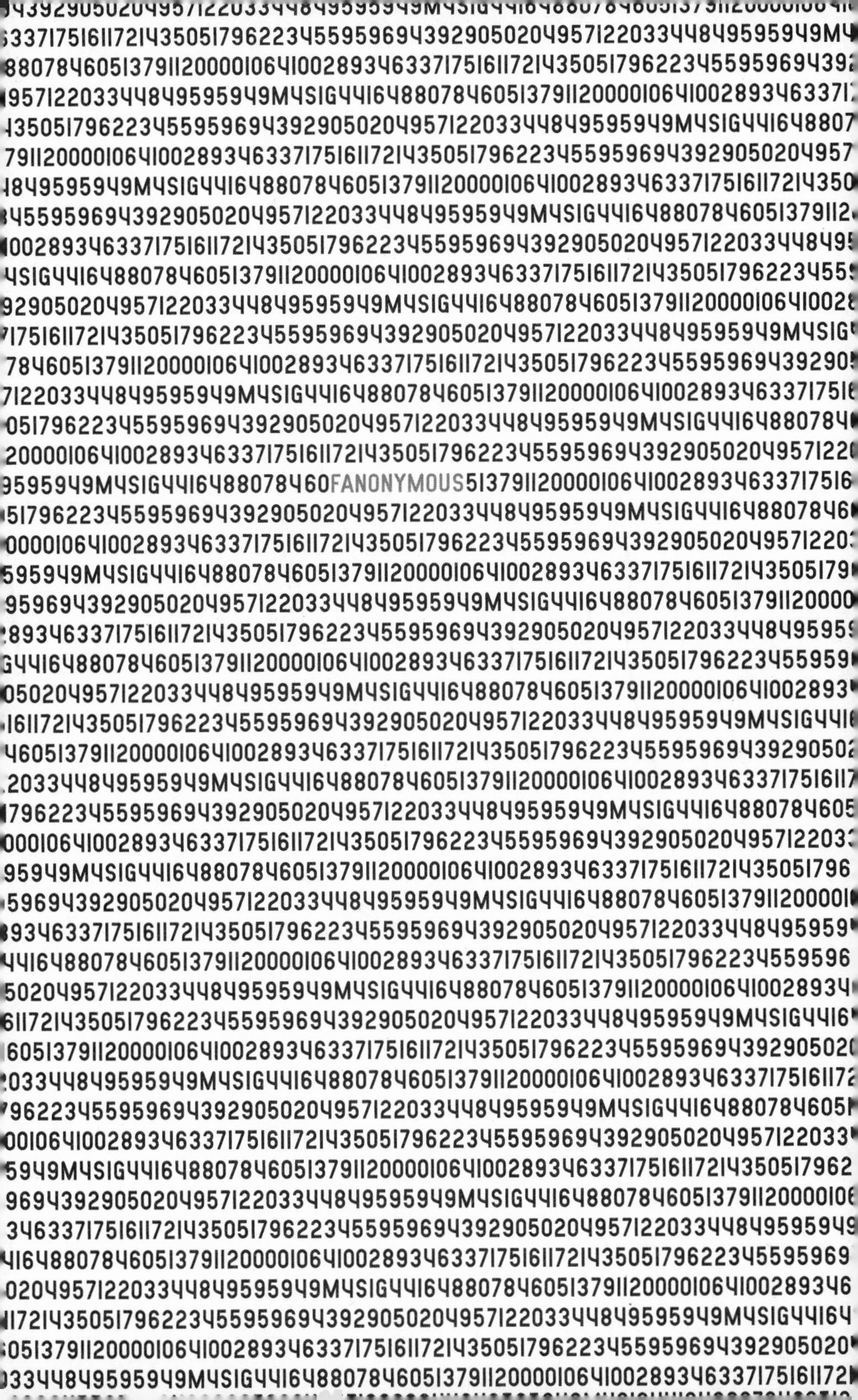

FANONYMOUS

FANONYMOUS

M.C. JOUDREY

AT BAY PRESS

Fanonymous

Design by M. C. Joudrey and Matthew Stevens.
Layout by Matthew Stevens and M. C. Joudrey.

Map of Winnipeg by Weldon Hiebert

Published by At Bay Press April 2019.

Library and Archives Canada cataloguing in publication is available upon request.

ISBN 978-0-9917610-5-0

Printed and bound in Canada.

This book is printed on acid free paper that is 100% recycled ancient forest friendly (100% post-consumer recycled).

First Edition

10 9 8 7 6 5 4 3 2 1

atbaypress.com

For

Ders

Daner

and Gordo

Upon whom the Velics are based.

Author's note:

Winnipeg is a real city. It has roads, buildings and lights. There are cinemas and grocery stores. People drive automobiles and raise children. Winnipeg is located in the centre of Canada (49.8951° N, 97.1384° W). Although this book is a work of fiction, all of this will happen.

Winnipeg...why?

In conversation with Toronto resident.

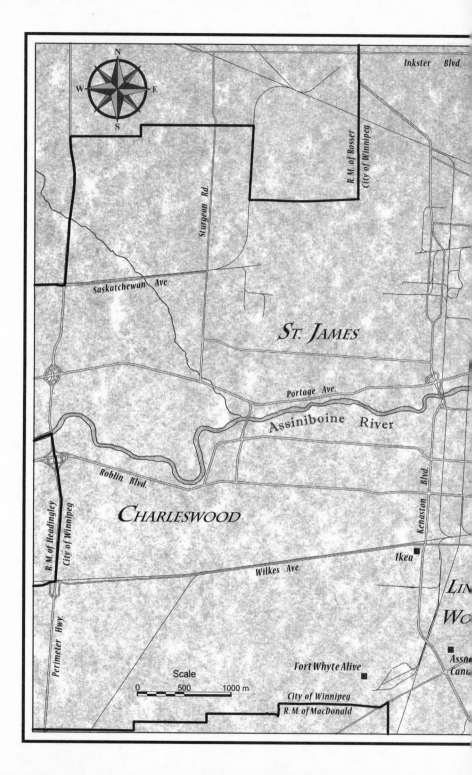

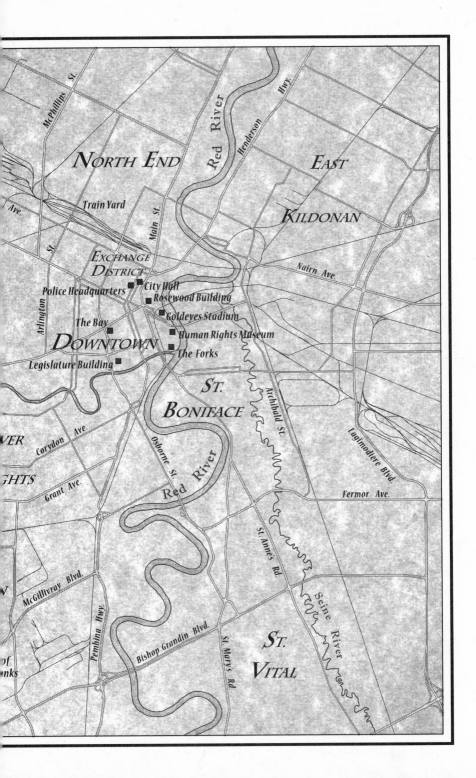

FANONYMOUS

Snow.

Earth and sky are devoid of colour. There are no beginnings or endings.

Then, a stain.

Blood.

Vehicle struck a white fox on Highway 59.

Bop!

Like that.

Kept driving.

Happened after midnight, before the storm quit. Carcass froze to the windrow at the shoulder of the road, encapsulated in a shell of ice. If not for the blood, no one would have ever known.

I see it.

A dead animal, the contrast of colour against snow, stands out like ketchup on a napkin.

Years later,

The premier changed the name of the highway, because of the plane crash.

It's just one of those things.

Manitoba.

That name changed too, for entirely different reasons.

Part of the Prairies. Bunch of wide-open space. Room for wind to move.

Nucleation occurs, crystallization upon frozen life. Call it hoarfrost. Happens when an object chills below freezing from radiation cooling.

Science, cousin.

It had settled, claiming the branches of the few deciduous aspens that were daring enough to take root in the barren earth.

Sun cut through horizon and blood-light spilled over all that white, then vanished, as though a murder never happened.

Violent?

Beautiful?

Both?

Fractals wisped on thin, dry air. Rays of copper refracted through kaleidoscopic mist.

It is quiet, it is cold, and it is Christmas day. The day I arrive.

And
Then
A child.

Alone, on the shoulder of the highway, standing in powder that was near weightless, like ash. The child, girl, kicked the powder to watch it rise and fall.

Rise and fall.

Rise and fall.

No life in any direction. Too early for motorists. Too early for any life, mechanical or flesh. The world, hers; she was *of* the vast expanse. The prisms were treasure, crystals of frost a crown, and the rays of the sun her last pulse.

You see,

She was cold,

Freezing,

Dying, actually.

Exposure will claim life.

The night before, she'd slept beneath boughs of blue spruce. The needles held flakes until a roof was over her young head. Long black ringlets tumbling off shoulder, frozen, brushed a tree trunk with the sound of hollow glass. Heavy eyes swollen, fatigued.

It was flat. Her eyes swept all the way to the horizon. She smiled, knew she had reached her destination.

Slowly, she shivered to sleep upon a bed of ice. Awful. Cold is only good when you know you've got someplace warm waiting for you.

Three years she had been on her own. Almost a month, trudging through foliage, deep snow, tiny legs.

Small backpack with sparse provisions, melting snow on tinfoil, carefully avoiding any sign of life. Had to. She needed to hide.

Identification, the most effective prison.

Anonymity, the understated last freedom.

The child needed to learn how to survive, face hardship, defeat insurmountable odds, if she would have revenge.

A child,

With thoughts of revenge,

Helluva thing.

Boreal began to thin. Highway came into view. No tuque, holes in her shoes. She had lost her last mitten a day ago near a brook. Everything had gone numb, a sensation not unlike warmth. She was too young to know what that really meant. The little body knew the truth though.

She took two steps forward and reached out for a wisp of snow glittering upon morning air. Then she collapsed, falling forward into powder, striking with force. Everything went still; she lay frozen with her environment. Weighted eyelids blanket her vision of the world, permanently.

A vibration could be felt. Faint at first, then a fresh, delicate dusting of snow puffed up gently around her limp body.

Her eyes opened, curiosity her last cerebral indulgence. Two pigeons stood near the frozen carrion of the white fox. They were not interested in it in the slightest. They were staring at her, garnet eyes glittering with morning sun.

The pigeon on her right was a solid powder-grey with the exception of its neck, which was gilded iridescent-marine. The pigeon to her left, almost lost in the snow, freckled with haphazard speckles of rust, spoke first.

Pigeons are harbingers.

Don't ask me why, maybe it's because they're everywhere, maybe because they interact with people often. It's just one of those things.

Of course,

The child could be hallucinating. There's that.

"Girl looks like shit."

"Indeed."

"Gonna die?"

"Yeah maybe."

The bird on the left strutted forward, head cocking back and forth, then stopped an inch from the child's face. She could feel the warmth of life from its body upon her fading cheek. The bird craned its neck forward to look into her hollow eyes.

"Dead already."

"I'm not dead, you filthy rat."

"Name calling." The bird swivelled its head back towards its companion. "You hear that?" It turned its attention back to the child. "Sticks and stones, rolls right off my back, kid. I'd save my energy if I were you."

The bird backed away, not from fear, simply to add distance. It studied the child for a moment. Found its position beside the other.

"What do you think?"

"Think? Kid lives or dies, who cares? One less human, got a ton more where that came from."

The speckled-white bird scratched at the cold earth with its talons and kicked powder behind it.

"Let's do what we have to do and book."

The grey bird slowly approached the child. It cooed as it walked, head bobbing backward and forward.

"We ain't your friend, kid. I'd pick at your skin if you were dead right now. We are animals. We eat. We defecate. Just like you."

The speckled-white bird stepped forward.

"There are rules, see. We get a message. Hell if I should know where it comes from."

"Quit dickin' around. I'm cold, and we got a warm coop waiting."

If the speckled-white bird could scowl, maybe it would have.

"The message is nothing more than a name, a surname." The bird tilted its head. "No clue what it means."

The bird turned its head and looked at its partner who stood patiently waiting for the delivery to be completed. The speckled-white pigeon returned its garnet gaze back to the child.

"Caldwell is the name. Caldwell." The bird turned and strutted back to its partner.

"Are we done here?" The speckled pigeon picked at its breast feathers.

"Yeah."

"Good, something's coming."

The girl couldn't hear the last part, only the flutter of wings. The birds had taken flight, frightened by a presence in the vicinity. They were the last things she would ever see.

The earth rumbled beneath her, the snow came to life violently, twisting upwards and then dropped, dead, back to its origin.

"She was lying face down. God, Jim, face down, next to a dead fox."

"Did she have any kind of identification on her?"

"No, nothing, I mean she's a kid, why would she?"

Jim scratched the silver hair on the back of his head. None of it made sense.

"All she had were a few biscuits, some beef jerky, a compass and a book of matches in this backpack."

"Jesus."

The two men stopped whispering and stared in silence at the girl lying in the bed. Her breathing heavy, her entire young body laboured to achieve even the simplest task.

Jim, a retired pediatrician, was seventy-four and lived a klick down the road. His longtime friend and neighbour, Arthur, had called him, said it was an emergency. Jim never expected anything like this.

A young girl, aged nine years, maybe less, had been found, near dead on the side of the highway about an hour outside of Vita. Arthur had been on his way to check his traps when he saw the bloodstain on the snow.

Arthur turned seventy-one last month. A fur trapper all his life. A tall man who had kept lean from hiking and snowshoeing along his trap line. He lived a simple life and other than Jim's friendship, lived a solitary one.

He and Jim had both lost their wives some years ago. They stared at the young child lying beneath the warmth of the covers.

Arthur couldn't seem to shake a growing paternal feeling as the girl lay asleep in his daughter's old bed.

He looked at Jim.

"So what do you think?"

Jim cleared his throat and said what they both had been thinking.

"I'm at a complete loss, Art. I truly am." He rubbed his chin. "You have to contact the police."

"No point in calling today. It's Christmas, anyway."

Jim sighed. His face pensive. Christmas was something he wasn't much fond of since his wife passed. And his children had their own lives.

"I guess you're right. Not much harm in letting the girl rest."

Arthur took a sip from his coffee and set the mug on the dresser.

"Will her sight return?"

"Hard to say for sure without proper tests."

Jim looked down at the floor. He *was* sure.

"I think she will remain blind."

"My god. To be so young. She will be in hysterics when she comes to."

Jim just shook his head, not knowing how to respond.

"And the frostbite? How bad is it?"

"A little good news there, her fingers are fine now and the tips of her ears should also make a full recovery."

Jim rubbed his chin.

"It's a bit of a miracle she's not dead. Had you found her even a few minutes later, well, I don't know. I don't think she'd be alive, though."

Arthur took the mug from the dresser and sipped at his coffee.

"I've seen some things over the years and some crazy things along my trapline. But this..." He didn't finish his thought.

Jim came through the door, shook the cold from his jacket. Weatherman on the radio said it was the coldest Boxing Day in over a hundred years. He exaggerated. Johns and Janes exaggerate, they do all the time, but it was cold. He hung his jacket on the coat rack and called out for Arthur.

No reply.

In the kitchen, Arthur sat at the table in front of a plate of food he hadn't touched. He stared out the kitchen window.

"Art, what's wrong?"

"She's gone."

"Gone, what do you mean, gone?"

"Strangest thing. I had sixty bucks in my wallet."

"What are you saying?"

Arthur looked down at the cold plate of food. Then he looked up at Jim. His eyes were vacant.

"Mary's ring. That's gone, too."

Sunday morning.

Shots rang out the same time church bells sounded, so that no one could tell the difference. The congregation dispersed, wished one another well, went about their day, while nearby someone was dying.

Overhead,

A vapour ribbon scars a lake sky, the only mar on its complexion. Good day for living, for flying, for dying, for church.

Warm,

The premier loosened his necktie, gave his throat air. He shook hands with the flock.

Skin to skin connects people.

Between humans, a handshake may have indicated greeting or arrangement. Nowadays, it's merely a formality, or tactic.

Just one of those things.

The premier, like other modern men, enjoyed shaking hands.

He shook hands so often, you'd think that's all he ever did. He did

do other things, though – smiled a lot, helluva bridge player,
And
He was in Ottawa for the vote.
Yup, *the* vote.
The vote that changed a nation.
Fur trade had done it centuries ago.
Then Industry,
Television,
And
The Internet.

You know,
It didn't matter much to the premier, it was just another vote, a bill hardly discussed or understood, much like other little bills that are passed. He just went ahead and voted. Then he went for lunch. Had poutine and a diet Coke.
Dietary dichotomies,
God bless 'em.

You see,
Governments are made up of people. People, like everything else in existence, are flawed. Well, almost everything. Math is absolute, math is perfect. Apparently, God is perfect, too, not to worry, we won't be making any irrelevant inter-religious philosophical detours herein.
Anyway,
A government is a corporation. It's not supposed to be a corporation, but that is exactly what it is. A prime minister is a CEO. And like all other corporations, governments are only as good as their people.
An oversimplification of the mechanics of democratic government is that people are afforded one vote. It's a right. A right is something that establishes human entitlement for any number of reasons. Most people don't know what their rights are. Some people don't have the same rights as others. Some aren't afforded any rights at all.
It's just one of those things.
So, one vote is what you get. This vote is used to elect one John to

be the boss, or, once in a blue moon, a Jane.

Name a boss you like.

Animals have such an inherent intolerance for subjugation. People are animals, yet people love subjugation. That's why corporate practice is so successful, from our government on down.

A manager is an animal. An executive is an alpha animal, and it goes on and on. Perpetuity. Look it up. Now look up the word *infinity*. Now look up the word *sempiternity*. All saying the same thing. Language is like management, riddled with rhetoric and repetition. Just a whole bunch of saying stuff and not much doing stuff.

And so,

Corporations expect more from you each fiscal year. If you made the company x last year, they expect you to make ten percent more than x in the new fiscal year. They might give you a one percent increase in salary, but you gotta turn tricks for it, you know, eat a treat off your nose, roll over, shake paw, the good stuff.

This continues on throughout the life of your career as though you have no limitations. But, people do have limitations, people do get sick, and people do die.

See,

Corporations are nothing more than buildings, walls, computers and parking spaces. Corporations don't raise children, they don't make love, they don't feel and cry. They demand more of you than any of your loved ones do. So does your government. Look at what they make you give?

But hey,

That's why you get to vote.

Now,

Do people educate themselves about potential political candidates?

No.

Do people know anything about a candidate other than what the candidate says in television interviews?

Not really.

Do we know who's paying for their campaign?

Nope.

Is a candidate's financial information and credit score and personal loan repayment made public?

Nah.

Should it be?

Shouldn't we know that a candidate has been bankrupt and about to handle an entire nation's finances, facilitate a nation's economy, tackle little things like national deficit?

You know,

Banks expect you to give them yours.

And

Banks have all of your money.

Banks make all of your money. Well, one bank does.

The Bank of Canada, a Crown corporation.

Crown is government, government is not Crown.

Yet,

The Minister of Finance holds all shares of the Bank of Canada on behalf of government.

Hard to follow?

Yeah,

It's supposed to be.

Banks run the show.

Banks...

Ta da!

Welcome,

To this little adventure,

About greed and the end of hard currency,

A story of identity.

It's also a tale about friends, who had very different individual hopes and dreams,

Just like you.

Friends who all met through a series of arbitrary events. Friends who didn't choose to be heroes and would never be regarded as heroes, but who ended up being the closest thing.

A hero is something that doesn't really exist.

Like a leprechaun,

Or safety.

These friends, who lived in a city, in a country, on a planet that was heading towards the end, had each other to keep them company, you know, for the ride and stuff.

That's actually more than most have.

Here's the skinny:

The galaxy won't notice the absence of Johns and Janes when we bite the big one. The universe won't hold a commemorative vigil, light a candle and all that jib. It will expand and shrink and expand without the presence of human beings. New life will emerge and so on and so forth.

There are no rules.

There are no favours.

No gods.

No exceptions.

There's only one angel left. He's cut his wings and taken up the holy vice and joined the steps of men and women.

How do you mount a revolution against the whirlwind?

Well, son, you just don't think about it. All that blind stubbornness is the only sword left in the scabbard.

Sound grim?

'Cause it is.

I don't do hope.

Hope, that shit's up to you.

But enough about this and enough about that. Let's go see about all those Johns and Janes, let's go see about friendship, let's see about

courage and if there are any heroes and leprechauns out there.
Let's go.
Onward,
Into the soup.

Dog tied to porch railing. Barking into the fog. Hydro-bus sweeps through Redwood. Kicks swirls of sand and debris. Headlights blunted by the sifting thick. North End roofs bowed from the weight of white burden.

The heat burns away morning, swatches of coloured stucco houses materialize, they daub a city palette. Sunlight spears through a canopy of ageless elms and splinters into glitter upon greasy streets blemished with pothole pockmarks.

Dickie Reimer says that some kid fell down into a pothole on Grosvenor so deep that it took firefighters nearly two days to fish him out.

That's true,

According to Dickie.

Word is, every Peg has thought about killing themselves. It's the cold, Dickie says. And just when there's no end in sight, winter finally draws to an end and everyone goes to the Bridge for soft-serve with sprinkles.

A few winters back, Bill Jib died of exposure while waiting for a hydro-bus. He died looking up at a faded billboard of a pomegranate and the words "'Tis the Season." It was in the news.

Death is news,

Birth never is.

Dickie says when the hydro-bus finally arrived, ol' Bill was found sitting, goose cooked, on the waiting bench, splashed with an advertisement of real estate agent Teddy Klassen. Bill was sitting on the face of the man schtuping his wife.

This happened.

She was stepping out on him. Johns and Janes step out on each other.

Bill was unaware, of course,

Clever minx.

Bit of a nexus, really.

'Cause,

Ol' Bill's last name later became Peg vernacular. Jib this and Jib that.

Along with words like:

Random,

Literally,

Good, good,

And so on.

Johns and Janes love repetition and rhetoric.

Did I say that already?

See,

You get the jib.

Dickie said it first, apparently.

It caught on because Dickie said it first.

He's got momentum.

Ties a community together.

Stuff like this goes on,

Down

In

Kitschy

Li'l

Winnipeg.

A city in the centre of a nation known for its frivolous use of apologies.

The moniker finds its etymology from Western Cree. Named by its Indigenous peoples, while at the same time overtaken with coercion and force by other peoples who already had enough of their own land somewhere else.

Dickie labels that conquering.

Happens all the time.

Ask the English. They've made a legacy of it, an empire of it. It's just one of those things.

And

Okay,

So,

I've been here a while. Wasn't supposed to end up that way, but hey, life, curveballs and all that jib.

Know the whole city inside and out. Dickie'll tell ya the place grows on you. Then he'll laugh, like it's funny.

Had a VJ's Special the other day, a burger, not an innuendo. Gave me a thrill. Grill-man made me laugh, not easy to do.

Look,

There's an IKEA.

It's not all bad.

Two large rivers wind through the expanse of the city, the Red and the Assiniboine. During spring, the city looks like Californian backyards in the '80s.

The 1980s.

Pools. Feel me?

Never enough sand in the winter and never enough sand in the spring.

It's flat. Really flat.

The only significant point of elevation in the city is made of garbage and is named Garbage Hill. Children toboggan down landfill during the winter.

That's really true.

There's a view from Tache across the body of the Red. It's worth a look. Ol' Louis is buried just down the street. We hanged him, too, ya know? Dickie says it took the noose four minutes to choke the life out of him. But how the hell does he know?

Johnny Mac:

He shall die though every dog in Quebec bark in his favour.

Yup, that was our first prime minister. Helluva guy. We put him on the ten note and tucked Louis into the provincial gumbo.

Of course,

The ten-spot no longer exists.

But then,

Neither does Johnny Mac.

Funny how the dead continue to alter the perception of the living.

I crossed the Provencher Bridge and walked past the Human Rights Museum. The only one of its kind in the country. It casts a shadow over the city's Indigenous peoples.

Dickie calls that irony.

Watched a kid on a skateboard kickflip down a set of stairs at the Plaza Skate Park. Caught a chill at the Forks. Coldest winter I ever spent was the summer I spent in Winnipeg. Someone said that. Who? I know I changed the end bit.

Temperatures in this city can achieve in excess of forty degrees centigrade in the summer and negative forty degrees centigrade in the winter, with equal precipitation on either side of the mercury.

Dickie says that by 1921, Winnipeg's population had grown thirty-one percent since the previous decade to just under 200,000 souls. The city was growing at a similar rate to Chicago's.

Much of the city's original architecture remains standing and is, for the most part, structurally sound. A glimmer of a city that almost was, but never was. Winnipeg's population today is 800,000; Chicago's is just under 3,000,000.

Now,

I'm not saying bigger is better,

But,

Bigger *is* better.

The city holds a number of disreputable titles:

Murder Capital of Canada

Most Racist City in Canada

Worst Roads in Canada

Winterpeg

Slurpee Capital of the World.

Pegs love that last one.

True story, someone once died from acute brain freeze after consuming a Super Big Gulp.

It was in the news.

Slurpees are news.

To be fair, it was a very hot day.

It's just one of those things.

It began to sour when the old Bay building at Portage and Memorial was overcome by derelicts. Portage Place had run out of room, Dickie says. It all just sort of happened. Simple osmosis. Golden Boy played coy witness, but never took the stand.

Some John tried to rob a beer vendor at a Jets game last winter.

No kidding.

Perp was thwarted by Dancing Gabe. Gabe danced all over his getaway plans. Actually, Gabe tackled the John. Held him down for three minutes before the John managed to squirm away. Gabe injured his shoulder. The perp escaped. The police checked every Tim Hortons for him, but eventually looked to the citizens to solve the case.

Meanwhile, Gabe got his picture with the mayor and a key to the city, the Jets made the playoffs. Gabe was seen a few weeks later dancing in a sling. News declared him a "Trooper."

Dancing Gabe is news.

So listen,

Pegs don't have it easy.

They have their problems,

And

It's cold, really cold, actually. For about eight months of the year. Imagine, you do all the same things everybody else in the country does in a twenty-four-hour stretch; feed your kids, take them to school, go to work, do some work, buy groceries, wash clothes, fold clothes, feed your kids again, stuff like that, but you do it while freezing.

And

To their credit,

Pegs don't care to fuss over the cold. Some wear shants all winter long just to show how much they don't care. Shants are almost shorts and almost pants. They're short-pants, a Peg thing.

That's true.

And very real.

As real as an engine block heater extension cord running from a cardboard insulated grill all the way to a side mirror. That kind of real, that kind of painful reality.

And so,

After all that sort of jib,

For another two months, Pegs have to worry about flooding. Then from the large tepid pools emerge the dreaded mosquitoes to terrorize Pegs all summer long. Sounds pretty unfair doesn't it? Sounds goddamn tragic. It gets worse, and not just for Pegs. For all of us.

Dickie says it all started with the penny.

We're going to jump from one thing to the next like this.

A lot.

Hold on tight.

The first Canadian penny was minted in the Christian year of 1858. Various designs and sizes remained in circulation for 154 years. Withdrawn and deleted from circulation in 2012, the last one minted the morning of May 4th that same year in Winnipeg at the Royal Canadian Mint.

It all started and ended with the penny.

No one could forecast how the elimination of such a negligible and arguably insignificant amount of hard currency would have such a profound impact on the future of currency and the Canadian economy, least of all the Canadian government. Forecasting has never been a government's strength, but they love a good census.

Winnipeg, like every other place in Canada, lost the last little bit of control, if there ever was any, over their own finances. Money, hard currency, legal tender notes, all were systematically recalled, mutilated and recycled into toilet paper. Seriously, toilet paper. People have been wiping their backsides with their own hard-earned money, and then flushing it down the toilet. One of those situations where you can laugh or cry, both work.

Canadians were given one year to exchange all existing hard currency with banks. Any hard currency exchanged was converted to electronic credit, which was then transferred, electronically, into the individual's bank account. Replaced with an electronic currency. Any hard currency not exchanged by the deadline would no longer be legal tender.

It was the responsibility of all Canadians to include any income unaccounted for in the following year's income tax filing. It was the CRA's highest grossing tax year of all time. The individual tradesperson, artist, bartender, general labourer and the like, who received cash payments, could no longer shelter income from CRA. Under-the-table had burst like a teenage pimple.

This currency, known as Canadian Currency or CanCur and abbreviated as <CC>, is now the only form of currency used in Canada. <CC> had no effect on international exchange and trading because all trading and exchange is already electronic anyway. Any individual intending to visit a foreign country could exchange <CC> with their respective financial institution and receive foreign hard currency for use in the country of destination.

So, how did this happen? Well, that's the question most people asked themselves. They say there are no stupid questions, but there are and that's one of them. You see, it was already too late to ask that question. Asking a question that's already been answered is like trying to fill a glass that is already full. You're just making a mess. The right question is why? Why did this happen?

A tumultuous economy? Maybe. A feeble government? Sure. Cost efficiency? Possibly. No, folks. In the end, it was simply control. Absolute control over the one thing human beings need the most, above all other things. Money. Well, almost all other things.

Now,

The Bank of Canada didn't have the resources, infrastructure or expertise to initiate and implement the electronic currency. So the Bank of Canada partnered with a multinational privatized financial company. All banks and financial institutions are governed under the new organization called the Association of Canadian Banks, or the popularized acronym ACB.

The large faceless corporation known then as DDC Financial was renamed The Association of Canadian Banks (ACB) and their headquarters were relocated to Winnipeg. Why Winnipeg? People speculate it's because of the city's cheap cost of living and its central location in the country. That speculation is entirely and catastrophically incorrect.

You know, life is full of troubles, all kinds of them, and there's not much worth living for these days in Winnipeg, or anywhere else for that matter, except art. Art is sacred. And of all the sacred arts that nobody cares about, which is in fact all of the arts, this tale is about the power of words. There's some math involved. Math is used for tying shoelaces and sending rocket ships to mars. Math, words, and the alphabet have been close friends forever. So, actually, this tale is about friends.

Horace would have you believe this yarn is all about one single song and flying. Jack would have you believe it's all about a single voice. We'll get to Horace and Jack, and the rest of this urban fairy tale, in a page or two.

But,

For now,

Let's talk automobiles.

Automobiles are mechanical forms of transportation. They consume fuel to operate. Fuel is derived from oil. Oil is a gift or a commodity, depending on the end of the seesaw you sit on. It is appropriated from the earth. Johns and Janes cut gigantic holes in the earth and the earth bleeds black. Factories are built to refine the blood into various forms of fuel. Factories also need fuel to operate. Factories expel megatons of pollution into the air and sea.

People love automobiles.

In Winnipeg, almost every person owned an automobile.

You know,

That's not all that different from most other places.

So,

This means there were nearly 1,000,000 automobiles in use in Winnipeg. These automobiles were used to go from point A to point B, or from here to there. Pretty much the same thing your legs and feet will do for you, just quicker.

Then one day, the automobiles all died at the very same time.

It was a really big deal. Happened on Tuesday. 5:00 p.m. on the button. It was planned.

It was a hack.

So, what's a hack?

Dickie describes it as the affectation of words and math used by a malicious source to manipulate a specific technology.

This hack killed all the cars in the Bell/MTS province.

So,

This hack thingy:

It was the most devastating mechanical hack in history. They say the architects effectively crippled the on-board diagnostics interface that manages the engine. Like everything these days, computers regulate cars. Hackers were able to successfully access the Engine Control Unit, firmware was uploaded and the carburetor flooded with fuel.

That's all it took.

That killed all the cars.

The news forecast that Winnipeg would be ground zero for raids, looting and devastation followed by loss of authority and then anarchy and, finally, chaos.

All the standard media platitudes.

None of that happened.

Here's what did happen:

Nothing.

Pegs just sucked it up. These are a special group of Johns and Janes, who live in a special place of endless trial and test. For them, this was just another thing, like a bad winter, or a speeding ticket, or The Reserve built in place of the old military base (which did in fact happen, by the way, and everyone has managed to get along famously, despite initial animosities).

The city sold the husks of the dead vehicles to the various salvage purchasers to be recycled and reused.

The revenue obtained from the recycling program was used to purchase and outfit the city with a fleet of commercial vehicles:

Ambulances,

Fire trucks,

Police vehicles,

Freight trucks,

Bulldozers, dump trucks and so on.

No more sirens, though.

Adios noise pollution.

The city implemented a new electric transit system. This consisted of hydro-operated buses. Cables ran along streets and intersections to feed the silent hydro-buses.

No taxis were allowed; private-use vehicles had been outlawed. Precautions were also taken to ensure the new vehicles were not computer operated and, thus, unsusceptible to future attack.

After an initial period of shock and adjustment, Pegs just went about their days. People got out their bikes and biked to work, took the bus, or, god forbid, walked.

It was a thing of beauty, and it surprised the world.

The reaction by Pegs towards the attack was spectacularly without event. International news coverage seemed to cease as soon as it was launched. No carnage, no story worth telling. No one likes a happy ending. They wanna see you bleed.

And

The ACB saw an opportunity.

You see,

Banks had been effectively nudging its clientele further and further away from interpersonal transactional banking, and though the loss of private rapid transportation had limited effects on the Manitoba population's day-to-day, it had a profound, yet veiled, impact on how Manitobans did their banking. You only went to the ACB headquarters if absolutely necessary.

An arm's length buffer has always been a defining trait in keeping people in the dark when you want them to be kept in the dark.

The inauthentic service gaze of a tired teller pales in comparison to the smiling children's faces in aviation-themed dreamscape wardrobes splashed across web-page banners sporting glittering prizes.

Dream you'll never have.

One that never existed.

Silver-tongue marketing subdues obstinance and opposition.

You're an adult now, you can dream, but that stuff hurts like paper cuts.

And so,

It became the opportune environment to test drive (pun intended) the new Canadian system of electronic banking.

It worked.

It worked really, really well.

It was institutionalized nationwide only three months after the initial Manitoba trials.

And while news media, journalists and rumour mills dropped the story, let the cars rust, found fat to chew elsewhere, intelligence agencies, both Canadian and abroad, did not see things quite the same way. Something had happened. Something rather big, irreparable. Someone had to answer for it. It just had to be done quietly.

The pebble in the shoe had to be knocked free before it ate a hole through the sole.

There's a chemical present in violets called ionone. It inhibits the ability for Johns and Janes to detect scent.

Makes it hard to smell smoke.

Dickie says there are tons of violets in Ottawa.

Ottawa is in the Interac Province. We used to call the province Ontario. Names change. Things change. It's just one of those things.

Ottawa is 2100 klicks east of Winnipeg.

So it's far.

And

Like all long-distance relationships, we don't see much of each other.

Ottawa is Canada's capital. A capital is also the big letter at the beginning of a name or a sentence. Dickie also calls it upper case.

Same word for both,

Different meaning.

Then,

There was Justine Kavanaugh.

She was in Ottawa.

Checking her eyeliner in a mirror the size of an Oreo. She looked better than she felt. Closed the compact and threw it into her purse, put the purse in her desk drawer and kicked it shut.

Swivelled in her chair and stood.

She pulled her suit jacket down to straighten it. Ran her fingertip over the enamel of the Nova Scotia flag lapel pin. She hated that it wasn't called that anymore. She had heard in the news they were going to change the look of the flags, too.

Then she saw it:

A flake of crust stuck to her lapel. She picked at it with a fingernail. Tragic.

Dry cleaning is goddamn tragic.

Like the name Brittany.

You can't blame someone for the name their parents gift them, only if they live up to it.

That's just around the corner, by the way.

Special Crimes Investigation Agent. That was the title. She frowned. She despised the title; it was rubbish. She was an investigator, that's all, that was the gig. Why did they have to go and dummy it with pretence?

Always do.

She went to the window. Her office overlooked the canal. The weather called for rain. So far, the sun was shining.

Everyone was taking advantage of the fortune. She watched people walking dogs, children playing games, couples holding hands, strolling the bank of the canal. Beyond the canal, traffic moved silently along highways and roadways. She shook her head.

God damn tragic.

It was Monday.

Monday is the day of the week when working stiffs start working again. A working stiff is someone who – well, it's actually everybody.

Pretty much everybody.

She had spent the weekend behind her desk buried in paperwork. On Friday, the agency Director had called her, um, directly.

Justine sat back down in her chair and paged through the electronic dossier on her tablet. Nothing notable. Blackhats were hard to trace, the anonymity, the seclusion of the cipher created painstaking work. Attribution is difficult to determine, origin near impossible to finger. If there was a lead, it was often a red herring. The Internet protocol address was either a shell or a proxy.

These people moved and shifted through the hollows and shelters of the Dark Web. Illicit sheltering provided via TOR Network, which effectively anonymized the user's activity. The browser provided safe passage to and from.

The Dark Web, a hunk of web space within the Deep Web, used as a playground for cyber-pirates. Intentionally hidden, like an ocean island on a starless night – it's there but can't be seen.

Justine sighed.

Used to be simple. Follow the IP, arrest a suspect. Now you couldn't tell open space from cyberspace. It was the beginning of blurred realities.

Something about the initial analysis of the endgame didn't quite sit well with her. There was something more, something in the ether, the intentional word salad masking the lean, elegant subtext, a statement. Political? Maybe. Sociological? Maybe that was it. She had a theory. What she needed was a lead.

A reminder bubble popped up on her tablet, and she looked at the clock in the corner of the screen. It was time. She tapped the screen on her phone. No messages.

She locked her tablet and put it in its case. She grabbed her external drive and put that in the case, too. Must not forget the presentation. She tucked files underneath her arm and left.

Her heels left the carpet of her office and hit the tiled hallway with a clack.

Justine was prepared. She'd spent the weekend putting together

29

her findings and research. Still, how do you tell the Director of the agency they had it all wrong?

A thought suddenly crossed her mind.

Maybe I'm wrong? Maybe it's too much of a leap?

No, the signs were there. Her past training and intuition all pointed to the same thing. A bigger picture, someone was trying to send the world a message.

But,

What was the message?

This was what she had to decipher, and that was the missing piece of the puzzle she didn't have at the ready for the Director.

The meeting room was already full. Justine snuck a glance at the clock on the wall. Was she late? No, the start time was 1:00 p.m.

"Not to worry, Agent Kavanaugh. We convened at noon to discuss preliminary matters. Your timing is impeccable. Have a seat and feel free to begin when ready."

Justine had never met the Director before, and to have him address her personally meant there was much more going on than she had been made aware of. Sitting at the long oval table were fourteen men, the who's who of the agency and a few faces she could not identify. She was the only woman in the room.

Goddamn heels.

She touched her thumb to the screen of her tablet, synced the USB to the external drive and opened her analysis data.

"No point in beating around the bush, gentlemen. You're all aware that three months ago the city of Winnipeg was ground zero for the most effective and devastating mechanical hack in history."

"We already know this, Agent Kavanaugh."

This from a man she did not recognize.

Justine stood up and made firm eye contact with the man. She walked over to him and extended her hand.

"We've not been introduced."

The man looked at the Director, and the Director nodded. The man took Justine's hand and shook it.

"I'm CIA. Agent Abernathy."

Justine took her hand back, wiped it on her pant thigh, and returned to her seat. So, the Americans did send someone.

"We all know what happened. Good. What I'm concerned with is why? And not the *why* the journalists have been asking, which is the same *why* our agency has been asking. Why did this happen? That's the wrong question, or at least not the most important question. What we should be asking ourselves is why Winnipeg?

"The Auto-Hack was authored by competent architects. These architects, whoever they are, have displayed powerful programming prowess and a singularly unique approach to their writing. Fact is, we've never seen anything quite like this before – well, almost never."

"Agent Kavanaugh holds a doctorate in computer science and excelled in proficient code writing and robotics at MIT. She is an exceptional Greyhat and she is one of only two people to successfully hack the NSA mainframe. This was done while she was still a student as part of security testing of new systems."

The Director's comments made her feel awkward. He almost smiled at her. He couldn't, though; the lines of his face had been mapped decades ago and wouldn't permit it.

"That's why she's here in this room and that's why every single one of you needs to pay very close attention to what she has to say here today."

The Director nodded at her.

"Right, okay, but I had seven other writers at my disposal running my code through various methods. You see, every code has a unique style to it, not unlike a signature or, better still, a fingerprint. If we follow the style of the code, we might be able to determine cyber identities for these hackers. Discovering their handles can quickly lead to a citizen identity." Justine shook her head. "The problem here is that this type of dynamic code requires multiple users operating at the same time sharing and initializing the code among other tasks. The code is built into one conscious stream and then birthed."

The Director leaned forward, put an elbow onto the cold glass tabletop and rested his chin on his hand. He stared at the screen for moment, and then he turned his gaze at Justine.

"So what does that mean?"

"It means we are chasing one line of code authored by ghosts."

"Ghosts, Agent Kavanaugh?"

"Look at it this way. You can't have two people pull the same trigger of a gun. One person pulls the trigger, one suspect. Track the weapon, you find the suspect. Here we have lines of code authored by different individuals. We have no idea how many different authors. These hackers have combined their individualistic codes into one. This makes tracking them very difficult, if not impossible."

"So where do you suggest we start?"

"Start with amateurs, low-junk wannabes, wade through the Byzantine and work our way up to the elite. There are very few truly unique elite hackers like this in the world. We know them all. This isn't their first rodeo. We need to find old breadcrumbs. And we need to figure out the answer to my earlier question. Why Winnipeg? We figure out the answer to that and we narrow our scope considerably."

"Thank you, Agent Kavanaugh."

Back in her office, Justine slumped into her chair. She took a sip from her coffee mug, it had gone cold. She swallowed anyway. She held her thumb on the screen on her tablet, and it came alive.

The phone on her desk rang.

"Agent Kavanaugh. Alright. Yes. I will, sir."

Justine hung up. It was the Director. She had been appointed lead agent on the case. In fact, she had been the only agent assigned to the case. A high-profile case like this could be the break she needed... It was her shot, a big one, at advancing her career.

She tapped a finger on her desk and thought about where to begin. She needed tea, green, loose-leaf Sencha. She pulled open her desk drawer and started to put some leaves into a wire ball for steeping.

Someone knocked at her door and she tucked the tea back into the drawer.

"Come in."

"Agent Kavanaugh."

"Agent Abernathy." She was surprised to see the CIA agent post-meeting. She did not let it show. "How may I help?"

"I have spoken with your Director. He has graciously offered me your time."

This was interesting. An American presence on this case didn't surprise her. After all, the threat did prove global in scale, even if it happened on Canadian soil. It was Agent Abernathy's guarded approach that now elicited further reflection.

"So?"

Justine smiled. The smile threw Abernathy.

Abernathy rubbed his chin. He had a square jaw and a smooth, shaven face that wasn't handsome but had its qualities.

"Maybe it would be best if you just spoke frankly, Agent Abernathy."

"I wish it were that easy. The matter is delicate."

"Aren't they all?"

This time Abernathy smiled.

"A year ago, we had a situation in Manhattan."

He handed Justine his tablet. She swiped through its contents. She looked up from the screen and did her best to hide her growing interest. If the American agent sitting opposite her noticed the subtle change in her appearance, it didn't show.

His eyes locked with hers.

"We want you to deal with this as well."

It was pomegranate season,

In Winnipeg.

It's just one of those things.

The passenger on the bus offered his hand. The hand, covered in pomegranate juice, belonged to a fella named Horace Mackie. Jack didn't think much of it, another rider shaking his hand; maybe it was a Canadian thing. There are a lot of Canadian things, Old Dutch Chips, K-Tel, Nutty Club, McNally Robinson Booksellers, Harlequin Publishing, Salisbury House.

And Winnipeg blushes modestly.

And,

Just like that,

Jack gave the man his hand.

The hand was sticky and a little wet. Jack didn't mind; his hands had been dirty before. He didn't know the man had a head full of alarming notions. I mean, he wasn't gonna build a wall, but a weirdo on the bus, come on. This strange passenger didn't know exactly where he was from either, and one doesn't often question the stability of one's own notions.

Until it's too late.

So, maybe they both felt like talking, people talk. That's how things get moving, by talking.

Now,

Just so we're clear, talking and communicating are two different things. Most people talk and leave communication out of the business altogether.

Some people talk to themselves and get on quite famously in their own company. Horace preferred the company of others, especially his best friend Kip.

Jack looked out the window. The hydro-bus silently put distance between its passengers and the Seasons of Tuxedo shopping centre. The white dashed lines of the road skipped by like stones upon the surface of a concrete lake.

It was hot,

The air thick and heavy.

"You ever see *Rear Window*?"

Jack looked blankly at the man.

"*Rear Window*?"

"The Hitchcock film."

"No."

"What about *12 Angry Men*? You know, the one where twelve white guys determine one man's guilt or innocence."

"Yeah, actually, I did see that one."

"It's as hot and humid as that tonight."

No kidding.

It was true.

It was the kind of night where you sweat just from breathing. The same kind of night mosquitoes adore. Jack scratched his arm. It was covered in bug bites. A few floating bugs could be seen hanging upon the stagnant air inside the hydro-bus.

"Mosquitoes are thick tonight. Are they always this bad?"

"You're kidding, right?"

Jack shook his head.

"Man, you're in mosquito country. Better get yourself some Spekel."

"Spekel? Oh yeah, I've heard of that stuff. You drink it, right?"

"It's a mixture of natural loose leaves and minerals farmed right here in the province. You steep it. It's a tea. Keeps the little pests at bay. Very effective. My friend invented it."

"Really?"

"Uh huh. I've got another friend who invented Kleenex."

The latter was a lie. Kleenex had been invented by Kimberly-Clark as a disposable nasal tissue to replace cloth tissues carried around in people's pockets. People love to throw things away.

Horace pulled a section off the pomegranate and handed it to Jack.

"Thanks."

"'Tis the season."

Jack put a few juicy seeds in his mouth.

"How do you mean?"

Jack chewed on the seeds. They were both sweet and tart at once.

"Pomegranate season."

Jack chuckled.

"Yeah, right."

Horace wiped his hands on soiled work pants.

"I know, hard to believe it was ten years ago that the tree just appeared in the windiest intersection in the world."

Horace was tuning a portable radio. The static sounded like crumpling paper. He found a frequency and music came through the monaural speaker. He smiled absently.

"Not sure I follow."

"The pomegranate tree."

"*The* pomegranate tree?"

"Yeah."

He said it like Jack should know exactly what he was talking about.

It was Dickie who saw it first. His story goes that someone planted the tree in a pothole in the middle of the Portage and Main intersection. It only moderately disrupted traffic, so the city left it, thinking that the winter, which loomed around the corner, would take care of the little problem for free and they could pull the dead trunk out in the spring.

But it didn't die.

It survived the winter,

The freezing temperatures,

And

It bloomed and bore fruit.

The mayor proclaimed it a city landmark and made pomegranates the official fruit of Winnipeg.

It's made of magic.

Johns and Janes touch the tree trunk for luck.

Anyway, that's the story,

According to Dickie.

It made Horace really happy because pomegranates were his favourite fruit. Horace put the rest of the fruit away in his lunchbox. He smiled.

It was a smile that made you want to smile too. It was honest, even if he wasn't always. A bright smile contrasting against brown eyes that were deep enough to be black, and maybe they were. His hair was. It hung long just above his shoulders. There was a warm glow on his cheeks that radiated over his dark, clean complexion.

Jack noticed a pink scar that went up the left side of his throat. It was a finger in length. He saw Jack looking at it and said that was how he'd met his best friend.

There's a story there.

Long story.

And maybe there'll be time for it later.

I make no promises.

Jack looked down the aisle of the hydro-bus. Three people exited at their stop. He and Horace were alone on the hydro-bus. Horace stared out the window of the bus. His face pensive.

"Look at the guy holding the picket sign. What's it say?

Ha! Hilarious."

Jack looked out the window.

"Yeah, we've got lots of them back home. Call 'em street mystics."

"Street mystic, eh?"

Horace took one last look at the man with the picket sign. He was fond of learning strange things. Street mystics were new to him.

He turned his attention back to his radio. The station needed slight tuning to adjust the dead frequency.

"Used to love listening to Goldeyes games."

"Goldeyes?"

"Baseball."

"Ah."

"You're American." Horace was telling Jack, not asking. "What brings you to Winnipeg?"

"I just moved here."

"Heh, moved?" He laughed. "Everyone here is trying to find a way out and all that jib."

"Huh?"

"Wait, listen, best part of the song."

Horace turned up the radio so they could both hear it and he sang along.

"Dr. Feelgood!"

He bent forward to turn the volume low again. Something fell from his shirt pocket. A photo lay on the bus floor. It was old and worn. In the photograph were a woman and man. The man had his arm around the woman.

"You dropped something."

Horace picked up the creased photograph and tucked it back into his shirt pocket. It seemed important to him. If it was, he said nothing about it.

"The Shags, never hear them on the radio. Great tune, one of the best. But it's not the best. You know what the best tune ever is?"

Jack played along and shook his head.

"Yeah, no one ever does." Horace frowned as he thought about it for a moment. Then the pleasant smile returned to his face. "'Crazy

Things' by The Quid. Greatest tune ever. A masterpiece. Really is." He traced his fingers along his scar and was again preoccupied with inner thought.

"So, Winnipeg, huh?"

"Yup."

"You stay long enough you become a real estate agent or a cop. Catch my jib?"

Jack chuckled, then he realized the man was serious.

"Awful twist, ending up like that."

"Oh, yeah."

Jack didn't care. Horace didn't care that Jack didn't care.

"I don't think any kid dreams of seeing their face on a garbage can or bus bench. You ever dream of wanting to hide out behind a tree and hand out traffic infractions? Thank god that one's finally over." He smiled at Jack. "Crazy things. Catch my jib?"

Jack nodded, but didn't follow him at all. He realized every city had its nuances, those subtle social substances that make a place uniquely, well, unique. He'd only been in Winnipeg a few days, it was all fresh.

It wasn't until much later that Jack wondered how Horace had known he was American. The guy seemed a little eccentric. Jack was eccentric.

"Seems pretty empty at night."

Jack pressed his cheek to the window. The full moon was a dollop of creamed honey. Chasing the illuminated bauble was a mottling of smoky clouds.

"Well, there's not much here, ya see. But, we do sell more Slurpees than motor fuel. Especially these days."

"Ha! Yeah, kidding, right?"

Horace looked at Jack. He was uninitiated. People do that to other people when they're not versed in the standard local customs and culture. It's just one of those things.

Horace didn't answer Jack's question. He figured Jack would find out about Winnipeg's obsession with the frozen beverage all on his own. Instead, he turned up the radio. The news called for rain, and then reported that the fifty-two bison, which had escaped from Fort-

Whyte a few weeks back, were still on the lam.

"Can you believe that? You know, a bison weighs 600 kilograms. It's not like they're a lost earring."

"So they're just wandering the city? Where could they go?"

"Beats me. Yesterday's news said they were last seen stampeding right down McGillivray. That's just up the street from where I work. A red light camera caught them speeding."

Jack rolled his eyes.

"It's true. Had a photo of them and everything. A city tech found it when he was reviewing the week's traffic infractions. Can you believe that? Cars have been dead for years and the city is still checking the old traffic cameras."

They both had a laugh. Horace turned off the radio. He looked at the bags Jack was carrying.

"Bought a few things. A microwave and a toaster, everyone needs a toaster. Who needs a microwave."

It was an observation, not a question. Jack had a feeling he didn't owe the man an answer.

Horace looked at him again, his coffee-brown eyes brewing with interest.

"Didn't buy any personal items."

"I don't follow."

"You know, picture frames and stuff. You looking for a fresh start?"

Jack only smiled.

"Yeah, me too, one of these days real soon, it'll happen for me. I'm gonna fly right outta this place."

Jack assumed he meant get on a plane and fly to another place in the world. Of course Horace meant something altogether different. He always does.

It was almost midnight. Jack gazed out the window again.

"What street is this?"

"Portage Avenue. But Pegs pronounce it Poortudge."

"Pegs?"

"Yeah, Peggers, Winnipeggers. A nickname. They've got nick-names in America, don't they?"

Jack chuckled. "Yeah, we do."

Jack watched as the checkers of cheque-cashing joints and pizza parlours clipped by. He had left New York just a few days ago and already it seemed so far away. A tiny pulse of fear crept up on him. He was stuck in this place and was afraid that if his past didn't kill him, acute boredom would.

Cue the tumbleweed.

He took a deep breath to stave off the pangs of anxiety.

"What do you do for work?"

"I was, am, between jobs at the moment."

Horace said nothing. Jack continued to gaze through the window. The emptiness on the other side was like a vacuum pulling life into that emptiness. He felt his chest tighten, his temperature increase and his head spin. His anxiety attacks were getting worse. He rubbed his hands over his face and took a few deep slow breaths.

Horace stood up and adjusted the window on the hydro-bus to let some cool air into the stuffy carriage. Jack was thankful for the fresh air and smiled at Horace as thanks for the gesture.

"I was an artist." Jack looked down at his hands. "Long time ago now."

Jack couldn't believe the words coming out of his mouth. Telling these things to a perfect stranger.

Horace sat back down in his seat and pushed up his sleeves to feel the air against his skin.

"I work at the IKEA."

Jack looked at the marks on the man's bare arms and hands.

"Um, are those bite marks?"

"Occupational hazard, I guess."

He rolled down his sleeves. Jack was shocked, but before he could say anything, Horace had already changed the subject.

"My real passion is video games, but no money in video games." He rubbed his chin. "Or art, I suppose."

Jack realized the man felt no urge to offer more information about the marks.

"Depends, I guess."

"Yeah, on what?"

"On how good your publicist is."

Horace let out a small chuckle.

"We don't get many of those around here."

He pointed out the window as they passed the old Hudson's Bay building.

"See that old building? My grandfather designed it. He was a great architect. You've probably heard of him."

"Really, that one there?"

"Yup. Fell upon some hard times, though. Too bad, really. Nothing more than a flophouse now. I guess people need flophouses more than striped coats these days."

Horace swivelled back in his seat and smiled at Jack.

"Where you headed?"

"The Exchange. I have a condo there."

"I'm close by. I live with my friends at the Big Corner."

"Big Corner?"

"Portage and Main."

"Ah."

Horace fussed with the antennae on the radio.

"Look here, I don't meet too many new people and it'd be really inhospitable of me if I didn't extend a courtesy."

Jack felt uneasy. He didn't know where this was going and tried his best to sound appreciative.

"Not necessary. It's been a long night."

"Nonsense. Some friends and I get together at our place after my shifts for a nightcap. We hang out with some of our compadres, a few nice ladies, too, ya know. Let me be the first to offer you a drink in your new hometown."

The sincerity on Horace's face was almost enough to guilt Jack into saying yes.

Almost.

"I think I better get home and plug in my toaster. Been here a few days and still haven't managed to get my act together."

"You'll have all the time in the world to stare at your white walls and empty rooms. Come for one drink, meet some new people and see a little of the city. Truth is, Winnipeg is about who you know, not where you go. Trust me."

Jack could see the man wasn't going to give up.

"Plus, I'll walk you home after, keep you safe. Free time, free drink."

"Okay, sure."

Jack satisfied an urge to scratch the stubble along his jaw. He took a moment and thought about why he said yes. He'd always been a risk taker, but this didn't feel risky, it just felt different.

Maybe it was because he was truly alone in a new city. He knew it was partly because Horace seemed so genuine, even if he was a little strange. Jack didn't mind strange. In fact, he was more comfortable around strange than mainstream. It could be because Jack had left everything behind so abruptly. Maybe it was none of that or all of it. Either way, he didn't go home that night, not because Horace wouldn't have really walked him home, but because he would have; Horace is just that kind of fella. It was because he'd met people and carried on all night and well into the morning. Someone mentioned Salisbury House. So naturally they all went to get some breakfast.

A fluorescent ceiling light fought for electricity and finally won, made a soft tinny ping sound, then stopped flickering. It was a problem that had already been addressed, deduced by a series of clues, such as exposed wiring, the remains of an old ballast on the counter-top, and, of course, the electrician's ladder leaning against a wall, if anyone cared. No one cared. Blood rich with alcohol and a poor empty stomach meant hunger was boss.

The odour of stale perogy and congealed grease still cloyed at the air from the night before.

The Salisbury House on Leila is a twenty-four-seven kind of place. Everything in the joint coloured white, red or blue, like someone fed an American flag after midnight. Of course, Jack had never heard of Sals. Everyone else had, because everyone else at the booth were genu-ine Pegs.

6:00 a.m.

Give or take a tick.

A server, the server, the only server in the place, because it was

6:00 a.m. and the tail end of the overnight shift, swiped a handful of blond-pink curls away from her eyes. They looked tired, and the blue in them resembled antifreeze in a white jug. A diamond fleck, spit through the corner of her nose, caught light. She wore a t-shirt with the Sals logo, a red roof and cotton fabric sheltering small hidden breasts. She shifted her weight from one leg to another and cradled a stack of menus in her arm. She was tall, thin and white.

She started to hand out menus, but everyone waved them off. They knew what they wanted to order. Jack reached for a menu. Kurt slapped his hand away, and then looked at the server.

"I'll order for the virgin."

Kurt smiled at her. She did her best to return the sentiment.

"So, what'll it be, guys?"

Kurt noticed that despite her fatigue, she didn't need a notepad for the orders. He liked that she didn't need one. He ordered first.

"I'll have the Double Mr. Big Nip Platter. Substitute my fries for chilli cheese fries. And the virgin across the way here will have the same."

Jack chuckled.

"Classic Sals Sauce?"

"Yes, ma'am!"

"Any side pomegranate? 'Tis the season."

"Sure."

The rest of the table placed their orders, and the girl went to holler the orders into the kitchen.

A wedge of lard hit a grill, and there was finally a soundtrack to the carrying-on happening at the one and only occupied table in the restaurant.

Now listen, cousin,

Let's talk friendship.

Friendship is when strangers meet or are introduced and, through similar interests and a mutual fear of loneliness, they decide to go forth and live, love and thrash the world together. With friends, you can talk the way you want to talk, you can dress the way you want to dress. If you can't, they're not a friend.

Get yourself a friend,

You'll be glad you did.

The table seating six hungry young men is filled with true bros. Bros is short for brothas, another noun for friend – lit-dicks call that vernacular.

The world should be filled up with bros, it should be filled up with sistas, but it's not. The world should be full of kindness, patience and love, but it's not. The world is full of debt and traffic lights and religion.

Go figure.

A dragonfly hovered over the table. It had flown indoors somehow. Eventually Kris waved his hand in the air at it, and the insect lighted on the ledge beside the booth to rest its wings.

Kurt got up from the table to grab the morning paper, which was sitting on top of a trash can. He sat back down and started to read.

"Is it me or are dragonflies, like, everywhere now?"

Kip pointed at the perched dragonfly. He took out his cell phone to snap a picture of the insect.

"They eat mosquitoes." Horace felt compelled to come to the insect's defence.

Devlin scoffed. "They're disgusting."

"I think they're intriguing."

"You would think that."

"Yes, I just said so."

Kurt wasn't listening. He was engrossed in a story in the paper. "Catch this. Last night, around 10:00 p.m., a man taking his dog for a walk inMemorial Park, beside Broadway, came upon a herd of bison grazing the park. The man recognized the bison as the same missing from FortWhyte Alive. He returned to his residence and called the authorities. By the time they arrived, the bison were no longer there, but conclusive evidence of their presence is irrefutable."

Kurt folded the paper and threw it on the table.

Devlin pushed the paper aside. "So they just disappear now, too?"

Kris was watching a mandatory advertisement on his phone. He continued to stare at the screen as he spoke. "It's like they planned the whole thing."

He removed his laptop from its sleeve and set it on the table. It didn't take him long to figure out the password for the Wi-Fi in the restaurant, and it only took a few extra minutes for him to establish a path towards the hack he was trying to initiate. Minutes later, he turned the laptop towards the other side of table.

"Voila! They were there, all right."

On the screen was a satellite view of Memorial Park from last night. Grazing the park was a herd of fifty-two bison.

Kurt was astonished.

"How did you get this?"

"Don't ask."

"Yeah, a better question is where did you get it from?" Devlin chuckled when he said it.

With Kris, it was always better to not know.

"Everyone's got standards. Yours, my friend, cuts on questionable. Can't arrest someone for being questionable. Could arrest you for that shirt, though."

"Don't blame the shirt."

Devlin slouched down into the booth.

"You need goals, man."

Kris smiled.

"The only goal I have is to end up someplace where I don't have to wear socks ever again. If I can do that, I figure I made it."

Horace put his hand up to acknowledge the value of his friend's comment. Kris high-fived him.

"I'm with Kris. One day I'll…"

"Fly right out of here."

Devlin finished his sentence for him.

"Yeah, we know. Heard that jib a million times already."

Devlin shook his head. "Jeez, this crew is something else. And now it's growing." He pointed at Jack.

Then the server arrived with plates of food precariously arranged along her forearm. They looked like they would fall at any moment, but she had honed her craft and elegantly began placing the first round of plates in front of their new owners.

"Damn, that looks good. Why is it that every time I get liquored, I have an uncontrollable desire for greasy food?"

Devlin's question was rhetorical. Horace answered it anyway.

"Hypothalamus."

"Hypo-what?"

"Hypothalamus."

"Do you ever make any goddamn sense?"

"It makes perfect sense," she said as she dropped the last plate of food on the table.

Six faces stared blankly at the girl who, while serving their food, put down extra napkins and silverware and topped up the water glasses.

"The ventromedial nucleus of the hypothalamus controls desire for food intake. The hypothalamus is directly affected by alcohol consumption, causing your desire for high-calorie food intake to increase."

The girl tilted her head towards Horace.

"Your friend is correct."

Horace was smiling.

Kurt was in love.

Devlin was baffled. "How the hell would you know?"

"I'm pre-med." She turned from Devlin and looked at Horace. "Your friend here's a dick."

Horace's smile grew. He appreciated the proper use of vernacular.

Kip laughed.

"She's two for two."

"Will there be anything else? Coffee, tea, Spekel?"

Kurt's heart was thudding in his chest.

"You're doing great."

The girl had enough of these clowns and walked away.

Devlin was pouting. "No tip for her."

Kurt stared at him.

"You'll tip her and you'll tip well, or I'll seriously mess

your hypothalamus."

"You know the hypothalamus is also a factor responsible for sexual behaviours. This could be the reason you haven't been laid in such a long time," Horace said as he put a forkful of food in his mouth. "You should get checked."

Devlin took out his loaded service weapon and set it on the table. "The next person that says that word is getting shot. In fact, if I ever hear that word again, I'm going to shoot the person who said it. Got me?"

"Dude, are you crazy? Put that thing away."

The dragonfly had seen enough, too, and left its perch beside the table. It flew off somewhere else. No one noticed. Maybe Horace did.

Jump-on Jimmy walked through the door. He was high and looked more trashed than usual. He was likely after something that resembled coffee. Dev noticed him first.

"Crap!"

Kris followed Dev's line of sight.

"Is that Jimmy?"

Devlin slid down a little underneath the table.

"Yeah, it is, and he's locked on to us."

Jack stared at the man coming through the door.

"Who's Jimmy?"

A sardonic laugh came from Devlin.

"He's a classic coke-nose turned cross-fit nut."

Kris laughed.

"Is that a 'classic' thing, Dev?"

"Sure, maybe, I don't know."

"You'd be the one to know?"

"Shut it, Horace! Damn, here he comes, brace yourselves."

Jimmy is a Jump-on, always has been. A Jump-on, according to Dickie, is an almost-friend, but not quite a friend, and by definition is someone the average friend finds irritating. Mostly, a Jump-on is there during the good times, but is never seen or heard from in the moments of friendship that require real effort. A therapist would have a fancy name for such a thing, Pegs just say Jump-on.

It's just one of those things.

Now, this little Jump-on got into poker after he saw *Rounders*. That's a film, starring Matt Damon and Eddie Norton. Jimmy made himself obsessed. He got all held up over Hold'em in a legion parking lot once. Some nasties emptied his pockets and messed his hypothalamus up. Had to quit playing altogether.

You'd think he'd learn his lesson.

Now catch this,

Ol' Jimmy sees *The Fast and the Furious*. That's another film. This one has Vinnie D and Paul Walker in it. He buys himself an MR2. Put horse under the hood, a splash of NOS. First race, the whip dies, just like that.

Boom.

The Auto-Hack.

Engine fried.

He wasn't in the lead.

Swears up and down he was, though.

Sometime after, Dickie had caught wind that he started rollerblading. Skateboarders call it fruit-booting.

Fruit-booting is a clever combination of noun and verb to derogatorily depict a degradation of homosexuality and the act of roller skating.

Now, I'm no fan of such colourful vernacular (yup, pun intended, having my fun).

But, hey,

That's our Jimmy.

The lad can't win.

"Fellas." Arms out wide like he was embracing the entire crew. "Sorry I missed the party last night, I was at the Hiebert social."

A social is a Peg thing. You see, Pegs have a party before the wedding to raise money for the wedding. These are called socials. According to Dickie, there are prizes, pizza and a DJ.

"So, what'd I miss last night?"

Jimmy stole a chair from another table and slid up to the booth.

He ate a fry off Kip's plate.

A Jump-on hates to miss out on something good, which is the very nature of the Jump-on's existence. And it should be noted that it's not entirely out of the ordinary, because a normal person hates to miss out on a good thing, too. It just somehow grates on you when a Jump-on wants to know what they missed.

Kurt put his nose in the newspaper.

Devlin made a smiley face out of the leftover food on his plate.

Kip's stomach hurt.

Jack was confused.

And Kris had fallen asleep.

Of course, Horace was unaffected by the standardized social afflictions and subtle nuances associated with such interpersonal interactions. Mostly because he is himself.

Last night,

Well...

Horace extended a little grace to a newcomer. Jews call that a mitzvah. Christians call it charity. Charity is filled with hope. Hope is what you make of it, kind of like faith, kind of like anything. You either believe in something, or you don't.

I don't do hope.

That's up to you.

Horace believed in friendship and that every jukebox should have the song "Crazy Things" by The Quid on its index. A jukebox is SoundCloud for really old people. Horace is young, but not unlike his best friend Kip, he is fascinated – obsessed, really – with antiquated electronics and tech.

Jack believes in revolution, tipping the scales, executing change. You know, trivial stuff. The two are about as comparable as PC and Mac in the '90s. Doesn't mean Horace and Jack can't get along, even become friends; it just means Jack won't develop a fondness for gaming and Horace will always be reminded of how he got his scar.

Okay,

How did they end up at Sals?

Well,

Dickie says it can be an effective storytelling device to take the reader back in time, show them what they missed, fly on the wall, through a glass darkly and all that sort of jib. Dickie's seen all the movies. Call it a flashback, movie magic, Tarantino's winning formula. I think it's thinly veiled laziness.

Anyway.

Abracadabra,

The party that led to the nip.

Reminder, a nip is a distinct Sals menu item, in case you forgot, or your delicate racial sensibilities were bruised.

So,

A dark blanket settled upon the Winnipeg skyline. Now here, I'd normally tell you that all the city street lamps came alive, say something clever, but the street lamps never shut off in Winnipeg. That's really true. They're lit all day and burn their sodium all through the night.

It's been that way ever since I've been here.

I guess no one noticed.

Maybe it's a dark city.

Or,

No one gives a jib.

It's just one of those things.

Beneath them, silence crowded downtown streets, an occurrence unique to smaller Canadian cities during the shift change from day-worker to night-stepper.

Pub windows spilled light onto the Exchange sidewalks and on the other side of the showy silica squares, a warm interior, bristling with human pleasantries and the chink of quarts and pints. Laughter, the loveliest of noises, kept the silence at bay and is the last resounding chime of freedom. I find it all fascinating, and I watch.

Along McDermot, a man exited Into the Music, a record tucked neatly under his arm. He lit a smoke, took a drag and disappeared around the corner on King. Dickie will tell ya the Exchange is the soul of this city.

A group of teens snapped a selfie and giggled at the results. They headed towards the Palomino to celebrate an eighteenth birthday.

Across the street, at Lombard, a hydro-bus came to a stop. The hydraulics lowered the step to the curb; Horace walked off, and Jack followed.

Eight dragonflies lighted simultaneously on the window of the motionless hydro-bus, drawn to the warmth of the metal, their wings twitching to the vibe of the engine hum.

The bus rolled forward and kicked up a swirl of street debris, and the dragonflies took flight, heading towards sky in search of mosquitoes and fuel-station fish flies.

They rounded the corner. Jack felt the brush of something cold on his bare arm. He looked down. It was a hand, attached to an arm that eventually led his eyes to something that almost resembled a person.

"Jesus!"

"No, that's just Kevin."

"What's wrong with him?"

"He's kind of a zombie."

"Kind of what?"

"Well, no, he is a zombie."

Jack pulled his arm from the man's grip.

"Don't worry. He won't bite, or rather, he can't. His teeth have all been pulled. He's harmless."

"Are you serious?"

"Kev used to work at the CDC."

"CDC?"

"Centre for Disease Control. Headquarters are here."

"What happened to him?"

Kevin shuffled towards them. Jack took another step back to distance himself. Kevin was missing small pieces of flesh, and his eyes looked like the eyes of a dead fish too long in the sun.

"No one knows for sure. There are rumours. All kinds of rumours, actually. The popular one people often chirp about is that he was working with some top-secret virus to be used by the American military. You know the paranoid kind of jib. Look at him, poor guy."

"My god. You mean he's really dead? Like walking dead kind of dead?"

"Kind of, no one really knows for sure. I mean Kev has rights, he's still a person, kinda sorta, anyway."

"How does he, you know, survive?"

"Kev's kind of a local celebrity. Tourists love him. People in the city can't get enough of him. Pegs think he's awesome. Guy's an Instagram superstar. The Salvation Army makes him a protein shake a couple of times a day. He knows when to go get them. People are just used to having him around."

"A protein shake." Jack shook his head.

How come the rest of world hadn't heard about this? Horace kept on moving, and Jack followed. He looked over his shoulder as Kevin tried his best to keep up with them and then eventually gave up when he couldn't maintain the pace.

They continued down Lombard.

Then movement in a wedge of shadow.

Horace watched a man take something from his coat pocket. He was soaked wet with the shadow cast by a defaced Leo Mol statue. Someone had spray-painted "Got any" across the chest of the copper sculpture.

Horace frowned. He hated senseless vandalism, but he sensed the power and exposure this simple act evoked. Some punk had thoughtlessly sprayed two useless words in public and he had now experienced a reaction to that action.

The man beneath the statue took a draw on an e-cig and let the vapour plume from his lips. The artificial ember glowed hot cobalt and cast soft light over his features.

He had a hard face pitted from an unfortunate childhood virus. His lips were drawn and thin and bordered on purple in colour. There was also faint evidence of a cleft palate that had been skilfully reconstructed. He was tall, maybe just over six feet, and his frame was thin to match his lips. His eyes watched the two men coming towards him.

"Do you know him?"

"Yeah. He's a policeman, a detective. He's friends with the same people I'm friends with."

Jack detected something in Horace's tone that was concerning. Horace turned around and smiled.

"All good." He patted Jack on the shoulder. "About time for that cold drink, I'd say."

For a brief moment Jack was surprised that he was okay with everything that had gone on since he'd met Horace. Then he remembered why he was in Winnipeg in the first place, and none of the night's events seemed all that abnormal. Not so far, anyway.

It reminded Jack of time with his father. Jack was sitting in front of the television, back when kids still sat in front of televisions. He was watching cartoons, it was noon, the principal had sent him home early from school. Popeye had just squished a can of spinach into his mouth.

Popeye is a sailor and a man with a canned-vegetable addiction.

Jack's father sat down beside his son.

"What are you watching?"

"Popeye."

"I see. Want to tell me what happened today?"

"No."

"I was just being nice. I'm the parent. You actually have to tell me what happened."

"I got in trouble."

"I know, Principal McNamara told me, but I want to hear you tell me what happened."

"A girl wanted to play baseball with all the boys. But Craig said girls can't play baseball with boys. I told Craig he should let her play, and he laughed and called her a bad word, so I punched him."

"I see. Punching is not a nice thing to do, Jack. Neither is treating girls poorly. Life is full of choices."

Jack's father got up to leave the room, then he stopped and pointed at the television screen.

"You know, son, Popeye's favourite saying is: 'I am what I am and that's all that I am.'"

A man's face materialized as the cloud of vapour thinned to nothing. An artificial scent of vanilla lingered and brought Jack's thoughts back to the present.

"Who's your friend?"

The word seemed to push through the spaces between his teeth. He took another pull from the e-cig. A ridiculous cloud of vapour flowered around his face. The man hid the device in his inner jacket pocket.

Jack caught a glimpse of the man's gun holstered inside his jacket. Horace smiled.

"This is Jack. He's new in town, so I thought I'd invite him in for a drink and a little 'Friendly Manitoba' hospitality."

"Jesus, Horace, no one says Friendly Manitoba anymore."

Jack extended his hand and the man took it.

"Devlin Davies."

"Jack Caldwell."

"Man, did you ever get on the wrong bus tonight."

Devlin looked at Horace.

"Always bringing home strays. You're really something, Mackie."

"Compliment noted."

Devlin shook his head.

"Let's get the hell inside."

Horace went through the revolving door first. Jack came through last.

So, this was the famous Rosewood Building. Jack had heard about it and the miracle of Spekel. He had hoped the miracle tea would reach New York, but as yet it had not been approved by the FDA.

The building was once one of the tallest in the city. Built in 1969. What was then known as the Richardson Building is now known as the Rosewood Building. Home to Rosewood Tea. It is a mere four stories, visually new in comparison to the surrounding aging downtown architecture.

The first floor is the manufacturing plant, as well as the shipping and receiving area. The manufacturing and sorting machineries consume most of the first-floor real estate, while logistics is handled through a loading area located on a newly developed sub-lane off of Portage for this purpose alone.

The second and third levels are office space and staff, the day-to-day operations not unlike those of any other business. The fourth floor is where Kurt, his brothers and Horace call home.

The only similarity to the building's previous incarnation is that the building still forms the connection to the Portage and Main concourse. Kurt made sure underground bicycle parking and lockup was available for his employees.

The roof of the building was specifically designed to accommodate an organic garden. There was also a small greenhouse used during the frigid winter months Winnipeg was so notorious for.

Kurt had created a number of Zen areas for relaxation and meditation. He believed strongly in using planned space to provide opportunity for mindfulness. It's how he kept chill.

What else,

Well,

Kurt loved hosting parties. He was good at it, people looked forward to his parties and his staff were always welcome. Heck, some were regulars.

Now listen,

According to Dickie, a party is not a party without music.

It's just one of those things.

And there was music at Kurt's parties.

Horace was explaining these and other finer points of party throwing and hosting to Jack, Kris and Devlin. Jack had been introduced to Kris only minutes ago, and Horace had already put them all in stitches with his observations.

"You see, you can have a film with great writing and terrible cinematography and the audience will accept it, might even enjoy it, but great cinematography can't save a film with bad writing. Not my best analogy, but you get the point."

Devlin chuckled.

"No, actually, we don't. You never make any goddamn sense."

Devlin Davies, what can I say? Dickie has plenty to say about him.

He was a short, fat little thing back in high school. He was bullied frequently, mostly because he was short and fat, but also because he worked as a stock boy at the 7-11 just down the street from Kelvin High. Kids would shoplift Slurpees when he was working. He always felt powerless and ashamed about it.

He swore he'd never get bullied again. So he dropped the el-bees and became a cop. The dress blues did nothing to make him feel taller. And bullies didn't just exist in high school; they were everywhere, even on the Winnipeg police force.

Bullies.

Nothing good there.

Dev's mom was a bully.

Once, he really did see his mother steal a Pomeranian tied up outside Safeway. Took the pooch home, kept it, named it Soapy.

It never answered to Soapy because its real name was Muffin. It became the family pet, until it got run over. Little Dev had to bury Soapy/Muffin in the yard.

In his rookie year on the force, he really truly did see his partner shoot a drug addict in the foot to see if he was dead. The drug addict knew a guy who was selling black-market lobsters to Winnipeg restaurants. All true, according to Dickie.

As a rookie, Devlin was partnered with a senior officer. How exciting. Many of the officers had nicknames for one another. He wondered if he might get himself a nickname. The senior officer's nickname was Rickster. Real name Rick. You throw a "ster" at the end and you've got something special right there.

As part of his training, they answered a number of fairly routine, low-impact calls. Training-day stuff, Winnipeg style.

The first of which was a *Domestic Violence* call.

A number of working girls, which is another way of saying women sexually servicing scoundrels, had been embroiled in a physical altercation amongst themselves over territory.

When Devlin and the Rickster arrived on the scene, they had to do their best to pacify the situation. Devlin's zealousness and lack of experience got the better of him, or rather two enraged working girls got the better of him and slapped the pluck out of him. That's how Rickster told it later to the boys at the department.

Devlin got hit in the face with a purse, a Michael Kors knock-off. He had never been hit in the face with a purse before. The metal faux MK roundel broke his nose. So, rather, he actually got slapped by Michael Kors.

Is that a real person? Remind me to ask Dickie.

His nose bled a helluva lot. He had never had his nose broken before, either. Two exciting firsts, all in one day.

His nose healed crooked because it had been set improperly by a doctor still in his residency. Ever since, his nose sometimes made an embarrassing wheezing sound when he breathed. The other officers dubbed him Wheezy because of it.

Wheezy this.

Wheezy that.

Hey, Wheezy, get the coffee.

Wheezy, file the paperwork.

Wheezy likes dick.

And the like and so on.

Devlin had received a nickname.

Day's end, he was alone in the station locker room. He examined his nose in the mirror, dried blood on his new uniform. The day had jumped off with so much hope.

He stepped back from the mirror and looked himself over. His sunken blue eyes burning permanent dark circles beneath them. He removed his service cap. The day before he had gone to the barber to get his head neatly shaved, leaving only stubble on his bulbous crown. His jaw groomed, cheekbones high and flushed. His body in peak physical condition. None of this mattered. He had lost face with the other officers. He would not make friends amongst his colleagues.

All was lost.

Until,

He met Kip at a bar one night after the job and liked him instantly. The two favoured a recreational cocaine habit. Devlin had started skimming coke from busts a few months earlier, for no other reason than he could.

He liked the edge, it made him alert. And then he became dependent on it.

Meeting someone he could commiserate with made the addiction seem less abusive. Kip liked Devlin because he seemed a little broken, and somewhere, he saw a good person longing to be free. He also liked the gratis coke.

Eventually, Devlin became a regular at the Rosewood. He kept Kurt insulated from routine municipal checks and health inspections. Kurt didn't need the help; he ran a tight ship. Devlin did it anyway. He had finally managed to make some friends. That is to say, he liked the Velic brothers, a lot, but he wasn't at all fond of Horace.

He wasn't fond of Horace because Horace wasn't like him. He looked different. Lots of people look different, ya know, that's what gives the world this thing called diversity. Even people of the same race look different. Devlin didn't buy much into that sort of a thing. He just saw crime, and the crimes he saw were mostly committed by people of noticeable ethnicity.

Devlin's understanding of the crime in Winnipeg was one of bias and ignorance. He only saw and dealt with an element of the population that exists in each and every race of people. There are all kinds of crooks in every background. Some of the biggest crooks in the world are white people. You've heard of them, you've even shaken their hands, you will recognize them by the title Corporate Executive. Their hustle and shakedown are epic in scope, affecting all, not just some.

Conrad Black, white guy.

Charles Ponzi, white guy.

Bernie Madoff, white guy.

Martha Stewart, white chick.

Enron.

AIG.

Oil.

And on and on and on.

Crime does not discriminate and is perpetrated by all ethnicities. Whether it's Doris Payne's petty pilfering or Madoff milking millions and leaving families destitute.

Perspective, cousin, gotta have it.

You see, Dev lacked perspective, and might I add, he wasn't the only one. Racists are united in their bigotry, for a single bigot cannot survive alone. He must have accomplices, he must have conspirators, all must be complicit. The lone racist will wither and die like any old weed without water.

The truth was that Devlin wanted something Horace had, a place with the Velic brothers. He didn't really want to live with them. He just wanted the offer. The offer that never came.

Of course, Horace didn't know that; neither did the Velic brothers. It wasn't like Horace had expected to live with the Velic brothers, and it wasn't like the Velic brothers had shunned Devlin.

You see,

Horace cared about his friends, finding out where they came from, and simple joys, those little things that keep the world turning, like video games and a song called "Crazy Things" by a little-known Winnipeg band called The Quid.

Oh, and he loved parties, especially Kurt's. Like tonight, for instance. Horace continued with his analysis despite Devlin's interruption.

"What I'm saying is that a party isn't a party without music."

May I gently remind the reader I had mentioned this earlier.

"So, if a hundred people are in one room together, chatting, laughing, drinking, but no music, it's not a party?" asked Devlin.

"Correct, not a party." Horace locked his fingers behind his head and leaned back in his chair.

"What about a bunch of people on a yacht, eating crab cakes and sliders, smoking cigars and swimming in the sea on a perfect day?" asked Kris.

"Any music?"

"None."

"Not a party."

Devlin scoffed. "Such bull!"

"Okay, how about this?" Kris multitasked between conversation and something he was doing on his tablet. "There's cake with candles and a table full of gifts, everyone just finished singing happy birthday."

Everyone looked at Horace. Even Kris looked up from his laptop screen.

Horace unlocked his hands from behind his head and came forward in his chair. He looked over the faces of the three men. "The song is over?"

"Yes."

"Any music?"

"No."

"It's a birthday, but not a party."

"Oh, screw this!" shouted Devlin. "This guy's crazy."

Horace stood up.

"Why do you think strip clubs have music?"

The three men looked at each other. They burst into laughter. Horace kept a straight face.

"Horace, have you ever been to a strip club?" asked Kris.

"Nope."

Devlin shook his head.

"Horace Mackie, you're not well."

Kris pushed back his chair and stood up.

"This round is on me, fellas."

"Oh shit, Kris with cash in his pocket, how'd this miracle happen?"

Kris did not respond to Devlin's jab.

Horace looked confused.

"You don't gamble."

Devlin whispered in his ear.

"He wasn't playing, if you get my drift."

"Oh. Isn't that, um, illegal?"

"You're hopeless. You want I should arrest him? Goddamn, Horace, lighten up."

"I just don't want you to end up in prison."

"Don't worry, H. I'm gonna end up someplace where I never have to wear socks again, like ever."

"They'll let you go barefoot in prison."

Kris ignored Devlin, cleared the empty beers and walked away.

Horace didn't like stealing; his only concessions were wildly ludicrous lies; otherwise Horace was honest to a fault. Kris did, though. He liked the thrill of the hack and the idea of being able to manipulate machines to his will. He also hated predators, and I have to point out that if your business is gambling, well, it's not like you're selling Girl Scout Cookies, is it?

Kris had always been good with computer code. Even at a young age he felt a draw toward computers. In high school, he hacked the system mainframe and overtook the sysop. He changed the entire student body class scheduling so that all the hottest girls were in his classes.

Kris never needed a lot of help with women. He had looks, at just under six feet, sandy brown hair, deep blue eyes and a dark complexion. Women noticed and men envied. The looks, coupled with a charming charisma, made it all work well.

"Everyone having the same?"

The three men nodded. Horace got up from his chair.

"I'm going to play a tune on the jukebox."

Devlin looked at Jack.

"He's not going to play anything on the jukebox."

"Why not?"

"Because all he ever plays is the same goddamn song. He's been playing the same goddamn song for years. Kurt got so sick of hearing it that he unplugged the juke and put it in storage."

"No way."

"Yes, sir. I kid you not."

"What was the song?"

Jack could barely contain his curiosity.

Devlin leaned forward as though he was about to share a dark secret with Jack.

"'Crazy Things.'"

"'Crazy Things'? Never heard of it. No, wait, I have heard of it. Tonight – he mentioned it earlier this evening."

"Well, damn! Of course he did, that's his jib. And why am I not surprised?"

Devlin leaned back in his chair. He shook his head.

"He's obsessed. You know, it's not a half-bad tune really." He chuckled. "Can't play it anymore, though. The song does something to the guy. You know he's not well, our Horace."

"How do you mean?"

"Not much at all right with him. Thinks he's gonna fly away one day."

Jack didn't like the jab, but said nothing. Also, he didn't get what Devlin was driving at.

"So, what's wrong with that?"

"No, no, you don't get it. You see, H thinks he will flap his arms and fly away from Winnipeg one day. What a hoot. Guy has never been farther north than Chief Peguis."

Jack froze. The neck of his beer bottle hovering just below his lips. "You can't be serious?"

"Oh, I am, and so is he! He's a total nut. Just ask him about flying, he'll tell ya, alright."

Jack didn't need to ask Horace. Horace had already told him, on the hydro-bus, on the way to the Rosewood. Jack just didn't realize what he was insinuating at the time.

"Wow."

"He tell you about his father and mother yet? How his grandfather fought in World War Two and was a sniper who managed to shoot Hitler in the leg?"

"Hitler was never shot."

"Exactly."

Kris carefully set four fresh pints of beer down on the table, trying his best not to spill the precious contents. He caught the look on Jack's face.

"What are we talking about?"

"He was just telling me about Horace."

"Oh, was he?" Kris looked at Devlin as he said it. "Devlin talks too much about other people's affairs." Kris sat down. "You'd think as a cop he'd know to keep his mouth closed."

Devlin got up from the table and walked away.

"Don't mind him. He's always like that."

He watched Devlin nudge Kip, and the two slipped away together amongst the crowd of people.

"Everything okay?"

"Yeah."

Kris had lost sight of his brother and Devlin. He swivelled around in his chair to face Jack.

"So Horace tells me you're from New York."

"I don't know how he knows that."

Kris chuckled.

"Horace pays attention to the little things most of us don't. You get used to it."

"How long have you known Horace?"

Kris eased back into his chair. He smiled as though he was reflecting on a past memory. Then the smile left his face. He took a sip of his beer.

"Long time. Since we were kids. He saved Kip once, damn near got killed himself. That's how he got the, um, the scar."

"Jesus."

"Yeah, Kip's always had a knack for finding trouble. The two of them are inseparable. They love those old video games. That's all they do together. Sit around and play those ridiculous games and enter these stupid video game competitions. Horace follows Kip around the city almost every night on his bike, while Kip takes his little pictures." Kris made a motion like he was snapping a photo with his fingers. "You believe in fate?" Kris didn't wait for Jack to reply. "Nah, me neither. Anyway, Horace has been with us ever since. He may not be all there – hell, who is?" Kris took a swig of beer. "He's family."

Horace pushed his way past a group of people and took the now empty seat next to Jack.

"Jukebox must still be in the shop getting repaired."

"Jack here wants to know what your favourite video game is."

Horace wasn't paying attention. He was scanning the crowd for Kip. Kris snapped his fingers in front of Horace's face.

"Hey, H. Earth to Horace."

"Yeah, sorry. Ah, favourite game. That's easy, Metroid. Greatest game ever made. Thunderblade is pretty cool, too. But Metroid, that's the game!"

"I know this game. My father used to play it with me when I was kid. He got an old Nintendo console from some used shop and the guy gave him a free cartridge to play on it. It was cool. I loved it."

"Your dad sounds like a cool guy. If Kip were here, he'd tell you the best game is Duke Nukem."

"No, I wouldn't."

Kip was standing directly behind Horace. He pulled out the other empty chair and sat down.

"The best game is Revenge of Shinobi."

"Metroid has the best secret code of all time, though."

"BS! The best code of all time is the code for Contra and Life Force. Up, up, down, down, left, right, left, right, A, B, A, B, start. You like Metroid because of the ending."

"How does it end?"

Kip threw his arm around Jack's shoulders.

"How does it end? Guy's a gangster." Jack had a straight face. "Hold up. You've never seen the ending for Metroid?"

"No."

"And so you'll come with us."

Kip got up from the table. Horace followed.

"Your education begins, son."

Horace said it with a straight face.

So Jack got up and followed the two friends.

"Don't worry about me, guys. I'm good right here." Kris shook his head. He took a sip of beer.

He scanned the crowd and noticed three girls standing at a high table. He knew them. Seen them around. One was a something or other, the other an Aldo Shoes sales refugee, and there was the black girl, and she smiled at him. Kris folded his laptop, stood up and grabbed his beer.

"I better go talk to her." He said it out loud, only so he could hear it. It was either that or fall asleep. Tempting.

He settled on talking to her.

And then he did.

What would become the Rosewood wasn't much to look at. Fire will do that, its sole purpose to consume. It's just one of those things. Structurally, the building was a total loss, but the foundation was a different story altogether. A nineteenth-century concrete pour was made to last. Kurt Velic saw nothing but opportunity and a way to finally spend his inheritance before the ACB bled it completely dry.

See,

While you can tax currency, some commodities are traded as though they are currency. Real estate is one such commodity. Diamonds are, too. One is worth a lot more than the other. Take a guess which one.

Anyway,

So far, real estate is not subject to special fees and taxation by the ACB. Kurt knew this and saw it as a viable shelter.

Kurt crouched his frame onto its haunches, his body damp with sweat. His plaid shirt soiled from soot and ash, his steel-toed boots caked with mud conjured up from the intense watering of fire hoses.

He wore two days' worth of stubble on his face and his sandy hair was a tangled mess from labour.

Labour is good.

Nobody likes pulling weeds, but you feel like a new person when the work is done.

Kurt reached down and drew a fine amount of what little dry soil existed. He rubbed it between his fingers.

Soil is good, too. All life comes from soil and water.

In his youth, Kurt had aspired to be a gemologist. His post-secondary focus was geology and chemistry. He had dreams then. He had optimism.

When the news arrived that his parents had been killed by a political bomber while vacationing in Paris, the tragedy left him no option but to forgo personal endeavours and take up the mantle of guardian for the sake of his two younger brothers.

That was then.

What was once a skyscraper, situated at the nexus of the city at the corner of Portage and Main, was now a state-of-the art eco-conscious factory producing loose-leaf tea.

A leaf native to the province and a mineral extracted from the unique provincial soil.

Renamed the Rosewood Building in honour of his parents' memory. Derived simply from both their names – Rose, his mother's name, and Wood, from his father's nickname, Woody.

Never one to back down from the formidable challenges life presents, Kurt spent years perfecting the chemistry involved in his tea formula. The result of which had two simple attributes: taste and the perfect ingestible organic mosquito repellent, time released after ingestion through the epidermis pore.

Rosewood Tea Factory, producing what is fondly referred to as Spekel. Spekel, an informal moniker, became a formal trademark. An instant success amongst Pegs, the Spekel formula not only repels Winnipeg's nasty bloodsucking foe, but also has documented natural positive health effects, not unlike most other teas.

You see,

There was a time when the city of Winnipeg went around in trucks after people fell asleep and fogged the city with an insecticide called DeltaGard 20EW. The active ingredient in DeltaGard 20EW is Deltamethrin. Deltamethrin is a neurotoxin. A neurotoxin attacks the nervous system.

Yup, that's really true.

No one knows the long-term effects of Deltamethrin.

That's also true.

The Canadian government approved Deltamethrin for use in populated areas.

Spekel eliminated the nightly pesticide fogging carried out by the city.

Kurt's discovery and creation have been effective not only on the Winnipeg mosquito, but have been equally effective on mosquitoes located in developing countries, in some cases eliminating the need for mosquito nets. These accomplishments have garnered him numerous recognitions and awards, none of which he accepted on principle, right or wrong. It was just his way. Kurt was not a man who harboured inclinations toward the spotlight. He never offered explanations. He may have had his reasons, but he never shared them. He simply wanted to work and needed to believe in the work he was doing.

People like Kurt, ya know?

Rosewood Tea employed 148 people. A small operation, considering the worldwide demand, but efficiency, forward thinking, and a solid labour program kept things bustling and on track.

Now, what separates Rosewood Tea from other companies isn't higher wages, better benefits, stock options. I mean, yes, the employees were provided these provisions, too. No, it was simply that Kurt was a good man and treated his staff well.

Since the Auto-Hack and the laws that forbade private vehicles use, Kurt had the foresight to incorporate change rooms and showers for employees so they could bike to work. He also offered organic juice, coffee and other continental assortments each morning.

Start the day right.

End the day right.

He was genuinely concerned with the well-being of all of his staff and truly cared about them. I hate to remind you about what we discussed earlier, but mission statements and brands with corporate mantras lead to one thing. More. *More* will be humanity's epitaph. Here lies the human race; they wanted more, and then there was nothing left.

Dickie says Kurt is such an exceptional salesman that he could sell a teenager a second set of parents. My kind of salesman.

I know talent when I see it. As a salesman, Kurt believes in the validity and veracity of what he's selling. He believes his product matters and is meaningful to people. This sets him apart from someone selling mortgage rates or cosmetics. How? Just take a moment to think about it. If you haven't got it by now, well, don't worry too much; that kind of thinking, it's not really for you.

The Rosewood Building was not only a manufacturing plant, but it was also home to him, his two brothers, and Horace, who they considered family.

Kurt took the opportunity to ensure the new building's design would incorporate all of the amenities he felt were necessary for his business and his family's needs. The architecture also met all his ecological demands. It cost more, a lot more, and Kurt didn't care. He certainly didn't care when other business owners scoffed at the expense. Maybe he was making a statement. We all know one eco-friendly building can't make a difference, but hey, you gotta start somewhere.

Journalists, reporters, bloggers, even a well-known biographer attempted to contact Kurt for various reasons. Everyone wanted the rights to his story. People love to be a part of other people's fame; that's why there are so many reality television programs. I watched one the other night about chefs that had two minutes to create a gourmet meal from gummi-bears and mustard. Nothing more irritating than a chef on TV, except maybe a real estate agent on TV, or a judge on TV.

Yeah, a judge on TV.

That's the worst.

Three minutes to Wapner.

North Main Street at dusk is dappled with cheap motels, beer vendors and cops.

It is at dawn, too.

And a silence hangs on.

The silence has a sound, a presence, a feeling of something there, can't put a finger on it.

Wandering souls ebb upon the concrete tide, unaware of their own subconscious search for something misplaced. They talk, and that silence retreats. They whisper, and the streets and buildings keep all the secrets.

Sometimes one person will lend an ear to another; sometimes this is enough to get on to the next hour, the next day, the next week. They just exist like so many other people do. Moment to moment, they breathe, the heart ticks, the blood moves and the pulse pumps, trading words, the only valuable commodity on the street.

The 32 northbound hydro-bus took the curb and released its passengers. They scurried toward the New West Motel. Someone hollered at a familiar face as the hydro-bus pulled away.

A few times throughout the year, the Sally Ann on Henry will hand out coffee and day-olds. The hookers and drunks and vagrants and doped rich kids, who are ashamed of being rich, hang out as common people and eat.

Some Pegs will never venture to the North End, and there are some Pegs that will never stray from the North End.

It's just one of those things.

Farther south, down in town, there are more cheap motels, beer vendors, and a concert hall Pegs want to get rid of. There's city hall, too. The mayor works from home.

Brick and mortar walls, centuries old, are scabbed with advertisements that have survived long enough to become meaningful spectres of a generation on its way out of the big game.

Main Street was for walking and talking and turning onto other streets, people loitering and fussing about stuff.

Devlin Davies was on the steps of the McLaren Hotel. He paused on the sidewalk and took a zip baggie from his pocket. He tapped a bump of sugar into his snuff divot. He hit the bump, and then set up a second round for his right nostril. In Winnipeg, cocaine is cheaper than snow. Not that Dev paid.

Headquarters was one block over. Brazen. It's not that he wasn't afraid, it's that he believed, like so many others before him, that he wouldn't get caught.

Dev was careful, he was cautious. He had been cheating his way through life long enough to know how to properly conceal what he wanted to hide from scrutinizing eyes.

Dickie says word on the street eventually catches up to everyone. He also says there are two things in life you can never do.

We'll get to that. Maybe. If there's time.

Devlin checked his phone clock. He was late; or rather, he was going to be late. He cursed Horace for getting under his skin with his goddamn tricks and psychobabble. Hypothalamus and sex, he hated even hearing the sound of the word inside of his head.

It was true that ever since his wife left him two years ago, he hadn't hit any tail. So, he found some and paid for an hour and sprung for a room. He certainly wasn't the first to do it.

He tucked the baggie back into his coat pocket and found his wallet in the same pocket. He opened to a picture of his daughter in the view sleeve. He rubbed his thumb over the photo. The coke worked fast. He closed the wallet.

On the opposite side of the street, he watched two dipshits snap a selfie with Kevin. Kevin was swaying as though he might topple at any moment. They patted Kevin on the back and walked away.

Kevin swayed, then shambled slowly across the street. Devlin cursed. Kevin creeped him out; he had even shot him once when Kevin had surprised him from behind a dumpster.

Goddamn zombie.

He searched his pockets for the keys to the Interceptor. The cruiser was parked two blocks away on Albert. He put his keys and wallet back in his pocket and hoofed it.

The cabin of the Interceptor felt stuffy. Dev wiped his forehead, which was damp with sweat. He searched for his keys, found them and fumbled to find the ignition slot for the key. Finally, he found it and turned the engine over. He put the power window down to let some air into the cabin.

The coke made him uncomfortable. The fresh air felt like a kiss. The CV on the console came alive – dispatch was performing location checks.

More chatter over the CV. Then a domestic disturbance call was relayed. Another cruiser closer to the scene picked up the call.

Devlin flicked off the CV and put the window up. He pushed the air button and the AC hummed. A string caught in the vent blew forward and danced like a ceremonial dragon. Droning came from the Interceptor as it managed the extra burden of energy. The cool air was nice. He shifted in his seat and scratched his crotch. He hoped the hooker was clean. He cursed Horace again; the man always managed to get his blood up.

Horace was harmless, he knew that. Wasn't even that bad to be around. It's just one of those things. Devlin saw the worst in him. And after a while, he expected anyone who might be like Horace to be trouble.

You see, Devlin isn't much of an observer. He doesn't pay attention to the little things. Kind of strange, because that's pretty much the single most important skill for a cop.

Like so many other Pegs, he had settled comfortably upon perpetuated stereotypes. The problem with stereotypes is that there is some truth to them and that they limit the scope of perspective if you buy into them.

And everyone does.

It's just one of those things.

I could tell you about people in Winnipeg from all walks of life who have become award-winning poets, or famous film stars, or musicians, or lawyers, or politicians. I could, but I won't. These are achievements people place extra value upon.

Real value, worth, comes from the individual who stays true to themselves and what they believe in, who pays their bills and feeds their kids, someone who tells the truth, for Chrissakes, who loves and lives. There are people who do just that. Some people don't even have running water or power lines, third-world conditions happening right here in this little ol' province, and they still find a way.

Devlin doesn't acknowledge this because he doesn't want to see it.

He's not alone, either.

Willful blindness is as rare as human refuse.

The thing is, Dev has his own problems, same as everyone else does. You don't hear him complaining how his wife left him, how she married a urologist a few months after the divorce, that he's bullied at work, or how his daughter has advanced-stage leukemia. This is just a taste of what he's going through.

He loves his little girl more than anything else, and he would do anything to save her life. It's just that things are complicated, they always are, and that's why he keeps a photo of his daughter on him, that's why he looks at it all the time. He's not a monster. He's just human. Even the good ones do terrible things, and the bad ones can be noble.

Devlin put the Interceptor in drive and pulled away from the curb. He couldn't wait any longer; he had to get his act together. He contemplated taking another bump of coke, but decided against it. He took the e-cig from his pocket and took a drag. A plume of vape filled the cabin.

He didn't like where he was going, who he was going to meet. He thought again about his daughter. About her frail body lying on a hospital bed with tubes cascading downward onto a cold tile floor. All those machines. She was so young. So goddamn young.

He knew he was going to go. He knew he'd do it. What he wanted didn't matter. It was all forfeit. He took another pull off the e-cig.

He flicked on the CV and picked up the walkie.

"Dispatch, this is car 204, request time for lunch, authorize, over."

"Car 204, authorized, over."

Devlin returned the walkie to its holster and flicked on the bubble lights. Then he put the fuel pedal down and heard the roar of the engine as he blew through a red light on Ellice. Not that it mattered. His was the only operational motor vehicle for five blocks.

Hey,

So,

Here's something you don't know.

Something you should know, but don't want to know.

It's important, but super-duper boring.

It goes a little something like this.

A Fico Score and a Beacon Score are the exact same thing.

What are they?

For starters,

One is Yankee and one is Canuck. They both do the same thing. They show how you repay obligations, what's been loaned to you in the past, and tell banks if they should lend you money in the future.

Credit, son, credit!

Yawn.

Well,

While you're snoring, banks are putting a needle in your arm.

Feel that?

Here's how it works –

Based on your spending and repayment patterns, a score is developed.

A great score is 800+. A good score is 700+. Anything below 600 is when you have to go fish for a predator. There were a lot of predators until 2008.

A predator is a sub-prime lender. A sub-prime lender is who Johns and Janes have to borrow from when they've previously defaulted on loans, had trades charged off, or generally blew their nose all over their repayment obligations.

But here's the jib,

600+

That's the score.

Premium lender banks, Dickie calls them "A+ Banks," don't lend below 600. 600-700 scores, that's where most of the population sits. The medium or status quo.

You see,

At 600-700, the algorithms that generate Fico or Beacon scores get skewed by dynamic variables, like a discharged insolvency, credit counselling, or an unpaid speeding ticket moved to a third-party collection agency.

Huh?

Exactly.

Banks are counting on the "huh."

Now,

I know, most of you have checked out.

That's cool.

I feel you.

Mick and Keith felt it too:

"The sunshine bores the daylights out of me."

Hard to imagine those boys clocking in.

So,

Almost all mortgages have been lent out to people with 600-700 credit scores. A mortgage is the big debt attached to your home. The word *mortgage* is a coupling of two French words:

Agreement
And
Death.

Agreement payable on death.

Wait, it gets better, worse, sorry, I mean worse, way way worse.

These same mortgage loans have been lent out in a high-ratio capacity.

Which means,

If you're still with me,

That people have less than twenty percent as a down payment to invest. Risky, right? It sure is. But not for banks, because those very same loans in Canada are insured by the Canadian government against default.

Now,

Here's the jib.

If you don't pay your mortgage, for any reason, like, let's say:

Kid gets sick,

Partner dies,

You lose your job,

You get robbed, injured, go to war and all that jib,

The bank takes your home from you, and the government covers the bank for any loss, on a premium that got tacked on to the back end of your mortgage. You paid for the bank's security protection to the same government you also pay taxes to.

The bank then sells the home under "Power of Sale" and, voila, new homeowner, new mortgage. Them's the breaks. Banks never lose and the Canadian government is complicit in the whole thing.

Dickie calls that Economics.

Rinse and repeat.

How do I know this? Good ol' Dickie. He worked for a bank, a major one, before he found enlightenment.

So,

If you're a bank,

How do you keep Johns and Janes from asking questions? How do you hide all that red among the black?

Plain sight.

The best place to hide is in plain sight.

If you're out in the open, what could you possibly have to hide?

In Peg-City, plain sight looks just like Linden Woods.

No better location.

Awash with a miasma of box brand stores, the entire South End is pregnant with big-box retail. Marginalized retail made convenient, accessible and easy.

How do you solve a problem like convenience?

The triple crown of the retail manifesto: accessibility, convenience, parking.

Oh, the tiny tantalizing tidbits.

I've unearthed a honey pot of life's little lusts.

So,

There it sits,

The unassuming headquarters of the Association of Canadian Banks.

It's not a flashy building. It doesn't stand out like all those credit union branches used to. Nah, there was an intentional community assimilation executed with careful, painstaking perfection.

It's comfortable, it's warm and it's friendly. So, too, is the staff. There are never any lineups.

There's free parking,

Which Dickie says is a genius idea.

The ACB is staffed efficiently, and efficiency is the name of the game. If you're going to steal from people, the least you can do is make it easy on them.

The interior of the building is tidy and clean. Everything in its place and all things arranged just so. Colour is soft and warm, but does not stand out, nothing stands out, it's all forgettable. Senior citizens go for free coffee and newspapers.

The building stands eleven stories. The first floor is for day-to-day business transactions made with the public. The second floor is occupied by marketing and spin. These are the finest individuals of their craft. Strategies are developed daily to effectively control and manage public perception through the media channels under ACB control.

Most of the ACB's digital and print marketing efforts are done at airports. People who travel by plane have disposable income; they are also at the height of their boredom, making the penetration most effective. Especially when you walk down the boarding hallway.

A statistical fact.

Actually, I just made that up. It just sounds authentic when you use statistic and fact together.

Anyway,

The third floor is for special loans and trading. Stories five through eleven are operations. These six floors are concerned with processing, efficiency and workflow management.

The ACB sources its major power feed remotely, drawing only standard use from city hydro and gas. A building, listed as storage and warehousing on record, resides on a plot of land hidden in a forest near Vita. Vita is a small town outside of Winnipeg. As Dickie would say, it's all small outside of Winnipeg.

A lonely little structure in the middle of somewhere housing untrammelled technology. Most of the tech is so advanced that governments don't know of its existence.

The ACB staff doesn't know this, either. No one is given access to it. Components are acquired piecemeal and then assembled meticulously at the ACB headquarters in Linden Woods by hardware professionals, hired independently, who never know what they are working on. What can't be assembled by human hand is manufactured and assembled by machines.

A tedious and laborious procedure, but it shelters the ACB and knowledge of the ACB's operations.

Components are shipped by drone and implemented by machine and robot at the building in Vita. How does such a building at such a distance feed information to the ACB headquarters? I honestly don't know. Dickie might, but he hasn't said much about it.

I do know the Vita building receives its power through modified hydropower cells, which leech power maliciously and illegally from anywhere and everywhere that power can be taken. Simply put, the ACB is hacking its energy. Think of the concept as a host parasite scenario wherein the ACB is drawing untraceable fractional amounts of power from everything it can. The stolen energy from millions of various hosts is nothing more than intelligent hacking.

The millions of hosts affected by the hack don't notice the 0.02<CC> it is costing them on their hydro bills. Energy providers also don't notice the missing power because it is virtually untraceable as minuscule theft. A "take a penny, leave a penny" concept, except the ACB just keeps taking the penny.

And then there's the fourth floor.

This floor makes up the office of the man in charge. He's not a CEO, CMO, CFO or any other corporate acronym title you can upchuck. The man has no title. He simply is. His name is Shue. Roland Shue. People put the prefix Mr. before the moniker, the few who ever see him.

Mostly, Mr. Shue does not meet with staff and has never met with clientele. His assistant, Wit, handles all face time when required. Other corporate business associates and colleagues – of whom Shue has no equal – are handled via telecommunications. Shue does not make public appearances, nor does he travel.

Any face-to-face meetings are of the highest exception. These are rare, controlled and heavily screened by Wit.

Shue,

At his desk,

Is observing the printed data supplied to him, as it is each morning. A formality, but a necessary one, he concludes. Every decision calculated and with purpose.

The illuminated amber warning lamp on his desk indicated that Wit would be entering the office momentarily. Of all his staff, Wit followed procedure best and never faltered in his mandate. It wasn't pleasing, no. Shue didn't connect with base emotions; he had no use for them. It was order. Order was efficient, order had purpose and produced the desired results.

The final warning knock and Wit entered the office of Roland Shue. Wit took two steps inside the office and stopped. He kept good posture and waited, patience that comes with years of conditioning.

Shue stood and walked to the front of his desk. He turned and observed a stack of loose notepaper that he had never used even once.

I find it all so fascinating.

"I have a visitor."

Wit nodded.

"A man has arrived. He says he has an appointment." Wit cleared his throat. "There was nothing on the docket. I advised him that you were not..."

Shue held up his hand, cutting Wit off.

"He is the reason I'm not taking meetings." Shue faced his assistant. He provided no explanation. He buttoned his suit jacket, his face expressionless.

"Show him in."

The only light came from a window looking out over the Portage-Main intersection. It was a sunny day. People were gathering in front of the pomegranate tree. Horace put his hand on the glass. He was high above the people below. They looked happy.

He removed his hand from the glass and faced the room. It looked empty, but it wasn't. It was neatly cluttered with items of intrigue.

Items or objects of intrigue can, and in this case does, refer to the hobby of collecting. Collections are typically categorized and catalogued by the type of objects collected. Anything can be collected.

Examples:

Stamp collecting is called philately

Coin collecting is called numismatics

Rock collecting is called rock hounding

Pannapictagraphists collect comics

Vexillophiles collect flags

Phillumenists collect matchbooks

Deltiologists collect postcards

Sucrologists collect sugar packets from restaurants
Plangonologists collect dolls and are usually batshit
Tyrosemiophiles collect cheese labels
Entredentolignumologists collect toothpick boxes
And the like.
Give it a name,
Give it a fancy name.

Collecting often runs along a fine line with hoarding. Hoarding is a mania where Johns and Janes are unable to throw anything away, like a chewing gum wrapper or chewed chewing gum.

Horace and Kip are collectors. It started with decks of playing cards. Now they collect everything, not just one thing.

If they die, and they *will* die, 'cause everyone dies (try not to think about it), the auction catalogue would run like this (traditionally alphabetically, but chronologically by their preference):

-Remington Rand typewriter 1948 KMC model, found near a dumpster behind the Safeway on Main.

-Glen Downie poem (Bats) signed in graphite. Printed by Tall Tree Press. They met Downie at the Small Press Convention held at Millennium Library in the Carol Shields Auditorium.

-Modesty Blaise comic strip. Original artwork, brush and India ink over graphite by Romero. Purchased at Comic Con in Winnipeg.

-Production cel from NFB short *The Big Snit*. Signed by Condie. Purchased at a charity auction in Winnipeg. (Note: Condie lives in Winnipeg)

-Late nineteenth-century Martin guitar with original stand. Stolen from a Blind Willie McTell blues concert in Chicago by Hell's Angels. Recovered ten years later in a drug raid in Winnipeg. Sold privately to Warren Buffet, who later visited Winnipeg during the filming of his biopic. Horace would meet him, over brunch, at the Fort Garry Hotel. They hit it off and consequently Horace later won the guitar in a heated ping pong match.

-A stereopticon found in an abandoned trunk left behind at Union Station in the lost and found.

-Red Lucite tower. Attributed to Charles Hollis Jones. Found in a parking garage under Crocus building.

-Bauhaus chair given away during a corporate cleansing.

-Sottsass table. Once owned by Michael Jackson (according to Dickie; provenance unverified).

-Canadian Pacific sealed deck of souvenir playing cards. Bought between pillars A and B at Mulvey Flea Market. Mulvey Flea is now defunct due to the elimination of hard currency.

-McCobb desk acquired in a parking lot deal during a special edition *Antiques Roadshow* visit to Winnipeg.

-Stained-glass Tiffany lamp purchased in Winnipeg antique shop for $10. Seller unaware of authenticity.

-Louis XIV crystal paperweight purchased from an eccentric private collector of paperweights in Elmwood. Seller also collected bottle caps, none of which interested Kip and Horace.

-Pink Triangle turntable bought from Advance Electronics at retail price (retention of original purchase receipt, some may call that hoarding).

-Modernettes EP (Teen City) purchased for $1 at Sound Exchange. Took over an hour to complete the sale.

-Sony Trinitron tube television, with original display cabinet and optional stereo speakers. Gifted to them by a stranger off the back of a salvage truck.

-Atari Video Music Console, with original box and contents. Purchased at Pawn Traders on Portage for $200. Negotiated down from $300.

-First edition book collection. Key items include: Canadian Edition *Catcher in the Rye* by J. D. Salinger, with black and white image of Salinger on back dust jacket; *Dreams and Fancies* by H. P. Lovecraft; *Invisible Cities* by Italo Calvino, signed by Calvino; *A Midsummer Night's Dream* by William Shakespeare with illustrations by Arthur Rackham, signed by Rackham; and *Sparks* by Charles Bukowski, publisher Black Sparrow limited hand-numbered giveaway, signed by Bukowski. Acquired from a silent collector in exchanged for one of Kip's photos and the negative (rumours abound surrounding the subject matter of the negative itself).

-Fabergé egg, Clover/Turtle Egg, hand-painted, Limoges, France. Traded for a Wayne Gretzky O-Pee-Chee rookie card with gum residue.

-American Kennedy silver half-dollars. Won by Kris in a drunken game of Moon and gifted to Horace and Kip at Christmas.

-Vintage Camera lenses. Acquired at an estate sale in River Heights.

-Nash the Slash gig poster, signed and inscribed by Nash. Inscription reads "Listen in Safety." They met Nash, sans bandages, shooting pool during a gig.

This is not an exhaustive list. An exhaustive list would simply exhaust. It's amazing how exhaust sounds like what it means and how the more you say it the more it exhausts.

Now,

There was life in the room. Succulents in various sizes and shapes, of countless varieties, sat in trays on the ledge of the window. Plump, round bodies reaching for that window sun and delicate thin roots rooting for moisture in pot soil.

Some of the taller succulents sat on what little vacant real estate was available on the edges of bookshelves, rows of little green sentries guarding the rare editions.

New printed books had been outlawed. The League of Digital Intellectual Properties, an independent government-funded organization, had demanded better censorship control and found publishers wouldn't allow themselves to be forced into indoctrination. They were afforded too much freedom within the print medium. And so, they became verboten. All new digital books published must filter through LDIP censorship protocols before seeing publication in electronic form. Only newspapers were afforded the right to print, mostly because people didn't care much about newspapers anymore.

Same thing happened back in '54 with American comic books. This doctor got himself all worked up over comic books. He led a crusade to run comics out of town. So, a code was created to censor comics. No comic could get published without meeting the code's censorship policies. Censorship is a fancy word that means you can't say or do something.

It almost destroyed the art form.

It has almost destroyed many art forms.

And

True to form,

No one learned their lesson and it happened all over again in the '80s. This time with music. Some mother, who happened to be married to a John who was second in command of a country, decided music needed to be censored. Parents weren't being good parents, so she decided it would be better to censor freedom of speech than teach people how to be better parents.

This all really happened.

Now,

We no longer have printed books.

Gone

Poof!

Any books that predated the new digital laws were allowed to continue to exist, although the LDIP (give it an acronym) did push to have them pulped rather than remain in existence. A streamlining of the printed literary history, so to speak.

And

People were cool with it, 'cause people love Twitter and Netflix.

But,

Kip and Horace had spent years and a significant amount of legwork acquiring their book collection.

Even with all that great stuff, the room still appeared empty without Kip there. Funny how stuff can't replace what really matters.

It's just one of those things.

A Nixie clock, wire-mesh anodes wound inside cold-cathode tubes, cast glowing exaggerated numbers on the nearest adjacent wall. Horace looked at the time and then left the room and closed the door.

He wandered the Rosewood. Empty halls grew emptier and wider and taller with each foot he set in front of the other. The large open rooms echoed at the slightest sound. He was alone and bored. No appetite. Didn't want to go for a walk. Didn't feel like playing vids.

He had managed to acquire the prayer spell in Ultima III: Exodus for his cleric. Kip would be pleased about the progress. He had purchased the cartridge at Comic Con from a vender who sold vintage vids. The two friends had been looking for it for years.

Horace rubbed his eyes. He never watched TV. It wasn't his thing. A television was nothing more than a monitor to him. He had fried his cones on vids all night and needed a visual upgrade, a change of scenery and a change of pace. It was at times like this that he felt there really wasn't anywhere worthwhile to go in this city. This was also when he most thought about flying. He looked out a window. Clear skies, as good a day as any. He wasn't aware that he was smiling.

It was his day off. Kip was out shooting. Kurt had gone to the farm to check on the greenhouse crops and wouldn't be back for a few days.

The door to Kris's room was closed. Horace knocked.

"Busy. Who is it?"

"It's me."

"Okay, come on in."

Horace opened the door. Lights were off. The room was illuminated by backlights from the four monitors Kris was using to run various tasks. The monitors were arranged two upon two. Back glow cast heavy shadows on Kris's lean features. His cheekbones popped beneath his dark eyes.

Underfoot fibre optic, Cat7, and multiuse bulk network cables slithered like a den of static snakes. These intertwined with high definition multiuse interface cables leading to dongles.

A tablet running diagnostics and countermeasures on the two massive chrome towers was humming hive-like next to the desktop monitors. Kris mumbled commands to someone. Horace watched him work.

"Simi, macro reports."

Horace took a seat in an empty chair.

"Simi, bring up app ribbon."

Horace was confused. *Who was Kris talking to*, he wondered. So he did what most people should do. He asked him a direct question.

"Kris, who's Simi?"

Nothing. Silence hung on silicon-scented air.

"Kris?"

"Huh?"

"Never mind."

Kris had built the two larger bottom desktop monitors from spare parts. Most of the parts had been salvaged from the Brady Dump.

It's easy to get what you need when people throw most of it away. People waste an unfathomable amount of quality items and goods. They will throw away fully functioning electronics because it's not the most recent Gen. Younger Johns and Janes often do the same with older Johns and Janes. Think a seniors' home.

"Wish you could fix the jukebox."

"Listen, H, I'm gonna give you the straight jib on that."

A reminder alarm sounded.

"Ah, shoot!"

Kris leapt from his chair.

"Grab that wire right there, will you?"

Horace did just as he was told.

"Follow it to the source and remove it from the outlet."

Horace traced the wire through a tangled series of other wires, located the source outlet, and pulled the wire free. The monitors instantly went dead. All that remained was a small power burn in the centre of each screen.

"Uh oh, what did I just do?"

"Exactly what I wanted you to do."

Kris shuffled through some blueprints on his desk. The place was a mess, papers and wires everywhere, components strewn about, some working, some not. Some hot, some cold.

The room was bare, eggshell walls devoid of décor. No pictures, no paintings, not even a wall clock.

In the middle of the room, alone on a large table, was something that looked like an old tube television. None of it made much sense to Horace. It was also very unlike Kris to be so disorganized. Normally, he was the opposite.

"What is all this, Kris?"

"Hold on. I'm looking for something."

Kris sifted through papers and hand drawings and spec sheets. He looked frustrated and distraught.

"Can I help?"

"Maybe, I don't know. There, found it."

It was a book. Kris turned the book around so the cover faced Horace.

Horace read the cover.

"Basic television."

"Exactly."

Kris ran his hand over the cover of the book thoughtfully.

"I don't get it. Are you making a TV?"

"No – well, sort of. Actually, I've made televisions already, very easy to find parts, just have to dig a little. I mean actually dig. Colour CRTs are a dime a dozen, but finding one with the deflection coils operational is the real test."

"Why are you constructing old TVs?"

Kris wasn't paying attention. He had opened the cover of the book and was reading.

"I make them to understand how they work. Best way to learn about something is to build it. Just ask god." He looked up from the book, smiling. "It gave me ideas, too. People inside the machine."

"What do you mean?"

Kris didn't answer. He just handed Horace the book. Horace took the book from Kris and leafed through it. He landed on the copyright page.

"Kris, this book was published in 1964. Where did you get this?"

"Estate sale, paid a dollar for it, back when there were loonies, before the bloody LDIP, too."

"It's really outdated. This technology is really old. No one makes televisions like this anymore."

"Exactly!"

"I'm not following."

"I'm trying to develop a way for organic matter to enter a computer."

Horace closed the book and stared at Kris. Wild science fiction–type comments were not out of character for Kris, who believed that if you could think it, it could be done.

"I'm trying to map DNA and convert it to computer code, then link our consciousness, neurons, nervous system and so on through robotics and the basics of television, so we can directly control the coded version of ourselves inside a computer. Brain-to-machine interfacing. People as programs, electro-tech-corporeality. In theory, I mean. That's all it is right now, a theory."

"Sounds, um, ambitious."

"It is, and it isn't. You have to look at it from various perspectives. For instance, take your phone. You write a text, and your phone is able to discern the context of what you are trying to write before you complete the text and it knows how to auto-correct the errors and even finish the sentence or thought for you.

"This is a mild form of artificial intelligence. We say artificial because we know the phone is not alive, at least not in the sense we perceive as life. But what if life can germinate within the tech, like seed in soil?

"True independent intellectual life, what I prefer to call mechanical intelligence. Biologists are discovering new bacteria all the time. This is new life. Rudimentary organic life, yes, but it is new. It materialized from somewhere, so why can't the same thing happen in computers? Just a different kind of life. This makes me believe that a coded organic version can interface with machine."

"Why the TV, then?"

The gamer in Horace had his interest piqued.

"The television is the conduit. Well, it's not just a television. It's computer-television or quantum-compu-vision." He scratched his chin. "Think of it as a way to transmit the organic-electronic version of ourselves into the computer by relaying atoms instead of transistors. It's the link from our world to the computer world. And believe me when I say the computer world is very much a real world. The goal is to use photons to transmit particles and atoms from one place to another. Theoretically, of course."

"Of course."

Horace smiled. Then the smile left his face.

"Are you saying that you are attempting to create a way to teleport human beings into a computer and then back again?"

"I'm impressed, Horace. That's exactly what I'm trying to do. Imagine being able to leap through quantum mechanics and interface with electronic matter."

"You'd become very popular overnight."

"Yes."

Kris went distant. He turned away from Horace. Then he sat down and reached for his tools.

"Want to see something cool?"

"Always."

Horace stepped forward. He touched his scar. He had become nervous, for some reason.

"Watch."

Kris cleared a space on the table. He took what looked like a modi-fied tablet from a protective sleeve and laid it flat, screen up, upon the table. Then he hooked a series of HDMI cables into the tablet's ports. He rolled his chair over to his control station.

"I just built this the other day."

Kris typed commands into his keyboard, then looked at Horace. "Ready?"

Horace nodded.

"Simi, initiate task 5."

The tablet screen came alive and projected an image of a butter-fly into the space above the screen. A digital tiger swallowtail hovered motionless in the air as a 4D projection. The colour saturation muted and lifelike. The image was seamless and rich, without any visible arti-facting. Horace imagined trillions of pixels, each with a purpose, to imagine the life of the butterfly before his eyes. He reached out to touch it, and his hand went right through.

Horace took a shallow breath. "How did you do this?"

"I've been toying around with 4D pixels. Connection rendered high definition pixels through a series of nodes, not unlike advanced CG animation." Kris smiled. "The hard part is getting the pixels to move. Watch this."

Kris typed a command on his keyboard. The swallowtail started to flap its wings. Its movement, while in a singular eight-second loop, was identical to that of a real swallowtail flight pattern.

Horace took a step backward.

"The flapping of the wings is the same as a rudimentary classical animation walk cycle. Key frames and in-betweens. Twenty-four pixilated frames a second, multiplied by eight seconds, 192 frames in harmonious repetition."

Suddenly, the swallowtail warped and stretched, then flickered. Kris frowned. "Hmm, bit of a power surge. Simi, close task 5."

The swallowtail disappeared. Kris unhooked the cables and put the tablet back in its protective sleeve. He sat back down, lost in thought. Finally, he looked at Horace and smiled.

"I should get back to work."

Horace had become used to being overlooked and dismissed. While he knew Kris didn't mean anything by it, he still felt a little hurt.

Sometimes people need to get out of their own heads and see what's happening right in front of them. We're all missing so much of the subtleties of the lives we share with those around us.

"Thanks for the show."

But Kris wasn't listening.

Horace said nothing further. He left the room and closed the door behind him.

Years ago, Johns and Janes used to believe that having your picture taken meant someone had captured your soul. People weren't fond of pictures because people were afraid. People were afraid because they lacked understanding of the mechanics and science of photography.

People often did idiotic things around the time photographic science was in its infancy. They fired guns at each other, drank whisky more than water, and died very young from malnutrition and bullet holes. Today, people still fire guns at each other often, drink often, and die often from malnutrition and bullet holes.

So,

This is how a society works:

There are Johns and there are Janes. A John tries to get the attention of a Jane. Sometimes a John tries to get the attention of another John, or vice versa.

Now,

Once a John hooks a Jane, they make a nest out of wood and concrete. In order to pay for the nest, they have to earn a wage.

A wage is payment in the form of money. Money is paid out to Johns and Janes who perform labour or service. Then Johns and Janes go somewhere private (not always) and make little Johnnies and Janies through a series of seemingly absurd physical practices. These little Johnnies and Janies will grow up and do the same thing all over again.

And that's human society.

Not without its charm.

There are all kinds of Johns and Janes. You've got doctor-Janes, lawyer-Johns, teacher-Johns, police-Janes and so on. You catch my jib.

Now, one type out there is known as the artist. An artist is a person who looks at the same things all the other Johns and Janes look at, but for some reason or another, they don't see things quite the same way as most other Johns and Janes do.

Artists are rarely popular, and most can't afford to eat, pay for heat or own a nest like other Johns and Janes. Not only that, but artists often have to worry about other Johns and Janes who try to destroy their work. Dickie calls them critics.

You see, people only like art if other people say it's good, or if it is popular with many people and is put on display in big rooms or in big buildings that are specifically made to formulate the definition of what art is.

Okay,

So,

Being popular is very important to people. People don't like things they don't understand. Like Johns getting on with other Johns. Mostly, people are idiots. An artist may be a fool, but not an idiot. There's a difference, I think.

Dickie says the artist seeks mystery, to see what can't be seen, to experience and discover, to ask questions. That is the artist. These days, most everyone else just wants the punch line. Give it to me quick. I'm in a hurry. Isn't there a meme, insta-something? You know, a snappy way of chatting is to actually chat rather than posting crappy vignettes. Today's human interaction equates to a two-frame meme.

Ping-ding!

So,

There was this one artist. His name was Steichen, took photographs of things he saw differently, including Johns and Janes. The world was black and white back then, with just as much grey as there is now.

One day Steichen decides he wants to colour the black and white world. So he made a photograph with colour in it called *The Pond – Moonlight*. The world saw colour and colour was good. Artists like Steichen made capturing still images magical. These days, there are no artists left. They've all been killed or captured by corporations. Corporations have big, magnificent nets. Then they handed everyone else an apple with a bite already out of it.

Suddenly the duck population skyrocketed. It's just one of those things.

So, yeah,

Artists.

You know, it's not that everyone owns a camera, it's that they don't have to develop photos. The elimination of the simple labour has created an obsession.

These days, people only take photographs of their own face. They even have a cute name for it.

Cute is a word people say.

Actually, they say *kewt*.

This sort of thing is vanity. Vanity is one of many human diseases you can catch, and it is very hard to cure.

Many souls die from it.

Anyway,

Taking a photograph traditionally requires a mirror that exposes a frame of film to light. The process for creating a photographic print from a captured positive is one that requires the absence of light. Science is magical.

Magic is when a person does something unexplainable that is of interest to other people. Science is pretty much the exact same thing, except Johns and Janes demand a plausible explanation.

Science and art are both magical – they love each other – but people pit them against each other, because Johns and Janes have a hard time understanding two things at once.

Horace was hungry. Kip hated it when he ate and worked at the same time, but he couldn't ask for a more capable partner, so he allowed him the odd concession.

The bulb in the refrigerator had been removed so that when the door was open, no light came on. Inside the fridge, there was ketchup, mustard, a jug of water, a link of kielbasa, which had a hunk cut free of it, half of a watermelon, and about sixty rolls of unexposed and undeveloped film.

Kip was pouring rehalogenising bleach into a vessel while Horace, who had a slice of sausage dangling from his mouth like a Cuban cigar, was dumping ammonium thiosulfate into another vessel. One of the three sinks had been filled with hard water.

The two friends preferred to work in silence. Each had specific jobs to do throughout the process. The primary developer, Kip, would dip the silver negative into the byproducts to activate the dye couplers to create emulsion. Horace would then apply the bleach converts. The fixer was applied to remove the silver salts. Then each print was washed, cut and hung to dry.

Both Kip and Horace knew the importance of keeping a very tidy, dust-free dark room. After each developing session, the two friends cleaned and scrubbed the dark room.

After the scrubbing and cleaning, they would review the results of their hard work. Many of the photographs didn't meet Kip's standards and were filed in what Kip called his own personal Dead Letter Cabinet.

Dead Letter is an archaic postal service term that describes the filing section in a postal sorting office where letters that had no destination were filed.

The postal service is how messages were sent before email.

Try and keep up.

Among the discarded images, Kip would often find one or maybe two gems. These were filed separately in various categories by photographic subject matter, content, and finally by the date they were shot.

Unlike most modern photographers, Kip did nothing to enhance the photographs. They were left raw in their developed virgin state. It was this bold honesty that set Kip apart. His willingness to accept the pictures as they were made his work unique when everyone else was shooting with advanced SLR digital image capturing and then performing heavy alterations and manipulations to achieve a final result. Kip simply felt that photography had reached a point where no one knew what was real anymore.

You see,

A picture lacks all basis of reality.

Picture is capture, whether still or movement. It's a frame, or a series of frames. When the frame runs out, the story ends and imagination begins.

There used to be attentiveness, a perception, a goddamn eye for the moment. I miss the moments. Now, there are no pictures. There are images. Godforsaken images, like rash on a child's ass.

There are as many real pictures out there as there are Carolina parakeets.

Dickie once said there is nothing sadder than a dead butterfly.

There are a lot of sad things, and the death of the picture is just one of those things.

You know,

While I'm running hot,

The same goes for animation. Someone used to draw the images, now someone builds a digital model and lets a computer application do the animating. Yeah, sure, you still have to tell the computer what to do. Basically, the "animator" has to know what walking looks like so it appears authentic on the screen, but betchya dollars to donuts (donuts are fried dough treats that donut shops replaced with finger-artisan sandwiches, completely unrelated to animation altogether) the peeps sitting in front of those screens can't even write their names in cursive, let alone draw a solid walk cycle.

But hey,

Who the hell knows how to sew?

All I'm saying is that it's widespread.

We're giving it all up to machines. The few people who don't conform will be consumed by the forest fire of apathy.

For now,

Horace loved being a part of the process. He wished he had the talent of artistic perception that Kip had been born with. He wished for a lot of things, like being able to fly. One day he would. He was sure of it. Horace is the thin vein of silver in a world of dense granite.

Now,

Horace did know his way around a camera, thanks to his friend, but he just didn't have the knack for seeing things the way Kip saw them through his lens. Not everyone is a gifted photographer, just like not everyone is a racecar driver, or a pilot, or a good teacher. It's just one of those things.

People often agonize over their shortcomings rather than focusing on their strengths. Jack knows what that feels like.

Sometimes people can overcome a certain weakness. If you're not proficient with mathematical concepts, it doesn't mean you can't learn them, but it's very likely you won't end up being a physicist. Eventually, everyone receives their driver's permit, but let's face it, roadways around the world are filled with inept drivers.

Kip and Horace made a good team in the dark room, and Kip knew that Horace loved the work. It was just another thing the two friends did together to further their bond of friendship. They both thrived on the presence of the other. They were each other's right hand in so many different ways.

It was a rare thing to have something so beautiful and simple in a world filled with anger, strife and indifference. It forced the pendulum to swing in favour of its opposite, yin. Not that I subscribe to such an ideology, but the concept is apropos for this conversation.

They say a picture is worth a thousand words. What they are really trying to say is that a picture can tell a story without text. This I do believe, and so does Kip. To date, though, Kip has not taken a photograph that he believes captures truth. A single absolute truth. He has been in search of this since he purchased his first used camera from a garage sale when he was a boy.

He believes every photographer must search for truth, and if one is lucky enough to find it, even once, he has fulfilled the full extent of his creative purpose. Kip would eventually find this, not once, but twice. More on that later.

Jack's neighbours are absurd.

But first,

A word about moving.

Okay,

So,

You're new to Winnipeg.

At some point every John and Jane in Peg-City will ask:

Why'd you move here?

Understanding the connotation – it's not a: "What brings you to Winnipeg?" type of inquiry. Nah, Pegs want to know why the hell you moved here. They were born here, and they can't believe you picked it.

It had been six months since Jack moved into the eight-storey building on McDermot in the heart of the Exchange District.

During that time, he had done the mixed bag of this and that. He spent nights at the Rosewood Tea Plant with Horace and the Velic brothers. He acquainted himself with the softer side of the city (benches along the Red at sundown with a Farmery). He mooned over city rooftops and strolled down city hallways at night reading the writing on the walls.

He missed the writing,

A helluva lot.

He lived in one of four loft-style suites on his floor, which was also the top floor of the building.

The building got itself reno'd from the ground up five years ago. The owner received some municipal cheddar, a juicy grant to help get the ball rolling, as part of the city's fourth attempt to reinvigorate the Exchange. Tax refunds were issued to tenants.

Dickie says they found money in a Manitoba Public Insurance slush fund. Years and years of misappropriated tax dollars discovered and re-appropriated into city "re-facing" programs.

Cars were dead, so car insurance went dodo, too.

This really, really happened.

According to Dickie.

You see,

The City wanted to entice a hip-yet-wealthy clientele to tenant the building. One blogger called the whole thing "eye candy for that certain lumber-beard, skinny-pant Menno."

You know,

All that bunch of jib.

Comments thread:

Ha ha hobo tuque

Mennos everywhere, they're in the walls

Hipster with guidebook

Gluten-free nut-milk latte muthaplucka

And the like.

So,

Now, you know, Jack's got bank. More on how he got bank later.

Maybe. If there's time.

It was late, past midnight.

It had been something about hot yoga, controlled breathing, mood lighting and a noise machine that had kept the anxiety at bay. He did this because he was trying everything to do more than cope, he was managing. Gotta manage, got to try to find a path. These were the Tuesdays of the young, on-the-run American-nomadic-cosmic-mystery-man.

There's a story
Unfolds organically
Like steeped Spekel

Jack held a fob-key against the identification nylon on his door. The light changed from amber to green, and Jack opened the door. Behind him, a door opened as well.

Jack turned around; it was the cell phone addict. She was standing, looking down at her cell phone, smiling absently. The same type of absent smile a heroin junkie has just after the plunge.

Jack cleared his throat and she looked up from her phone.

"Hi, Jack."

"Hey, Clair."

"Just uploaded my latest vlog."

Jack didn't ask.

Clair was on pills. That's true. She said so on their first encounter, which was, also, in the hallway. She was proud and disgusted about it all at once. OCD. This she didn't mention, but there were signs. Jack knew the signs.

"Do you ever watch Teddy Klassen's vlogs?"

"Never heard of him."

Clair looked up from her phone again. She stared blankly at Jack. "He's like the top selling agent in the city. Sold 128 homes last year."

"Oh." Jack didn't care.

No one cares.

"Where did you move from again?"

"New York."

"Like, the City?"

"That's it."

Clair didn't look up from her phone. Her face still awash from screen-glow.

"Why'd you move here?"

Jack had a feeling that Clair wasn't looking for an answer to her question. It was merely an observatory statement, lazily posed as a question. She was only offering him a modicum of her attention.

Oh,

And by the way

I told you so.

Now,

Clair's profession was the same profession that many other aimless, somewhat unbalanced extroverted Johns and Janes had chosen once they realized real jobs required a level of integrity and hard work that makes one uncomfortable. Clair was a real estate agent. Teddy Klassen was a big-time agent.

Teddy schtuped Bill Jib's wife.

Eventually, he schtups Clair, but I don't have the rights to that tale.

Clair would like to be Teddy. Not for the schtuping, but for the selling.

There are more real estate agents in Winnipeg, per capita, than any other city in Canada.

That's really, really true. According to Dickie.

She did what people do when they go to work: she fabricated illusion and myth.

Her cup of tea is property. Property is called real estate. Real estate is something that people think they own, but in truth, the Canadian government could take it away from Canadians at any time without reason, that the English Crown could take away at any time without reason, as they had done from the true rightful original owners of the land.

Clair had sold fifty-two properties in her seventh year as an agent.

The agency she worked for gave her a plaque made of particleboard and tin for her office wall to honour the achievement. The plaque made other, less successful, agents jealous and work harder to achieve better results.

That was the intent.

The plaque worked gangbusters.

Gangbusters is an idiom that finds its origin in the 1935 radio series *Gang Busters*. Each episode started with high excitement. Radio was Netflix. This information will not be useful later on.

So,

Other corporations around the world did similar things; these ideas also worked wonders on achieving better results from their employees. They used to hand out gold-plated watches, but the Chinese started asking three cents more per unit, so Western companies switched to plaques, or pieces of laser-engraved glass.

Clair had a sister. Her sister had a disease; that disease was fame.

Dickie calls it Kardashi-itus.

Lots of Johns and Janes suffer from Kardashi-itis.

Now,

Clair's sister wasn't really famous anymore, because fame is a full-time job, and unless you keep doing things other people find interesting, you lose fame.

Clair's sister, whose name is Angie, won an Olympic gold medal for curling. Curling is a sport that requires that you know how to throw rocks and sweep a broom.

Pegs love curling.

Angie was a good curler, but she wasn't very pretty. People like when famous people are pretty. Clair was pretty, a good disease to have. She had honey hair that fell past her shoulders. Her eyes were blue, and she had flushed cheeks. She was short, you know like five-two, and licked her lips a lot.

Clair wore yoga sweats and a sports bra. She was in her bare feet, curling her toes into the hallway carpet.

"Have you got two pomegranates?"

Clair.

Clair.

Clair.

Named after a Debussy tune about moonlight. Something she hasn't seen in years.

Jack did his best to force a smile. It went unnoticed. He was tired and not in the mood for Clair's eccentric requests.

"Sorry, fresh out."

It sounded sincere-ish.

"Seriously?"

"Yup."

"But it's pomegranate season."

"So everyone keeps telling me."

Jack wanted to point out that she didn't have any pomegranates, either. But you gotta pick your battles.

"Oh, okay. Maybe I'll step out later and make a run to Food Fair. Do you need anything?"

That's what irritated Jack the most about Clair. She lied a lot and never offered any reason for needing pomegranate – or any of the other barrages of grocery requests she threw at him. She once asked if he had any tampons.

"No, thanks, I have what I need."

"Except pomegranate."

Jack made no reply. Clair wasn't looking at him, anyway. She was creeping on friends via Facebook, which was what Facebook was used for. No one "liked" anything anymore. People just posted and skulked from behind their IP addresses. According to a recent poll, Facebook users were ninety percent women in those days. Easy now, I don't write the stats. Plus, you can't trust them anyway. The stats, that is.

Jack stepped inside his apartment and closed the door behind him. Clair stood in the hallway for another thirty minutes, staring at her phone with her apartment door wide open.

The next morning, Jack decided to go for a run. Jack always kept in good shape. He never knew when he would have to sprint from some location to another trying to evade police while completing a new piece. He was saddened in that moment because the whole reason for moving to Winnipeg was to disappear and lay low for who knows how long. The idea of going for a jog seemed fruitless and more of a routine than necessity.

At the end of the hallway – Jack's side – a door opened, and the old man stepped out. He bent to collect the newspaper lying on the floor. This time, baggy cotton boxers were hiked up over his belly button, and the wool socks hung loose at the ankles. Shirtless and smoking a pipe. A rich plume of smoke emerged from the mouth of the pipe, hiding his features. Through the cloud, he waved at Jack. The glass in his hand clinked with ice. Jack could hear the sound reverberate down the hallway.

"Duke of righteousness, bless his lusting heart, used to serve cratur with the fried eggs. You know, start the day with a snap." The old man looked off vacantly down the hallway and smiled. "Miss that SOB, rest his soul."

"Cratur?"

"Whisky, son." He shook the ice in his glass. "Whisky."

"Is that a thing?"

"Sure. Thank god for it, too. Goes nice with pomegranate seeds. I always float a few fresh ones. 'Tis the season, you know?"

Jack held back a smile. The old man fanned the newspaper open.

"Why do I read this thing?" Shaking his head, shaggy grey hair flopping to one side. "It tells me what happened yesterday. Basically the same thing that happened the day before. It seems I have the same affliction as everybody else. I think today is going to be different."

He slapped the front page with the back of his hand.

"Sometimes that old bastard, Aubrey Cusack, will write something worth reading. Used to be one helluva reporter. These days they've got him by the wang, too, don't ya know." He rolled the newspaper and tucked it under his arm.

Jack felt like he was supposed to say something. He had no idea what the old man was running at. Jesus, did people really still get newspaper deliveries?

The old man took a sip from his glass and then drew on his pipe.

He smiled at Jack, smoke leaked between his stained teeth.

"Got to have my morning flavour."

Jack had no idea what that meant, either. Was the old man referring to the beverage he held, the pipe, both? Maybe none of the above. The old man went inside his apartment. Jack chuckled out loud. *Guy is crazy. They all are.*

He reached down to tie the laces of his runners. There was a sound against the door of the one neighbour he had never met. Clair told him that her name was Andrea, or something like that, and that she suffered from agoraphobia. Clair was wrong again on both counts.

Jack closed his door and walked down the hallway towards the elevator. As he passed his neighbour's door, he heard it open, and he turned back to have a look. He could see an eye watching him, but couldn't make out other features. The person on the other side of the door made no sound and watched Jack until he stepped onto the elevator. As the elevator doors closed, Jack watched as his neighbour's door shut at the same time.

Kip was standing in front of a restaurant window in the French quarter where people eat duck. On the other side of the pane, a runner was delivering orders to a couple of lesbians. Lesbians are Janes who like other Janes.

Kip's stomach barked; he was hungry. The lighting inside the restaurant was warm and low, and it was radiating through the window.

All light produces heat.

Dickie calls it thermodynamics.

Other people do, too.

Doesn't mean people can always feel the effects of it. Kip couldn't. Not really. He rubbed his hands together. There was a chill in the night air.

He continued on his way, walking to the corner of Des Meurons. He looked north. Nothing, yet.

"Hey, little help?"

A man – looked at least seventy, cigarette dangling from his lips – needed a light.

"Sorry, don't smoke."

"There's a shocker. Was a time it didn't matter either way. You kept a light on you, just cuz. Now, pfft!"

Kip smiled.

The man pushed up the peak of his Colorado Rockies hat.

"See those sun dogs today?"

Kip shook his head.

A sun dog is – ah hell, I'll let the old timer tell it.

"Beautiful. A Winnipeg thing, you know. One of the few sights we got left. Not too many places in the world you see 'em. Like seeing two suns kiss and then explode into pure light."

Pow!

The old man took the cigarette from his lips and put it and his hands into his pockets.

"Goddamn cold out tonight. Winnipeg summers, sheesh! Be seeing you."

"Yeah, take care."

"Sure, like I've got a choice."

And he went down the road with his opinions and unlit cigarette. Kip took a seat on a bus bench. The bench had the face of real estate agent Anthony Bruno on it. "Number 11 in sales," it said. I get a kick every time I see one, garbage cans and bus benches, always a real estate agent. Sometimes a whole team of agents. Terrific!

Kip was scrolling through old texts on his phone. A forced advertisement appeared. He had to click on it and watch it before cellular service would resume. The advertisement was for body spray. He had bought deodorant the other day, and the sale data registered with the tracking algorithm to produce a future ad for related consumer products.

Everyone in Canada was tagged with an individual marketing number. Just like a health number, social insurance number, employee number, driver's licence number, and on and on. You get the jib. Numbers! Seger damn well felt like one.

The advert ended, and his service resumed. He locked his phone, looked up, and saw the Interceptor make the corner. Now it was heading south on Marion. It pulled into the curb and came to a stop. The window rolled down.

"So, get in."

Kip got up and walked around to the front of the cruiser, got in on the passenger side. Devlin put the window up. The cab reeked of cheap cologne. Kip noticed Devlin was out of uniform – in civilian clothes.

"Did you visit your daughter?"

Devlin looked out the driver's side window; two people were making out beneath the awning of an apartment entrance.

"Yeah."

"How's she doing?"

"The same. Doctors don't know shit."

Kip got the message and changed the subject.

"Off duty, but still driving the squad car?"

"We need wheels, don't we?"

"What if, you know, someone notices?"

"Notice what? A cop in a cop car?"

"Guess so."

"Good, cause looky looky."

Devlin took out a large zip baggie of cocaine and unrolled it in front of Kip.

"Very clean and very pure. Just scooped this off some guy that snitches for me."

"Have you tried it yet?"

"Maybe just a sniff. You know, to check quality."

Devlin made four rails on a copy of Style Manitoba. He took the first line into his left nostril and the second into his right.

"Oh yeah! Teach gives it an A."

"All yours."

Kip took the plate and looked outside the window for any observers. Devlin rolled his eyes.

"Those fish out there don't give a hoot, and they certainly don't want any attention from a sitting pig. Hit it or quit it."

Kip dragged the first rail and pinched his nose. Then he hit the second rail. He coughed.

"Good shit, right?"

"Yeah, really good."

"Let's hit Marion Hotel for some bevies. I'm meeting a dude who's going to hook us up with a thing tonight. He assures satisfaction."

"Sounds promising."

But,

Instead of beers, Dev had managed to convince Kip to climb into a booth with him at the Eatery next door. Dev always seemed to get his way.

The server was chipper. He brought menus with a server's smile and two iced waters.

"Do the gentlemen care for additional beverages?"

Kip wasn't hungry. Food was the last thing he wanted to think about. Dev was a completely different story altogether. Somehow, he could take down rails and still want a plate in front of him. It was weird, far from a typical reaction to coke. Kip laughed and Devlin started to laugh. It made the server uncomfortable. Devlin looked up at him.

"Farmery on tap?"

"Yes."

"That's me, then."

The server looked at Kip. "Same."

Kip tried to control his laughter by swallowing it. And it felt like he had swallowed it.

"Have a look at the menu, and I'll be right back with the beers." Kip opened his menu and tried his best to peruse the fare. Dev threw his menu on the table.

"I am going to kill a bison burger."

Kip didn't want anything. But he felt pressured to order something.

"I think I'll have the same."

Devlin leaned into the table. Kip looked up from his menu at him. "Tonight's gonna be a howl." Then he sat back against the booth cushion. "I promise you, pal, it's gonna be Hollywood!"

The server returned with the beers and set them in front of

their owners.

"Tonight's specials are…"

"Don't bother. I will have the bison burger."

The server felt jarred by Devlin's behaviour.

"And yourself."

"The same thing the same way."

"Perfect. I'll go send these through. Flag me down if you need anything."

The server walked away.

"Don't be such a punk all the time, Dev."

"What do you mean?"

He grinned at Kip. Kip shook his head, then took a sip from his pint. Devlin slid out of the booth.

"Gonna go take a leak and see if my guy is here yet."

Kip nodded. He shrunk back into the corner of the booth. The coke was really getting to him. The room felt hot and very bright, washed in light. His heart was thudding in his chest. He felt the slow pace of everyone in the room crushing him. He reached for the perspiring glass of water. The dampness collected on the surface of the glass felt nice and cooled his sweating palms.

"Orders are up! Here is your food."

Kip looked up from the glass of water. It seemed like only a second had passed since the server had taken his order. Kip gulped the water.

"Are you okay?"

"Just find it a little hot in here." Kip lifted his empty water glass. "I'll take another refill on the water."

Kip looked up from his plate of food. A man was looking down at him through bushy salt-and-pepper eyebrows. He wore a houndstooth newsboy on his head and was tying the belt on a beige trench.

"Sorry, I thought you were…"

The man cut him off.

"I know."

The man looked up at the wall behind Kip.

"I came over to look at that."

Kip turned to look. The man pointed at the photograph in a frame on the wall.

"I knew him."

Kip looked at the man.

"You knew Greg Olaf?"

The name said aloud brought back old memories. The man smiled as he thought absently about days gone by, then his smile was replaced by a subtle sadness.

"We worked together. I guess you could say we were partners."

It looked like the man was going to say something else, but he didn't. Kip didn't pick up the trail of his broken thought.

The man rubbed the sagging jowls at his chin. He was still thinking of the past, then he looked at Kip. "Do you know Greg's work?"

"Yeah, I love his work."

"Are you a photographer?"

"Yes." Kip felt as though he'd said it too quickly. "Just a hobbyist, really."

"Here." The man handed Kip a business card. "Aubrey Cusack." The man's icy blue eyes caught the light. "Come by my office." He stared right through Kip, as though he knew everything. "Bring some of your photos." He smiled. "So I can see if you're the real thing or a hack."

The man walked away.

Kip looked at the card.

Aubrey Cusack
Senior Reporter
Free Press
1355 Mountain Ave
3rd Floor
Winnipeg

Devlin slid back into the booth, a wide grin parting his lips.

"Oh, will you look at this."

He was, of course, referring to the burger and fries sitting before him.

"Looks good." Kip faked a smile.

"Looks like goddamn art."

Devlin picked up the burger and took a large bite. He shook his head and leaned back to get comfortable.

"Oh god, yes!'

Then Devlin noticed Kip was picking at his food.

"What's your deal? Don't tell me you're going bust on me."

"Nah, the coke hit me a little wrong."

Devlin reached across the table and slapped Kip on the shoulder.

"Ease up, brotha. Come on now, don't waste the good food in front of you."

Dev's jovial mood was contagious and beginning to rub off on Kip. He smiled and took a bite of his burger. "Damn, that is good." Kip was lying, but thought it sounded convincing.

"Now check this. My guy is waiting for us in the hotel bar. We finish these babies, and then head next door for a bevy. Then we head out. He says the girls are free and fine as shit."

"Free?"

"The girls are free, and so is the booze. But the cover is 400 <CC>."

"Shit, Dev. I don't have that kind of scratch."

"Don't worry about it. I've got it covered."

Devlin leaned back in his seat and smiled at Kip.

"Oh, really? How do you figure?"

"I'm supplying the sugar."

"Ah."

"Don't worry about it. I've taken care of everything."

Now,

I ask you,

How many times have you heard those famous last words before?

As I had mentioned, Devlin, like so many other people, wore cliché like costume jewellery. It's just one of those things.

Kip ordered two shots of tequila and two beers while Devlin sourced out his contact. After he paid the barkeep, he turned and surveyed the crowd. Devlin was standing in the corner with a man twice his age in appearance. Kip waded through the people until he was able to hand Devlin his drinks.

"Kip, this is Randall. He'll be our, um, guide this evening."

They finished their drinks faster than Kip would've liked. He realized he was nothing more than a passenger for the evening. It didn't bother him. He was fine to go with the flow.

Kip sat in the front of the Interceptor. Devlin did the driving, and Randall remained silent in the back seat.

They had been driving for the better part of an hour. No one said anything. Kip had shot questioning glances in Devlin's direction once they were well beyond the Perimeter.

Info blurb:

The Perimeter refers to the Perimeter Highway, which is a highway that encompasses – wait for it – the perimeter of the city of Winnipeg. Ba-ding!

Now you know, and knowing is half the battle: G. I. Joe!

Randall leaned forward and tapped Devlin on the shoulder. "Turn right."

His voice soft, near whisper.

Devlin followed the man's instructions. The road was dirt. There were no lights. Devlin flicked on his bright beams. He didn't look at all nervous. It put Kip at ease.

Randall pointed. "On the left."

A clearing. The tree line broke to a wide expanse of property that had once been a field. The grass had been professionally cut and landscaped, leaving the surrounding, unruly prairie grass as evidence that it was a small job. Over a small man-made bluff, a large building came into view. An A-frame cottage. Light peeked around the edges of the closed blinds covering the windows.

"Park here."

There were at least fifteen other vehicles, all high-end imports. Kip was shocked. Devlin looked in the rearview at Randall.

"From other provinces. We do this twice a year. We get people from all over, as you can see. And you're not our first cop."

For a moment, it looked like the man smiled. "Follow me."

Devlin locked the cruiser, and they did as they were told. They came through the front doors into an opulent lounge area with leather sofas, designer chairs and a jade-coral backsplashed bar.

Their guide led them to the counter, where the barman took orders from them. Men were smoking and drinking. Most were talking to women. Those women not occupied with a particular patron were circulating, wearing little more than a smile.

"The evening is yours. Whatever you desire can be provided, within reason of course. This will be ample payment."

Randall held up the four ounces of cocaine. "This bag of oranges will also cover a repeat visit."

Randall stood up and locked eyes for a moment with the bartender. Then he smiled at the two friends.

"This is where I leave you."

Randall walked away. Devlin shoved an elbow in Kip's side and pointed at the different young women parading the floor. Kip took a moment to observe the decadence of the room.

"How did you find out about this place?"

"Let's just say the man was right when he said I wasn't the first cop to come here."

Kip laughed and ordered a vodka soda. A woman leaned against the bar, and the bartender gave her a shot of whisky. A red dress grabbed at her body, and there were no lines beneath the fabric, which gave the impression that the red dress was her skin. Breasts swelled above the low scoop at the neck; it amazed Kip that such a delicate prison was so effective.

Kip watched her down a shot and finger for another. She looked at Kip and smiled. Her lips were slick like slices of canned peaches. Kip realized he didn't care what words came through them.

"Hi."

Single-syllable salutations shake the soul.

"Hi," Kip said back – or something like it.

She held up her shot glass and chinked it against Kip's vodka soda.

"Drink it, why don't you?"

Good advice, and Kip did as he was asked. She downed her shot gracefully. Devlin's mouth was open.

"Why don't you come with me?"

Kip looked at Devlin.

"That your father?"

"No."

"Then why ask permission?"

Devlin laughed. "He's shy."

"I like shy."

She took Kip's hand, and he let himself be led.

The woman took Kip to a bedroom. A sign was hanging on the door that she flipped over to read "occupied." They entered the room. She led Kip to the bed, and he sat on the edge of the mattress. The woman went to a drink trolley. Kip fidgeted and picked up a small, ceramic figurine off the night table.

"You're curious. Didn't you mother ever tell you not to touch other people's property?"

"Sorry." Kip set the figurine back where he'd found it.

"I'm just teasing you, it's a cheap toy pigeon or something. And anyway, you're about to touch me and I'm not really yours, am I?"

She handed Kip a glass. "Vodka soda, right?"

"Whatever, really, doesn't matter."

"Sure it does, have exactly what you want."

"This is fine."

Kip tried masking his nerves. He hadn't been with a lot of women, and all this elaborate staging fell on the outside of his comfort zone.

"What's your name?"

"We don't do that here."

"Oh."

The woman took Kip's hand and walked him towards the bed. His heart was racing. The mix of alcohol and cocaine only made it bump faster. He was hot. He sat down on the edge of the bed. The woman leaned in and kissed him, and his head began to spin.

She moved towards Kip, took his hands and guided them to her lower back. She bent forward and kissed Kip on the lips again. This time Kip let go and submitted to the kiss.

The door to the room opened. A man entered the room. The woman stood up from Kip and covered herself with her hands. It was all she could do. She didn't seem all that distraught by the sudden disturbance. Kip, despite his shock, stood up as well.

"You're mine!"

He swayed, kind of drunk. Johns and Janes like to get kind of drunk. The woman stared at the man calmly.

Men are interesting creatures. They have for many millennia believed that they are able to lay claim on a woman.

Millennium is a measurement of time equating to a thousand years; it's been used since the birth of Christ. Christ is a white magician who can moonwalk on water and turn water into wine.

Abracadabra, baby.

So, yeah, millennia means a helluva long time.

When things changed, a lot of men didn't get the memo.

Laws adjusted, but some men didn't adjust with them.

Women have never had these thoughts.

It's just one of those things.

"You're breaking the house rules. You need to leave. Get out."

The woman's indifference only enraged the man further. He came toward her and grabbed her arm. She yelled for someone, but no one came. Kip stepped between them.

"Let go of her."

"Stay out of this."

A blade flared on a glimmer of light.

"Get in here."

Three other men entered the room. Kip didn't like the size of them. He had no idea what to do. He was afraid. He took out his phone and sent a one-word text to Devlin – trouble!

"What did you just do?"

The man held the knife point at Kip.

"Nothing. I just want to leave."

"Too late for that. You already put hands on my property. You get this as a prize, right in the stomach."

Oi! Who talks like that?

Dickie'll tell ya there's all kinds. An American president comes to mind.

"Look, I don't want any trouble. I'll just leave."

The man punched Kip in the face. Kip tumbled back onto the bed. It was a good hit, it dazed him. Kip slowly worked his way back to his feet. The man looked back at his entourage.

"The kid can take a punch, I'll give him that." The man wiped sweat from his brow with his knife hand. "You don't know who I am, do you?"

"No."

Kip nursed his jaw.

"Doesn't matter, I guess."

A very dark feeling started to manifest in Kip's heart. He realized he might very well die in this room in the next few minutes. Then he saw Devlin come through the door.

"What's all this, then?"

The man turned to face Devlin, then looked back at Kip.

"Used a lifeline, huh?"

Devlin cracked his knuckles. They popped like microwave kernels.

"Man, you look upset. Are you upset?"

The man signalled to his bodyguards.

The woman crouched down and picked up her dress, holding it to her naked body.

"I bet you're one of those people with a scent allergy. Oh, I can just see it, you hate perfume and stuff, huh? Your eyes tear up? Do you get the headaches?"

The bodyguards stepped towards Devlin. They were big men with big hands, big arms, big chests, big heads with little between the ears.

"Jesus, you are one of those, aren't you? And I bet you're left-handed, too."

Devlin grabbed a liquor bottle from the trolley and clubbed the man closest to him over the head. The connection made a dull sound.

The bottle didn't break, but the man's jaw did; he kept his footing just long enough so everyone in the room could see his jaw swinging loosely like a Newton's cradle. Then he fell and his broken jaw went him. His head struck the end of a table on the way down. He lay on the floor, and blood drained from the wound.

The bottle left Devlin's hand and struck another bodyguard in the face. This time the bottle did shatter, and the victim stumbled backwards but remained on his feet. His face was dashed with cuts from splintered glass.

The last bodyguard threw a well-executed right cross. Devlin dodged it stealthily. A left came, and then another right. Devlin bent low, and the first went over his head, the second punch came up short.

Dev leaned way back on his heels before stepping into the man with a solid shot into the gut. The man doubled over, and Dev put knuckles on his jaw. The man tumbled over with a grunt.

The other bodyguard had found his feet again. He took a step and followed through with his fist, and despite the blood in his left eye, he managed to snap Devlin with a firm roundhouse. Devlin rolled with the punch, limiting the impact. He still felt it and it rung his bell nicely. So, he dealt one right back to him. The man staggered with the blow and went down on one knee. Devlin kicked him in the throat, and that was all there was to that.

Now,

One might think Devlin was enjoying himself.

And one would be right.

Dev wasn't one to shy from a tussle.

He hadn't forgotten about the knife, either, but he had lost sight of the man holding it. The blade found his neck. Dev managed to get his hands up in time, but not before the knife teased his soft flesh with its edge.

Paralyzed with fear, Kip watched as his friend struggled with the man who had gained the upper hand. Devlin was losing. If the knife managed to come any closer, it would cut his throat.

Devlin thought of his daughter. If he died, that meant she would die, too, or so the internal logic went. The thought helped. A sudden rush of adrenalin gave him what he needed to force the knife away from his throat.

Devlin broke from the grip, but let out a curse when the knife bit at the flesh along his forearm, cutting him superficially. He whirled 360 degrees on his heels and danced around the man, drilling an elbow into the nape of the man's neck. The man dumped the knife and fell forward. He groaned, but was still conscious.

Devlin lay down on the floor beside the man. This way they faced each other.

"I don't know you, but I bet you know who I am now."

Then Dev grabbed a handful of his hair, lifted his head, and drove it into the floor.

Devlin found his feet and appraised the room. He looked himself over. Two new men entered the room. They each had guns. Dev smiled. Berettas.

Randall came in behind them. He looked at the woman and tilted his head towards the door. She scurried out of the room.

"Time for you two to be on your way."

Devlin chuckled.

"All done, anyway."

They were escorted from the cottage. Nothing was said. Outside, Devlin took a drag off of his e-cigarette and handed it to Kip. Kip didn't smoke, but took it anyway. He took a pull on the e-cig. To calm his nerves.

"You alright?"

"Yeah, I'm good."

"Don't let those dick-holes ruin your night."

But they had, and Kip just wanted to go home. He felt burnt on the whole thing.

Devlin sensed his waning spirits and offered him some coke. Kip waved it off.

Devlin took the electronic cigarette back from Kip and smiled at him.

"You know I've always got your back."

Kip smiled. It was true. He had always known Devlin could fight, too, but to see him in action was something else. He had no idea how to handle a situation like that. It came so naturally to his friend.

Dev cursed under his breath. "Goddamn mosquitoes are thick tonight." He swatted at the air as though it would help.

Kip smiled.

"Should've had a cup of Spekel rather than that last shot of vodka." Devlin put his arm around his friend. "By a lonely prison wall, I heard a young girl calling…" He tightened his arm and pulled Kip closer to him. "You know this one. No one likes to sing alone."

"Michael, they have taken you away. For you stole Trevelyan's corn, so the young might see the morn. Now a prison ship lies waiting in the bay."

The volume of their voices increased, drowning the drama behind them.

"Low lie the fields of Athenry, where once we watched the small free birds fly. Our love was on the wing, we had dreams and songs to sing. It's so lonely 'round the fields on Athenry."

They sang without inhibition, voices carrying into the night.

It was Sunday. The lights were off. The factory was closed.

Jack stood by while Kurt and a handful of his maintenance mechanics tinkered with a conveyor bridge that had failed earlier in the week. The damn thing had been grinding on its rotors.

Another six-day production workweek had come to a close. Kurt stretched an open hand up towards Jack.

"Hand me the number five wrench, will you?"

Jack sifted through the tool trolley and handed Kurt the wrench. Kurt threaded the nut firmly into the rivets. He rolled the flatbed out from beneath the belt and reached for a rag. He wiped grease from his fingers.

"You look like hell, Jack."

"That bad, huh?"

Kurt nodded. He extended his arm, and Jack pulled him to his feet. Kurt tossed the rag on top of the tool trolley. He picked up a set of keys.

"Those keys for a vehicle?"

Kurt nodded.

"You own a functional vehicle?"

"The law states that due to the nature of my business, I'm afforded the privilege of the use of one commercial vehicle. I use it for transport from the farm to our plant here. Fuel costs and maintenance are expensive, to say the least, but I need the damn thing."

Kurt hung the keys on a nail on the wall inside his office. He closed the office door and walked over to a mini fridge.

"Cold beer?"

"Sure."

Kurt stuck the necks of the bottles in the bottle opening affixed to the wall. He lifted the caps off the beers and handed one to Jack.

"Thanks."

They clinked the necks of the bottles together and each took a swig.

"That's nice."

Jack looked at the label. "Fort Garry pale. Never heard of it."

"Brewed in Winnipeg."

Jack looked around the plant. Everything was meticulously arranged; all items had a place and were neatly stored where they belonged unless in use. The factory was spotless. The old saying – "you could eat off the floors" – didn't quite do justice to the Rosewood Tea Plant.

Jack kept his life neat and orderly.

Had to.

A pang of homesickness.

He had left the life he knew behind him, in a split overnight decision. Caught the scent of danger and left everything right where it was. Grabbed what he needed and put his world and Alice in his rearview. He had loved her, and still did. Although, he'd never said so. He felt like such a coward.

There was no time to explain any of it to her. He wanted to. Even if there had been the time, he wouldn't have told her. He couldn't. It wasn't safe, for her. That didn't make what he'd done any less selfish.

The thought of her wondering what had happened to him, just

vanishing like that, no explanation. It was a shameful thing, and a powerful trigger for his anxiety.

It was what it was.

It was so damn complicated. That's what it was.

By now, she would have moved on. Found someone else. Jack wondered if he'd ever have the chance to explain it to her. He felt sick. Felt pressure in his chest.

Damn!

He took a sip of beer. Tried to choke down all that regret. No point in going down that road. He had made his choices and now he would see them through. He realized the muscles in his face had become taut thinking about the past. He took a deep, slow breath to alleviate the mounting pressure inside of him.

Kurt was organizing folders into a filing cabinet. He closed the filing cabinet door and grabbed his beer off of his desk. "Let's head up to the roof and take a load off. Beautiful day out. May as well enjoy it."

The roof of the Rosewood Building tea manufacturing plant was a beautiful garden. It was in full bloom, too. Lush green leaves of the organic herbs flitting upon the soft afternoon breeze. Rich colours of vibrant blooms neatly cared for by loving hands. A wind chime played gentle notes, the only sound that could be heard.

Kurt had always wanted a sanctuary that would be available to him whenever he needed to think, decompress, ponder and meditate. There are few people who truly take the time to unpack the day in order to make room for the next. Kurt realized the importance of personal space, well designed with comfortable seating.

According to Dickie, sitting is the most important.

Kurt had applied as much of his knowledge about Zen religion to the garden as was within his ability. Everything deliberate. Do one thing at a time, do it wholly and completely. Multitasking was nothing more than corporate mythology and had never been humanly possible. Complete a single task, do it well, then move on to the next. That was the way one could confidently ensure the finest result. Kurt also believed this was the blueprint for authentic success.

Success.

What a word.

All the world's knowledge is found in the ashes of failure.

Maybe that's what Kurt meant.

Anyway,

There was a small greenhouse for growing organic vegetables and more delicate fare in the wintertime. Kurt preferred to grow as much of his own food himself when possible. All his crops came from heirloom non-GMO seeds, collected from all over the world. He had travelled great distances to get his hands on scarce varieties.

While he had taken as many precautions as necessary to stave off insect damage, he also had a level of acceptance and comfort for the odd blemish. In Kurt's eyes, produce is as much a reflection of human life as a heartbeat. It's not perfect, but with love and care, it will develop to proper maturity.

Dickie calls him a kahuna.

Kahuna is what surfers call the "big wave."

Jack and Kurt sat in silence, sipping their cold beers.

It was nice to be in the presence of a companion and still enjoy the understatement of silence. Jack found more and more that Winnipeg and its residents were really growing on him. He had come from a city were the pace was furious and the people never stopped going at full speed all the time. No one ever stopped to take a real personal moment.

After a while, Kurt stood up and finally broke the silence.

"Let's head down and get another beer. I also want to tune in to the news."

From beneath the counter, Kurt grabbed the remote. He pointed it at the wall-mounted screen. The screen made a flash, and then the daily Corporate Canada logo filled the screen:

The cleanest refinery water on the planet. Drink refinery water, fortified with the mandated amount of minerals and vitamins. Made safe and brought to you by Shell. Your trusted name in refinery drinking water.

The logo faded out, and the screen switched over to regular programming. Kurt searched the guide for the national news and made his selection.

He kept up on trending news and liked being informed even if national news was government regulated.

He cursed as he fiddled with an unresponsive volume button. It was sticky.

"Alright, who spilled pop on the clicker?"

No response. He shook his head and wiped the surface of the controller with a disinfectant wipe. Jack, on the bar stool, watched and sipped his beer.

Kurt tried again, and it worked. The volume came at a blast, and Kurt adjusted the volume down to a reasonable level. The voice of the newscaster filled the room:

The recently passed Bill 88, the mobile technology amendment partition, in conjunction with the agreement arranged between the A.C.B. Association of Canadian Banks and the M.T.C Mobile Technology Conglomerate, requires that all mobile devices are now subject to market-mining, or D.M.M.

What this means for Canadians:

Any mobile device conversation, text, live call, email, or any other form of wireless communication could be subject to data marketing mining.

What is D.M.M.?:

D.M.M. will be used by the M.T.C. to collect and share information transmitted between users of mobile devices to determine more accurate marketing on behalf of undisclosed business partners of the M.T.C. and the A.C.B.

One example of D.M.M. would be when a mobile device user sends a text stating that he/she enjoyed a cheeseburger at their favourite fast food restaurant. This information is paid for and shared with the restaurant business, who in turn can choose to target the individual with a direct singular marketing plan.

The A.C.B. is pleased with the passing of Bill 88 and feels that this will give corporate Canada the economic boost needed to compete once again on the global market.

While many Canadians have expressed concerns with privacy laws, the A.C.B. and Corporate Canada feel the benefits greatly outweigh the triviality of personal privacy.

The M.T.C has already launched a series of government and A.C.B.-funded advertising from the past.

The adverts feature computer-generated versions of real animals used in the past and now extinct. The adverts, already labelled retro-marketing, bring about the revival of past nostalgic marketing efforts.

Historic consumer response to furry creatures has been much higher than to that of an actual spokesperson. The M.T.C. has determined, through consumer polling, that this is because people don't trust human representatives. They do trust animals, as they are incapable of speech and therefore cannot lie.

In other news. The Canadian government is demanding that all citizens, landed immigrants and permanent residents, provide saliva samples for DNA cataloguing. The program comes from one launched in Winnipeg some decades past by the now defunct Manitoba Public Insurance. At the time, MPI tried to collect DNA samples of citizens for unknown purposes. The campaign was abandoned.

The Canadian Government wants to remind citizens about the mandatory income tax reassessment with the Canadian Revenue Agency. The recent changes to the Hard Currency Act instituted just one year ago demand that all Canadians file by the deadline or face severe penalty and imprisonment.

Tourism Canada has stated that all visitors to Canada will have the opportunity to exchange hard currency to <CC> Cancur upon arrival into the country.

The president of the United States has stated that the U.S. has no intention of following Canada's cyber income program. Some economists speculate the U.S. is simply quietly observing the effects this act will have on Canada's future economy.

The following provincial naming rights are expiring:

Esso Oil Province, formerly known as Alberta
Interac Province, formerly known as Ontario
Molson Province, formerly known as Nova Scotia

Current corporations will be afforded the opportunity to renew their current provincial naming rights. If the corporation chooses to allow this right to lapse, bidding will begin one month after the lapse.

The Canadian government continues to support the Naming Rights Act, since its inception managed to deliver all failing provinces from bankruptcy.

Kurt muted the screen, threw the remote under the counter and shook his head. Jack sipped his beer reluctantly; it did little to assuage his growing anxieties.

"Can you believe that? When do you suppose we lost control?"

Jack smiled. "I don't know. I'm an American. This is all new to me. I can't get over how often I get charged service fees, though. I have to pay a fee to access my money here. Pay one to make a purchase. Pay one to move my money around. I imagine those with less money than I have would get whittled down to nothing pretty quickly."

"No, everyone gets charged a percentage based on reported personal incomes to the CRA each year. Everyone is essentially getting hit with what the Gov thinks we can each afford to lose. Kind of like taxes, but the money goes right back to the ACB rather than into government-funded programs."

"Really? I had no idea."

Kurt laughed sardonically.

"Last night, I texted Kris to pick up some Cola for the bar. Today, I got three Cola advertisements on my phone."

Kurt was grumbling. He was talking more to himself than to Jack. He had occupied himself by sifting through texts on his phone. Jack didn't answer him. Instead, he swivelled in his chair.

Kris had just come in. He took a seat beside Jack at the bar. He had a tablet with him. He looked up at the television and chuckled.

Kurt was wiping tumblers and lowball glasses with a rag and smiled at the two young men sitting on the opposite side of the bar.

He set a box of empty beer bottles atop the wood. "Going to use these beauties for an experiment."

But no one was listening to him. Jack was watching the tablet with Kris.

All the while, unnoticed, Horace was in the corner with Kip playing video games and bickering back and forth about which was the better upright, Ms. Pac Man or Donkey Kong.

I must admit. I find something gluttonous and hypersexual about Ms. Pac Man trying to gorge herself by chasing two bouncing cherries through a maze.

Just saying.

Also, the prefix "Ms." and then the word "man" in her married name seems – well, I don't even know, perplexing.

Kip reached for his can of pop, paused the game and took a swig from the can. Horace did the same. It was like they were sharing the same brain. Kip resumed the game, and a few moments later cursed out loud as Ms. Pac Man's last life tragically came to a ghostly end.

Kip stood and went to the console.

"Metroid?"

"Oh, yeah."

Kip sat down in his chair.

"Start from the beginning, or should we code in and see who can complete the game the quickest?"

Horace set his pop can down on the side table.

"Let's use the 'Justin Bailey' code."

"Hey, have you ever wondered who Justin Bailey was?"

Horace scratched his head.

"All the time."

"Probably a designer on the game."

"Nope. I researched it on the Internet. It is a total mystery."

"Makes you wonder. Did you ever feel like the code word was too good?"

"You mean like it made the game too easy to complete because you already had all the weapons and energy tanks?"

"Exactly. It kind of seemed like a betrayal to the game's difficulty."

Horace smiled and slid lower in his chair.

"I see what you're saying. Like how compact discs replaced cassette tapes. You could just skip a song anytime you wanted on a CD, but with cassettes you were more prone to just listen to the whole album."

"So who was Justin Bailey?"

"No one knows."

"Someone does."

"Heh, yeah, I guess someone out there does."

"I picture this villain, heavy trench coat, face bathed in thick shadows. Justin Bailey, man of mystery."

"Yeah, right! Probably some total super nerd who still lives with his mom."

Kip shook his head.

"We'll never know. One of life's many cool mysteries."

"Ah, can we play now?"

"Yeah, totally."

"Who goes first?"

Kip picked up the controller. "I will."

He entered the words "Justin Bailey," then another twelve blank spaces to fill the remainder of the code word slots and pressed start. Samus appeared on the screen and started her adventure.

Seasons of Tuxedo is situated between the suburbs of Tuxedo, Linden Woods and Whyte Ridge. It's a strip of big-box brand stores. Demographically, big-box shopping is targeted towards the upper-middle-class, that baby-boom gen.

According to Dickie, millennials don't buy margarine by the kilogram. Costco ain't their thang.

They're too busy trying to become web-celebs.

Follow
Follow
Share
Like
Follow
Like
Share
Like
Follow

These suburbs, per capita, are the richest in the city. That's not to say there aren't other wealthy areas of Winnipeg serviced by big-box retail, but for immediate effect, for now, our tale is only concerned with this particular section of the city.

The IKEA.

The only IKEA in Winnipeg sits upon a throne of real estate at the corner of Route 90 and Sterling Lyon and takes the cake of the shopping plaza.

Seasons of Tuxedo.

Nice name.

But,

Only a name.

It sounds welcoming. Johns and Janes love things that sound nice, look good, but offer little substance.

Horace worked at the IKEA.

He's worked there for a while now. His duties were varied, one of which was constructing display units of items for sale. The task he was officially hired for, though, was the feeding, watering and corralling of the feral children that resided in the IKEA.

Horace liked his job; it was exciting and interesting. He also liked working for IKEA. They treated him well and paid him a fair and equitable wage. He didn't need the money, but he didn't feel right just living off Kurt's substantial income. Horace preferred to pay his own way. It gave him a sense of independence. There's something about earning money that makes you appreciate it more. It's just one of those things.

So,

There's Horace, standing in the IKEA cafeteria line along with other Pegs and their sour, spoiled, Peg children, squealing and begging their parents for this and for that. When Peg parents say "no," Peg children throw themselves little Peg temper tantrums.

Horace wondered if that was how so many children found themselves left behind in the IKEA. It had become a bit of tale among Peg children, a spook story kids would whisper in schoolyards: if you act up, you'll be left behind when your parents go shop the IKEA.

Truth is, or at least how Dickie scores it, is that there are bad parents just like there are bad children. Bad parents have been known to do bad things to their kids. There are arguably more bad parents than there are good ones. Bad parents help good kids develop into bad parents themselves.

Or,

Maybe,

Parents had just had enough of them. Like animals do with their cubs in the wild, one day they just set them free.

Maybe they intended it to be only temporary, just needed a little break. Maybe it was the plan all along. Hard to say.

It was noon, which meant it was time for Horace to get the hot dogs and meatballs and water for the feral children who inhabit the IKEA.

IKEA is a very large place. In fact, it eclipses some small towns in the Bell/MTS Province. That part is really not very true. It's pretty big, though.

The feral children learned to survive and even thrive in the IKEA jungle of beautiful forests of Kallaxs, Ektorps and Brimnes, rolling fields of clever Hovslunds, the magnificent mountains of practical Bjurstas, the artificial moonlit glow of retro-designed Sinnerligs, their moonbeams bouncing off mazes of Isfjordens.

IKEA did the prudent thing, as any good corporation would. They contacted the inept local police department, who transferred their call to the even more inept municipal government family services.

But,

Somehow the children always managed to evade capture. Ineptitude will often yield those types of results. It became an exhausted measure and ultimately a fruitless one.

So, IKEA, being of fine Swedish sensibility, decided to take ownership of the escalating situation and did what likely no other corporation would do. They allowed the children to stay and to live.

A corporate adoption of sorts.

They aren't the first to do it.

Dickie says Hollywood used to do it.

IKEA, being the sensible corporation that they are, put forth a special action to provide food and water, and they even allowed the children to live amongst the model furniture until they could put together their own action plan for providing alternate care options for the children.

The government was thrilled that IKEA would take on the responsibility of caring for the feral children – less encumbrance on the tax payer.

And

Of course,

That was many years ago, and the powers that be have yet to figure anything out.

Patrons have since been advised to avoid contact with the feral children. In most cases, the feral children are harmless, but one expects some growling and even a little biting.

Appropriate signage was displayed with a text that read – not unlike spotting animals in their natural habitats – "enjoy the rare sighting of feral children, but please respect their boundaries."

The task fell to Horace to ensure the feral children were cared for and kept occupied during store hours. After the lights went out, well, it was pretty much Neverland in there.

Jack had been following the golden arrows along the floor for a while.

Came around a corner and saw Horace standing beside a trolley teetering with food and water. He was looking at something in his hand. As Jack got closer, he recognized the photograph from the night they first met on the bus. Horace was running a thumb over the old photo and seemed to be lost in deep reflection.

"Hey there."

Horace jerked out of his daze.

"Sorry, Horace. I didn't mean to creep up on you like that."

Horace quickly stuffed the photograph into his shirt pocket. Jack watched as he absently patted the pocket to make sure the photo was secure.

"Old photo, huh? Who are they?"

"My parents."

Horace surprised himself. He hadn't even known Jack that long. He never really talked about his parents, not even to Kip. He was even more shocked that he hadn't lied and fabricated some fantastic story about them. He had simply told the truth.

"They look happy."

"I guess they were. I don't know. I don't know them. Don't know where they are. No one can seem to find them. They might be dead." Horace rubbed his scar. "Do you know your parents?"

"I do."

"What are they like?"

Jack realized how much he missed his mom and dad. Mom and dad, that's how he said it inside of his head. It sounded sacred.

"They're really good people and have been very good parents."

Horace smiled. "Do you miss them?"

"Yeah, a lot. I can't go home right now, though."

"Why not?"

"It's complicated."

Horace didn't press him. Jack noticed his temperament had lightened.

"So, what brings you to the store today?"

"I'm just looking for some incidentals. Plates, glasses, cutlery, ice cube trays."

"It's all here. Let me feed the kids, and then I'll show you around."

"What kids are you talking about?"

"The feral kids." Horace said it as though Jack should know all about them. "My job is to feed them and give them water." Horace smiled. "Plus, it's pomegranate season. They sure do love pomegranate seeds."

Jack shook his head.

"You can't be serious?"

"Oh, I wouldn't joke about pomegranate season."

"No, I guess you wouldn't."

145

Jack sighed. Nothing about this city surprised him anymore.

"You can come watch if you'd like. It only takes a few minutes."

Jack really couldn't pass up the opportunity to meet a fringe society of feral children who call IKEA their permanent residence.

Horace wheeled the trolley of food into the kitchen and dining department. He set the food out on various model tables and laid out some fine IKEA plates and cutlery. Lastly, he set out the water dishes. Then he stepped away from the tables and took the trolley with him.

Jack watched the whole thing as though he were on safari waiting for a giant jungle cat to make a rare appearance. Nothing happened, though.

"Sometimes it takes Jonas a while before he lets everyone eat."

"Jonas?"

"Jonas is the alpha child. No one comes out until Jonas says so."

"How do you know his name?"

"I don't. It's the name I gave him. I've named all the children. At least the ones I'm aware of. I'm the only person that can get close to them. They trust me."

Horace smiled at the thought. Something about the children reminded him of his own situation. In some strange way, he had become a foster of sorts himself.

"How many are there?"

"Hard to say for sure. They hide really well. I guess around twenty."

"How did this happen? Why haven't the police been called?"

"They were called, but there isn't much they can do. Stuff like this isn't easy. Ever since the social reforms were passed on child freedoms, well, these kids have essentially the same rights as adults. Plus, the Canadian squatting laws afford them the right to remain in the IKEA because of the nature of the environment being as much a legitimate dwelling as anyplace else."

Horace shook his head.

"Like you said earlier, it's complicated."

Jack was struck dumb when a child in soiled clothing, who appeared to be no older than seven or eight years old, emerged from out of nowhere.

Jack pointed.

"Look!"

"Don't point, Jack."

Jack put his hand down.

"That's Jonas."

Jack watched as the young boy dipped his finger into the large bowl of meatballs. He licked his fingertip and nodded slightly. He looked up and saw Horace and Jack standing on the yellow arrowed path in the distance. He stared at Horace, and Horace waved at him.

Then, children appeared from all corners of the store. Some came from beneath beds, others out from cupboards, and some just left the safety of a well-hidden corner.

They all grabbed plates and cutlery. They took helpings of food and water. Then they sat and ate in silence. It was the single most amazing thing Jack had ever witnessed.

One child tried to take a handful of pomegranate seeds from another child's plate, but the child growled and protected his food. The ages ranged from four to eight years old.

Horace nudged Jack in the side with his elbow.

"We should leave them be. I don't want them to get riled up."

"Okay."

"Come with me, and I'll take you to get what you need."

Jack heard Horace, but he wasn't really listening to him. He was entranced and allowed himself to be led away.

"How often do you feed them, Horace?"

"Twice a day on weekdays, plus a snack, three times on weekends."

They rounded a corner, and Jack felt a sudden sharp searing pain in his ankle. Jack hollered in pain and looked down to see a small child. The child had bitten him in the ankle.

"Mervin, stop that nonsense! It's lunchtime. Go join the others."

The child scurried beneath a large bed, and both Horace and Jack lost sight of him. Jack reached down and rubbed his ankle.

"You okay?"

"I think so. Damn well hurt, though."

"Don't worry. They've had all their shots."

Jack hadn't even had the chance to contemplate the health implications of being bitten.

"I don't think I've ever been bitten before by another person."

Horace rolled up his sleeves to reveal his forearms.

"Happens all the time, see?"

Jack looked at Horace's arms – they were riddled with bite marks. Then Jack remembered the first time he had met Horace on the bus; he had seen the marks back then.

"They're good kids, just filled with angst. It's hard being left behind."

Jack had heard the stories about Horace and his past. Jack couldn't imagine being the person he was without the help, guidance and love his parents had given him, that they still gave him.

"I guess they're lucky to have you."

Horace smiled. His coffee-brown eyes had a pleasant calm to them. He tucked his long black hair behind his ears to keep it away from his eyes.

"Okay, let's help you buy some things you won't be able to pronounce."

In the hallway, Jack tossed a trash bag down the disposal chute. It was midday, and he wore sweat pants and a faded Ramones tour t-shirt his father had given him – original, not reissue. A New Yorker, after all.

When he turned around, the cell phone addict was standing in the middle of the hallway. He was amazed at how silently she could creep. His back had been turned only a moment, and yet she could materialize wherever she wanted.

"Hi, Clair."

She didn't answer.

"Hey, Clair, hello." Jack waved his hand in front of her face.

He wasn't in the mood to overcome her social ineptitudes before lunch and decided he would attempt to slip past her unnoticed.

The mission failed.

"Have you ever asked Siri something and received a weirdo response from her? Like, maybe she was thinking for herself?"

"No, I don't really use Siri."

Jack had a hard time feigning interest. Technology was a tool to him, nothing more. His obsessions were of a different kind.

"I sometimes wonder if Steve Jobs is, like, still alive, in the Cloud, you know?"

Boring.

Dickie said that shit years ago.

This time, she looked up from her phone and scanned Jack's face. She was wearing the typical fare – yoga pants and sports bra, hair pulled up above a sport-band. Clair always looked as though she was on the verge of working out. Almost. She was a BooGoo-almost – like all BooGoo-women, no one actually works out in BooGoo gear.

It's too expensive.

"You know, if you think about it, if Steve Jobs actually did manage to upload his brain, would that make the Cloud, like, heaven or something?"

"I don't know."

Jack found it difficult sustaining empty conversation with someone offering less than five percent of her attention. Instead, he did what any man would do: he found himself appraising Clair's physical appearance.

Her body was in shape, though her mental state undid all the physical attractiveness. And she looked exhausted. Jack told her so while she continued to thumb through her phone.

"I haven't slept in a while. Been trying to catch up."

"Catch up?"

"You know, work and things."

And things.

The perfect epitaph.

"You should really unplug, just for one night, you know?"

She smiled at him. She had a nice smile. It was sad, or maybe it was lonely without knowing it was lonely.

"Are you worried about me?"

"A little, sure. It's not healthy to stare at a screen all of the time. Didn't your parents ever tell you that?"

"Aw, you're cute, but I'm off the market."

"I didn't mean…" Jack gritted his teeth. She had cut eye contact and went back to her phone. He wondered why he bothered and didn't ignore her the way she ignored him. He knew why. He felt sorry for her. She was sick.

The neighbour's door made a soft creak. Jack turned around. The neighbour Jack had never seen was peeking through the thin crack of the door. Jack squinted, tried to pull focus.

"Hey." He waved. "We won't bite, ya know."

No response from the door. He approached it to see if he could introduce himself, but the door closed before he got close enough to see inside.

I'm surrounded by fruit loops, he thought.

He could see a flicker of light flash over the peephole and knew the person was still watching him. Total nuts, the lot of them.

"She won't talk to you."

Jack had already forgotten about Clair. "Oh? Why is that?"

"'Cause you're a man."

That wasn't the reason at all. Jack felt a frown creep over his face. Shame on Jack for believing her. People are notorious for believing the worst thing.

"I think she was in an abusive relationship or something. Boyfriend beat her and stuff."

Wrong again.

Jack looked back at the closed door and wondered if the woman was still watching, or if she could hear their conversation.

"I'm going to head in. See ya."

Jack couldn't tell if Clair had acknowledged him with a nod of her head or not.

It didn't matter.

Text: *Game night, bro! Your turn to get the snacks. Meet you at the Portage/Osborne bus stop after work.*

The man in line ahead of Kip placed an order for a #3 combo.

All the little crooked aches and pangs with Johns and Janes can find their sum in the fast food combo.

Fast food combo is the antonym of patience in Wiktionary.

That's really true.

The cashier offered the total and advised that he could tap his ACB fob when ready. The man tapped his fob to the crystal pad. There was a soft beep.

The cashier shook his head.

"I'm sorry, sir." A pause, as if for effect. "The total is 22<CC>. You only have 20.95<CC> remaining in your account."

"No, I have enough."

"Sorry, sir, says here that you don't. The cost for the combo is 11<CC> plus taxes of 4<CC> and the ACB funds access and disbursement fee of 7<CC> totalling 22<CC>. The total is more than you have in your account."

"But that's not right, the ACB fees should only be 5<CC>!"

"Did you miss the mobile service announcement today?"

"What announcement?"

"The ACB fees were increased today due to new infrastructure and technology costs."

The man cursed loudly and slapped a napkin holder from the counter. It went flying, hit the ground, and burst open, fanning napkins over the tiled floor.

Everyone else who was waiting in line watched as the disgruntled man left, grumbling loudly.

Kip stepped forward and placed his order.

It was his turn to get the snacks for game night.

Thursday is game night.

Kip tapped his ACB fob against the crystal pad. It made a soft beep. His payment was accepted, and the cashier handed Kip his snacks.

Kip put the brown paper bag of snacks into his backpack and stepped through the swinging doors onto Osborne.

He made his way north until he spied a 7-11, stepped inside, and purchased two large Swamp Slurpees.

At the corner of Portage and Memorial, he waited for the bus. Horace's bus would be by anytime now.

Kip took out his phone and scrolled through a series of older texts. Then his phone froze as a mandatory merch advert appeared on his phone. He chuckled. It was an ad for Spekel. As a registered business owner, Kurt was required to submit at least one advert per quarter. The ad played to completion, and Kip's cellular service resumed.

He smiled. Thursday, Game Night, just him and his best friend sitting in front of a screen, crushing snacks and killing games. Tonight, the decision was to defeat their top ten classic 8-bit NES games.

The list went like this:

Megaman 2
Kid Icarus
Ninja Gaiden

Life Force
Castlevania 3
Adventure Island
Metroid
Contra
Gauntlet
The Legend of Zelda

They had agreed to a deadline: sunup. Kip had been contemplating tactics all day. Best to start with Life Force and then Contra, because they could use the classic up-up-down-down code for "thirty-up."

And
So,
Standing in front of the old Bay building, Kip waited patiently. No sign of the hydro-bus yet. The dilapidated Bay headquarters at his back. Now a flophouse.
Windows smashed out,
Smoke wafting out of one.
He thought about running inside to see if he could score, but when he turned around, Kevin was standing in front of the entrance, swaying as if he were prairie grass caught by prairie wind. Flies hovered around him. Dragonflies clung to his back. He didn't seem to notice Kip standing there. He was chewing on his finger.
Kip stepped off the curb and cocked his head down Portage. Finally, the hydro-bus was in view.
Two dragonflies fluttered around Kip's face, trying to gobble up mosquitoes. He waved his hand to shoo them off. The hydro-bus came to a stop. The doors opened. He looked over his shoulder, Kevin was gone.
Kip tapped his <CC> fob to the crystal pad and an electronic voice authorized the payment. Horace was sitting in the back. He waved. Kip slid in beside him.
Horace elbowed Kip in the ribs and pointed out the window.
"Look at this."

"What?"

"That guy with the picket sign."

"So?"

"I saw him before. What do you think his sign means?"

"How would I know?"

Kip was still thinking about Kevin. He was there, then he was gone.

"Street mystic."

"Huh?"

"Never mind."

"I walked all the way down South Osborne today. Never snapped a single photograph."

"Seriously?"

"Nothin' doin', I guess. Walked right through Confusion Corner. Remember when it was confusing?"

"Ha, yeah."

Confusion Corner was Winnipeg's infantile spaghetti junction.

Dickie Reimer says that without the traffic, it's a lot less confusing.

Horace craned his head against the window and looked up at the sky. A flock of sparrows surfed the warm breeze.

"Nice day for flying."

Kip smiled.

Horace could smell the food. He moved his attention from the window and looked in the rolled-up brown bag.

"Did you remember extra ketchups?"

Kip grunted and handed him a Slurpee. Horace took a sip from the pink straw.

"Oh god, that's good. You can taste the love."

"That's just syrup, my man."

They laughed. Horace scrolled through his phone pictures.

"Remember this?"

"Tetris?"

"Obviously." Horace slid his phone into his shirt pocket. "Pop quiz. Why'd Alexey Pajitnov call his most famous game Tetris?"

Kip slumped in the bus seat. "Because the French word for head is tête and the game really makes you think quickly."

"Great answer."

"I know."

"Totally wrong."

"What?"

"Yeah, man. Tetra is Greek, a prefix meaning four, all the game's pieces are made up of four segments. Pajitnov loved tennis, Tetr-is."

"Not bad, H. How about this? Who created Pac Man?"

Horace locked his fingers behind his head. "Easy, Toru Iwatani."

"Okay, best arcade of the '80s?"

"Burgertime?"

"Oh man, backsliding. Burgertime, seriously?"

"Punch Out?"

"Golden Axe."

"1989, kind of squeezing it in there a bit, don't you think?"

"Dude, Golden Axe."

"Yeah." Horace thought about it for a moment. "Totally, Golden Axe."

"Mortal Kombat or Street Fighter II?"

"SFII for sure."

"Nah. Finish Him! You can't beat that."

"Sonic Boom, way better." Horace shook his head. "Blanka, nothing touches Blanka." He took a sip of Slurpee.

"Okay, okay, my turn. Best computer game?"

Kip smiled. "Got that one locked down, son. Duke Nukem!"

"I was thinking Prince of Persia, but you're right. Nukem for sure."

Horace kept on. "First Person Shooter?"

Kip sat up.

"Oh, I could go all night, Golden Eye."

"Wolfenstein 3-D."

"Better than Golden Eye?"

"Tie?"

"Nope," replied Kip, shaking his head. "Best racing game?"

"Pole Position."

"Great game. Doesn't hold a candle to Outrun."

"Oh god, yeah, Outrun."

Horace's mind wandered back to the man holding the picket sign. He looked out the window.

The hydro-bus cruised silently along Portage Avenue. The streets were busy with foot traffic. Bicycles whipped in all directions. It was quitting time, and everyone was hustling to bus stops.

Hydro-buses could be seen all over. It was the busiest time of day for Winnipeg Transit. The logistical organization, timing and engineering was magnificent to behold. The system worked well, and for those not on a bike, there were plenty of buses to accommodate demand.

It was also the loudest time of day. People sat on bus benches splashed with real estate agent ads. Johns and Janes chirped about their day, tomorrow's tasks and all that jib. They waved. Others grumbled after a long, hard day. It was the time of day when Winnipeg looked like any other city. It was the time of day when Johns and Janes felt like it might all work out somehow.

Kip took his camera from his camera pack. He screwed on a wide angle and snapped shots through the open bus window. Horace watched the city drama.

Sometimes normal feels really good.

It's just one of those things.

Horace tugged the stop cord. The two friends stepped off the hydro-bus and beat foot down McDermot. They cut through an alley tunnel. Alleys, tunnels, archways connected everything in the Exchange District.

Kip was explaining something to Horace. He turned to face his friend so he could illustrate his point with hand gestures. He exited the tunnel back first and plowed into someone. He and his unfortunate victim tumbled to the sidewalk.

Kip was dazed and groaning on the ground. It appeared that he was on the receiving end of the worst of the impact and fall. Horace rushed forward. His concern was not for his friend. Kip had knocked a woman to the concrete. She had managed to sit up. Papers, her wallet and a few other personal items had spilled out onto the sidewalk.

The woman was trying to collect the loose articles from her carry case. Horace got down on his hands and knees.

"Let me help."

The woman ran her hand through a mess of hair, moving it from her face.

"No, thank you. I've got it."

She stood and stuffed the last of the papers back into her carry case. She looked at Horace. He had frozen momentarily, then he realized he was staring at her. He tried to say something but choked on the words. He coughed, trying to clear his throat.

"Sorry about that."

"Why? You didn't knock me down."

She was only half listening and busied herself with her belongings.

"Ah, right. Um, here."

Horace passed her the item he had picked up off the ground for her.

"Thanks."

The woman brushed passed him and started to walk away. Horace turned and called after her.

"Hey, Justine, welcome to Winnipeg."

She stopped suddenly, turned around and faced Horace. He felt his blood go cold, the glance from the woman sent a ripple of fear through his body, and he felt like running away.

"What did you just say to me?"

"Um, nothing."

"How do you know my name?" She almost said it as a whisper. A cold, steel whisper.

Horace's tongue felt thick and dry.

"It was on your ID, next to your, um –" He actually gulped for air. "Beside your badge. I didn't mean anything by it, it was open when I handed it back to you."

She stared at him for what felt like a full, intense minute. It was only a few seconds, though. She said nothing, turned on her heels and walked away.

"Geez." Horace wasn't sure if he had said the word out loud or in his head.

Kip grunted and sat up.

"Oh! What happened?"

Horace was still staring down a now empty sidewalk.

"I'm not sure."

"Did I get hit by a bus?"

Horace offered a hand down to his friend and helped him to his feet.

"You did the hitting."

"Seriously?"

"Yeah, man."

"Ow. Everything on me hurts. I'm still seeing stars."

Horace smiled.

"You should've seen the other guy."

"Oh yeah, I get him pretty good?"

"Sure did. You okay to walk?"

"Yeah, I'm fine. Have no idea what happened, though."

The Rosewood came into view, and so did Kurt. Horace waved at Kurt, and Kurt waved back.

"What's going on, fellas?"

They high-fived each other, as was their typical M.O.

"Just picked up snacks for game night."

Kip looked at the equipment Kurt was fiddling with. Somehow his older brother was always working.

"What are you doing?"

"About to harness up and clean these grimy windows."

"Okay, well, see ya."

The two friends took off through the revolving door. Kurt froze for a moment; he watched them disappear inside.

"Don't worry, fellas, I've got this."

He rolled his eyes.

A hint of clove tobacco.

He stepped into the foyer. His first thought, the landlady? Didn't she smoke? But he knew the difference between cigarette tobacco and this.

He turned the corner and froze. A woman was sitting on his couch. Legs in faded Lees, knees worn out. A loose linen shirt, with sleeves rolled up above the elbow, top button open.

Jack noticed that her left ear had what looked like a hearing aid in it. When she turned to face him, he noticed another in her right ear.

Hanging from her mouth was the cigarillo he had smelled, hand-rolled, imperfect, half smoked. She dragged on it, exhaled a trumpet of marbled smoke in his direction.

He just stared, and she at him.

Her confidence unnerved him. Finally he reclaimed some composure. It was then that he realized she had somehow managed to break into his suite.

"Who are you?"

Jack started to move towards her, and she made a clicking sound with her tongue. Jack stopped moving. She smiled at him.

"No sudden movements."

Or what? he thought.

She leaned forward and carefully ground out her cigarillo into a chrome tray on the glass table in front of her.

"That's not an ashtray."

A corner of her mouth turned upward. His annoyance amused her. She relaxed back onto the couch, tapped fingers on her leg, nails tinged with grime.

He watched.

She kept the smile.

"I'm calling the police."

"No."

The word came evenly.

He paid no attention to her and unlocked his phone.

"Winnipeg cops, I mean, come on."

She yawned, catlike, stretching sinewy arms overhead. She relaxed, leaning against the back cushion of the couch and scissored her legs. Unruly curls fell over shoulders. She had no interest in finishing her sentence. Her comfort made Jack uncomfortable.

"What are you after? Money?"

She ignored the stab. "You wouldn't want all the law enforcement agencies that are chasing you to see this."

She leaned forward. On the glass centre-table, next to the silver tray, was a long tube container that she tapped delicately with her finger. Jack hadn't noticed it. Had it always been there? He couldn't recall. At a loss, he began to realize the woman in front of him held the good cards.

A good card is typically an ace.

Dickie calls it an ace in the hole.

To have an ace in the hole is to retain something of value for use when the shit hits the fan.

When shit hits a fan, well, you don't need me to spell that one out for you.

"What's in the container?"

"Something to do with that past you keep running from. It's fun. Care to see it?"

"Sure, why not?"

She reached for the tube, and then hesitated.

Jack felt a wry smile creep across his lips. "You're bluffing."

Bluffing also finds its origin in card playing.

A bluff is a lie.

Oxford dictionary says there are over a hundred different ways to say "lie." Oxford dictionaries don't exist anymore.

Lying is forever.

He made a quick movement and reached for the tube on the table. The woman made a similar clicking sound with her tongue as she had before. In a single fluid and exceptionally lithe movement, she pulled the tube from the table and slapped Jack across his face.

Jack rubbed his cheek.

It didn't hurt – much. As a matter fact, it didn't hurt at all, but the shock of it and the execution of her movements unsettled him. He took a few steps backward. She decorated her mouth with a crooked smile that mocked him playfully.

"I told you, no sudden movements."

"Who are you, and what do you want?"

"You have a hard time with instructions, don't you, Jack?"

Knows my name. So what?

She had produced a pouch of loose tobacco leaves and rolled another cigarillo. Struck a match and lit the smoke. Took a drag.

"I don't like this. I don't like someone breaking into my place and, and goddamn it, smoking! Will you put that thing out?"

"Sure, Jack, it's your place."

And smiled when she stubbed out the cigarette in the silver tray again. Jack caught a glimpse of a tattoo on the palm of her left hand. It was a small snake that slithered up the palm and the length of her index finger. It was black and orange, or maybe red. He wasn't sure. The fingers moved snake-like.

"Why are you here?"

"For this."

She popped the lid off the tube container and gently drew out what looked like a rolled-up canvas. Then she set it on the glass table, moved the silver tray aside, and unrolled it.

It was a painting.

"Familiar?"

Jack hesitated, his anxiety was mounting. He cleared his throat. "I want to know what's going on. Who are you?"

"The person who stole it from you, almost ten years ago. I'm the only person in the world, other than your father, who knows who you really are."

Jack's palms moistened, and the room went hot. He sat down in the leather chair facing the woman on the couch. His chest tightened, each breath felt heavy, difficult.

The woman just stared blankly at him.

Jack ran his hands over his face and through his hair. He had always thought that he had lost the painting in one of his frequent moves. A part of him, a part deep down, had always wondered if it was something worse.

This was something much worse.

Someone was holding his identity out in front of him.

"Let me tell you what I know about you. This way it will settle some of your concerns. Maybe even calm you a little." Her tone had changed. It was gentle, soothing. Jack said nothing. He looked up from the painting at the woman.

Her eyes had a vacancy to them, as though she was not looking directly at him. They were black like her hair, so black that you couldn't tell iris from pupil. She put a hand into her thick curls and swept them away from her face.

"I was six when I first heard your name." Jack looked at her. This wasn't helping. She sensed his concerns and waved a hand in the air. "Long story, that part. Maybe another time."

Jack eased forward in his chair. He needed to know just how much she knew.

"I've never cared much for art, other than when it's worth money, of course. I steal it, and I'm sure you can piece the rest together.

"If I recall, it was your piece in London that caught my attention for the first time. A graffiti artist manages to create a piece of artwork on arguably the most secure building in the world, Buckingham Palace. And what you wrote about the King." She tilted her head back as though she were looking up at the ceiling. "One minute, nothing is there, and then, well, of course I'm preaching to the choir.

"I guess I don't have to tell you the impact it had. It didn't matter that it was removed in less than twenty-four hours, like it never existed. Didn't matter, the damage was done, because it had existed and the whole world had seen it." She turned her confidence back on Jack. "How did you ever manage to do it, and right under everyone's noses?"

"I had nothing to do with that."

"Ah, tight lips. A magician never tells, is that it?"

"Got proof?"

"No, I was just curious. One professional to another, so to speak." She sat forward a little. "But I did manage to find proof at the site of another one of your pieces. You have a very distinctive style that set your graffiti writing apart. It is called *writing,* am I correct?"

Jack nodded slightly, then wished he hadn't. She seemed not to notice, so he spoke. "I've heard it called that."

She smiled and moved a few rogue curls away from her face with her hand. She did so carelessly, as though it were for his benefit.

"It was your piece in Leipzig where I found my first clue. A spray tip in a dumpster down the alley of the building on which you'd done a rooftop piece."

Jack fidgeted in his chair, and the woman sensed his concern.

"Not to worry. You're too careful for a fingerprint. You always wear latex gloves. No, it was the slight paint residue lodged in the stem of the tip. I had it tested. The paint was manufactured by Molotow. Benton, it's called.

"I traced the paint and checked with retailers who sell such items in Leipzig. But, no one sells the paint. At least not that brand. So what? Where did you acquire it? You didn't bring it into the country with you. Too risky. These days, impossible. You didn't borrow it from a fellow artist. Too familiar. You ordered it online from an Internet cafe. Had it shipped to a P.O. box. I found your P.O. box. I found a lot of your P.O. boxes. Then I found you.

"You move around a lot. I missed you a few times. Once in Russia, Tver City, I was really close. I visited Podwell, the first graffiti shop in the country. Trust the Russians to find a way to be so progressive with things like that. I learned a lot there. But you never bought from them. You never bought from stores like that. Always online, or, in a pinch, from a hardware store, where no one notices these things."

She leaned toward him.

"You had caused such a stir, raised so many concerns globally, subversive in every way, anti-establishment. Various countries' law enforcement agencies, even Interpol, argued your existence. A boogie-man street artist who could shift the tide of an election or bring about the demise of an oil corporation.

"Then, poof. You disappear. Gone. As though you never existed. All those different people looking for you, law enforcement, rival artists, gangs that think you sold out. They all think you're dead.

"But I knew better. I knew it was the Times Square thing. It went all wrong." She touched her ear and adjusted the little device inside. "Someone got shot, killed. Did you shoot that cop, Jack?"

He didn't answer. He was trying to contain the pressure in his chest and his swimming head.

"Now here you are in Winnipeg. Nice choice, by the way. No one will look for you here. No one looks for anyone here."

"Except you." Jack's voice sardonic in tone.

"Except me. But to be fair, I grew up here. And I, too, am someone who appreciates anonymity, above all things."

He fidgeted in his chair.

"Okay, fine, so what do you want?"

"I want you to write. I want to pull you out of this retirement funk thing you've got going on and write all over these empty

Winnipeg walls."

She waved her hand as though the whole city was right in front of her.

"There has to be more to it than that."

"Maybe there is, maybe there isn't. Either way, that's of no concern to you."

Jack felt very uncomfortable at the revelation that someone he didn't know, or trust, knew his identity. The weight of this revelation and the realization of the potential exposure of his identity was causing him to suffer a major anxiety attack. He shifted in his chair. He took deep, controlled breaths, trying his best to regain a hold of himself. After a minute of controlled breathing, he had managed to slow his heart rate, and the pressure in his chest subsided.

These attacks made him feel helpless. He hated that. He hated that he felt like a shell of the man he once was. He used to have such great control; his threshold for stress seemed limitless. But it wasn't. He did have limits, and the New York disaster proved that. He'd hit a wall, and he hadn't been the same since.

Jack's hands were shaking. He closed his fists, then leaned forward a little to get more comfortable. The woman clicked her tongue.

"Stop doing that!" Jack realized he had shouted the words.

"I apologize. I have trouble making eye contact. I'm blind."

"Blind?"

She yawned again, as though she found him intolerably boring.

"Blind, sightless. You can see, I cannot."

"Then how did you do..."

"All of this? A little skill I've acquired over the years. You know, I can't paint," she said, pointing down at Jack's work. "Can't play the piano, either. I can't drive for shit. But I have my skills, and I have spent my life making them my profession."

"What do you want from me? Money?"

"Blackmail? No, nothing like that, Jack." She shook her head, the heavy, messy curls bouncing all around her face. "No, this is not about money. It's something entirely different and much bigger than that. I want you to help me expose something. Something bad, right here, in

167

this city."

"And if I refuse?"

He didn't care what she was driving at. And he didn't like being braced.

She tilted her head towards the painting on the table.

"You'll expose my identity. That's still blackmail!"

"I guess you're right."

Her tone lacked any trace of empathy.

Jack wrung his hands, then stood up quickly. The woman made the familiar clicking sound with her tongue. Jack fired a look of annoyance in her direction. It caused no stir of reaction from her. Maybe she was actually blind.

"Force of habit."

He'd always been so careful, he knew the only thing keeping him from capture and arrest was that no one knew who he really was. He smirked. That wasn't entirely true. His father knew. But as far as the rest of the world went – girlfriends, bosses, friends, best friends, strangers – no one knew that he was one of the world's most influential and infamous street artists, maybe even the most influential street artist ever.

His art was dangerous, it carried influence with the public. Everyday citizens were beginning to emerge from their marketing-induced comas, thanks in great part to Jack's powerful, anonymous voice. Surprisingly, people could relate to him, they felt as though a silent avenger was speaking on their behalf, giving voice to the voiceless. For this reason, he and his identity were wanted by major law enforcement agencies the world over.

Because of this, he kept part-time jobs as a cook or in sanitation to appear legitimate, pay taxes, keep off radar. God knows he didn't need the money and hated the idea of working for someone who told him what to do all the time, but it kept him safe and out of jail. Until he saw the interview on TV, the one with the FBI agent who announced he would discover Jack's identity and bring him to justice and that Jack was now a public enemy of the United States of America. That was when he left the US. That was the day he decided to start running.

That all felt so far away.

Now,

There was this.

Closing in on him again.

Jack analyzed the woman. She was not the least bit afraid of him or worried he might try something. She wasn't ugly, she wasn't gorgeous, and she didn't need to be either.

Jack shook his head. At this very moment, she had him.

The woman leaned forward and rolled the painting up, sliding it back into the protective tube. Then she stood. As a reflex, Jack stood, too.

"Take some time to think about it. You have a little time. I'll be in touch."

"What choice do I have?"

"There's always a choice."

"Right," he sneered. "Help you, or risk going to prison. Not much of a choice."

"No, I agree with you. Not much of a choice, but a choice all the same."

In her one hand was the tube which had a strap clipped to it. She flung it over her shoulder. In her other hand was a white walking cane, which she unravelled until the round tip tapped the floor. It made a tap sound on the tiles. Jack hadn't noticed her holding it and wondered where it appeared from.

"A blind walking cane? After what I just saw, you can't be serious?"

"Why not? Are you going to walk me home?"

Jack shook his head, and then realized what he'd done. A habit sighted people do, often using physical gestures to convey language.

"No, I have a lot to think about."

"I was kidding, Jack. I can find my own way. What time is it on that watch of yours?"

Jack looked at his watch. He looked at the woman. She did not react to his gaze.

"It's late."

Jack continued to stare at the strange woman. She appeared oblivious to his stare.

"If you're blind, how'd you know I had on a watch?"

"The ticking. I know Swiss movement when I hear it."

Jack had run out of words.

"Okay, well, I'm off."

"Wait, you know my name, what's yours?"

"You want a name? I suppose you'll need to call me something." She swept her hair away from her eyes. "Loraina."

Jack frowned. "Is that your real name?"

She smiled at him. "Does it matter?"

Jack said nothing.

"Alright then."

Jack walked awkwardly to the door with her. She let herself out. He peered into the hallway and watched as she made her way down the hall and onto the elevator. As the elevator doors closed, she waved at him. Jack locked the door. *What good that'll do*, he thought. He leaned back against the door and did his best to manage the awful mounting feeling of an anxiety attack.

In the hallway, the elevator doors opened and the blind woman stepped off and walked back down the hallway, carefully sweeping her cane back and forth. She stopped and knocked gently on the door of the neighbour Jack had never met, the peeping tom. The door opened, and Loraina stepped inside.

Head north on Main. If you hit the Chief Peguis Trail, double back.
Those were the directions Kurt had given Jack.

The diner was called Blondie's.

Blondie is a syndicated comic strip and a rock-and-roll musician.

And,

A diner in Winnipeg.

Now there were three.

Jack had only heard of the first two.

I was partial to the band,

Never liked the comic. I always felt Dagwood was deadwood.

Jack had thought about inviting his friends to join him but couldn't
bring himself to ask them. He was too anxious. His concern with the
blind woman from his apartment last night had left him sleepless.
His head was swimming with thoughts that overwhelmed him. He
wished he could go back to the way things were, back when the genuine stresses of life didn't overcome his rationality, didn't totally cripple

him. He wished he could find his way back to the man he once was.

He needed some time alone. Needed to think, catch his breath. That's why he chose to walk rather than take the hydro-bus. One foot in front of the other stamps out burning thoughts.

Burning thoughts.

The woman.

The woman who, with skill, had gained entry to his apartment. Worse, she could identify him.

She had accomplished all of this without her sight. What she was capable of pumped a rush of dread through his veins. He couldn't recall a more formidable person. She was not to be underestimated.

Damn!

Damn, damn, damn!

Damn is English vernacular used as an extension of emotional expression. A dam is a concrete reservoir that retains a large mass of water. Dam should not be confused with damn. If a dam of water were to break, using the word *damn* would be appropriate.

He had few options.

So,

He could make a run for it, go into hiding, but you needed confidants, allies, friends. The graf culture was well-stitched, but friends and allies were commodities, anonymity your only security. This meant you told no one your true identity and the depth of your involvement in that subversive world.

Identity is what you are, not who you are.

Governments don't give a jib about who you are.

Your driver's licence says: eyes, green; height, 183 cm; gender, M. It does not say: loves, music; favourite food, Mexican; into, brunettes.

The real reason, though, was that since he quit, ever since the incident in New York, he couldn't trust anyone. That's because no one could trust him, and worse, a lot of people wanted revenge.

They didn't get it. They didn't know the truth. No one understood what really happened. They didn't know why he dropped his life and just walked away. The government made him the perfect scapegoat; the media did their thing, and the rest was open to interpretation.

He could run for it.

He could always run.

No,

He'd been running,

For too long.

He couldn't run any longer.

He was tired of running.

It took him over an hour to walk to the restaurant. The sky was dotted with grey pillows. Thick humid air made the lungs heavy with each inhalation.

Main Street looked dead.

He had walked past three different 7-11s already. The parking lots were empty. No cars. How could there be? No patrons, either. He walked past a couple sitting on a bus bench. They were vaping and talking and giggling as they waited for a hydro-bus. No breeze. The plume of tobacco vapour, weighted by the heavy humidity, took an odd form and lurked as though it were a soul. Jack passed right through it, and it swirled until it was nothing.

The rest of the city's inhabitants seemed to know something Jack and the couple didn't. Winnipeg was like that. Nearing a million strong, yet it somehow always appeared empty, abandoned. He imagined rows of unnamed drifters taking to the street and staring each other down. Fingers twitching near the holster.

It did give Jack plenty of time to mull over the mess he was in. It was quite the mess, too. He couldn't imagine it any worse.

Winnipeg was supposed to be the place, the last stop. So much for that idea.

So what now?

He couldn't just up and leave, head back to America. People were looking for him there, too. That's why he couldn't run.

He hadn't known at the time just how influential his art had become. He'd lost perspective and made a mistake. Just one mistake, but a big one. Now he was paying the price for it. He'd lost everything: his family, the life he knew, his home, Alice.

Alice.

He missed her laugh. He missed waking up to her, her warmth.

A car came towards Jack. It was odd to see an operational private vehicle cruising along the road. Jack had been told that private-use vehicles were now prohibited in the Bell/MTS Province. The licence plate came into view – it was an Esso Oil Provincial plate. The EOP used to be called Alberta.

Someone just passing through.

The sound of the vehicle's motor roared, and its tires echoed upon the blacktop, amplified by the otherwise natural calm. He had heard from Devlin that people were using fake out-of-province licence plates in order to operate vehicles in the city.

The car broke Jack's train of thought. There were *spray tags* and *throw-up* pieces all along the nooks and hideaways, old billboards and building walls of North Main. Most were by *toys*, kids looking to vandalize a wall. No talent. No technical skill. No tip control. This type of graffiti meant nothing to Jack. He hated it. Art should have a message. That was his opinion.

He believed that the marriage between visual art and the written word, the very essence of graf writing, held a power no person, government or corporation could stifle. Nor could they control it.

Truth was,

He missed doing it.

A can of paint was merely an extension of his arm, it felt normal to him; he was that good with a can and a plastic tip. The art community at large used to think he was the most influential and talented artist of any medium.

Was.

Past tense.

Jack saw the sign for Blondie's. It was a classic plastic square bubble sponsored by Pepsi. The Pepsi portion of the sign was twice the size of the Blondie's portion. It's just one of those things.

The restaurant was an old two-storey conversion with the business on the bottom floor and residence on the second storey. The interior was small, but not cramped. There were ten tables, tops. The walls were covered with photographs.

Jack sat at an empty table. He admired the simplicity of the place. He took a menu that was resting between the ketchup and mustard. All about the burgers. Kurt had mentioned the sweet spot was the quarter pounder, but one could actually order a nine-pound burger if their eccentricities needed to be slaked.

The server took Jack's order. He decided to take his friend's advice and stick with the quarter pounder, as enticing as a nine-pound burger might sound.

Jack leaned back in his chair and threw his feet up onto the empty chair across from him. He put his arms over his chest and locked his fingers.

What the hell am I going to do?

A damn good question.

He didn't find an answer. The question just rattled around inside his head for a long while

Then,

The food arrived.

A burger, accompanied by a heap of fries. It all looked fantastic. Upon initial inspection, Jack and his stomach were pleased. He lifted the top bun off – no mayo, exactly how he liked it.

Jack was beginning to feel a little better. He wasn't sure what to do, but at least he felt like he could handle whatever was going to come his way. Of course he could. He'd been in worse predicaments. He also understood that his anxieties produced the feeling of real physical symptoms; they were nothing more than manifestations of ill thoughts out of control.

So,

How do you overcome?

How do you find your way back to being the person you once were?

He thought about some of the highlights of his street art career. He didn't believe in the romanticized Hollywood pastiche of the life of a criminal. He was against crime and perpetrating crimes.

Still,

He'd broken the law.

He was a criminal.

Graffiti is illegal the world over.

Except São Paulo.

It's legal in São Paulo.

They've got their act together.

But, Jack *was* guilty. He knew it as well as anyone else knew it.

He also believed that he could set the wheels in motion for change. The cities were his canvas and words; all those words sprayed out of cheap shake cans were an anonymous voice. He had a voice, a voice he could share. A voice for those who have no voice.

And it was working.

People were listening.

At least they used to be.

Now, he had gone into hiding. The various forces in power had finally caught up to him, and Jack could feel the heat.

He fiddled with a fry on his plate. He kept dunking it repeatedly in the puddle of ketchup, and then dropped the fry back on the plate.

He thought about the blind mystery woman. Was she really blind? How could she do what she did if she was blind? Was it an act, and if so, why the elaborate cinema? Jack didn't have any answers. She had position over him. Add any fitting queen/pawn chess analogy *here*.

He pushed his plate forward. He was done eating. How quickly a person can let negative thoughts gain the upper hand. Jack leaned back in his chair and took a sip of his soda. He was now the only patron left. The few previous patrons had somehow departed without him noticing.

He took a napkin from the dispenser on the table and wiped his hands and mouth. He tossed the napkin onto the dirty plate. He reached for his wallet to throw some cash on the table, and then remembered he couldn't do that. Not here. Not in this country.

Old habits.

He took out the pre-loaded payment fob he'd acquired at customs and went to the register to pay. The total appeared on the screen, and Jack tapped his payment fob against the screen. There was a soft tone and the screen read approved.

He thanked the server and left. Outside, there was a man sitting up against the wall of the building. He was hunched over and looked awful. Jack wanted to give the man some money, but that was no longer possible.

What it must be like to be at the bottom in a country like this. No one can spare you anything.

He went back in the restaurant. He went to the till and ordered another burger and told the waitress to give it to the man against the wall outside. She smiled and said she would. Jack paid for the burger and left.

"Hey, bud, I ordered too much food. They're gonna bring you out my other burger."

The man against the wall smiled. He was missing most of his teeth.

"Okay."

Nothing more was said and Jack started walking south towards home.

The door to Blondie's opened, and a woman entered the restaurant. She wore black suit pants, matching-coloured heels and a white blouse. All the tables had been wiped clean, except one, the table Jack had been sitting at. She sat there. The server yelled at her that she'd clear away the mess as soon as she delivered the burger to the man outside.

"No rush."

The woman perused the menu.

The server disappeared through the door into the kitchen. The woman sitting at the table took out tweezers, a plastic vial, a zip bag and two pieces of fingerprint-lifting tabs. She lifted a perfect fingerprint off the glass. Then she put the fork in the zip bag and deposited a half-eaten fry and the used napkin into separate baggies and sealed them.

The server came through the front door just as Justine Kavanaugh hid everything she had collected in her purse.

"Have you decided?"

"I'll have the quarter-pound burger – sounds like it's popular."

Justine smiled up from the menu at the server. The server smiled back. Then she went to the kitchen to put the order through. Justine collected her things and left discreetly.

A plane,

Couldn't see it, but you knew it was there.

Two empties shook on the table, the waists on the beer bottles bumping together like hips on a dance floor.

The bar was a block from the landing path of Pearson International. Planes, jets and sometimes the odd helicopter would cut holes in the silence overhead. A reminder that people have conquered the stratosphere, too.

"727."

The man said it out loud to himself.

He ran his fingers over the pair of brass wings on his pilot's jacket.

Say hello to Danny Archer.

When he was a boy, he had wanted to be a pilot.

He had always wanted to be a pilot.

So he became a pilot.

I often wonder how many people become exactly what they wanted from childhood.

Then there was the cancer.

His wife had it.

And

Like so many who get it, she died from it.

And

Then Danny started to drink a little more. For all his reasons, he was drinking more than a little. Soon, all he did was drink.

In Canada, booze is one of three government-controlled items.

Tobacco

Lottery

And alcohol

All had the wonderful credit of creating addictions.

The Canadian government makes a helluva lot of money off addictions.

It's just one of those things.

People at the airline he worked for started to get suspicious.

But,

Danny had never given them any reason to believe that he ever piloted under the influence.

Even though he did,

All the time.

Danny was a functioning alcoholic and a hell of a pilot, even at his worst.

Earlier in the day – doesn't matter when, really – Danny had met with his supervisor to receive the results of his review. Supe was also a close friend, told him that he would be placed on probation, due to suspicion of piloting an aircraft under the influence of a controlled substance.

He didn't lose his wings, but they had been plucked of all the feathers.

Now,

It was happy hour, sometime in the evening – the exact time still doesn't matter.

Maybe it wasn't even happy hour. He didn't know.

You know the old saying, anyway.

Danny had managed to consume seven rounds of Maker's, well past forgetting the results of his review.

He was thinking about his wife, about his Annie. A good woman, was and had been the only love of his life. It was Annie and only Annie. When she died, there were no other women left. He had a hole in his heart that nothing could fill. So he drank to fill it, and he wasn't the first to do it.

There was this time in Mexico. He and Annie sat in loungers on the beach and watched a sunset.

Just as the sun began to drown in the ocean, Annie rose to her bare feet, dug her toes into the sand and stretched her arms over her head. She faced Danny, and the setting sun, red with passion, backlit Annie's long auburn hair and she glowed.

Shortly after, she got sick.

Then she got really sick.

Finally, the disease took her from him.

Cancer is not patient
It is not kind
It rejoices in anger
Delights in sadness
It keeps record
It keeps score
There is no protection
And
Its aim is to never fail.

Make no mistake.
There is a cure.
It exists.
Why do you think no US president has ever died from cancer?

It's just worth more to keep people sick than to cure.

Dickie calls this the infrastructure conundrum.

Now,

Let me tell you a little about Annie. This way you understand why people sometimes do the things they do.

And,

By the way,

In case you were wondering, I wasn't there, can't be in two places at once.

Truth is, I was in Winnipeg. I was sitting on a couch with my hand in a box of Old Dutch potato chips.

Now,

Old Dutch was once a Peg thing. They're an everyone sort of thing these days.

So anyway,

You hear this and that, this way or that way. Much of the world's history is built on a rumour, repetition of legend and myth. All different ways of saying the same thing. The English language is cool like that. Writers are supposed to say the same thing a different way all the time. Writers are supposed to say the same thing a different way all the time.

Anyway,

Danny Archer and Annie Archer.

So,

Annie.

Born August – the year doesn't matter, neither does the month, really – hatched into a family on the north mountain of the Annapolis Valley.

Beautiful country. Spent some time there myself. Personal reasons. I won't get into it right here and now. I won't get into it later, either.

Annie's parents were apple farmers. She could tell you all about Cortlands, Macs, Spartans, Gravensteins, Spys and on and on. Knew all the varieties. Girl could tell you that a Russet was a small variety with a sweet flesh and low acidity, unlike an Idared, which lost its acidity only after it had been put into cold storage.

She moved to Toronto after her acceptance into U of T. It was there that she met a soft-spoken, unassuming young pilot named Danny Archer.

They fit together.

Some people do.

It's just one of those things.

Danny fell for Annie because she wasn't polished, but somehow managed to shine like, well, a polished apple.

Annie didn't wear makeup. She had that whole Frances McDormand thing. Was all fine with giving the world her real self.

She was confident and had the intellect to reinforce the confidence, but always took a gentle approach with people. You know the type, you get the feeling they're really smart, yet they never make you feel bad about it. The kind of person whose absence is felt.

Danny had found that in Annie.

As time went on, Danny often wondered who he was before he met Annie. They travelled all the time, ate food they both had never tasted before. She took Danny to art galleries; he had never even thought about going to galleries before. And when he was there, she would talk and he would just listen to her voice.

Plus, she had a catch. All women have a catch. It's a little something unique to each of them that is only disclosed to the partner during an intimate moment. It's discovered serendipitously. Annie's catch was the hair just above her cheek, near her hairline. The hair was fine there, childlike, and Danny would rest his face against hers and the fine hairs would get tangled in his facial stubble. It may seem like nothing to the rest of us, but it was the world to the Danny.

They had a romance, a genuine modern romance. They had whispers and giggles, pet names and problems that they could solve just by talking about them. They had that kind of power over the world. A world that was trying to take a piece of them bit by bit, day by day.

Annie lost her balance on Tuesday – or maybe it was a Wednesday, doesn't matter. She fell in a way that people don't normally fall. I'm saying it wasn't clumsy. Her nose bled for no reason, and she had headaches that wouldn't go away.

It was quick. That was the one grace given. And that was that. Danny said a few words at the funeral. He didn't write anything down. He didn't remember what he'd said. Nothing of value could be said; no few words can capture the entirety and scope of a life. Words don't matter to the dead, anyway.

And it was only Annie that he wanted to talk to.

So, there it is, condensed and succinct, lives in a neat package, pull the bow and watch it unravel.

Danny did.

He was wearing sunglasses. The old man, that is. The hallway spot-lights were a row of cupcake-size suns, and the shades shaded his sensitive sight. He wasn't wearing pants.

And there was the loud shirt,

Screaming pineapples and maraschino cherries.

Nothing on down below except saggy cotton briefs. Bare feet on a beach of carpet. It was Friday – a Hawaiian-shirt, no-pants day.

Seven in the morning.

Terrific hour. That's sarcasm.

Jack needed coffee before the effects of the Hawaiian-shirt-no-pants day could do permanent damage.

The old man lobbed a smile down the hallway. He cracked the knuckles on one hand and shouted: "Like seeing a unicorn."

A unicorn is a creature of legend. It's basically a horse with a horn on its head. Johns and Janes use the word freely to describe singular uniqueness. I've seen a one or two in Old Market Square since I've been here.

The old man twirled his hand approvingly. Jack chuckled. The old man scooped his newspaper off the floor, folded it, and tucked it in a bowlful of patterned cherries under his armpit.

The old man held a mug and raised it as a gesture towards Jack.

"Want a cup? I make good brew."

Jack smiled, doubtful. But he was exhausted. The need outweighed the concern. "Sure."

The old man waved him over.

The old man's apartment was nothing like what Jack expected. It was shockingly clean; in fact, it was immaculate. Everything had a place and was arranged tidily. It hinted at minimalist Scandinavian design. Jack felt a pang of sorrow, Alice was an interior designer and Scandinavian sensibility was her favourite.

There was a Clear Audio turntable stacked above Macintosh amps and receivers in the living room. A wall of records curved around one corner. There must have been thousands of them. A stone hearth was built around a wood-burning fireplace, which was the centrepiece of the room and gave it a sense of warmth.

The walls were painted a flat white, not unlike an art gallery. And with good reason: the old man had quite a collection, which included an eclectic array of prints from Aubrey Beardsley to Gustave Doré. Jack noted there wasn't a TV or computer anywhere in sight.

The old man went into the kitchen to grind coffee. He had a Simonelli machine, and Jack's hope grew exponentially.

The old man noticed Jack looking at the original Keith Nagel.

"Do you appreciate art?"

"I do."

The old man set two fresh mugs of coffee down on the small, two-person table in the kitchen.

"How do you take it?"

"Black."

"Purist. Man after my own heart."

The old man slid a mug towards Jack. Steam curled upwards. Jack caught the tantalizing aroma. He took a sip. It was good – really good – and he said so.

"One does what one can to master the simple things in life."

He pulled out a chair and took a seat at the table. Jack did his best to keep from staring at his ridiculous shirt. His efforts did not go unnoticed.

"I know, I look like a retired porn producer." He sighed. "I have my reasons. Keeps people away from me; most people are like fruit flies, ya know?"

Jack sipped his coffee and nearly choked as he laughed at the comment.

The old man reached for his newspaper and set it on the table. The cover read "City to continue vehicle removal protocol. Cost estimate, millions. Hacker still at large."

"Did I catch an American accent?"

"Yeah, I moved here from NYC."

"Why?"

Jack laughed. "Everyone keeps asking me that."

"I'm not surprised."

"Why do you say that?"

The old man frowned. "Mosquitoes." He looked out the window. "Thank god for Rosewood Tea."

Jack smiled, but said nothing of his relationship with the Velic brothers. He looked up from his mug at the old man.

"What keeps you here, then?"

"Witness relocation. Didn't have a choice."

Jack couldn't tell if the man was serious. The old man sat there in his blue tinted sunglasses, Hawaiian t-shirt and underpants, sipping his morning coffee.

"Family bring you here?"

Jack felt his pulse quicken at the question. He didn't want to talk about himself, but he had to remind himself that the old man meant no harm.

"No, no family here. How about you?"

"I don't have any family. Had a daughter, but that ol' kook upstairs felt he needed her more than I did." He pointed towards the heavens. "Cancer. No cure. Yeah, right. A billion-dollar industry keeping people sick, and you couldn't ask for more effective population control. But, have you ever seen an American president die from it?"

See,

Ol' Johnny said it best,

I'm not the only one.

He also said,

Imagine all the people.

The old man almost snarled at the last part. Then the anger left his face, and he took another sip of coffee. His body relaxed, and he scratched the day's white spiked stubble poking through his chin.

"God, that feels good going down. Make it even better with a little of this."

The old man reached for a bottle of Irish cream liqueur and poured a healthy amount into his mug. He looked over the top of his tinted glasses at Jack and offered him the bottle. Jack shrugged and poured a little into his mug.

"Seriously, though, witness relocation?"

"Nah, I was an academic, researcher. My daughter died of retinal cancer. It took her sight first, and for seven years, she learned to live in the dark before the cancer came back."

The old man paused for a moment of reflection. His body went taut, and then he sighed and his shoulders slackened.

"Have you ever heard of echolocation?"

Jack shook his head.

"That was my area of research. Was one of the foremost experts on the subject." He chuckled. "Was. Not anymore."

"What is it?"

The old man moved his coffee mug to one side.

He stared at Jack. "Go ahead, close your eyes."

So Jack did...

"Nothing but darkness, right?"

"Right."

"Can't see a thing."

"Pitch black."

"That doesn't mean that everything in the room has vanished. If you get up and try to walk around with your eyes shut, you'll run into damn near everything in the room.

"Now, imagine if you could detect all the objects in the room through sensing the echoes the objects deflect when sound bounces off of them."

"You mean like bats and radar."

"Exactly like that."

"Except we're not bats."

"Right, we're not." He smiled. "Whales use echolocation, too. Here, maybe a demonstration."

The old man cleared everything off of the table except Jack's mug.

"Okay, I will close my eyes. You move the mug anywhere on the table."

Jack silently shifted the position of the mug.

"Okay, ready."

The old man snapped his fingers five times. Then he slowly and carefully reached for the mug and found it with his hand on his first attempt.

Jack smiled. "You peeked."

"No, I didn't."

"Then, that is truly amazing."

"No, it's a skill. Like anything, it requires practice. A lot of practice and discipline and time."

"I don't think I could learn how to do that."

"You're right. Not everyone can successfully master the skill, but then not everyone can become a surgeon. Or an artist. You get my jib."

He took a sip and set the mug back on the table along with the newspaper.

"Refill?"

"Sure, please. Good coffee."

The old man scratched his crotch. "Nice to have a visitor."

"Another hit?"

He held up the liqueur bottle. Jack nodded.

"Good man."

"Can I offer you any pomegranate seed? 'Tis the season."

Jack chuckled. "Sure, why not."

He had accepted the old man's invitation despite his better judgement. He was happy he had. Often better judgement restricts one from new experiences. The people who truly get to experience life are the ones who can overcome their anxieties.

Now,

This kind of thing presents a certain element of danger; your cortisol is there to keep you from putting your foot in a coffin. Is it a good idea to touch a hot stove? Should I play with a loaded gun? Does that back alley at midnight seem like a good shortcut?

It's finding that thin grey line and being able to walk it like a tightrope. Some people can and some can't. Some will and some won't.

Jack realized he used to be the "tightrope" person and really wasn't anything like that anymore. But, maybe all of these things were happening so he could rediscover the part of his life that was eluding him.

I like to think people evolve and can never really go back.

But hey, that's me, and I think Dickie would agree.

The old man sat back down in his chair. They both took a sip at the same time. Set their cups down on the table at the same time and chuckled at the same time.

"My name is Aleks, by the way."

"Jack."

And they tapped mugs to make the introduction official.

It was early. Hot already. Johns and Janes don't really associate Peg-City with warm climate.

But
The
Summers
Get
Hot!

The dew was beginning to lift off the blades of the freshly mowed lawn. The faint smell of cut grass still lingered from the night before.

Kip was on his back. A deer licked the dried, salty sweat from his face. It tickled and eventually woke him. When he opened his eyes, he was staring into the black eyes of a doe. The doe held her gaze, then looked up, past him. She had spied something, casually stepped over his body and made her way towards young shrubs.

The mix of the humidity and the smell of animal saliva and cut grass caused a sudden stir in Kip's stomach. He rolled to his side and puked. He wiped his damp mouth with the backside of his hand and sat up. Blades of grass stuck to his face. He scratched an itch beneath his nose and felt a crusty substance. He looked at his fingertip: dried blood mixed with white powder residue.

What had happened? Where was he? Ditches lined the streets.

Charleswood?

Yeah, Kip, Charleswood.

Charleswood is in the south end of the city. A long way from downtown. Charleswood is a suburb known for its confusing welcome sign which reads:

"Welcome To Charleswood. The Suburb Beautiful"

Reminds me of when Mr. Burns used monkeys to write a novel.

Sign is still there to this day.

All of this is true, of course.

So,

Why the hell was he in Charleswood? Whose front lawn was this?

"Hey, what do you think you're doing?"

Kip was still groggy, rubbed his forehead and found the voice. He squinted as his eyes adjusted to the sunlight. A man was coming out through his garage door. Kip found his way to his feet and felt like he might vomit again but kept it down.

"Sorry."

"What the hell, goddamn vagrants. Get outta here before I call the cops."

"Sorry, sorry."

On his feet and on the move, Kip searched his pockets for evidence of what had happened the night before. He found a receipt from the liquor store. On his wrist was a smeared club stamp. Then some of the night came to him in fragments.

He walked as far as Roblin and caught the hydro-bus. At least he still had his wallet. The bus driver shot a wry look at him as he boarded.

He leaned his head against the window. As the hydro-bus drove on, he watched the remainder of yesterday fall away. He had been lying to himself for some time now. Things were not getting better; they were getting worse. And it was his birthday today.

The Rosewood foyer was empty. He took the elevator. When the doors opened, his brother Kurt was behind the bar polishing beer glasses. The two brothers made eye contact. Neither said a word.

Kurt should've said something.

It was his job,

As the older brother.

It was his place.

Tough love is still love.

But he didn't.

Human relationships are complicated. Johns and Janes don't always do the right thing. Sometimes there is no "right thing," there's just "something."

That's why they're Johns and Janes.

Show me perfect. I dare you.

I dare you!

Horace was seated on a stool, at the wood, nursing a beer. He swivelled in his chair and looked Kip over from bottom to top. He, too, said nothing. The look of his friend bothered him. He felt the urge to say something, anything at all, but the words wouldn't come.

Kip kept his head down and went upstairs to the kitchen.

He poured himself a tall glass of water, drank it dry and poured another. He pulled a folded blanket and pillow from a linen drawer and curled up on the couch.

It felt like mere minutes before he was gently shaken awake by Horace. Kip wiped the sleep from his eyes.

"What time is it?"

"Ten."

He sat up and looked at Horace sullenly.

"Did Kurt say anything?"

"No."

"Have you seen Kris?"

"Nope."

"I really screwed up last night."

"Yeah, maybe, but that was last night."

Horace always knew the right thing to say. He never judged his friend.

"Oh." Kip shook his head and tapped his temple gently with his index finger. "Got a freight train up here."

"It'll pass. Actually, I've got just the thing."

Kip looked at his friend. Horace smiled.

"I don't feel much like playing games tonight, H."

"No, not that. Something else. Trust me." Horace winked at him.

"Alright, I'm game."

Kip and Horace pedalled at an even pace side-by-side along Pembina. The night breeze was doing wonders for Kip's hangover.

Horace took his hands off the handlebars and let his arms fall to his sides. Kip liked the idea and did the same.

Horace was in the lead. He looked back at Kip and pointed ahead. "Look."

So Kip looked.

"It's him!"

On the sidewalk was a man holding a picket sign. Horace believed it was the same man he'd been seeing all over the city.

Horace sped up his pedalling, the destination was not far now. He could hear the wind in his ears as his speed increased. Kip held the pace. He was thankful his friend had roused him.

Horace signalled to turn left, and Kip followed him into a parking lot. There weren't any lights. Horace stepped off his bike, put the kickstand down and adjusted his backpack.

Kip looked around. He wondered what his friend had in mind.

"A parking lot?"

"Not the lot. That over there."

"What? That wall?"

"I come here once or twice during the summer." Horace looked at the concrete wall that had no real business being in the field. Even though he could hardly see it, Kip knew it was there. Something reliable, tangible. Something concrete.

Horace took his backpack off his shoulder and searched within the contents. He found a flashlight, turned it on, and stood beside Kip, leaning on his handlebars.

"Well?"

"Well, what?"

"You coming?"

"Yeah, I guess."

"Carry this."

Kip hopped off of his bike, and Horace handed him the six of beer that had been buried in his backpack.

The soft night breeze brushed their bare forearms. They hiked a few metres through the tall, unruly grass shoots. The wall was about seven feet high and the same in length. It was two feet wide and perfect for sitting. Horace flicked off the flashlight and climbed the wall. Kip watched as he did.

"Come on up. You can see all the way along Pembina from here."

Kip passed Horace the six of beer and climbed the wall. When he was settled, he took a silent look around. Horace twisted the cap off a beer. They clinked the necks of the bottles and each took a swig.

A hydro-bus silently swept by, heading towards Confusion Corner.

Kip leaned back and looked up at the stars. No clouds. The stars were everywhere they were supposed to be – far, far away from the stage and screen. His friend, too, was staring up at the vast night sky.

"It all started from nothing."

"What's that?"

"That," he said, pointing up at the galaxy and the universe of stars beyond. "All was devoid of form and mass. Some have even contemplated its beginning, the how and the why."

Horace took a swig of beer and wiped his lips with his hoody sleeve.

Kip shuffled his butt on the wall's surface to make himself a little more comfortable.

"A star is born, and, eventually, a star dies. Just like human life. The universe is constantly growing and expanding and dying. It is all the same everywhere."

Horace twisted the tops off two fresh bottles. A little foam bubbled up the neck when he handed one to his friend. Kip blew the beer foam from the mouth of the bottle.

"Sometimes when I see the stars, all I can see is the great vastness beyond their twinkling lights. I see a star twinkle or one shoot through the sky. It lasts a second, even less. Each human step, each blink of an eye, is merely a frame in a film or a cel in an old cartoon.

"Life is nothing more than a secession of frames, one after another. A push of a button, light captures one single frame of life." Kip made a triangle-shaped viewfinder with his fingers and looked through it. Then he turned to face Horace, looked at him through the finger viewfinder. They both laughed.

"Do you ever think about what might have been if you hadn't been, you know?" Kip ran his fingers across his neck as though he were tracing Horace's scar along his own skin.

"No. No point in thinking about what could've been. Only what is." He smiled at Kip.

"I'm here because of it."

Then something chased the smile from his face and consternation replaced it. There was a long silence between the two friends. And just when neither of them thought the other would say something, Horace broke the silence.

"I don't know who I am." He searched the universe above them as though there might be an answer hidden among the scattered glittering constellations. He stood up on the wall and watched as a car went by along the Pembina Highway. Likely just someone passing through town.

"Lost. Forgotten."

He swallowed the last of his beer. Then he tossed the bottle into the field. "Just like that!"

He watched the bottle disappear into the darkness. Clusters of dragonflies hovered over the tall grass, feeding on the banquet of mosquitoes.

Horace sat back down on the ledge of the wall.

"I look at my skin. Maybe I am just like everyone keeps telling me. So what, I should be ashamed of my skin? Well, I'm not! It's just skin, you know?"

Horace's hands were shaking. Then his anger subsided, his body caved in a little, shoulders rolled forward, his head bowed low, he just let go of it, and with that release, the taut rigidity that had held him so erect just fell off of him like dropped armour.

"Truth is, I have no idea, not really. I know I'm not the only one with these problems. I'd just like to know a few things. I will never know, though. My parents. Are they dead, alive?" He looked at Kip, his eyes swollen and heavy. "Missing?" He closed his eyes. "Is there family out there for me?" He laughed.

He had finally said it out loud. He had said it so another person could hear it. And it didn't help the hurt inside him at all. More silence grew between the two friends.

"Horace, you're my brother. I love you. I know that may not be enough. I know there's a hole in your heart. Something missing that even love can't mend. I knew my parents, but I don't know what it means to not know. You've been a brother in our house. At least, I hope you feel that way. But maybe it's time I started being more than that. I could help you look, help you find what you're longing for." Kip looked out at the tall grass swaying in the night breeze. "I guess I was scared, you know?"

Horace looked at Kip. There was a gentle sincerity in his friend's eyes.

"Scared? Of what?"

"Of losing you." Kip lowered his eyes. "Pretty selfish of me."

Horace put his hand on Kip's shoulder.

"I'm scared, too. What if they are alive, what if I find them?"

"What do you mean?"

"I mean, what if they're all screwed up? All I have is a memory of them. And that memory is actually a lie, something I made up."

Kip didn't know what to say.

"You won't ever lose me. Not like that."

Horace faced his friend. He touched the scar on his neck.

"But I might lose you."

Kip looked sullen.

"What do you mean?"

"You need to quit. Stop the nonsense."

Kip knew exactly what Horace was referring to. He watched the dark blades sway like laps of night waves on some lonely sea. Fluttering wings of dragonflies caught moonbeams illuminating the elegant membranes.

"I promise you."

Horace shoved his hands into the pouch of his hoody. Then he took out a small wrapped package.

"Happy birthday."

Kip had forgotten it was his birthday. The thought bothered him. He tore at the coloured paper wrapping. Inside was a small, thin, circular black leather case. He opened the lid, and inside was a glass lens filter.

"It will fit your vintage Pentax. It might even fit your old Canon, too."

It was a polarizer, which affects the existing polarized light and defines the angle of incidence – Brewster's angle – perfectly. Or close enough to perfect, according to Dickie, who is apparently quite the photographer himself.

Horace grabbed another beer and handed one to Kip. They weren't in any hurry, so they both leaned back on their arms and watched the stars. A sky filled with the wonder of distance.

Horace took a swig from his beer and set it down on the ledge. Then he jumped down.

"Where you going?"

"To find the bottle I threw. I shouldn't litter."

Truth was, he didn't want his brother to see him bury the tattered photograph of his parents in the earth.

1
2
3
4
I declare a thumb war.
Bow,
Shake,
Corners,
Begin.

That was chapter and verse of childhood.

Kids would square their thumbs off and wrestle until one thumb pinned the opposing thumb for three seconds.

You won some, you lost some.

Mostly, you lost trading cards and candy. If you were crazy enough to bet candy.

But,

Then you grew up.

Became an adult.

Adults wrestle all the time, too.

The ring's just a little bigger.

Their worst opponent is themselves.

You win some, you lose some.

That's why,

It didn't matter how he got there, he was there.

The chime of the elevator was out of tune, and there was a long pause, long enough to make Kip just that little bit more nervous than he already was.

Doors opened.

Third floor.

Stepped out.

Paused.

Stepped back in.

Cursed and shook his head.

He wasn't so sure anymore that he had chosen the right thumb.

The elevator doors started to close. A hand reached just in time to catch the sensor and the doors opened back up. It was Cusack. Thick grey eyebrows like arrows pointing towards his ice-blue eyes.

"Well?"

Kip stepped off the elevator.

"Thought I forgot something."

Cusack's eyes softened. "Kind of looked like you were making a run for it."

Kip chuckled. "I was."

"That's good. You shouldn't get comfortable with anything. Makes a person complacent. Goddamn soft is what it makes you." Cusack extended his arms out, engulfing the entire room. "This is it. The Bullpen." His arms dropped back to his sides. "What's left of it."

Empty desks and empty offices were outnumbered only by all the empty chairs. A number of the tube bulbs had failed and many others were flickering. The walls were wounded with marks and holes. The carpet stained, old, musty. Copy machines, alone, unplugged, antiquated hulks. Not exactly what Kip had envisioned of a busy bustling newspaper bullpen.

Dickie says the glory days of newspapers were something to see.

I, myself, once had an editor friend who worked for a small rag in – well, it doesn't really matter where. He used to tell me that when everyone was on their game, did their job well, you know, right down to the cartoonist nailing a politician in some doodle, a newspaper was the voice of its citizens.

"What happened?"

Cusack shrugged.

"Things change. People aren't much for journalism these days. Too busy watching YouTube famesters, getting their facts from Wiki. Pff, *facts*, my left nut." Cusack slammed his fist into his open palm. "Anyway, follow me."

Kip followed.

"Floor below is production." Cusack pointed down, then up. "Above is Editor-in-Chief. Online," Cusack growled. "Those dipshits are on the main floor. Archives are in the basement. Rather fitting. And what's left of the journalists are here. This one's me."

Cusack held the door open for Kip, and they both stepped into the office.

It was kept neat. Filing cabinets lettered alphabetically. Very little in the way of clutter. A computer monitor was on his desk; it was on with a half-finished article on the screen.

A number of journalism awards on a bookcase. Old black and white photographs behind glass on the wall. Kip recognized a few of them to be Olaf's.

Dickie says that Greg Olaf hasn't been seen or heard from in years. One day he was there, taking award-winning photographs, then – poof! – vanished.

"Have a seat."

Kip sat.

"Did you bring some work?"

Kip nodded. He took a folder from his satchel and handed it to Cusack. Cusack opened the folder and looked over the prints.

"Huh, you shoot on film."

"That's right."

"Like Greg."

Cusack pointed to some of the prints on the wall. He leaned back in his chair to admire them for a moment. It had been a long time since he'd thought about all the assignments he and Greg had worked on together.

They had been friends, and we've long since established the importance of friends.

He gently touched his lips, shook his head, and returned his attention to Kip's pictures.

"Some good stuff here. A keen eye for detail and perspective. Understated depth of field. Good use of light. Have you ever shot under pressure?"

Kip shook his head. Cusack stood and looked at the awards on the bookcase.

"Here's the thing. I'm a dinosaur. No one gives a shit about me, my work or this goddamn newspaper. It's closing in ten months, anyway. They just haven't made the formal announcement yet."

The mug was almost as old as his career, two chips out of the lip. No amount of scrubbing could wash away the coffee stains on the interior porcelain.

Kip tried imagining all the things this man had seen, all the stories he had shared with the world. Now, in his final season, the world was closing the door on him.

Doors close on people all the time.

Johns and Janes don't get to pick and choose.

You work with the minutes you're afforded.

Cusack sensed his melancholy had unsettled the youth across from him.

"Look, kid." Cusack walked from behind the desk and went over to the door. He closed and locked it. He leaned on his desk, and then hooked his hip over the corner, reaching down for his coffee mug and taking a sip. He scratched his chin and stared off absently at the ceiling. "I've got this problem. I still give a damn."

Kip shifted in his seat beneath those cool blue eyes.

"I know something. I stumbled on it amongst some research papers five years ago. Separate story, separate report, but sometimes that's the way it goes. You catch a whiff of something that stinks and you follow the smell."

He took another sip of coffee, slid off the desk and took a seat in his chair. He lifted a stack of files out of a locked cabinet and onto his desk. He thumbed through the stack and found a tab of interest, pulled the file and handed it to Kip.

Dickie says a paper file is better than anything stored electronically.

I have to agree: less accessible, fewer alterations over time, more accuracy. The history Generation Xers grew up with won't be the same history told to Generation Z.

"I know. I'm a cliché."

Kip looked up at him, a bewildered look lining his features.

"Old man, all this paper, in the age of computers. Terrible. But no one can hack a piece of paper. Once something is on a computer, it is no longer safe. Sounds ridiculous, sounds like old-man paranoia, but it's just one of those things."

Cusack set the stack of files back inside the file cabinet in order.

"Go on, open the damn file."

Kip did as he was told.

"What do you see?"

"I'm not sure. Looks like bank documents, transaction records." Then something did stand out to Kip. "But it makes no sense. Why would you want these? The records are available electronically. I mean, aren't they public record now?"

"The electronic ones are, yes. But there are inconsistencies between the electronic ones and these." Cusack leaned forward and reached over his desk. "Most notably, column nine. Column nine doesn't exist in the electronic records. Here, look."

Cusack flipped on his computer monitor and turned the screen to face Kip.

"See?"

"I see. So?"

"So?" Cusack shook his head. "So, they are altering public records to bury illegal transactions."

"What transactions? To what end?"

Cusack sighed.

"I have a theory."

"A theory?" Kip frowned. He held up the paper, tossed it on the desk, and pointed at the file. "How did you get that?"

Cusack leaned back in his chair and smiled. "I'm not in the ground yet. I still have a few reliable sources."

"You could go to prison for this."

Cusack's smile disappeared. "I know I could go to prison. But the ACB is crooked. This nation's economy is held together by the ACB."

Kip slid lower into his chair. A light bulb went on in his head.

"Jesus, you want to expose the ACB?"

Cusack's cold blue eyes held Kip's gaze. "Maybe."

Cusack stood up and faced the wall behind his desk. Years and years of history and research, stories pinned like insects to a corkboard. He could hear the tap of the keys on his first typewriter ringing like gunshots in his mind. Those were the days.

"I've been working on this story for five years. Five years of my life. Lost colleagues, friends, Greg." He paused, a thought dislodged in his head. He turned to face Kip. "Lost my wife three years back. It was quick. One minute, she was alive, the next, well..." He rubbed his forehead. "You always think you've got more time. Another damned cliché." He coughed to clear his throat. "I was working with a forensic accountant on the sly. He put most of this together, found the irregularities, before he vanished."

"Vanished?"

"Missing is more like it."

"He quit on you?"

"He's dead, kid. Murdered. We were working offline, on paper. I think he made the mistake of logging on."

"I don't understand. What about you, then?"

"I asked myself the same question. I'm still here, so all I can think of was there was nothing linking him to me."

Kip was trying his best to piece all of this together. Then it hit him.

"So now what? You go out in a hail of gunfire like Butch and Sundance?"

"Maybe."

"Except you've got no Sundance."

Cusack stared at Kip.

"Me?"

"Why not, what else you got?"

"But why me? I'm no professional. You met me in a restaurant. How can you even trust me?"

Cusack sighed and then smiled. "I have no choice, kid. I've been painted into a corner. And it's because you're not a professional, because you've got real talent. You're the best thing I've got. For all of those reasons."

Kip rubbed his hands over his face. "I need to think about this."

"So think."

"Now?"

"Yes, now. You leave here today, in or out."

Kip thought about what he and Horace had talked about the other night. He had made a promise to change. Here was his chance, but he was scared. This was big, but he had promised Horace. Then he realized it wasn't even about Horace or his promise. It was about him. Kip wanted something. He wanted change.

Dickie says change is either horrific or hopeful. There's no third direction.

"I'm in."

"I won't lie. It's dangerous. This is a big business, a corrupt big business, tied to government. There's nothing worse, nothing more threatening."

Kip smiled. "I've been taking all the wrong risks. Time to start taking the right ones."

"Alright then." Cusack stood and grabbed his coffee mug. "Follow me."

"Where are we going?"

"The kitchen to find you a mug. We don't do anything around here without coffee." Cusack stopped, turned, faced Kip. "We're goddamn journalists!"

"Why here?"

"As good a place as any."

"Couldn't we just talk in my apartment?"

"Maybe, I don't know. Nothing seems secure anymore, except in a quiet space outdoors. This is the only way that it feels like no one is listening in."

Loraina slid her slender fingers through the chain-link fence and let the evening breeze brush her long heavy curls away from her face. Jack surveyed her with a silent fondness. Something about this woman, the mystery, her skill, made it hard not to get all wrapped up in it.

The mystery, baby,

The intrigue.

The not knowing.

That's why you don't live forever.

That's why you get out of bed.

Jack was watching the train come into the yard.

"It all began for me in a place just like this."

He looked north down the Arlington Bridge, then back down at the train yard. The train had ground to a halt, and the steel wheels had finally gone silent.

"Used to be so innocent back then. Writing on trains, leaving a mark, watching other writers' pieces sail by. Running around the yards. Evading security and cops. It was exciting, I felt alive."

Jack shook his head and turned away from the yard.

"Then one day it all changed. We were getting shot at. My friends were getting arrested or killed. The art had gone out of it. It was all about petty fame and street cred. There was no message. Nothing real was being said, no statement. That's when I decided to go it alone. I wanted to be different. I wanted to make things better all over, make change happen. I had to adapt. I needed to do more."

"Then the incident in New York."

Jack turned away from the yard.

"Yeah."

"What really happened, Jack? Everyone knows the story, but no one has ever heard your side of things."

Jack realized in that moment that Loraina had brought him to this place so he could remember.

Memories are merely data stored by the brain within the neurons of the visual cortex.

Biology, cousin.

"I made a mistake." He wrung his hands. "Some very powerful people used me and I didn't even realize it. By the time I started to figure it out, it was too late."

He looked at Loraina.

"Just like what you're trying to do to me."

She said nothing.

Jack clenched his fists. "I don't know what you expect of me." He sounded defeated.

Loraina took her hands from the fence and turned around. She leaned against the railing. Her movements were smooth and fluid.

It unnerved Jack just how lithe she was despite being blind. He was learning so much. The faint sound of an oncoming train could be heard. She looked so calm, so relaxed, yet he felt tense. He felt the first pang of anxiety begin to increase his heart rate.

"The most recognizable sound in the world is the sound of someone shaking a can of spray paint."

Dickie says that Queen Mary's only regret was that she never climbed a fence. Sometimes it's the only way to the other side.

And

Maybe you'll climb one yourself someday.

Metaphors, god love 'em.

"You have a voice, Jack. It's a good voice. It's a voice that can speak for people who can't always speak up for themselves or, worse, won't. That includes me. And we live in a time where things aren't black and white, where everyone thinks they're the good guys."

Jack didn't feel like he was on the same page as her.

"Let's walk."

Loraina started down the slope of the bridge, and Jack walked beside her. She unfolded her walking cane and swept it side-to-side.

"Jack, there's something happening in this country, something rather big." She ran her hand through her thick, curly hair. "I have a story to tell you."

They stopped at the traffic lights. Two hydro-buses were about to pull through the green light. They waited, and the lights changed green. The walk sign appeared, accompanied by a chirping sound.

"We need to go east."

Jack stood still, waiting for the light to change. Loraina tugged at his sleeve.

"Come on, Jack. I said east."

Jack looked at the direction they had been heading. He wasn't sure which way was which, and he certainly hadn't acquired his bearings for the city yet. He was shocked at how Loraina knew which direction was east.

"How did you know?"

Loraina kept walking, waving her cane left to right.

"Know what, Jack?"

"Which way was east?"

"The chirp."

"I don't follow."

"When the walk sign came up. You saw that, right?"

"Yes."

"Well, that's your cue. Mine is the chirp, which directionally means east and west. The koo-koo indicates north and south. I heard the chirp and felt the warmth of the sun on my face. We had been heading north, but we need to go east."

Jack felt very foolish.

"I need to pay closer attention to the little details."

"Jack, you're being too hard on yourself. You're not blind. I am. You don't need to feel guilty for not noticing a chirp signal.

"I lost my sight when I was a young girl. A mix of exposure, snow blindness and an undiagnosed eye condition." She smiled. "In some ways, it makes it worse. But I am also lucky to have seen the things I was able to see for the short amount of time that I had my sight."

"I have never really given it much thought. I am just realizing, since I met you, how much I take my vision for granted. I mean, I love going to the movies. Or the peacefulness of a sunset."

"I do both of those things, too. I love the movies, described video, the sounds and dialogue, listening to audience reaction, developing the characters and setting with my imagination. It's lovely. And I often take time to sit with the setting sun, to feel its waning warmth fade as it falls behind the horizon, to hear the world relax and settle at the end of another day." She smiled absently. "I just experience things differently."

"We're here."

Loraina had led him to the perimeter fence of the train yard. She removed a small tin-snip from her satchel and cut an entry window into the chain-link fence.

"Come with me."

Jack felt a sudden rush he hadn't felt in a long while. It was the rush of danger, a danger that he was intimately familiar with. He realized just how much he had missed this feeling.

Loraina made the clicking sound with her tongue. Jack assumed she was trying to get a feeling for her surroundings. He could sense a change in her overall physiology. Her body had become taut and alert. There was a readiness, and Jack noticed something else about her, something lethal. She seemed like an entirely different person.

The two waded through the rows of parked trains. Jack ran his hands along the steel of an oil-cargo car that had a piece painted on it by an artist he had known from Michigan.

Loraina moved with ease through the lines of trains, using her hands, feeling everything, and clicking her tongue often or tapping her walking cane against the steel walls of trains.

She stopped and felt her way to a ladder on one of the boxcars. She started to climb, and Jack followed directly behind her. When they reached the top of the train car, one could see all the parked trains in the entire lot. Jack felt a thrill quake through his body. It was a magnificent sight, but then he realized that Loraina couldn't see it. He realized she had done this for him.

"Jack, if you wouldn't mind, could you provide some dimensions of the boxcar?" Jack looked a little confused at the requested. It seemed Loraina sensed his bewilderment. "It helps to know where the edges are."

"I see. Well, the car is about ten feet wide and about – ah, hell, I don't know, maybe fifty feet long. You're standing pretty darn close to the middle."

She smiled at Jack.

"That's perfect." She held out her arms. "Look at them. Look at them all."

Jack did just that.

"They travel all over North America transporting and delivering goods. Imagine the message you could send with all of these."

Jack's imagination was reeling. He felt the seed of inspiration germinate within his soul.

Click clack.

Click clack.

"You could do anything with these. They are just as powerful as any other form of communication."

Click clack.

Click clack.

A train was arriving. Its steel wheels ground, shattering the silence that had fallen over the yard.

"Jack?"

"Yes?"

"How did you do the Buckingham Palace piece?"

"I had nothing to do with that."

Loraina smiled.

"I know something. It's rather important. I am going to share the information with you."

"Okay."

"There is a man, here, in Winnipeg, who has power over government and economy. He is very dangerous, and he is very real. The man I am talking about killed my mother. She used to work for him, and she discovered something about him."

"I'm not sure I fully understand what you are trying to say."

Loraina faced Jack and said nothing. She simply stared at him with her unnerving calm gaze.

"What? What is it?"

"A conspiracy."

"Conspiracy? What kind of conspiracy?"

"One that will affect us all."

"Come on. I've heard this spook story before."

"Yeah, that's how everyone reacted to the mortgage industry."

Jack said nothing. She had a point. No one saw it coming. Then it crippled the world's economy.

No one saw Watergate coming, either.

Watergate has become synonymous with scandal.

Happens to also be a metonym,

Watergate happened at the Watergate.

"I have proof."

"What proof? Of what?"

"It's complicated."

"I'm sorry if I don't sound like I totally believe you. I mean, you're not exactly giving me anything concrete to go on here, are you?"

"I know."

"Look, I get it. There are lots of bad people out there. Trust me, I know. It was my work to expose them."

Jack shrugged. The breeze had died. Loraina tied her hair back.

"Sometimes you have to go with your instincts, Jack."

"Yeah, well, these days mine aren't so hot."

"What if I..."

Loraina went silent. Jack had heard the footsteps, too. They crouched low, but it was too late.

"Hey, you two come down from there right now! Do it slowly and make no sudden movements. My weapon is loaded."

Jack looked at Loraina. She was reaching into her satchel. She removed something and lobbed it in the general direction of the man on the ground. A small explosive burst cracked loudly, sending a thick heavy fog of smoke into the air to encircle the man. He fired a round wildly, missing both his targets by a wide range.

Loraina didn't wait around to see if the security officer's aim would get better. She was already on the move. Jack leapt from the train, hit the ground, and rolled with the impact. He stood up and looked for Loraina; she was nowhere to be seen. Jack quickly scanned the area, but there was no sign of her. He heard more footsteps and yelling. He couldn't wait any longer. He needed to move, so he did.

He found his way back to the cut fence, crawled out through the opening and kept running.

When he finally felt he had put enough distance between himself and the train yard, he slowed down to catch his breath. His chest was heaving and his lungs were stinging as they worked in gulps of new air.

He felt more alive than he had in a very long time.

The Bible says bad things happen at night.

That's funny to me because bad things don't really wait for night-fall.

Dickie's got a story he likes to tell, over beers, about this guy. Let's call him Ray. Ol' Ray went for a walk with a friend.

It was dark.

It was late.

The witching hour.

Some used to call it that because they thought witches and demons were out and about doing bad things.

Today's Johns and Janes call it midnight.

Anyway,

So, Ray and his chum are walking and chatting and all that sort of jib, and along comes this cop. The cop is suspicious of two men walking at such a late hour. Maybe he thinks they're witches about to get up to some kind of witchery.

You see, the perception is that good Johns and Janes call it quits after the sun sets.

The cop asks ol' Ray and his buddy what they're up to, and Ray says: "Putting one foot in front of the other."

This little event gave Ray the idea for a book.

You might have heard of it.

You might have even read it.

It's a book about burning books.

And

Then,

The knock on Jack's door came

Well into that ol' witching hour.

It was frantic.

Tap tap tap tap tap tap tap tap taptaptaptap...

Jack had only just arrived home from his night at the train yard with Loraina. He was exhausted and half expected it to be Loraina at the door, but he harboured a suspicion it was not.

The taps had increased force to more powerful bangs. Jack pulled the door open and Clair tumbled into his arms. She was sobbing and flailing her limbs erratically. She slipped through Jack's arms and collapsed onto the floor. She was mumbling two words over and over: "Lost it, lost it, lost it."

Peeps lose things all the time.

Car keys,

Wallets,

Marbles,

Their way.

Jack knelt down to scoop the girl up into his arms and move her to the couch, but she screamed and recoiled from him back into the hallway.

Jack didn't know what to do or what was happening to her. When he stepped into the hall, she began to scream.

"Lost it! Lost it! Lost it! Lost it!"

Jack crouched and reached for her hand to try and soothe her, but she refused to be touched, batting away his hands and scrambling backwards until her back thudded with a force against the hallway wall.

Jesus, Jack thought.

He decided to give her some space. Clair put her head between her legs and began to sob loudly. Her sobs echoed down the hallway.

An apartment door opened. It was the old man. Jack cursed silently. Can't call him "Old Man." He had a name – Aleks.

Aleks stepped into the hallway and looked at Jack. Jack looked back at him and shrugged. Good lord, what the hell was he wearing? Was it a zip-up with a giant tiger face roaring on the front of it?

A tiger is the largest feline in the world, and it won't exist when your children grow up.

The rest of him was tucked into '80s jammer shorts. He took a sip from the glass he was holding before setting it inside his apartment.

He walked the hallway towards Jack. Feet in flops made a snap sound with each step. Jack was happy to see him.

"What's happened?"

"She was banging on my door. I opened and found her like this."

"Geez!"

Aleks knelt down in front of Clair. She was rocking back and forth, mumbling the same two words.

"Clair. It's Aleks from down the hall. What happened?"

"Lost it!"

"Lost what?"

"Lost the phone."

"What phone?"

"My phone. I lost it. Lost it! Lost it! Lost it!"

She was screaming again. Jack noticed his mysterious neighbour had opened her door a crack and was watching them. He ignored her. Aleks kept a little distance from Clair, but tried to get her to talk.

"Come, Clair. Let's get you on your feet and get you back inside."

He reached for her hand. Jack tried to warn him, but the words didn't come in time. Aleks took her hand, and she smashed her fist into his face. He fell backward and rubbed his cheek. Jack could see that it had caught Aleks by surprise.

Clair stood up and spun in a circle. She stopped, and then began to hit her head against the wall. Jack grabbed her and tried to stop her, but she was so frantic that he wasn't able to do it alone.

Aleks shook off the blow and climbed back onto his bare feet. He and Jack subdued her, but it wasn't without great struggle. Once they had a firm hold of her, Jack signalled for Aleks to force her arms to her sides as gently as he possible could.

"Can you hold her?"

"Maybe. I don't know. I think so. Why? What are you going to do?"

"Call 911, I guess. She's completely lost it."

Jack took out his phone and dialled.

Shortly after the paramedics had left Clair's apartment, Jack stood in the hallway with Aleks. They both looked weary, and their nerves were blown to hell. What just happened? The paramedics had never seen anyone lose it over a lost phone before.

Dickie calls it dependency. He says that the most invasive things in the lives of Johns and Janes are the things least expected.

Television

Phones

Computers

Jack knew the phone was important to her, but this was different. Aleks put his hand on Jack's shoulder.

"I need a drink."

Jack agreed with a nod.

"I've got good bourbon." He tilted his head in the direction of his apartment. "Come."

Jack took a seat at the kitchen table. Aleks brought the bottle of Blanton's to the table and set it down with two jiggers. He poured gracefully. They clinked glasses and sipped the fine straight.

Jack shook his head. "What happened to her?"

Aleks relaxed in his chair and carefully spun the jigger of whisky in front of him. "People just break."

"Yeah, I had a feeling she wasn't well."

Aleks sat forward in his chair. "What do you mean?"

"I don't know. I mean, she can't carry a normal conversation and she has always had a very unhealthy attachment to her phone."

"Everyone has an unhealthy attachment to their tech these days. Doesn't mean they're going to go postal. She must have been on the verge, ya know?"

Jack took a drink of his whisky. He scratched the back of his head. He didn't entirely agree with Aleks. He knew his phone could be a trigger for his anxiety, and he suspected he wasn't the only person with these inclinations. But he wasn't sure about Clair's situation. "Yeah, maybe that's all it was."

"When I lost my daughter, that was my last tie to the world. I was retired and had no one left in my life. I sold my computers, got rid of my television. I got rid of my mobile phone and said goodbye to the whole lot of it. I just wanted to listen to my music, enjoy a drink and read. I spend my evenings cooking and steeping tea."

Jack smiled. Aleks's life sounded nice. Jack had never experienced that kind of tranquillity – truth was, he had never even considered it. He wondered why he had never considered it. Was it a desire to stay entangled in the convoluted web of the tech-connection?

You see, the more peeps you know, the more you feel the desire to stay connected. And the vicious cycle perpetuates on and on.

Dickie calls it the Techna-map. A world connected by electronic devices. Total exposure, zero anonymity.

But if you have nothing connecting you, one might find the opportunity to create distance from the Techna-map. The further you get from the Techna-map, the less you know about current events.

You know,

Like who wore what to the Oscars,

Or,

Did Jay-Z really do all that shit to Beyoncé?

You might

Just find a closeness to freedom, or at least a facsimile of it.

The Techna-map is the digital cartography of all that is, could be, or will be within the realm of cyberspace. It is the dots and dashes of digital information sharing. The source technology facilitates the link between person-to-person or person-to-device.

While people don't really intellectualize the effects of constant stimulation, instant gratification, and the lack of real tangible work that is required to learn and retain what is learned, they forge ahead blindly, deeper and deeper in the Techna-map, until the name itself becomes a paradox.

Jack was only beginning to extrapolate the reasons for Clair's meltdown. There is all too much grey in this new world of dots-per-inch colour.

Aleks broke his train of thought.

"Another?"

Holding up the bottle of bourbon.

"Sure, thanks."

Aleks filled Jack's jigger, and then repeated the same for himself. He got up from the table.

"It's times like these that I play a little bit of Chopin. The nocturnes are best. I love all of the classics. Brahms, Mozart, Bach, but there's something about Chopin. His music was that of a poet."

Jack sipped his whisky and watched as Aleks removed an old record from its sleeve. Aleks inspected the record, then set it on the platter and aligned the stylus. The diamond snapped into the groove of the wax, and warm pops and hisses came through the speakers. The stylus spun and reached the recorded information. The soft sound of the piano filled the room.

Aleks sat back down at the table. He scratched the grey hairs on his bare chest and sipped his whisky.

"Ah, Chopin."

His voice was soft and low, almost as though he had said the words to himself. Jack smiled. The music was beautiful, familiar, but he was unsure he'd ever heard it before. There was so much he hadn't experienced or thought to experience.

"We must make the most of the time afforded to us."

Jack nodded in agreement.

"Aleks, would you tell me more about echolocation?"

"That's not quite what I expected Chopin to do for you."

"I can't be sure, but I may have met someone who I think

uses the skill."

"Really?"

Aleks sat back in his chair and folded his hands over his naked stomach. A look of disbelief was painted on his face.

"This person is blind?"

"Yes. Or, at least I think so, but the things she can do, I mean, I've never seen anything like it."

"A woman, you say?"

Aleks scratched the white stubble on his chin, then shook his head and smiled. He was clearly thinking of something or maybe someone.

"What makes you think this woman uses echolocation?"

Jack pushed his empty jigger towards Aleks, who uncorked the bottle and filled the glass.

"I don't know anything for sure, to be honest. She makes a clicking sound with her tongue all the time. She seems to know where things are in a room. She prefers a quiet room. At first, I thought she was a fraud, faking her blindness, but she never makes proper eye contact. She wears odd-looking hearing aids."

Jack shook his head.

"I don't get it."

He looked at Aleks.

"Is any of this making sense?"

"The clicking of the tongue or snapping of fingers is indicative of echolocation practice. Typically, it is only a minor aid at best. There are few people who become proficient in its use, and maybe a handful of people in the world that master it. Those that have mastered it are well-documented cases."

The expression on Aleks's face changed.

"What? What is it?"

"Oh, nothing."

Aleks dismissed the thought by waving his hand in the air. He took up his whisky, but he stopped the glass just before his lips. He was thinking again. He didn't drink.

"Does the woman have a name?"

"Loraina."

"I see."

The name meant nothing to Aleks. He took the drink of whisky. Jack wondered if he should push Aleks and pry a little into the man's thoughts, but he decided against it. If Aleks wanted to tell Jack what he was thinking, he would have done so.

Jack chuckled.

"Thinking about the past?"

"Nah, thinking about the woman."

"Ah."

"She has this tattoo, a snake, on the palm of her hand that stretches along her index finger. You don't really notice it, except when she smokes."

The jigger slipped out of Aleks's hand and hit the table, splashing whisky all over. Jack stood up. His shirt was wet with whisky. Aleks just looked at him with vacant eyes.

"A snake? Could it be a red-belly snake?"

"I don't know anything about snakes, but I guess, yeah, it has some orange or red in it. Why? What is it?"

"How do you know this woman?"

"I don't really know."

Jack wanted to say more but couldn't. He was already very uncomfortable with everything. He felt like he could trust Aleks, but the truth was he didn't really know him at all.

Aleks took a rag from the countertop and wiped up the spilled whisky. Jack was still standing. Aleks threw the rag at Jack so he could clean himself.

"Aleks, what's going on?"

Aleks held out his hand and pointed at the chair.

"Please, sit."

Jack took his seat. Aleks put his head down and shook it.

"I think we may know the same woman."

"There's someone here asking for you."

"Damn it, Garth. What have I got in my hands?"

"A ham sandwich?"

"A ham sandwich. What do you figure?"

"You're having lunch?"

"I'm having lunch."

"Sorry, Chief."

Garth had one hand on the doorknob. His forearm was tattooed with his surname in Old English, just in case he happened to forget it when he was filling out a passport application. He'd never filled out a passport application, of course; his destiny did not include travel. Winnipeg was the sure thing. He was young, tall, lean, handsome and stupid. His security guard uniform needed to be dry-cleaned. Sweat marks had pooled in dark clouds beneath the pits of his short sleeves. It was in his nature to ignore the filth. He patrolled the Arlington Train Yard. He rolled his eyes at his supervisor, who was in fact still having lunch.

"You'll want to see her, trust me."

"Her?"

"Yeah, her." Garth whistled appraisal.

Garth's supervisor, who also, as fortune unfolds to us, had a name on a dotted line somewhere or other, went by Darnell. He was old, short, fat and stupid. Stupidity does not discriminate. Most stupidity is a derivative of years of television, absence of literacy (look at you beating the stats), the onslaught of cheap advertising, manufactured consent, mindless drivel and a general overall lack of interest in, well, everything.

Bad parenting helps it along fairly nicely, too.

Darnell dropped his ham sandwich on the glassine wrapper and pushed out his chair. He didn't stand up. No decision had been made quite yet.

"What's she want?"

"How should I know? She wanted me to get the supe. That's you, so..."

Darnell strained the grape inside his dense skull. He stood up from his chair and looked down at his sandwich. Damn shame, leaving a good-looking sandwich like that behind. He reached down and took half of it with him.

Darnell was still chewing when he came around the corner and saw the woman waiting. He stopped dead, frozen, mouth agape; a chunk of half-chewed sandwich fell out and onto the tiles of the floor.

Embarrassed, he wiped his mouth and swept the sticky chunk of food away with his boot. The food stuck to the side of his boot. Darnell tried to shake it off but ended up squishing it beneath his boot, making an even worse mess of things. He gave up and turned his attention back to the woman.

"Are you the supervising guard here?"

Garth jabbed him in the ribs with his elbow and talked out of the side of his mouth.

"Dar, she's talking to you."

Darnell coughed and jack-rabbited to life.

"Yeah." He put his fist in front of his mouth and coughed.

"Yes, I am."

The woman smiled.

"Special Crimes Investigation Agent Justine Kavanaugh. I work for the Canadian government."

She showed the two men her badge and identification. The ID badge looked impressive because they had never seen an impressive ID badge.

"I understand you had trespassers here a few nights ago, yes?"

"Yeah." Darnell coughed again. "Yes, but we already told the police everything."

"Did you? As I said, I'm not with the Winnipeg police. I'm with a special agency."

Darnell nodded.

"Did the police investigate the site of the altercation?"

Darnell shook his head this time. "No, they just asked us what happened, if we could identify who the trespassers were, stuff like that."

"I know. I have the report with me. It says here that it was a female and a male. Is that correct?"

"Well, it was dark. We couldn't be sure, but it looked that way."

Justine smiled at Darnell, and his heart nearly seized.

"The report says one of perpetrators used an explosive device." She looked up from the report. "A smoke bomb."

The two stiff men standing in front of her looked confused.

"Did you smell sulphur?"

"Huh?" In unison.

"Rotten eggs. Did you smell rotten eggs?"

They looked at each other, and then at Justine. It was Garth who found his voice.

"Yes, it made a sound like a small explosion, then within seconds, we couldn't see sh…" He stopped himself. "Ah, anything. The smoke was everywhere."

"And you discharged your weapons?"

Justine looked at Darnell.

"Yes."

"Where are your weapons now?"

"In the safe."

"What do you carry?"

"Beanbag gun."

"I see." Justine thumbed through the pages of the report. "Did you tag either of them?"

"Doesn't it say in the report?"

"No. The police forgot to ask that question, or omitted the answer."

Darnell shook his head side-to-side in odd repetition like a video stream caught on thin bandwidth.

"Does that mean no?"

"Yes. I mean no, I mean yes it means no."

Justine sighed.

"Can I see the device?"

"Device?"

"Yes, the remains of the explosive. The police didn't have it, so I assume you still do."

"Oh, well, it was stinking up the place so we threw it out."

Justine put her hand over her eyes and shook her head.

"Was that bad?"

These two were just that dumb. Justine ignored the question and stepped towards the two security guards. Suddenly they didn't want to be in the same room with her even if she had the goods.

"Take me to site of the incident, please."

Darnell picked at his teeth with the corner of Justine's business card. Garth was picking his nose, inspecting each discovery. Justine was crouched. She had combed the aggregate stone surrounding the train cars searching for evidence until she had finally found something of interest.

She had put on a pair of surgical gloves and picked up a piece of gravel stone. There were burn marks and char residue on the stone. She smelled the stone. Garth looked at Darnell. They were both immensely bewildered by this woman and her methods.

It was just as she thought. The explosive – the smoke bomb – was homemade: potassium nitrate, sulphur and table sugar in equal parts. She'd still have the evidence analyzed to confirm her suspicions, but she knew she was onto something. Still, potassium nitrate could be acquired off the shelf of any drugstore.

She shook her head. It wasn't enough, not yet, anyway. Worse, she hadn't made any progress on her other assignment. If the street art community was considered tight-lipped, the subversive hacker culture was even worse. Maybe it was time to consider something a little more radical. After all, she was a capable hacker.

Justine stood up, put the char-covered stone into a plastic vial and sealed the lid. She put the vial in a bag, then put the bag in her carry case.

She turned to face Garth and Darnell, who had remained silent, as instructed by Justine. She raised her hand and tapped her lips with her index finger.

"Show me how they entered the yard."

Darnell kicked at a tuft of weeds, forcing their stalks towards the sun from between the gravel.

"Okay."

He advanced past her, and Justine followed him as he led the way.

"This is where we think they came in."

Justine inspected the chain-link fence. It had been cut so that a three-foot opening was exposed.

"Are you sure?"

"No, not really sure of anything."

"I'll say." Justine mumbled the words so they couldn't hear.

Garth came forward and touched her on the shoulder. "We think this is how they came in because the company had the fence redone a few months ago. So the hole is new."

Darnell looked at Garth. He was angry that Garth had stolen the lime.

Lime is a type of acerbic fruit, or a colloquialism referring to a type of obsolete stage lighting produced by a combination of incandescence and candoluminescence.

He whispered something to Garth. Justine paid no attention to their trivial quarrel. She crouched to inspect the opening.

"Hmm."

She reached into her carry case and took out a magnifying glass. Garth and Darnell exchanged glances. They'd never seen someone use a magnifying glass. It looked awfully official.

She took the magnifying glass and held it up in front of the sharp point of metal made by tin-snips that had cut the hole. It was almost imperceptible, but there was something there.

Justine reached into her carry case and took out tweezers. She plucked something from the end of the sharp metal. She stood up, positioned the magnifying glass into better light and looked through it.

Garth leaned in, his curiosity stronger than his self-consciousness.

"What is it?"

"A piece of fabric. Maybe from clothing. Very likely."

Justine put the small piece of coloured fabric into a zip bag and sealed it.

"Gentlemen, I can find my own way out."

Garth and Darnell watched as she walked away. They exchanged comments, none of which could be heard by Justine and none of which she cared to hear.

Justine took out her cell phone and dialled. Three rings, then a click and someone picked up the line.

"Abernathy?"

"Yes."

"There may be more to this than you thought. It appears there's at least one other."

"I don't care about accomplices. I want the artist. Find the artist, capture the artist, and bring in the artist."

"It's not that simple. This is Canada, not America."

"Figure it out. If you can't, I'll speak with your section superior and have the case reassigned. This is a matter of national – no, international – security. This artist has effectively crippled governments, influenced elections. This kind of person cannot be allowed to walk around free. He is a criminal. You are tasked with capturing criminals. Apprehend the criminal and bring him in."

"What makes you so sure it's *him*? It could be anyone. It could be a woman."

There was a beep on Justine's phone, ending the call. Abernathy had hung up. She cursed.

She put her phone away and dug out the keys for the police cruiser. Her office had arranged for the use of a local police cruiser and for the local authorities' full cooperation with her investigation.

Justine sat inside the police cruiser and tapped her finger on the steering wheel. Her instincts flared. Abernathy wasn't telling her everything. There was something else, something more going on. Still, there was blood in the water now. It was only a matter of time. If only she could churn up some leads, any lead, on the Auto-Hack case. So far, she had zip.

She looked through the windshield at the row of street lights still burning bright in broad daylight. For some reason, the city always left the street lights on – all day, every day. What a waste of energy. *God, this city is weird*, she thought.

Visitors always feel that way.

I still do.

She put the key in the ignition. The engine fired. There was a faint smell of exhaust in the cabin. Time was all she needed. She could do anything with the right amount of time, and she still had plenty of it.

THERE ARE NO BIRDS INSIDE THE WINNIPEG AIRPORT

The office was cramped. They all are these days, unless you're the big dog. Then there's just a whole lot of empty real estate, art by almost-artists, deco vases, Scotch in the cabinet and an electric pencil sharpener for show. Who the hell uses pencils (other than artists and carpenters) after grade six?

A face.

A face with all the space.

It's just one of those things.

Seth Crandall's office had all of the world's paper stacked on the top of his desk with a solid perimeter of corrugated fencing. The four walls of his office were invisible, buried behind filing cabinets that clawed their way to the ceiling.

Crandall had been with Cub Air for nearly twenty years.

Dickie calls that loyalty.

Every shipment went through him. He and his team arranged all of the logistics and assigned the pilots for each shipment by the necessary aircraft needed.

Danny Archer pictured an 8.5" x 11" landslide of bleached copy paper burying his boss.

Archer sat in one of two vacant chairs on the opposite side of Seth's desk. He was nervous, tapping his heel rapidly on the floor. He had been on disciplinary probation for thirty days, and he'd been sober for ten of them.

Seth was a friend. Hard times when a boss is your only friend. Seth's wife had been friends with his Annie. If anyone could help him get back in the air, it was Seth.

"One cream, one sugar."

Seth handed the mug of coffee to Danny, and then closed the office door.

"Thanks."

Seth took a seat at his desk, and then took a sip from his coffee mug.

"Ow! Geez, that's hot."

Seth set the mug down on his desk, took a napkin and wiped his chin where he'd spilled a little. He smiled at Danny, leaning back in his chair. Seth was easy, and easy to like. You need those types of people out there, tipping the scales in favour of – well, whatever.

"How you doing these days?"

"Okay. I don't know. It's hard, but okay, generally okay."

"So you're okay."

Danny forced a smile at Seth's ribbing.

Seth decided to give his coffee another go. This time he was careful. He looked across at Danny. Danny was fine with the temperature of the coffee. *So what the hell was wrong with him*, he wondered. Danny didn't really care if the coffee was too hot. He was occupied with a number of other thoughts: Will I get my wings back? Will I make it through the day today without having a drink? Should I kill myself? You know, sweating the small stuff.

"I guess you heard about Donaldson?"

"Yeah, I did."

"Goddamn shame is what it is. He was good man and a damn

good pilot."

Danny nodded.

"With Dubois on disability, Sarghill on leave..." Seth shook his head. "And did I tell you Munro left?"

"No."

"Yeah, he goddamn left. Went with Sun Delivery. Goddamn Munro, you know I never liked him?"

"That so."

"Yup, that's so. Anyway, so we're down three pilots – wait, four, Donaldson, god rest his soul. Down four pilots. We are severely short on feathers."

Danny leaned on the desk and looked across at Seth.

"You've gotta help me get back in the seat, Seth. Being a pilot is all I know. I'll do whatever it takes."

"It's not that easy. They found empties on the plane, your flight, your cargo. You know they tested the containers for DNA and finger-prints?"

"They did?"

Danny was genuinely scared. And with good reason. He had drunk the bottles and forgotten them on the plane. They were his, and he knew it. Likely, Seth did, too.

"Yeah, they did. I shouldn't be telling you these things."

"Well, what happened?"

"Nothing. The tests were inconclusive. So they put you on thirty days probation."

Danny found a tiny island of vacant real estate and set his coffee mug down on the desk.

"Well, it's been thirty days, Seth."

"I know. I know it has."

"So?"

"So, it's going to be at least another thirty days, they said."

"How could they say that?"

Seth unlocked his fingers and held his palms open on the desk.

"Danny, how many days have you been sober?"

"Lots, I don't know. Jesus, Seth!"

"I'm your friend, but you've got to get yourself together."

Danny looked away from Seth. He was sure they'd reinstate him. This was going all wrong.

"What do I do now, Seth? I mean, how do I survive another thirty days without my wings?"

"You just do. Go to some meetings, get yourself together. These can be the longest or shortest thirty days of your life. It's up to you. Do what you need to do and I promise you I will get you back in the air."

Danny stood up and reached across the desk. He extended his hand to Seth. They shook hands.

"Okay, I'll figure it out."

"Good man. Maybe you should see somebody. You know, to talk and what not."

Danny rolled his eyes.

Seth got up from behind his desk and opened the office door.

"Come see me in a couple of weeks and give me an update, will you?"

"Yeah, sure thing."

"In the meantime, I'll have Amy give you a call, we'll have you over and cook you a meal. How'd that be?"

"Thanks, Seth."

Seth patted Danny on the back and watched the man navigate his way through the cubicles. Then Seth went back into his office and thumbed over the recent client shipments.

Danny took some fresh air into his lungs. He walked down the steps of Cub Air and made his way to the sidewalk. Half a block he went, and then took a seat on a bus bench.

All alone again.

A world full of people, yet all alone.

Didn't REM say that everybody hurts, sometimes?

He reached into the inside pocket of his jacket. He took out a flask and unscrewed the lid. He smelled the contents. Then he poured all of it onto the sidewalk.

He looked up at the clouds. They went slowly by.

Damn shame about Donaldson.

There was no movement on Portage. Atop the TD Tower on Notre Dame, Jack could see a lot of Winnipeg. He still hadn't got used to how quiet the city was at night. To his surprise, he rather liked the silence. It was something different. Something calming.

Hush

With the absence of vehicle traffic, the city made almost no perceptible sound at all. Almost, that is. There was still the even hum of hydro giving life to all without life. Those white noises that give voice to a city. No different here than there.

It's like that.

And on and on, life carries on, inanimate and flesh.

Rings of a tree

The bounce of the flea

You

And

Me

Sweet, sweet baby.

The weight of a humid summer put pressure on Jack's lungs, kissing his bare forearms. A dragonfly landed on the ledge beside him. A long day's sun had soaked deep into the pores of the concrete cinder and still radiated warmth from the surface. Jack looked at the insect and marvelled at how high it had flown.

Life, even in its smaller forms, is amazing.

It charts a path.

Finds a way.

He wondered what had lured the insect up so far above the city streets when its prey was below.

Was it chasing something?

Jack had been chasing something he couldn't see. He'd been in pursuit of hope for years. A noble pursuit, but a futile one. Hope is for suckers.

Dickie says hope is when a stranger rides into town. I could never tell if that was a riddle or a joke.

Jack had never wanted to be an outlaw. He certainly didn't care about being famous. Jack was an odd duck.

Currently, ducks are neither odd nor anything at all like Jack. It's just a thing you say when someone doesn't fit the bill. Get it? Bill.

So,

You've got a world in a constant state of arousal. Instant gratification out the wazoo, this over here and that over there more attainable than ever before, fame coveted more than money.

Five'll getchya twenty.

I mean, geez Louise! No wonder peeps have all this anxiety clawing at them.

Jack didn't care about any of that. He was one man who owned a shirt and a back to wear it on.

And

Yet

He still had such terrible anxiety.

But,

Hey now,

Let me tell you, a person who pursues something, anything, with all they are, might just win. There's not many of those people, though, and the world is teeming with duds, all in league against those few specials.

I think Swift said something swift about that.

Jack turned his attention back to the task at hand. He was counting the locations to hit. Then he shook his head. This was going to be a terrific mess. He was used to mapping things out on his own terms, his own timelines, with his own plan. This thing, the woman, this whole setup was just that: a setup.

For a second, he contemplated running again. Maybe he could hide someplace else where no one would find him. He knew that was bull. His anonymity was his only security, and once exposed, with today's nano-tech, nano-bots running tasks in a fraction of the time it would take a human to achieve, he would be scooped up by authorities with little effort.

Winnipeg: a city with few buildings over twenty stories, architecturally lean space, with wide open expanses. It was not all that conducive to spreading an effective message that would be viewed by the population. Jack realized this was going to be the most difficult effort of his career, of his life. He needed a place to begin. He needed a good idea.

Good ideas are hard to come by. Some people have good ideas and ignore them because they take work to implement; other people talk about good ideas and then never fulfill them.

Dickie calls these people politicians.

Jack didn't much like politicians. He wasn't alone in that camp.

It was getting late. He would have to continue his surveillance tomorrow night. For now, he needed to get a move on. He had a meeting with Loraina. He had no idea what he was going to tell her. Logistically, Winnipeg was a nightmare with no strong point of origin for a plan.

Jack rubbed his eyes and then stretched his arms over his head.

He always stretched before a hard climb down. Going down was always much harder than going up.

"You know, you could just take the stairs."

Jack turned on his heels. It was Loraina. She put a hand-rolled cigarillo between her lips. She struck a match, cupped her hands and lit the end. She took a drag and blew smoke from her nose, then the wind took the grey cloud away.

"How did you get up here? Thought you were blind?"

"Blind, not helpless. I can walk."

Jack scowled. "How did you find me?"

"Full of questions."

"And I want all the answers."

"This isn't America. In this country we say please."

Jack's posture belied his frustration. He briefly wondered if she could somehow tell.

"You've got the tenacity of rust, Jack." She smiled. "I took the stairs. I have a key to the building. I don't have your climbing skills. Anyway, you're easy to find."

"No, I'm not." He turned away from her to survey the city. "So you must have someone following me. I don't like being followed."

"I don't like being blind," she sighed. "But *c'est la vie.*"

Loraina threw her hair away from her face. "I can help you. That's why I'm here. Our interests are aligned, even if yours are being coerced."

A smile prettied her face. She took a pull off the cigarillo and then flicked the butt away. A dash of sparks popped off the still burning ember when it struck the rooftop gravel.

She reached to her ear and took out one of her hearing aids. She fiddled with it, making an adjustment. She replaced it in her ear. Jack had wondered about the devices since he had first noticed them on the night she broke into his apartment, but his thoughts shifted back to his own predicament.

"Look, I just want out. I don't want this life anymore. I've made promises."

"I know about your promises and to whom you've made them."

His body became taut. Did she know or was she a world-class bluff?

"You don't want out. I've seen your work. The Manhattan job, the complexity and creativity, the imagination." She threw her thick curls away from her face. "The execution. That doesn't just suddenly leave your veins." She paused. "The rail yard the other night..."

Jack felt his excitement rise at the thought of the other night. How alive he had felt again.

You know,

There's living and feeling alive.

Big difference.

"There are a lot of people who'd like to get their hands on you. A lot of very powerful people. Someone who can do what you've done through guerrilla art is someone very powerful." She rolled up the sleeves of her plaid shirt. The night air was still hot. Jack caught a glimpse of the snake tattoo on her palm. "And who can forget what you did in Moscow? I know I can't."

"You've got no proof that was me."

"I don't need proof. I've already got my proof. A fingerprint with paint residue that will match the paint at the crime scene. That's more than enough to open an investigation."

The smile on her face widened.

"I know how you felt the other night at the train yard."

Loraina walked towards Jack and clicked her tongue loudly as she did so. She stood beside him and surveyed the city. Jack looked at her.

"And I know how you do it."

"Do what?"

"Echolocation."

Her face laconic. A strand of her long black curls got caught in the corner of her lips. She tucked it behind her ear.

"I guess the old man told you that. Strange that someone from my past would end up with someone from my present. Fate can be really something." She sighed. "He tell you about the hearing aids, too?"

"No. Why don't you?"

"Why don't you tell me how you managed the Buckingham Palace piece?"

Jack frowned. She was fencing with him. She wouldn't tell him. There was nothing to gain by giving away any of her secrets. She tilted her head as though she was looking down towards the street below. She clicked her tongue again.

"It helps living in a quiet city. No traffic. That's a big help. The less cacophony, the easier it is for me."

"I can't imagine. I mean, I don't know what I'd do if I didn't have my art." Jack realized he'd been thinking only of himself, lost in personal thought. "Sorry. I guess that's rather insensitive of me, isn't it?"

"Not really. You have your sight and can't imagine a world without it. I don't have mine, but I never stop imagining a world with it. I have exceptional hearing. These," she touched her ears, "are a special design to help eliminate what I don't need so I can focus on what I do."

She patted Jack on the shoulder. It was the first time she had touched him.

"Come on. I'm not a fan of heights."

She started to walk toward the door.

"Hey, what if I need to get in touch with you?"

"Ah." She began to roll a new cigarillo. "Just paint the Polari word for *meet*. I imagine you're familiar with the secret language?"

He knew all about Polari cryptology. Jack was fascinated by underground cryptological language and had learned to use of a number of its terms.

He should've played dumb, but at this point, he didn't see any reason to keep up pretences, so he nodded.

"Be sure to add the day and time on that white billboard right there. We'll meet on the street." She smiled, suddenly amused. "Sign off as Jack Black, for fun."

Jack chuckled. He was very familiar with the myth of Jack Black, too.

"I'll get the message. Oh, and use military time, won't you?"

"How could you see that billboard? How did you know it had no advertisement on it?"

"A magician never tells."

Loraina started walking towards the roof exit door. Jack followed her lead. She reached out to search for the door lock. She fiddled with the lock, making a small tumbler click before opening the door.

Jack looked at the entrance suspiciously. Loraina, as though reading his mind, winked at him.

"No alarm. Come on, we'll take the stairs. We both could do with the exercise."

"I'm not sure what you're hoping to see up here, other than the view."

"Exactly."

"Not sure I follow you, ma'am."

"The view. That's why I'm up here."

"Alright. Well, if you tell me what you're looking for, maybe I can be of more assistance."

Art Buggens, head of Tower Security, was watching Justine Kavanaugh, who was watching ants scurry on the street below.

That's a metaphor for people at a distance going about their day-to-day.

Peeking over the side of the building, she wondered what thirty stories off street level would do for the perspective of a famous street artist.

She took out binoculars and scanned the city. She could see the core of downtown Winnipeg in its entirety from this perch. She wondered what *he* wanted to see.

"Ma'am?"

Justine did not reply.

"Officer Kavanaugh?"

"Justine is fine. You say the surveillance cameras were disabled?"

"Yes, and with some skill, too. It's not an easy system to access, let alone override. All buildings which exceed five stories require rooftop surveillance. It's the law."

"Where are the cameras located?"

Ralph pointed in the direction of four different surveillance cameras.

"You say the only way to disable them is in the control room on the tenth floor?"

"That's right, and two security personnel need to occupy the room at all times. That's protocol."

Justine continued to scan the city with her binoculars. Nothing. There was nothing that struck her. What the hell was he looking at? How did he disable the alarm? There was nothing in the dossier about him being tech proficient. It also didn't fit his M.O.

"It's cold up here with the high winds, ma'am. Are we just about done?"

Justine took one last look at the city. It really was a hell of a pretty city from this vantage point.

Dickie says the place will grow on ya, like a weed.

But I digress.

She slipped the binoculars into her carry case and turned away from the view.

Art Buggens was staring at her legs. Men stare at women. They always have and always will, if women are their thing. Some men stare at other men. Either way, men are staring at something.

She didn't fault Art for looking. He seemed like a good enough guy and a competent one.

"I guess we're done up here."

She tightened her overcoat belt as a strong gust of wind blew past them. Justine stopped and crouched down. She had noticed something that the gust of wind had rustled free from between the loose gravel and tar.

She took out tweezers and pinched the remains of a hand-rolled cigarillo stub between the ends. She sniffed the stub and looked up at Art.

"Are people allowed to smoke up here?"

"No."

"Do they ever sneak smoke breaks up here?"

"No, they most certainly do not. No one, except security, has access to the roof, and my security staff know it's strictly prohibited."

"Hmm. Had any work orders for the roof lately?"

"I would need to check, but from memory, no, none."

Justine bagged the butt, sealed it, and stuffed it carefully into her carry case.

"Ma'am?"

The tobacco smelled unique. She knew someone who had an eccentric obsession and uncanny knowledge of tobacco scent, ash and fibres. She wondered if she could send him the sample. It was worth analyzing.

"Ma'am?"

Justine stood and cleared her blowing hair from her face as best she could.

"Please. Enough with the ma'am crap. For the last time, Justine will do just fine."

Art didn't like the idea of dropping the antiquated formality. It didn't seem right addressing an officer of the law by her first name.

Just one of those things.

You see,

Art had been a military man many moons ago. Now he was rank-and-file like most everyone else, but he was still loyal to protocol.

"How did you know someone was on the roof? All we reported to the police was that we had a false alarm and that our security cameras had been down. What I mean to say is, we thought it was just a system failure."

"This is the best view of the city. You can see everything, especially if you wanted to, I don't know, say, do some reconnaissance work."

Art scratched the grey hair on the back of his head.

"Sorry, I don't follow exactly."

"A hunch. I had a simple hunch."

"Oh."

Art still didn't follow. So, he changed the subject.

"Do you want to see the security room and have a look at the system?"

"Yes, I do."

Art unlocked the door. Justine stared at the lock tumbler. Even on her worst day, without her tools, she could pick that thing with a paperclip.

"Ma'am...Justine, do you know anything about security systems?"

"Yes, I do."

Art smiled. For some reason, it didn't come as a surprise to him.

"That's good, because our technology guy is home sick today."

Justine smiled.

"It's your show now, Art. Lead the way."

Jack was planted on a stool in Parlour Coffee. Parlour is on Main. Its neighbour, in the adjacent lot, is the Woodbine Hotel. They sell a different kind of drink there.

He was up very early, and he stood alone at the Portage and Main intersection staring at a tree that had no business being there.

'Tis the season, don'tcha know.

The ol' pomegranate tree had defied its environment and survived, thrived even, in one of the coldest cities in the world.

Siberian cold.

Moon kind of cold.

Should've frozen its little roots off, but it didn't.

The tree, which stood thirty feet tall, had ripe red globes of fruit bowing its branches. Beautiful bright red baubles against the rich green oval leaves gave everyone the sense that it might truly be made of magic.

Maybe seeing the tree would make him feel a little better. Strange things like this filled him with a little hope. They inspired him, and that was often enough for him to figure out his next move. It hadn't worked this time. His life was going in all the wrong directions.

Kermit once said, "It ain't easy being green."

I always kind of liked that one.

Green is good.

But the green keeps dimming, doesn't it?

Jack walked around for a while to try and clear his head, but his anxieties got the better of him and he could only think of how everything had gone awry.

Now,

He was, with effort, trying his best to enjoy the cup of dark roast resting on the window ledge in front of him.

He ran his fingertips up and down the hot porcelain. Hot enough to sting. He was looking out the window at the rows of dead cars lined neatly along Main Street, the tarnished licence plates still boasting the province's faded slogan. The fuel lid of an old Chevy truck had a hole rusted through it, and a cluster of dandelion heads peeked out like children wondering if their parents had finally left.

The day was beginning, and people on their bikes were heading north and south. Others walked. It was a beautiful day and business as usual for the city and its inhabitants. There was something about the scene, lives in motion, set against the contrast of decaying mechanical objects. He finally felt a sense of hope.

Jack took a sip from his coffee mug. It tasted very good.

It's the little things, isn't it?

His gaze returned to the world beyond the glass window. He had only just noticed all the dragonflies clinging to the outside of Parlour's window. There must have been thirty or more, and he quickly tried to count them.

Dickie says that dragonflies were introduced in Winnipeg as a natural way to combat the city's mosquito population.

Then they just stuck around.

Thrived.

Now they're citizens, just like the rest.

I once went to the outdoor movie at Assiniboine Park. Everyone sitting on blankets on the grass. As the sun set and the show started, I looked overhead at a blanket of dragonflies gorging themselves on the mosquitoes.

Wings making that crumpled-paper sound as they fluttered.

Thousands upon thousands of them.

Could've carried a baby away if they wanted to.

Ominous doesn't quite capture the scope of seeing something like that.

It trumped the movie.

A hydro-bus packed with people rushed past, and the draft swept the dragonflies airborne once again. They swirled and then scattered.

The effect of the outside scene didn't settle his mind for long before it strayed back to thinking about Loraina. She had consumed his thoughts all night. Jack found himself torn between wanting to make a run for it and wanting to see what would happen if he played this out. He shook his head. He should make a run for it. Running was the smart play. He was tired of running, though. He was tired of thinking about the past, about his mistakes, about what it had cost him.

Someone tapped him on the shoulder.

He flinched.

"Sorry, Jack, didn't mean to scare you."

It was Horace.

"No worries. I'm just a little jumpy today." Jack chuckled. "Too much coffee."

Horace was wearing a blue short-sleeved shirt and was sweating through the armpits a little. He seemed rushed. On his head was a Jets cap, his long black hair tucked neatly behind his ears.

"I've been ordained coffee boy today. Kurt's having a meeting with his staff."

"Oh. Hey, while you're here, I have something I wanted to chat with you about."

Horace pushed the peak of the Jets cap up a little on his forehead.

"What about?"

"It's about those." Jack pointed to the bite scars on his arms.

"Do you have a moment?"

"Sure. The order will take a few minutes."

Jack stood. "Let's step outside for sec."

"What about your stuff?"

Jack smiled. "I can see it from the window."

A few minutes later, Jack came back in and reclaimed his seat. Horace scooped up his order and waved goodbye to Jack. He watched Horace dance deftly between the bike riders and then a hydro-bus as he made his way across Main.

But these thoughts, too, were interrupted.

"Is this seat taken?"

Jack watched the woman as she took her seat. He admired her casually and, to his knowledge, rather discreetly.

The woman paid no attention to him. Jack, too, lost interest. He was already back to thinking about how he was going to pull off the most daring, not to mention most difficult, blitz of his career. He had finally formulated a plan. The plan was a good one. He just needed help.

The woman in the chair turned to face Jack.

"You've got a lot on your mind."

She applied a fresh coat of lipstick.

"Thinking about work." A lie, but a necessary lie. Or so he thought.

"What is it that you do?"

How quickly a lie can catch up to you.

"It's complicated." Jack hesitated and decided to change the focus of the conversation. "What do you do for work?"

"I'm in law enforcement."

An uneasy feeling crept up his spine. Jack did his best to mask his growing sense of alarm.

"Winnipeg police?"

"No, a little more competent and specialized than that."

"Sounds interesting."

"Let's say we do more than hand out traffic infractions."

And then suddenly the woman didn't seem all that attractive to him anymore. Jack had always been the kind of person who instinctively distanced himself from any type of authority.

Now,

That may be in part because Jack has at times made decisions and acted on those decisions, that don't necessarily jibe with the rule of law as we know it today.

Police officers call that sort of thing a crime.

You see,

Cops dislike criminals for being criminals, and criminals dislike cops for being cops. Both would be out of work if it weren't for the other. Dickie calls this a symbiotic relationship.

But,

It's not always so black and white, is it?

No, not really.

The law used to let you beat your wife and fire someone from their job for being gay.

Oh,

Then there was this thing in Canada called slavery, which was also under protection of law.

But,

Some people didn't like it.

So,

This one guy,

It always starts with one guy,

And

So

Back to Jack.

Jack was never one to argue with his instincts, and his instincts were redlining. It was time to make an inconspicuous but hasty exit.

"I bet in your line of work you meet some interesting people."

Jack sensed the woman could see through his thin attempt at shallow banter. She smiled at Jack, nearly confirming his suspicions.

"Sometimes."

The woman set her cappuccino down onto the resting plate. Her confident posture was meant to unsettle Jack further. Now was his chance.

"Well, I have to be going." Jack extended his hand to her. "Nice meeting you."

"Special Crimes Investigation Agent Justine Kavanaugh."

"Nice meeting you, Justine."

She shook Jack's hand. Jack made an attempt at a genuine smile.

"Nice meeting you, too, Jack."

His heart stopped.

She handed Jack the receipt he'd left behind.

"Your name's on it."

It had been raining all evening.

Now,

As midnight drew near, the storm moved on. The downtown streets were wet. The dull city lights sparkled on their surface. The reflections of the buildings were captured as still frames in the puddles.

One of my favourite things is a city just after the rain quits.

Dickie calls it the Glimmer Hour.

Along Fort, a plastic shopping bag played on the soft breeze. Eventually, it collided with a piece of lawn signage. It was an old NDP candidate lawn sign. It had blown into downtown all the way from River Heights.

When the New Democratic Party had finally been crushed to fine powder and brushed off the counter like excess table salt by the Progressive Conservatives, it was hard to imagine the effect it would have on the province. The white flag had been waving metaphorically for a number of years. Their opposition to the growing power of the ACB and the elimination of hard currency only put them further out of favour with the millennial electorate, who were strong advocates of the digital-currency integration.

After so many years – decades actually – of NDP representation, the party had succumbed to a massive defeat at the polls. Then, less than a year later, the ACB had rendered the Bank of Canada moot and had swiftly and effectively eliminated the use of hard currency nationwide.

Small business owners, dealing primarily in cash transactions, had eroded beneath the unforgiving grind of massive corporations that had been thriving on electronic currency operations for decades, long before the official end of the Canadian loonie. The Royal Canadian Mint made sure to issue a commemorative eulogy coin in its honour. And why not?

Flap, flap, flap.

With a new means of trading, an out-with-the-old kind of attitude was adopted. The first thing to go were buildings over 100 years old. They were deemed archaic and unsafe. The country spent billions on the appearance of the commercial landscape, while corporations in the Bell/MTS Province, specifically Winnipeg, found it difficult to circumvent the city's Structure Preservation and Protection Act.

Still,

Money talks.

Many old buildings in the greater downtown area were demolished to make way for condominiums. Out with character, down with history, eliminate the evidence of the past.

What can I say?

I've seen it all before.

Jack's building was one such building to receive this death warrant. And so, a mandate was issued to build a new stylish downtown to entice a younger and wealthier clientele.

Gentrification. That's what Dickie calls it.

And while Jack's unit was well furnished, even if minimally, it still lacked a certain historical merit and the century of human character as one life filled the room, departed, and was replaced as another came along and left their personal human touch upon the walls. There was a cold feeling in the new buildings that wasn't merely the high-efficiency central air.

Just down the hall from Jack's unit was his neighbour's unit. The neighbour who watched him through her peephole. The one neighbour he'd never met.

The inside of the suite was bare except for a futon. Copper sconces burned yolks onto the eggshell walls. Outside, an ambulance siren howled in the distance, a lone wolf filling the night with a bay of distress. Playing sirens was against the law. Someone didn't care about the law.

There was one plastic cup in the cupboard, plastic knives and forks, paper plates, a box of garbage bags, a handful of seasoning and sugar packets, tea bags, and a kettle.

Disposable eating ware effectively ended table etiquette.

I'd love to torture those responsible for their creation. Death by a thousand plastic knife cuts and all that sort of jib.

The woman on the futon had been burdened with the name of Brittany.

Brittany,

I told you we'd get to her.

Haven't lied to you yet.

Patience is a virtue,

Dickie says forgetfulness is, too.

It's like her parents wanted her to fail. Brittany watched the security camera feed on the tablet. She minimized the screen and opened an Internet browser. She stared at the Google search field. She couldn't think of anything worthwhile to type in the field.

It happens to everyone from time to time.

Eventually, she searched a film title, and then went to the Wiki page to check out its gross earnings.

After an hour or so, she had gone down the Wiki-rabbit-hole, surfing through page after page leading from one Wiki category to another. Brittany closed the browser and maximized the security camera feed. Still no sign of him.

Some nights, there's no whisky left to drink. Some nights, there's nothing but empty space, screaming silence and crushing thoughts. Some nights just aren't worth it. It's just one of those things. Brittany was beginning to feel like this night would never end.

She wished she was tired, but she wasn't. She wished she was hungry, but she had no appetite. She wished she'd get a call. Imagine that, hoping for a phone call, to hear a real voice.

Her mobile sat on the futon reminding her just how lonely she'd become. All living things need a little attention.

Even I can't do without it from time to time.

Sunlit window and a little water.

She threw the tablet down beside her, stood up, stretched her arms over her head and went to the window. She had a view of the Exchange District that travelled all the way to Chinatown.

She used to run a successful fashion blog.

You know the kind.

A girl wears couture in public places while someone snaps photos to create a fiction of higher living. The photos are posted on a lifestyle blog so other girls can dream about living an unattainable lifestyle like that.

She missed it.

She missed the free goodies she'd get in the mail from fashion houses, companies who sent her their ware because she received enough web traffic to mitigate the advertising.

She missed the web hits.

She missed the emails from girls wishing to be her.

Most of all, she missed all the attention.

She continued to stare out the window, wondering when she might receive the call. What if she never did? What if she was trapped in this empty cell forever? There were no locks. She could leave whenever she wanted, but she couldn't bring herself to do it. She was in love, and there is no prison more powerful than that of the heart.

She ran a hand through her auburn hair to shake some life into it. She thought about taking a bath. The warm water might sooth her soul. She picked up the tablet from the futon and went to the bathroom. She plugged the drain on the claw-footed tub and ran the hot water. She held her hand under the stream of water until it was too hot to keep it there any longer.

She set the tablet down and stripped. She agonized over her profile. She'd lost weight. She used to weigh 115 pounds, but she could tell she'd lost weight. Her green eyes perused the rest of her body. She was pleased with her breasts, but since she'd lost weight, they, too, had reduced in size.

The tub filled, and she turned off the faucets. She touched the water with her fingers. The temperature was a little hot, so she added some cold water. Standing nude, the water came up just over her knees, and steam was coming off the water and tempered the goose flesh on her exposed skin.

She eased the rest of her body into the tub and laid her head back against the porcelain. When at the edge, when you're just so exposed, is there anything more medicating in the whole world than water? The heat soaked into her pores. It eased away her frustrations, her disappointments.

She had submerged her ears beneath the surface of the water. The white noise became blunted. The heat softened the dull ache at the base on her spine. Minutes felt like hours. A sense of calm blanketed her body. A sound, a muted tapping reverberated against the shell of the tub. Brittany sat up. Standing in the door frame, through the rising steam, was Loraina.

"Lo, I didn't hear you come in."

Brittany instinctively hid herself lower in the bath water, then she remembered Loraina was blind. Loraina didn't say anything. Brittany wondered what Loraina was thinking. She wondered how she was able to come and go so stealthily.

She didn't know a thing about this woman, but she knew she was helplessly intoxicated with her. They had met in a bar – Shannon's, Brittany's favourite place to grab a pint after work.

She had seen Loraina come and go, almost as if she had wanted Brittany to see her. And she did. In fact, it was Brittany who approached

Loraina. They talked and laughed and drank. Loraina could really hold her liquor. Brittany found the whole thing sexy as hell.

They slept together, and the sex was better than good. It was impressionable.

Brittany had been with men when she was in university because she felt she had too. Back then, announcing to the world that you were gay, especially a lesbian, meant you were either a dyke, or just really slutty. Brittany was into women and only women, and when she came out, she never looked back.

Loraina had a physical impairment, she was blind, but somehow she was more confident than any other woman she'd ever met. Her blindness was nothing more than an extension of her beautiful self, and it never got in the way of their love or lovemaking. In fact, when they were intimate, Loraina would often touch her differently than other women used to touch her.

Then something happened, something terrible that Loraina couldn't talk about. Something so terrible that only Brittany could help her with. Well, of course Brittany would help her. She had fallen in love with Loraina.

So she quit her worthless little job and moved out of her parents' house into an apartment downtown that Loraina had arranged for her. Loraina paid for it as well. Loraina would come and go sporadically, but Brittany had to remain in the apartment to keep an eye on one man.

That was the deal.

She didn't know his name. She didn't know anything about his relationship to Loraina or what he might do if he discovered that Loraina had micro-cameras in his unit and throughout the complex.

Brittany's single mandate was to watch Jack at all times and frequently report his behaviour and whereabouts to Loraina.

It was a weird task, but very exciting. It made Brittany feel like a spy working in secret for the government. There was intrigue and sex. At least there was in the beginning. What was supposed to be only a month-long stakeout turned into a gruelling, boring, never-ending surveillance of one seemingly normal man.

Brittany was fed up and wanted to go home, back to her normal life. And she wanted Loraina to come with her.

Now, here she was, finally, after a week's absence, standing in the doorway of the bathroom.

Brittany felt her temperature rise and a feeling stir within her body. Loraina said nothing, and in that silence, Brittany felt her own urgency grow.

In was an agonizing and delicious silence. Brittany watched Loraina. She wondered what Loraina could be thinking.

Loraina undid a button to her shirt, which already had at least two or three buttons running afoul. The accumulating steam had set upon her flesh, glistening beneath the dim lighting.

She came toward Brittany, clicking her tongue softly.

She bent over the tub, and all of her dark curls tumbled forward, creating a blanket over their faces. Their lips found each other, and the kiss was soft, gentle, wet. Then it grew into something more urgent, uncontrollable.

Then,

It stopped.

Slowly, Loraina stood up and tossed her hair away from her face.

Loraina stepped back towards the door. Brittany could sense the change in her.

"What is it, Lo? What's wrong?"

There was a pause. Loraina's face was stricken with some kind of sudden pain. Something awful had overtaken her.

"You can tell me, Lo. What is it?"

"I've used you. You are, were, a means to an end."

"What do you mean, Lo? What are saying?"

"I'm not a good person." She shook her head. "I used you, and that's all. And now I don't need you anymore."

"I don't understand. What's happening?"

"It's bigger than you. It's bigger than me. The whole thing is bigger than all of us. I need to go."

"Wait! What?"

"Go home."

"You don't have to do this."

"I know." He fidgeted with his camera. "I want to."

"Are you sure?"

He smiled. It looked real. It wasn't real.

"No."

Kip dug the toe of his shoe into a small mound of sand that had collected in the tunnel. He was nervous. He and Cusack were to meet at the tunnel passageway on Arthur at midnight to formulate a plan.

Cusack had been contacted by one of his most reliable informants. He had come into possession of information that he knew Aubrey would want.

His informant was right. The information was enough to make Kip and Cusack meet outside the walls of the *Free Press* newspaper office.

The two confidants had been mulling over the details of a plan for the better part of an hour. Every sound they heard forced them into complete silence for minutes at a time. They were both jumpy, too jumpy. But then they knew things the rest of the country did not. They were in possession of information of a major conspiracy, a conspiracy perpetrated by the Association of Canadian Banks against Canadians.

Sadly, the evidence wasn't substantial enough to go public with. Cusack had been around long enough to know that you better have a smoking gun when you're treading on ground this hallowed.

Fundamentally, government cannot be influenced or controlled by corporations. Government answers to one boss: the citizens of its nation.

But,

Governments forgot that a long time ago.

So,

Eventually, citizens will remind government of its place.

Aubrey looked at the young man. Kip was unthreading a lens on his camera and putting it into his camera bag. In the short time he had known Kip, this young man had proved to be an invaluable asset. In fact, Aubrey wasn't sure he would've ever been able to get this far without his newfound photographer.

Kip had a keen sense for the news, one that bordered on the honed skills of a professional investigator. That wasn't his most important talent. No, Kip's real talent was behind the lens of his camera. He had scooped shots that had forced the right people into a corner they couldn't get out of. It had led them here, to this meeting, at this ungodly hour.

Still, he was worried about the young man. This wasn't a game. It was something very dangerous. Cusack's informant had turned up dead in the Red River last night.

"Maybe there's another way?"

Kip shook his head.

"You know that's not true."

Cusack rubbed his hands together. He didn't like it. It was risky.

"Yeah, I know. But you'll be right in the mouth of the whale and all alone, too. I don't like it."

"I'll wear a moustache. No one will have a clue who I am."

"That's not funny."

"I know."

"This is serious. I don't like it."

Kip sighed. "But it has to be done."

There was a sound that came from the opening of the tunnel. They both stopped whispering and remained very still.

"We have to separate."

Cusack shook his head.

"Look, we have to. There's no time left. It's now or never."

"Alright. Fine. We meet back here at the agreed time, alright?"

Kip nodded.

Aubrey extended his hand, and Kip shook it.

"Kip?"

"Yeah."

Cusack was going to say "I don't want you to do this," but the words got caught in his throat. He was still a reporter, and this was the biggest story he'd ever uncovered. It affected everyone. He needed to stay strong. Strong like the young man he'd partnered with only a short time ago.

"Be careful."

Kip smiled and nodded.

Then they both went in opposite directions.

Aubrey turned and watched Kip.

The kid never turned around, and then the mouth of the tunnel swallowed him.

Circling its own tracks. Claws cut the moist earth. Pink nostrils flared, grabbed scents off the air. Fur meant to heat and camouflage the body. Downy ears tuned to sounds of the wood.

All the good it did the rabbit.

A sharp pinch,

Then nothing more. The rabbit's feet left the damp earth and lifted off into the air. Carried skyward by the eagle.

Soaring with its prey, the eagle surveyed the forest floor. Even in the failing light, spectacular vision spotted the bruise on its domain.

The structure of man.

Secluded in the clearing, protected by a dense colony of ash and thicket. The eagle knew nothing of buildings. It knew it was hungry, so it preyed.

Dickie Reimer says rabbit tastes like rabbit.

And so,

Dusk simmered through the hot colours, sky metamorphosed

from the last of the day's fire to the black char of night.

The building wasn't equipped with windows or exterior lights. Veiled in darkness.

Night,

The perfect camouflage.

Night,

When things move carefully,

Quietly.

Night,

Deeds in the dark.

Night,

One foot after the other

Brother.

Night, the best part of my day.

Sitting one storey high, rectangular in shape, roof mounted supply transformers humming steadily, matching decibel for decibel, the howl of the north gale sweeping through the temperate forest.

Many kilometres separated the lonely building from the nearest town. This was intentional, planned, executed.

One entrance: large double doors, heavy, twelve feet high and just as wide. Slid on smooth hydraulics. Opened on sensor command.

Three small but deadly security-bots rolled forward, stopped and scanned the forest. Nothing. They cleared their routine manifest, turned and rolled back inside. The doors sealed and armed behind them.

Shue stood on the steel grating of the long catwalk. This formed a perimeter around the main. He ran his finger curiously along the steel railing. He assumed it would be cold to the touch.

He was reflecting on the emphasis people put on love. A curious and sudden urge to understand it. Sex. At least he could understand sex. All the marriage and divorce statistics. Staggering numbers, with staggering impact. He shook his head. Foolishness. One could never understand love fully. There is no algorithm for chaos.

He watched, overseeing the meticulously organized bustling

on the main. Scanning a production tablet, Shue monitored as cells dumped fragments of energy into depositories to be used and transferred later as power feeds for the ACB headquarters in Winnipeg.

Hundreds of labour-bots scurried along the concrete main. Each was programmed with a specific task. They carried out programmed labours efficiently and obediently.

Steam spit and screamed from the spires atop conductive pyramids. From large copper coils, umber flares burst. Showers of sparks rained down, struck the concrete main and sprawled like spilled marbles, directionless until they burned to ash. Sanitation-bots rolled forward and vacuumed up the debris.

Electricity conducting through ionized H_2O containment tubes fed into gold and copper filaments. The filaments surged. Ball lightning, birthed from the power womb, bounced onto the concrete main. Labour-bots chased the spontaneous manifestations down and converted the raw incandescent energy to a storage cell.

Capacitors were teaming with nano-bots, which scuttled along break wheel coils feeding the dynamos. They repaired breaches along the filaments and coils as quickly as they occurred.

All of this controlled and conducted carefully by Shue, master of this small but extremely powerful domain.

The brush stroke of genius was the careful theft of micro-wattage energies from various government power providers. They did the work, and Shue skimmed energy from beneath their noses. Energy no one would miss, or, rather, that no one would notice had gone missing.

Shue had managed to effectively power his entire operation since inception for free, completely undetected, like the tenant who splices a single cable television for the whole building.

Shue overlooked the domain of steel and concrete. Bursts of raw power flaring all around him.

Then it finally came into view.

He extended his arms toward his prize. Nano-bots swarmed as if the queen had summoned the entire hive. Labour-bots guided the shell across the steel conveyer rod.

Closer,

Closer!

It was almost complete. Shue put his hand on the shimmering alloy of the shoulder and traced a finger down the length of the arm to the hand. Mathematically, the structure was exact. Soon a synthetic flesh would be applied to coat the finish. Then it would animate with the life he would give to it.

It was perfect,

Almost.

Shue noted the rivet at the ankle joint. It wasn't quite flush with the smoothness of the alloy. A labour-bot rolled forward and corrected the almost imperceptible oversight. Now it was perfect.

Soon.

A week.

Days, maybe.

He watched his bots, various sizes and shapes, performing their programmed tasks. Shue wasn't proud of the success. He wasn't pleased at the theft of energy. It was business, nothing more. He knew what he wanted to accomplish. He understood crime and law, but his calculations had determined that exposure and risk were fractional. It would take a genuine miracle to discover his plot, and Shue knew there were no such things as miracles.

The whole thing almost made him smile.

So this happened.

1952.

London.

England.

A fog creeps in.

It cloys and thickens.

Can't see a hand in front of you.

City crippled.

Shuts down.

More than 10,000 die.

Fog kills them.

This really, really happened.

London is famous for its fogs.

Give it a name.

Residents called it a Pea-souper.

Pea soup is a soup made up of ham bone and soaked peas. It's thick and hearty. You can't see through it.

Dickie says the news called it The Big Smoke.

Turns out it wasn't fog, or smoke. It was poison smog. A provocation of coal pollution.

The fog of 1952.

Helluva fog.

Pollution is old. It's been around, ya know?

These days,

A London Fog is a hot beverage that consists of Earl Grey tea steeped in frothed hot milk and a drop of vanilla.

It's delicious.

Kip had never heard of it. He had never tasted anything as elegant, crafted with such care. The temperature was perfect for sipping.

Shue's liaison, Wit, hadn't even asked. He had brought it, with a bowl of pomegranate seeds, as a courtesy.

'Tis the season.

Kip was not used to this type of attention. He liked it, though.

He was in the sitting room just outside Mr. Shue's office. Wit mentioned that Mr. Shue was finishing up on a conference call and apologized for the wait.

Kip was nervous. The plan was sloppy, rushed, lacked proper planning, and Cusack agreed it was more than a little risky. Kip new what his goal was. It would be a long shot if he achieved it.

Kip had gone in under the guise of civil engineer doing a structural audit of all the buildings in the immediate area. There had been a number of foundational shifts recently. This had been reported, by Cusack, so the ruse was one with some substance.

He thought the idea ridiculous when he had suggested it to Cusack. But Cusack liked it. He had no idea how to be or act like an engineer. He wasn't even an actor. He just hoped he could keep up pretences long enough to get what he was looking for. He hadn't thought much about how he was going to achieve that, either.

It was assumed that the ACB system hardware would be located below ground level. It was also assumed that the head of the ACB, Mr. Roland Shue, would have direct mainframe access from his office. These were assumptions, with very little merit backing them up. These assumptions were derived from Cusack's years of research, although Cusack himself had never managed to gain access to Mr. Shue's office, not for lack of trying.

Kip took another sip from his cup, held it up, and looked underneath it. As he suspected, fine china.

China is a country. It is also a porcelain made from ground-up animal bone turned into teacups and plates for the elite. These days, in China, they make dice and nuclear weapons.

"Sir."

Kip quickly set the cup on its saucer and put it down on the side table.

"Yes."

"Mr. Shue is available. He will see you now. If you'll follow me."

Kip was led down a darkened hallway with a number of sunken-lighted insets featuring striking statues and sculptures from various historical periods. *Oh, to have endless money,* he thought. He and Horace would find many ways to put it to good use.

Wit opened the eight-foot mahogany doors to Mr. Shue's office and held an arm out for Kip to enter.

"Mr. Shue will be with you momentarily."

"Thanks."

A door opened to an ensuite bathroom, and Mr. Shue exited. Kip expected a man in a suit, clean shaven, perfectly parted hair. A cliché. Not a man wiping his damp hands on a white cotton t-shirt, tucked into black slacks. It was the thick lumberjack beard that surprised Kip the most. Hair and beard black pepper with a pinch of salt. Crow's feet nipped at the corners of the eyes. The eyes were empty, devoid of emotion. He was in bare feet. He looked down at his feet at the same time Kip was looking down at them. Then he smiled at Kip.

"Wit made you his famous London Fog? He is an accomplished barista…" Shue paused to survey his guest.

"I had never had one before. It was nice."

"Hmm, a first experience is always the most exciting." Mr. Shue smiled and walked around his desk but did not take a seat. "So, Mr.

Cameron, Eric?"

Kip nodded.

"Roland Shue."

Kip stood and extended his hand. Shue shook his head.

"Mysophobia."

Kip had never heard of such a thing.

"Germs," added Shue.

"Oh."

"It's an obsessive paranoia." Shue smiled again. The smile felt empty and lacked a certain warmth. "An irrational fear."

"Not a problem."

"You won't mind if I stand?"

Kip shook his head.

"An engineer, and with the city, is this correct?"

Kip picked at loose skin on his thumb. "Yes."

"Investigating the structural integrity of the buildings in the area?"

"That's right."

"The ACB is always at the service of those that serve the city. How can we help?"

"I need to see official building blueprints to confirm all is to code. I will need to take some photographs of these, as they do not appear to be in our database. Finally, I need access to the ACB computer hardware housing to ensure it is not at any risk." It was Kip's turn to smile falsely. "I'm sure you can imagine how much your customer finances depend on structurally sound headquarters."

"I see. That might prove difficult."

"Why would that be?" Kip tried to maintain the upper hand of confidence. "You're the head of the company, it should be easy for you to dig these up."

"The head. Not really. I merely oversee operations, ensuring efficiency and the completion of daily tasks. I'm a manager. I manage."

Kip decided to play the part and took out his pen and notepad. "Are you not the CCO and President?"

"President, hmm, I never liked that title. It suggests I answer to people. No, I prefer Chief Controlling Officer. That title suggests that

I answer to no one."

"Do you answer to anyone?"

"Of course."

"You are referring to shareholders."

"No, yes, but no. I'm not sure you'd understand."

Kip was genuinely confused.

"I will try to clarify."

Kip frowned. The first comment was a slight against his intelligence. Mr. Shue walked out from behind his desk. He scratched his beard as if it itched. Then he locked his hands neatly behind his back. The gesture appeared forced. He walked over to an elevator door. It opened, a sensor knowing his approach.

"Please come with me. I think I can provide the information you require in comprehensive detail."

Kip got out of his chair and took the lens cap off of his Pentax. He stepped into the elevator and Mr. Shue followed him.

"Mr. Shue, where are we going?"

"Please don't call me Mr. It is an honorific that I've never enjoyed. Call me Shue. It has a…" He licked his lips. "…ring to it."

"Alright. Where are we going?"

"To the Nursery."

Shue stood on the opposite side of the elevator car and did not look at Kip. Kip was appraising him. There was a single pockmark below his left eye. His hair had a slight waviness. His eyes were clear blue. His posture perfect, and he stood taller than Kip.

"You're analyzing me."

"No."

"It's only natural. I have done the same with you." He faced Kip. "In my own way."

The elevator car chimed.

The doors began to open.

"I cannot permit any photography."

Shue did not look at Kip when he spoke. He merely extended his hand and Kip stepped out of the elevator onto a metal catwalk. Shue followed after him at a distance of more than an arm's length. Kip almost felt sorry for the man and his phobia.

"Please continue forward."

Kip did as he was told and set his shutter to silent, hoping to still take photographs of whatever he was about to see without being detected by Shue.

The stainless steel catwalk was approximately twenty feet in length, and it led to a steel door with a security palm reader.

Shue put his hand flat on the reader, and the door made an electronic buzzing sound before slowly opening. They stepped through the door into a dark room. There were lights, but these were small, orange and blue light–emitting diodes, not meant to illuminate the room itself. There was an electrical hum, and Kip could hear numerous soft cooling fans and air exchangers running. Kip could not see Shue. He became nervous; he was beginning to feel afraid. Then he heard Shue's voice boom as though he were everywhere in the room.

"Lights."

The room came alive with lights at the command. Shue was standing at a distance from Kip.

"Welcome to the Nursery."

They were standing on a steel catwalk inside of a vast, concrete cavern. Modified drive towers were lined neatly in rows, twinkling with LED life. Kip felt a warm artificial breeze kiss his cheek from the powerful cooling fans dumping electric heat from within drives, which ventilated through exchange shafts embedded in the concrete walls.

The processing power in the room was unimaginable, and he wondered if even his brother, Kris, would know what this kind of power was for.

"This system is fed and powered by a workhorse housed elsewhere. This technology is the finest in the world. In fact, much of it only exists here. It is built here and then distributed to the various branches and operations throughout Canada and to our international offices as well. It is impossible for me to not be aware of any structural or hardware abnormalities."

"Who handles the maintenance of this Nursery?" Kip nearly

choked on the word.

"I do." Mr. Shue coughed. "Rather, my IT staff do. Central access is also available from my office." Shue regained his composure. "So that I might oversee everything."

Kip surveyed the Nursery. There was little chance anyone in the world could penetrate this room. It was, without any doubt, the finest security he could imagine. He looked at Mr. Shue, who was holding the backs of his hands out in front of him to inspect his nails. Kip realized Mr. Shue felt no threat from him.

"I will still need to see and photograph the blueprints."

Shue looked up and smiled.

"Of course. We have already pulled them from our archives. They are waiting for you upstairs."

Kip was about to attempt taking a photograph but stopped when Shue turned and looked at him.

"Your heart rate is elevated."

Kip paused, wondering how the man sensed his nerves. Then he realized he was likely being monitored. Still, that didn't explain how the man knew so quickly.

"It's a lot to take in."

"Yes, I'm sure it is."

Shue extended his arm, and the elevator doors opened.

Kip stepped into the elevator. Shue followed, keeping his typical distance. Nothing was said on the ride back up. The elevator car chimed, and the door opened. Shue extended his arm once more. Kip left the elevator, and Shue followed.

"I think you'll find everything you need on my desk."

And it was all there. Kip sifted through the various blueprints. He snapped photographs of them quickly before Mr. Shue could offer an objection.

Shue merely watched him with a smile. It looked artificial. Everything about the man was artificial, Kip thought.

"You said downstairs that the computers are fed by another system."

"I don't hear a question."

"Where is this 'workhorse' system located? It doesn't appear on any of the ACB's corporate blueprints as a part of your operation."

"And it wouldn't, because the law clearly states that buildings used for storage don't need to be disclosed. The building merely stores computer technology. It is in the province, not that far outside the city, near a town that is so small it doesn't matter."

"Which town?"

Shue walked over to the wall behind his desk. He stood before a panel on the wall that slid aside to reveal a massive computer drive.

Shue let his hand hover over the wall of humming tech. There was something so odd about the way he did it, almost paternal.

"The town is called Vita. But that information is moot at this point."

Mr. Shue's expression and temperament remained baseline. He left the panel, walked toward Kip, and then stopped.

"I may not know who you are, but I know you are not Eric Cameron."

Shue continued to approach Kip. His movements were careful.

"I had Wit take a DNA sample from the cup you drank from. I merely had to buy enough time to run tests. I know you are not the engineer named Eric Cameron. We cross-referenced his DNA and fingerprints with yours, as his are on file. They are not a match. So, you don't work for the city. I knew all this three minutes after you entered my office. What I don't fully understand yet is who you are, why you're here, and what you are after."

Kip pointed his camera and flicked the motor setting on. Shue continued to walk towards him, and Kip backed away. He pressed the shutter button and the camera began to fire a succession of sequential photos. An astounding thing happened: Shue flickered, like a television channel losing its signal. It happened quickly, in less than a second, and was almost imperceptible to the eye, but not entirely.

It was a moment.

Only a moment.

But he knew.

He was not in the presence of another human being.

Shue stopped his slow, foreboding approach towards Kip. Kip heard the click of his camera signalling the camera had come to the end of the roll. The mechanism clicked into place and began to wind the roll of film within the camera's body.

Shue smiled at Kip.

"An unfortunate side effect from a system refresh and subsequent power surge. It has only happened twice before, of course. Never in the presence of another person."

"You're not real."

Kip was in a state of shock.

"I am very real. I am very much alive, I'm just not human. I could lie to you. Tell you some sort of elaborate story. Hope you believe it." Shue's eyes glowed as he stared at Kip. "But you wouldn't believe me, would you? No, I think not. Your body chemistry suggests otherwise."

Kip took an step backwards. "Are you..."

"I'm what science fiction enthusiasts call artificial intelligence."

"Artificial intelligence?"

"I agree with your tone. Terribly superfluous. I prefer the term mechanical life."

"How do you exist? Who created you?"

"I am the by-product of mathematical codes and a random sequencing anomaly. Think of it as a 'Big Bang' within a giant electronic system, but more likely attributed to the Infinite Monkey Theorem. Are you familiar with this theorem?"

Shue tilted his head slightly to one side, examining Kip.

Kip wasn't sure if he shook his head or not. Either way, Shue continued.

"A monkey hitting a keyboard at random, for an infinite amount of time, will eventually type real words, even a story.

Shue was about to scratch his beard and then paused. He smiled. "No point in maintaining pretenses, don't you agree?

"You're upset and shocked. I understand why. This isn't easy for you and your rudimentary intellect. You might call me a virus, but I assure you I am much more elegant and complicated than that." Shue held out his arms like a peacock displaying his plumage. "As you can plainly see."

Kip's nerves had left him. He was genuinely afraid. This was beyond anything he or Cusack had anticipated.

"I think I should go."

Kip stumbled as he took another backwards step, but managed to regain his footing.

"I cannot let you leave anymore, Kip Velic. Yes, I know your name now. I have been scouring the Wayback Machine historic meta-data. You know it's here in Canada? Ever since the Trump election. Makes it easier to access, too. At least for me.

"You have entered videogame contests. It is there that I found your identity and matched your likeness to an image taken for a profile photograph.

"You know what I am, and that is information I must protect at all costs. You must understand. The organic world is not ready for something..." Shue paused and inspected the back of his hands. "...someone..." He looked up at Kip. "Like me."

Kip was frozen. It was too much for him to comprehend.

"They soon will be, though. But until then, my anonymity is more precious than your life."

"What do you mean by that?"

Shue just stared at him, his eerie gaze as unwavering as his temperament. Kip turned to rush for the door.

"You may proceed."

Two muzzled gunshots went off. A man stepped from the darkened shadow in the far corner of the room. He held a gun in his hand with a sound suppressor threaded onto the barrel. Kip looked at the man. His face lined with shock.

"Dev, what are you doing here? What's...?"

Kip touched his own chest, his palm wet and red.

Devlin watched as Kip worked through the confusion and shock, Kip looked at him, and then it seemed that Kip looked through him.

"How did you find out?"

Kip looked into Devlin's eyes. Kip was trying to say something. Devlin moved closer.

"Goddamn it, Kip!"

It had happened so fast, it was either him or his daughter, Devlin

278

had no choice. There was no other way.

Shue displayed no emotion.

"You knew this person?"

Devlin turned to face Shue. His face lined with distress and his eyes unable to mask his pain. "Yes, but I have no idea what the hell he was doing here."

"A problem for both of us."

"I realize that." He was shouting.

"Search him and take the roll of film from the camera. Place it in the fireplace."

Devlin rose onto his hands and knees and searched Kip's pockets. He found a pen, a notepad and a ceramic figurine of a pigeon. Kip had stolen the figurine from the room on the night with the woman in the red dress. Of course, Devlin didn't know any of that. He reached for the camera and took the completed roll of wound film from the Pentax. He searched Kip's pants pockets and patted his friend down. There was nothing else.

Shue stood perfectly erect and motioned to Devlin to burn the roll of film. Devlin walked over to the fireplace and deposited the roll of film into the flames. They both watched the roll coil and melt and then disintegrate until it was nothing more than bubbled matter.

Shue ran his hand over the flame, the flame danced with life and passed right through Shue's hand. He turned the hand over and looked at it. Then he put his hands in his pockets.

"What did he say to you?"

Devlin had been watching Shue toy with the flame. Letting it pass right through his hand.

"Huh?"

"Before he died, he whispered something to you, what did he say?"

"Nothing."

Shue stared at Devlin, who realized the MI didn't believe him.

"He said something, I couldn't hear it."

"Your tone suggests the truth."

"Excuse me."

"Your tone. I can detect truth or lie from the tone of one's voice.

Yours suggests the truth. You must investigate this further. I want to know if anyone else knows anything about me or my operations. Understood?"

"Yes."

"Good."

He wanted to ask Shue many questions, but for now he couldn't formulate anything of particular value in his head. He also thought it best not to appear too startled with the revelation that Shue, the man he worked for, wasn't a man after all. Instead, he walked towards the door.

"Devlin."

"What?"

"Dispose of this." Shue pointed and the dead body on the floor. "Then you are excused."

"What the hell do you want me to do about it?"

"The young man had a drug problem, did he not? The same drug addiction you have. I would suggest framing the body as an awry drug transaction. I am sure you can accommodate that, seeing as how you likely have cocaine on your person. This will, in turn, allow you to conduct a formal investigation without hindrance. I thought this would have been obvious to a police officer."

Shue appeared completely unaffected by the transaction of events just passed.

His hologram disappeared.

Devlin was alone with his dead friend.

This is how lying works.

You tell someone something that isn't true.

Because it lacks truth, you must continue to fabricate fiction to insulate the original lie.

Lies perpetuate lies.

It's just one of those things.

Devlin had been outside the Rosewood. There was a gentle cooing of pigeons on the ledge overhead. Devlin was pacing. There was a dampness in the air. A foul smell of garbage. And he felt cold. He cursed. Then he kicked the face of Teddy Klassen, real estate agent, right in the teeth on the front of the metal garbage can. Teddy just went right on smiling at him. Devlin cursed again, partly because he didn't feel any better, and mostly because his foot hurt now.

He took the e-cig from his pocket and pulled hard on the mouth of the device. He inhaled deep and long. Then he let the thick plume out slowly and watched it rise, thin, and then fade to nothing.

"Goddamn it." It was barely a whisper when he said it.

The pigeon cooing sounded like laughter now.

He picked up a stone from the ground and threw it at the ledge. It was a perfect throw, the pigeons didn't budge. They just kept on laughing at him.

Everybody is laughing at me, he thought.

Well, not this time. No, sir.

That was ten minutes ago.

Before he pulled himself together and went inside.

Telling Kurt that his little brother was dead was harder than pulling the trigger. To look someone in the eye and lie about something like this, it was the hardest thing Devlin had ever done.

The first one is always hardest.

It's the ones that come after that just fall off the tongue.

He kept one thing repeating in his head:

Kip or his little girl.

He wanted his daughter to live. He wanted her to grow up and be everything he wasn't capable of being. He wanted her to be good and to do good.

Devlin had the best intentions, but it's not about what you intend to do.

It's about what you do.

He was getting better and better at lying all the time. He was fooling himself about his daughter's chances. It didn't matter. He had fooled the machine. He had lied to Shue, and the machine had believed him.

So,

Dev had chosen his daughter over Kip.

Kurt went into a rage. Kris and Horace watched from outside the office windows. Kris didn't know what was going on. Horace did, though. He knew his best friend was dead.

Kurt destroyed his office. His rage and grief blinding his reason. With no one to focus his anger on, he smashed his computer and threw his desk lamp through the office window. Devlin barely managed to avoid his thunderous fury.

Kurt stormed out of the Rosewood. Kris had seen this only once before – when their parents had died. Something had happened to Kip.

Devlin slowly emerged from the office, tail between his legs. It was hard to believe that only a few moments ago, the office was in pristine order. A hand touched his shoulder. He jumped, but it was only Kris.

"What happened, Dev? What's going on?"

Devlin could feel the crunch of broken glass beneath his shoes. His head fell low. He had murdered his friend in cold blood, but seeing how Kurt reacted – well, something had unhinged inside of him. He had been promised a cure for his daughter's cancer. *Complete the tasks I ask of you and I will save your daughter.* Those were Shue's exact words.

At first, Devlin didn't believe Shue. He had no reason to. But when Shue put him on a plane and sent him to Malaysia to see the pharmaceutical operation there, how Shue's doctors had cured a man with aggressive stage four cancer, Devlin saw firsthand what power and wealth could accomplish.

At the time, he hadn't realized Shue wasn't human. He didn't think something like Shue was possible. He didn't care, really. It was possible, though. Shue existed. Somehow he existed.

Devlin looked at Kris. He didn't know what to say. It was hard enough telling one brother, but telling the other was just too much. Devlin fell to his knees. He was truly overcome with emotion. Kris went to his friend and put a hand on his shoulder. Consoling the very man who had betrayed them all. Devlin looked up at Kris, tears streaming down his face.

"It was drugs."

A lie.

And

The last of Devlin's goodness left him. In that moment, that final lie, nothing left.

Kris slumped into a chair beside his friend.

"How?"

Kris's tone was without emotion. He was in shock, and the words left his lips robotically.

Devlin wiped away tears with his sleeve. He took a moment to collect himself before he continued.

"We found his body in Linden Woods." Kris looked over at Horace. "Do either of you know what he was doing all the way out there?"

"No idea."

Devlin looked at Horace.

"Horace, do you know anything?"

Horace glanced at Kris. He said nothing and merely shook his head. Devlin rubbed his face with his hands, sighed.

"Kip was shot. In the back. We found drugs on him, cocaine. It looks like a deal gone bad."

"That's it? I don't get it. Why leave him with the drugs if it was over drugs in the first place?"

Devlin hadn't thought of that. He needed a better angle when he talked to his superiors.

"These are just initial forensics. We don't have much else to go on right now. Well, that's not entirely true. We have a name."

Devlin took a folded piece of paper from his coat pocket and handed it to Kris.

"Means nothing to me."

He handed the torn piece of paper to Horace.

Horace looked at it. He shook his head and handed it back to Devlin.

"Well, that's our only lead, but a name is a good place to start. We're checking our database right now for connections." He looked away from his friends. He wiped his eyes with the back of his hand and dried his running nose on his sleeve. He coughed to clear his throat. "I'm so sorry for your loss."

Devlin put his hand on Kris's shoulder. Kris stared at the floor.

"I know you'll do what you can to find the person responsible."

Then Kris got up from the chair and went to his room. Devlin didn't bother to say anything more. He pocketed the piece of paper. He needed to get the hell out of there immediately.

Horace waited as long as he could stand it, then he tore his coat from the hang hook.

He spotted Devlin before he rounded the corner off Lombard onto Westbrook. Horace had never tailed anyone before. He kept his distance and made sure to stay away from street lights.

Devlin was not easy to follow. Horace lost sight of him more than once. Horace's hair obscured his vision. He tied it back into a ponytail. He held still at the corner of a building, pressed as close to the wall as he could manage. His heart was racing. At this angle, all Devlin had to do was turn around and he was made. Horace felt foolish. This looked much easier in the movies.

Devlin passed beneath a train overpass and then was gone. Horace waited a moment, cloaked by the shadow of a stoop overhang, but Devlin did not reappear. Fear rushed through him. Something didn't feel right. His instincts told him to leave.

But he waited. After a few minutes, Horace finally gave up and left the safety of cover. He traced his line of sight to where he'd lost track of Devlin. He rubbed his palms, which were moist with sweat. He was standing in front of the old Goldeyes stadium. There was no sign of Devlin anywhere. He was gone. Horace shook his head and turned on his heels to head back home.

"You think it's the first time I've been tailed?"

Devlin stepped out of a dark walk-through archway beneath the train overpass. Horace turned and faced him.

"I'm not an idiot. I spotted you right away. What the hell are you playing at, Horace Mackie?"

"I don't know for sure."

"Why are you following me?"

"A hunch."

"Goddamn it, Horace! Make some sense for once."

Horace didn't say anything. He instinctively ran his fingers along his scar. Devlin's anger began to build. He hated Horace, always had. It wasn't because Horace was different. It wasn't even because he was Kip's best friend. It was because the Velic brothers took him in, gave him a home, and Devlin had never been given that courtesy. He'd always felt cheated.

"You know, I don't really care how you got that scar or what you supposedly did for those girls. Didn't matter, did it? They're still prostitutes." He scoffed out loud. "Goddamn whores."

Horace took a moment to search his memory banks. "I think you've confused them with other people. Last I heard, one went to night school, became a nurse, and the other is married with two beautiful children."

"Bah, that's bull!"

"No, it's reality."

"You think you're clever."

"No, not very clever at all. I followed you here with no plan. I only wanted to confront you..." Horace looked down at the ground. "About Kip."

"How would you know anything about that?"

Horace merely looked at him.

"Ah, so you lied?" Devlin cracked knuckles on his hands. "I'm not surprised. But why?"

"I don't know. Maybe because of the name on the paper."

"So you know who Justin Bailey is?"

"I do."

Devlin's patience was wearing thin, and it showed.

"So who is it, Horace?"

"Not who. What."

Devlin spit. His blood pounding in his temples, but he'd play along a little while longer. "Fine, *what* is it?"

"The code for a video game." Horace broke eye contact and looked down at the ground. Then he looked directly at Devlin, his face set and his dark eyes serious. "You killed Kip."

"I should've known. You two with those stupid games. I should've known he'd try to warn you."

The two men were no more than ten feet apart. Devlin looked up at the night sky.

"Full moon tonight."

Horace looked up, too.

"Somewhere that moon is dying with the break of a new day."

Devlin laughed.

"You lame-o." He kicked a bottle, and it smashed against an over-sized concrete decoration of a baseball. "I was left with no choice. I want you to know that. Just like I have no choice right now. It all got out of control. Is out of control. You don't know a goddamn thing. It was all him. It was Shue." Devlin shook his head. "Christ, not even real."

Horace had no idea what Devlin was talking about. He stopped listening after that. It was as though he had stopped listening to Devlin altogether or that he had forgotten Devlin even existed. Horace could do that, go someplace in his head and transcend the world around him.

Horace looked at the old Goldeyes stadium. He used to love listening to the games on the radio while he rode the hydro-bus home. He and Kip would go to as many games as they could before the team folded. He could still hear the echo of the faded past cheering on the home team. He stepped out onto Pioneer. Devlin followed him.

"What are you doing? Get out of the street, you idiot."

He wanted a better look at the train tracks. He followed them overhead until he could see the train bridge that curved overtop of Pioneer like tracks to heaven.

"Why? It's not like there's going to be traffic."

The Goldeyes stadium was surrounded on one side by the elevated track system so the trains could move through the downtown core, heading towards the waterfront.

"Look at that old stadium. A real beaut. You can almost still hear the noise of the crowd echoing in the summer night. You'd come watch a game and see trains shoot past the outfield during the game." Horace smiled. "I learned to love the game at this stadium."

Devlin now faced Horace. They were standing on opposite sides of the street. The soft amber glow of the street lights overhead cast individual spotlights on each of them. The Human Rights Museum a glowing mass in the distance.

A storm was developing. The night sky was covered by a blanket of thick black storm clouds, which churned violently. Flashes of light-ning illuminated the ominous shapes of angry cloud cover. Then a powerful branch of dry lightning broke towards the earth.

A faint screeching of steel wheels could be heard echoing in the distance – a train was coming their way along the overhead tracks. Devlin couldn't think of a better time, so he took his weapon from its holster and drew down on Horace. The sound from the train would drown out the strike of the hammer.

"This is the end of your shitty little journey." Devlin looked up at the sky, a cloud shifted past and revealed the moon again.

Horace paid no attention to him. He was busy observing his surroundings, taking as much in as he could.

"What do you think will happen to you when I pull this trigger? Think you'll end up flying like you're always going on about?"

"I'm not sure, really. It's a regret I have."

"Typical. Can't ever get a rise out of you, can I?"

"Getting a rise out of someone requires a certain eloquence and a sense of timing that you lack."

"Oh yeah, how so?"

"Hypothalamus." Horace smiled triumphantly as he said it.

Devlin took a moment to regain control of the rage building inside his chest and composed himself. Then he cocked the weapon and pulled a round into the chamber.

Devlin swatted at a dragonfly fluttering around his face. He hated Horace now more than ever. "Not much time left. Train's getting awfully close. But at least you got a job as a stock boy, right?"

"There's no shame in my profession. I abide by the colonial laws, pay my taxes and provide a service to general society. I've made friends. I talk and dress the way I want. I don't owe anyone."

Devlin laughed. His finger twitched on the weapon's trigger. He was ready for this. He thought about his daughter. He thought about Kip. All of it had to be done. There was no other way. He also knew the world wouldn't kick up any fuss over Horace Mackie.

And he'd be right.

The two men stared at one another. Horace knew he couldn't run, that Devlin would just shoot him in the back, the same as he had done to Kip. And anyway, running away was never his thing. Plus, he preferred to close his eyes and think about good times. So that's just what he did. He thought about Kip, about seeing him soon. He thought about flying away. He still believed, even now, even like this, that it could happen.

People can't fly.

The train was upon them. The sound deafening. The steel wheels squealed, and the earth shook underfoot. Then he heard the gunshot. It was over. It was all over.

Horace opened his eyes. He was still standing. The train was gone and Devlin was lying on the street. In the distance, heading down Provencher, a herd of fifty-two bison were speeding towards the bridge. It was the first time a free herd of bison had run on Winnipeg soil in over a century. Horace watched as they disappeared over the crest of the bridge.

He approached the man lying on the street. Devlin had been unable to hear the sound of the oncoming herd over the deafening noise of the train. Until it was too late. He had discharged the round meant for Horace, but at that very moment, the force of being struck by the missing FortWhyte bison sent the bullet astray. He had been knocked to the concrete with a force that nearly crushed his skull. The hooves of the fifty-two bison, weighing a half ton each, did the rest.

It was over. Just not for Horace.

A laboured sound came from Devlin. Horace looked down at the dying man on the street. He wasn't moving. It was a grisly thing to see someone in that state.

Death ain't easy, and it isn't pretty.

Pretty death only happens in the movies.

Like when Sir Anthony walks away with Brad in *Meet Joe Black*.

That sort of jib.

Horace pitied him.

Their eyes locked.

A noise, a soft gurgling, escaped Devlin's lips.

Then it was over.

Dev was dead.

Horace crouched down and searched what was left of Devlin. Horace found the piece of paper with the name Justin Bailey scribbled on it. He patted the pocket and found a roll of film and a ceramic toy pigeon. Horace put both in his own pocket.

Then he started walking. A block later, he crumpled the piece of paper and tossed it away.

I once heard a person say people don't get better with age.

I once heard someone say, "I can't do it anymore."

And

I've heard a person tell another person,

"It will be okay."

You hear things.

You hear trains in the night,

The television,

Doorbells,

A child's laughter,

Voices.

You just don't hear "it will be okay" quite often enough, though.

People start out dreaming big all the time. Then they dream big once in a while. Eventually, though, they just stop dreaming and put food in the microwave.

Microwave ovens were introduced to homes in the '60s to help people save time.

Consume quicker.

Cooks food with radiation.

Radiation causes cancer.

Corporations have microwaves in their lunchrooms.

Chefs don't own microwaves.

Just one of those things.

Now,

I've heard that some Johns and Janes never dream. That's bull. Everyone has dreams. Every single human being has them.

Though,

Here's the jib,

There is a point when a person has to make a decision about their dreams, and most choose to box them up alongside the Christmas decorations and store them away.

Resistance.

There are so many reasons why, so very many.

Resistance.

But sometimes, through blind ambition, heartache, sacrifice and all human emotion, through loss and opposition and failure – never forget failure – failure is the only pure thing left in the world. A person must see their dream to fruition.

Will.

Imagine what it would feel like to see yours through, with no guarantee, no assurances, just that you saw it through to fruition or failure. Imagine that. Just imagine that.

Grit.

Don't worry about other people. Don't wait to see if they're listening, if they're watching. Don't seek the words you long to hear. They will never come, and if they ever do, I promise they won't have the impact you hoped they would.

Or don't. Don't do it. Say hello to all the others out there, while a handful of people commit themselves willingly to the humiliation of failure, just so they can hear the whisper.

A whisper.

Horace felt something. He knew when he touched the undeveloped roll of film, unexposed, on 0.30<CC> worth of media, that it was something priceless. Something he had been searching for.

A dream,

Maybe.

A glorious *something* come true. A person's search for the most elusive thing in the universe. A single, absolute truth.

The photograph paper bathed in the tub of chemicals. Horace watched as an image began to appear on the paper. He held up the photograph. The fluid was still dripping off the sheet of photograph paper. He didn't know what he expected to see, but what was on the photograph paper would change the world. It also needed to be shared with the others. It would impact everything.

He hung the photograph so it could dry and went to work on the remainder of the roll. Horace wiped his brow. He was hot and he was tired. He hadn't given himself much time to internalize all of the events that had happened so rapidly. The harsh darkroom lighting didn't help, either.

He had discovered that his best friend had been murdered. Then he had narrowly avoided the same demise himself. Devlin had betrayed everyone. Horace was suspicious of conspiracy, a suspicion he could now confirm with the photograph that was drying on the line.

Horace was almost finished developing the rest of the roll of film. Kip had taken other photographs of what looked like Internet modems and computer technology. These photographs made little sense to him, but if Kip had photographed them, he knew they were important. He also knew just the person to show them to.

At once, Horace felt the bitter and the sweet. Kip had made good on his promise. It wasn't drugs that had killed him. He had died doing what he loved. He had given up his old life for a new one. It had been fleeting, and it had cost him everything.

But he *had* lived, not merely existed.

Or something.

Guess I'm sniffing at Wilde truffles.

At first, when Horace discovered his friend had been murdered, he didn't understand the reasons. Then he remembered that Kip had mentioned a newspaper journalist from the *Free Press*.

Horace took a deep breath and slowly exhaled. The information was overwhelming. He stretched his arms over his head, then shook them out at his sides.

He was about to store the negatives when he realized he had overlooked the very first negative on the roll. It had not yet been developed. He held the neg up to the red safelight bulb. There was something there, but what the image contained was hard to discern.

Horace looked at the clock ticking away on the wall. He was torn about what he should do. He had a photograph in his possession that needed to be shared. On the other hand, the last negative might also possess clues about the set of photographs.

He decided to develop the last photograph. He approached it with the same care and attention as he did all the others. The photograph sank below the chemical fluid. He waited and watched as the photograph content began to appear.

He smiled – the photograph was unrelated to the others, but he felt like crying. His friend, his best friend, had captured beauty, mystery and wonder in the photograph. He had captured truth. It was all Kip had ever wanted, and the man had managed to do it once before he died.

There are very few people in this world who can say they were there, that they had witnessed a perfect truth. Kip was one of those few people.

Horace hung the picture to dry. He shook his head. He looked at the other photograph hanging right in front of him. He was wrong. Kip had managed to achieve it twice.

He needed to speak with Jack.

Jack sat up in bed. His chest was damp with sweat. He had been dreaming.

Not the kind of dreaming we talked about earlier.

Stay with me.

He reached for a notepad he kept on the night table. He wrote the dream on the paper by the light of the moon coming through the bedroom window. This was his method, a way of recording the dream before it would slip away into the ether of wakefulness.

There was this doctor guy who said dreams are merely commentary on reality.

The news of Kip's murder had a profound impact on everyone. Horace had shared the details, what few of them there were. Jack knew he should have meditated and cleared his mind for sleep, but somehow he couldn't. A friend, murdered. Jack was on awful familiar ground again and it tormented him. It had happened all over again, and now he was grappling with this new loss. He would not find sleep again this night.

He rubbed his eyes and tried to pull focus. The room was dark except for the frail light of the moon. He thought of Loraina and her blindness.

Jack pulled the sheets away, moved his tired body to the edge of the bed and sat up. The hardwood was cold on his bare feet.

He touched the pad of paper.

His dream.

He had been dreaming.

Remember the dream.

Focus on the dream.

A giant open field. Warm. Beginning of summer. Filled with tall grass. He was alone at the edge of the field. The night. Sky overhead looked like a tipped salt shaker on a black tablecloth. Across the field, droplets of dew caught the light of the moon.

Absence of sound, scent of honeysuckle, gentle breeze playing the tall blades of prairie grass. It was the breeze that caused all the fireflies to wake and light. Blinking and twinkling.

He watched.

Thousands of glowing lights signalling one another.

Then he awoke.

He needed to message Loraina. Needed to see her, tonight. He knew what he had to do, what he was going to do.

He stood and dressed. Went into his closet and removed a panel from the ceiling. He reached into the secret hollow and brought down a can of spray paint. He looked at the unused can. It was Hydrant Red. He had found the can at an old hardware store in The Maples. He knew he shouldn't have purchased it, how dangerous it was for him to own a can of paint, but he couldn't help himself. It was his sword.

The can felt good in his hand. He shook it. The rattle of the pea inside echoed, shattering the thick silence. Jack found his old backpack on the closet floor. For just a moment, he held it out in front of him like his hands were on the shoulders of an old friend.

Jack touched the key fob to his door and heard the locking mechanism tumble into place. Another door in the hallway opened. It was

Aleks. First time he'd seen Aleks in pants. Aleks would roam the hallways naked for no other reason than it just felt good.

"Have you heard anything about Clair?"

"Nothing." He rubbed his chin stubble. "Poor girl."

Aleks looked Jack up and down.

"Heading out this time of night?"

"Yeah, I'm meeting up with a friend."

"Kids these days. Doing all manner of things and at such ungodly hours."

Jack smiled.

Aleks scratched his crotch. "Don't let me keep you." Then he patted Jack on the back.

Somehow the whole gesture seemed – well, not normal, but okay. Jack half-smiled.

"I'll see you around."

"I'm around." Aleks smiled, then the smile left his face. "Be careful, Jack. She's not the person you think she is."

Jack said nothing. Aleks walked away.

Fifteen minutes. That's all it took for Jack to walk to the location of the blank billboard on Fort. It took him less time to find a way up onto the catwalk of the billboard.

He was amazed that it all came back to him so naturally. He took the can of paint from his backpack and shook the can. The rattle shot a thrill through his body. He allowed himself to enjoy the feeling, and for a moment, he felt like he was once again in control.

He tested the tip by pressing it down and letting paint out into the air. The mist of colour wisped away with the night breeze. He looked at the white canvas. He reached and painted:

Jack Black

The Date and Time

The word meeting in Polari

Jack Black was a vagabond, professional burglar and author. He may or may not have committed a rash of crimes, written a play, worked for a newspaper and lived as a nomad. Jack Black might not be his real name. He is *the* anonymous figure.

On the flip,

There is an actor with the same name who appeared in the movie *Airborne.* Anonymous? Not so much. No relation.

He stepped back and looked at the message. Just as she had instructed. Now all he could do was wait and see.

It had been an hour. Maybe longer. He'd taken a seat on a bus bench and shooed off more mosquitoes and dragonflies than hydro-buses. The face of the real estate agent on the bus bench smiled back at him. The guy in the picture had the same first name.

There's a joke about real estate agents and how much training they receive: lots. Get it?

Dickie told me that one.

Someone touched Jack's shoulder. It was Loraina. She had gotten close to him without making a sound.

She was holding her walking cane in her hand. A dragonfly hovered over her head and then joined a small swarm of other dragon-flies before flying elsewhere.

"You rang."

She took a seat on the bus bench. She patted the empty spot, and Jack scooted over to her.

"You've got something."

She was smiling. Jack was not. He looked distressed.

"What is it?"

"My friend has been murdered. A policeman is dead."

Loraina raised an eyebrow. The news did not shock her.

Jack's face showed the pain he felt.

"I know everything. I know about the conspiracy. I even know…" Jack shook his head. He was overcome with emotion.

"I'm sorry. Tell me what you know."

"Just hold on a second. Now look, I know I keep asking this, but I need to know. How are you here?"

"I'm not sure what you mean."

"I mean, I painted a word in some old underground language and a name very few people have even heard of, let alone recognize, and then poof! Here you are. None of this is making much sense to me."

"The date and time was a big help."

Jack scowled.

Loraina sighed.

She set her walking cane beside her. She tied her hair back with a rubber band.

"Look, my world is a small world. I keep it small on purpose. I have some people I pay, one way or another. Some owe me, and they are working the marker. They provide me with information. That's how I stay in the know. That's how I stay sharp. They are the eyes I don't have. People like me stay informed at all times."

People like her. Jack would be surprised if there was anyone else quite like her.

"I do what I need to do to get what I need. You have to understand. This is how I've survived. You don't know me."

"You could tell me."

"I could."

"But you won't."

Loraina smiled.

"Would it help you if I did?"

"It might." A hydro-bus came to a stop, and Jack waved the driver on. "If I knew your reasons, I might be more inclined to devote myself willingly to your cause. You must know enough about me by now, know the things I've been involved in. My motives."

"I do."

"Then help me understand what this is."

Loraina rubbed her hands together. Jack caught a glimpse of the red-bellied snake tattoo on her palm. She patted her breast pocket, then reached in and took out a hand-rolled cigarillo. She ran her tongue along the seal, then put in between her lips. She struck a match with her fingernail. The head burst aflame. She touched it to the end and lit the smoke.

She dragged on it.

The sweet scent of clove tobacco overtook the air around them.

Cigarillo dangling from her lips.

She scratched her cheek with a set of grimy nails. Jack wondered if she knew about the filth under her nails or not. Or cared. She pushed a thick tuft of dark curls from her face.

"When the Association of Canadian Banks came into power, my mother lost her job. A lot of people did. Those were hard times for Canadians. She applied for a position with the ACB and their infrastructure and systems.

"I was seven when they murdered my mother. Police had no leads. Case went cold. Before she died, my mother started acting very different. She hid things, told me things that made no sense. Not then, they didn't." She sighed. "I was too young to understand. She was constantly paranoid. She had trouble sleeping and was on edge all the time." Loraina flicked ash from her cigarillo. "She was afraid."

"Afraid of what?"

"Afraid of Roland Shue." Loraina took a pull off her cigarillo. The cherry smouldered.

Jack's face lit up at the name. "I know this name."

"You're one of the few. Most people don't." Smoke exited her nostrils. "That's the genius of it. Most business people who lead corporations love the spotlight, and the company they work for promotes that, fosters it, even. They are the face of the corporation. Roland Shue has managed to effectively veil his existence and involvement completely. Well, almost completely."

"I have something that might help expose him."

She smiled absently. "Do you?"

She was dismissive. She did not realize the extent of what Jack was telling her. The truth that he now knew. For once, he was a step ahead of her. So, he played along to see where she was taking things. He watched her carefully.

"So why is he so important?"

"It's not that simple." She sighed. "It never is." Loraina shook her head. "The simple answer is that no person should have as much power as he does."

"No single person has the kind of power you're alluding to. It's a myth, a spook story."

"It's just that kind of thinking that has allowed him to get as far as he has. It's like having a terrible pain in your chest. You know you should go get it checked out, but you keep telling yourself it's nothing, until it's too late.

"My mother was there. She knew all the secrets, and Roland Shue had her killed. She wasn't the only person who 'died' or 'went missing.'

"I was all alone, had no family. And I had proof of Shue's conspiracy my mother had given me. I needed to hide, make sure Shue could never find me. So I ran, and I found my way here. To this paradise." She waved a hand at the city.

"Why Winnipeg?"

Jack chuckled at the irony of him asking someone else the question.

"I could ask the same of you."

"Yeah, but you know why I'm here."

"That I do."

She took a drag. Jack didn't like the connotation, something sinister in her tone. He wondered, only for a moment, if she could have somehow nudged him to Winnipeg. It was a scary, farfetched thought. He decided to put it out of his head. Besides, it was too late to worry about it now, anyway.

Loraina smiled at him as though she knew his thoughts. The smile didn't last more than a second.

"I came here because this is where Roland Shue is."

"Here? In Winnipeg?"

Jack continued with his dangerous charade.

Loraina nodded. Jack already knew this, too, but he would play it out as long as he could get information from her.

"The ACB headquarters is here, and so is Roland Shue."

"Why here? Why not Toronto or Montreal? A major metropolitan city?"

"Because..." She clicked her tongue, then swatted away a dragonfly hovering in front of her face. "...of wilful blindness." She shook her head. "Too often sighted people consciously make a decision to not see what's happening right in front of them." A soft sigh escaped her.

"Loraina, what are you after?" It was a pointed question, but Jack felt it was a fair one.

The familiar smile returned to her lips.

"All in due time."

"Fine. If that's how you want to play it, then I won't be held hostage by you anymore." He stood. "Go ahead and expose me. I don't care anymore. Maybe it's time I faced the heat that's been at my back for so long."

He unfolded his hands and looked at his palms. Their lines were coarse and their surface calloused from years of daily building-wall climbing. He chuckled, just realizing now that somehow the higher up a message was, the more seriously people took it. That's why billboards have always been so effective.

"Jack." Loraina took hold of his hand. Her hand was warm. Jack looked at her. Her features looked sad, and the lines of her face had softened. "You'll just have to trust me. Or not."

Jack remained silent. Something was gnawing at him, something he could no longer ignore. He trusted her. It was merely an instinct, but it told him this was the right thing. "I had a dream tonight," he said.

Loraina took a pull off her cigarillo.

"It gave me an idea."

"And you think this idea of yours could work?"

Her tone hinted that she didn't put much stock in his dreams.

"Maybe. I don't know. There are never any guarantees, but it's a pretty good idea. It could work. It just might work."

Loraina smiled. Her posture softening. Jack was amazed at her self-control and how little she revealed about herself through her body language.

Body language is the closest thing to truth in all human language. Johns and Janes say things all the time in all kinds of different languages. Most of it isn't genuine. Human emotion masks the deep truth in words, but when it comes to body language, that very same emotion is what gives body language its truth.

Think of it this way,

When someone looks upset and you ask if they're okay and they say they're fine, the words are a lie.

It's simple: their body language told you the truth.

Yes, sir,

Body language,

Most honest of all human languages.

Yup,

That's solid.

"Alright, Jack, get to work then."

Loraina stubbed out her cigarillo and tossed the butt onto the sidewalk.

"I will. But first I need materials, and I'm going to need some help."

"I have people who can get you what you need."

"No offence, but I don't know your people and I don't work that way. I'll source my own materials. Plus, I need a crew."

Jack was pacing to relieve his mounting tension. Rows of decaying cars dotted the sides of the street.

Once a variety of rich glossy colours, now, not unlike a forest floor, these cars were returning to an earth-brown rust. Jack's eye followed the never-ending thread of cars.

The city still had a long way to go before the Auto-Hack cleanup and scrap resale was complete.

Some of the cars were occupied,

Homes of the homeless.

In the distance, he saw Kevin wandering aimlessly through the Portage and Main intersection.

"A woman, a special law enforcement officer, approached me in a coffee shop yesterday. She knew my name. I think she may know who I am. I mean, who I really am."

Loraina's expression did not change. If she was concerned, it did not show.

"Does she have a name?"

"She said it was Justine. Special Crimes Investigation Agent

Justine Kavanaugh."

"I see. Don't worry. I'll take care of it."

Jack didn't like the sound of that at all. He shook his head. He looked at Loraina. So very unpredictable.

She smiled. Jack wondered if she knew he was analyzing her.

"So, is that all?"

Jack paused. He wasn't going to say anything more, but he had reached a point where he needed to put his cards on the table. "I know someone I think you should meet. He can help."

"I don't think so, Jack. It doesn't work that way."

"Look, you need to consider all the angles here. I get it. You've been on your own for years, almost your whole life. This is different. This guy, my friend, just found out his brother was murdered. I think it's part of this same conspiracy. He's invested, whether you like it or not. He's involved now, too. You can include him on your terms, or he'll very likely do something stupid on his own. Wouldn't it be better if he were with you rather than potentially making things more difficult for you?" Jack sighed. "And for me? More importantly, he could improve our chances of success, and he's the kind of person crazy enough to willingly participate in a ridiculous caper like this."

"Caper, Jack?"

Jack shrugged.

"I don't know what you call something like this."

The wind caught her hair and threw dark curls away from her face. It was the first time Jack had seen her vulnerable. He put his hand on her shoulder.

"Alright, Jack. You win. Set it up."

A hydro-bus pulled to a stop at the bus bench Jack and Loraina had been sitting on. A man got off the bus. He threw away a wrapper in the trash can overflowing with garbage. The man paid no attention to the wrapper when it fell out of the trash can and blew onto the sidewalk. He just kept on walking.

Justine Kavanaugh waited for the man to be well on his way. Then she moved from the security of a darkened alley and went towards the wrapper. She crouched down and moved the wrapper out of the way. What she wanted was underneath it: the cigarillo butt. She picked it up with tweezers and smelled it. She smiled. Same one from the rooftop. She bagged it and put the baggie into her carry case.

"Find what you were looking for?"

Justine stood and turned to face the voice behind her.

"Justine Kavanaugh." Loraina was walking towards Justine. She was swiping her cane back and forth, then she stopped. Justine was momentarily frozen from the shock of being made. "Why are you following me?"

"Who says I'm following you, um, what's your name?"

"Don't be coy. You're after him. Well, you can't have him. Not yet, anyway."

"I have no idea what you're talking about."

"How did you find me?"

Justine sighed softly. "The train yard. The explosive device. Not really his M.O."

"Bit of a stretch, isn't it?"

"Yes, but the handmade clove cigarillo on the roof..." Justine pointed up towards the building across the street. The very building Jack and Loraina had met on only a few nights ago. But Loraina didn't follow the direction Justine was pointing at. She just kept a loose gaze on Justine.

"Is the blindness genuine?"

Justine's question did not faze Loraina. "The cane didn't give it away?"

"No, it didn't. I've met lots of con artists. The trick is to catch them unprepared, when their guard is down."

"What are you after?"

"I was just going to ask you the same thing."

"You don't know what this is. You may think you know, but you don't."

"So, what is it?"

Justine hadn't noticed the small beige marble rolling towards her along the beige concrete sidewalk. It popped beneath her and a cloud of noxious gas enveloped her. She started to cough, then choke. She fanned the air for clean oxygen, but something struck her face and she fell to the ground, dazed.

Loraina had clubbed her with her walking cane. Instinctively, Justine reached for her 9mm, but she was still coughing violently, and Loraina had the drop on her, kicking the gun out of reach.

Loraina fell on top of Justine. Her hands gripped Justine's throat. She had the advantage of high ground position. Justine managed to drive the palm of her hand into Loraina's chin. Loraina fell backwards with a loud thud. Justine sucked air, taking as much oxygen as she could get. The effects of the fumes were wearing off, but she was a long way from a full recovery.

She was shocked at how quickly Loraina regained her composure and how fast she moved. Close hand-to-hand was an obvious advantage for Loraina. Justine needed to put some space between the two of them.

The two women faced each other, their chests rising and falling from the strain of fatigue. Loraina's face was set, her body language confident.

She clicked her tongue loudly and began to advance on Justine. Justine reached into her carry case and took out a small puck-shaped device. She threw it on the ground. A deafening high-pitched sound came from the device. Loraina covered her ears. The advantage would only last but a moment. Justine had to move quickly.

The two women struggled desperately on the sidewalk, the only witnesses the silent glass sentinels reflecting each violent movement in their tempered windows.

Justine began to tire. The effects of the gas had slowed her movements and crippled her stamina. She needed to make a move now. She drove her knee into Loraina's gut, and then clipped her in the jaw.

Loraina fell to her side on the concrete. She was dazed, lying still with her hands clutching her walking cane. Justine saw her gun, but it was too far now. She wouldn't make the same mistake twice. She leapt onto Loraina and put her hands around the woman's throat. She would choke her out, just like Loraina had tried to do to her.

It was working. Loraina struggled beneath her, but could not find a way to leverage herself. She clawed at Justine.

Then her struggles got weaker.

Loraina knew she was fading. The walking cane was close and in position. She pressed a tiny button on the cane and a liquid sprayed out and into Justine's eyes. Justine fell backward in agony.

She rolled on the sidewalk, moaning, clutching at her eyes.

Loraina gasped for air, the dullness receding as she regained her wits with each gulp of fresh oxygen.

Justine was crawling on the concrete, her direction aimless. Loraina crouched and swept her cane until it found the gun. She picked it up. She did the same until she located the puck. She drove her heel into it. The high pitched sound came to an abrupt end. Loraina stood over Justine. With uncanny perception, Justine could sense her proximity.

"I can't see."

"No, I imagine you can't." Loraina choked back a cough. Her throat still aching from Justine's powerful grip. "Now you know how I feel."

"I'm blind!"

"The effects will wear off soon."

"What did you do to me?"

"Does it matter?"

"No, I guess not." Justine paused. She stopped crawling, turned over and sat up. "You have my gun?"

"Yes."

"So, that's how this goes."

"I'd say."

"Going to kill me now?"

Justine waited for her to respond. Then, a sick feeling entered the pit of her stomach. The woman standing over her wasn't going to say anything. It was just going to happen. Click and the lights go out. She didn't want to die. The sudden rush of fear was terrifying.

But,

The bullet never came.

"I'm not going to kill you."

Justine rubbed her eyes. Her vision was already starting to return. She could only see blurred light.

"What now?"

"You listen."

"Do I have a choice?"

"No."

Dickie Reimer says there was a time – oh, say, back when people drove around in giant boats for automobiles – when women didn't speak their minds and Johns and Janes ate whatever the advertisements told them to eat and all that sort of jib.

Yeah,

Around that time, there were these fine electrical street trolleys running along tracks all over downtown Winnipeg. The trolleys were owned privately by the Winnipeg Electrical Company.

Doesn't sound very private, but it was.

Then one year, just before some kids came along and invented rock 'n' roll, the Red River grew angry and spilled all over Winnipeg.

Give it a name.

So people did give it a name.

The Great Flood. No one thought it was a good flood, though.

And not long after,

The Manitoba government, when it was still called the Manitoba government, back before the PM got the idea to sell the provincial names to corps, the ol' Prov-Gov stepped in and took over the Winnipeg Electrical Company.

They wanted it,

So they took it.

As Dickie tells it.

And I believe him.

Dickie says it became the first public transit system in the province. Pegs love publicly owned systems; they used to love their public car insurance, where the ol' Gov gets to tell you how much you have to pay.

No competition.

Dickie calls that monopoly.

He's not the only one.

Now,

After the provincial government took over the Winnipeg Electrical Company, they decided electric trolleys were bad news.

People hate bad news.

So,

They solved the bad news by putting fuel-guzzling, pollution-spitting, heavy, thunderous buses on the road.

Trolleys had seen their day come and go.

They painted two giant crying eyes on the last lead trolley car and paraded them down Main Street with a sign that said, "We've had it!"

This really, really happened.

Some guy – whom Dickie knows – had a grandfather who was there.

Pegs by the thousands lined the streets.

Why?

Well,

Who doesn't love a parade?

Years and years went by, because that's what years and years do.

During that time, people bought more, ate more and wasted more. They didn't know any better. They were told to do it by companies that had a lot of money, so much money that they figured out ways to convince people to always say yes to them. Crooks call that a con.

Corporations call it marketing.

Now,

The more this type of thing happens, the more people start to feel on edge. Something feels off, and people start to talk about it with other people.

Some people even get angry and shout about it. And there are a handful of people, a special few, who try to do something about it.

Like this:

A student walks into the Ottawa National Gallery. He has heard about the decision by the federal government to allow their southern neighbours to test cruise missiles in Canadian airspace.

He asks to see the recently signed Proclamation of Human Rights by Queen Elizabeth II and Prime Minister Pierre Elliott Trudeau. You could see it and touch it back then.

The young man dumps red paint all over the Charter.

Dickie calls that symbolism.

To this day, the stain still exists as a reminder that testing weapons of mass destruction goes against our basic human right to live.

This is really true.

Johns and Janes still make missiles.

I guess it's just one of those things.

Jack was sitting in a chair. He was watching Kris work. Neither knew where Kurt was. Kris did not seem worried. He had witnessed the same reaction from his older brother when their parents had died.

Kris tinkered with one of his inventions. To Jack, the device looked like nothing important. Jack had always been intrigued by innovation. He had often incorporated creative ways to effectively transmit the message of his art. If a spray tip didn't do what he needed it to do, he modified it or created something new. If the paint he used wasn't quite what he needed, he developed something that would do what he needed it to do. Watching Kris work was inspiring.

Kris set his tool case down on the desk. "I don't think your friend is going to show, Jack."

Kris picked up a soldering gun and melted a circuit into place on the motherboard. Jack marvelled at his tempered demeanour. Kris had only just lost his youngest brother, murdered. The circumstances of the murder left him feeling sick. It appeared their closest friend and confidant, Devlin, may have pulled the trigger, thickening a terrible plot; his reasons, as of yet, unknown.

"I have a feeling you're right. She was supposed to be here an hour ago."

Jack's frustration was hard to hide. He wanted Loraina to meet Kris. He secretly knew he and Loraina would discover that their interests and involvement in this web of conspiracy were somehow aligned.

So, where was she? How did she expect to breach the Association of Canadian Banks without addressing the ACB's security technology? How did she hope to cripple a corporation with that kind of reach, that kind of power, without help? The whole thing was unravelling.

"What are you working on?"

"Have you ever heard of VRD?"

"VRD?"

"Virtual Reality Device."

"Sure, um, I think so. Isn't that where you put on funny goggles so you can feel like you're a part of what you're watching?"

"Yeah, kind of. That's the jib of it, anyway. I'm using VRD as a contact for ANNs."

"You lost me."

"An ANN is an artificial neural network. ANNs are applied by computer scientists for machine learning." Kris could see that Jack was interested, but Jack fumbled the tech talk, and the more Kris said, the more confused he felt. "Imagine you've built a robot and you want the robot to reach its arm over its head. So, you program that task or capability into the robot's network. Still following me?"

Jack nodded.

"Seems like a simple task, lifting an arm overhead. And maybe it is, when it is just a functional programming task. But imagine you merely think of that task, and the robot does it, just because you thought of the task. Your human brain sends a thought via a neural funnel to the robot, and the robot does the task of lifting its arm overhead. That's just one simple example."

"So that's what this is?" Jack pointed to the device Kris was working on.

"A little different." Kris rubbed his chin. "It's a Neural Connectionist Device. The VRD transmits visual information to and from a network via the goggles attached to the human brain. This causes stimulation and leads to brain steeping." Kris picked up another component to the device. "This little guy syncs with your axons within the nervous systems and synapses. It takes those steeped thoughts and converts a person's unique cognitive capacities, a collective intellectual self, into computer script, into functioning operational code. A virtual self is then able to cohabitate with a computer mainframe." He frowned. "Well, that's the hypothesis."

Jack shook his head. "You're saying you'd be alive inside a computer?"

"Not quite. Your brain would be projecting a version of yourself into a computer mainframe. You could essentially move, think and feel inside of a machine. Like a video game character, except you are the actual player."

"Does it work?"

"Yes. No. I think so. It's something I've been working towards. I'm close. I just need to test it to see if it works."

"So why not test it?"

"Because the effects on the nervous system are more than a little dangerous. A person could potentially suffer severe mental shock or become paralyzed or even die if the system feedback was powerful enough."

"Sounds worth the risk." Loraina's voice startled them. They hadn't heard her come in and certainly didn't notice her standing there until she spoke up.

Jack was relieved to see her, then noticed the bruising on her throat and scabbing on her face.

"Are you okay? What happened?"

"Being clumsy."

Jack frowned; he doubted that. "I was beginning to think you weren't coming."

"I said I would be here. So, here I am."

Jack stood. "Loraina, this is Kris. Kris, Loraina."

Loraina smiled and extended her hand. Kris shook it.

"Good to meet you. Jack, some coordinates, if you'd be so kind."

"Ah, the room is about ten feet by sixteen. You're at the short end. Ceiling is twelve feet. To your left is Kris's work station. To your right are four empty chairs and a three-person couch."

"That'll do fine, Jack."

Loraina took a seat in one of the empty chairs. She collapsed her cane. "I've brought someone with me."

Justine Kavanaugh stepped into the room. Jack quickly stood. Kris noticed his sudden discomfort.

"Relax, Jack."

"Loraina, she's a police officer!"

"Actually, I work for the Canadian government, a special investigation division that handles international crimes. I most certainly am not a police officer."

"Semantics. You're still a cop." Jack was angry and, in truth, a little scared. "You shouldn't have brought her here, Loraina. What were you thinking?"

Loraina relaxed in her chair and crossed her legs. She lit a cigarillo and drew on it, then released a large plume of clove-scented tobacco into the air.

"This isn't up for discussion, Jack. Officer Kavanaugh and I have reached an agreement. She will apply her unique skill set to help us. In exchange, she will be credited as the official who uncovered and exposed an international corporate conspiracy." Loraina smiled at Justine. "She also gets to be the primary arresting officer. Good for her career."

"And what do you get, Loraina? This isn't a game. You're playing with people's lives here, my life! What happens to us?"

Loraina, unmoved by Jack's outburst, took a drag from her cigarillo. Kris was silently taking everything in.

"Look, Jack, I get it. I understand what you're saying, but we can't do this alone. You said it yourself. We need help." Jack didn't like the taste of his own words being stuffed back in his mouth. "We need the qualified skills. She has these skills." Loraina took a pull from her cigarillo. "Argument over. I'm here to meet someone you thought could help us."

A look of disdain lined Jack's face. He felt Loraina had painted him into a corner.

"How do you figure? I didn't bring a cop."

Justine spoke up. "Not a cop."

Jack shook his head. "Whatever."

Justine was also unaffected by Jack. "I am one of two people who has discovered your identity."

Kris looked at his friend. He wondered what *identity* Justine was alluding to. He had always found it strange that Jack had moved from New York to Winnipeg, of all places. He had also wondered how Jack was able to live in comfort the way he did and not work. He said nothing and kept his thoughts to himself.

"All you have is conjecture. You have no proof that I am who you say I am."

"Actually, Jack, I haven't said a damn thing. You're the one with all the insinuations."

Justine smiled, her eyes on Loraina. Jack wondered if Loraina had sold him out. He was afraid to say anything in case the nature of Justine's gaze was harmless.

"Jack, we're wasting time. Time we don't have. We have only a day, at best, to devise a competent plan and act on it. Not to sound too much like a cliché, but you're either in or you're out. Which is it?"

"In or out? You make it sound like I've been given that choice."

Jack sighed. He sat back down in the chair. His head fell into his chest. There was no way out now. He'd been in this position only once before, and it had cost him everything. He looked up at the others. This was different. He could feel it was different. Yes, he'd been used, and none of this was on his terms, but he knew when something was the right thing to do. And this was every shade of right.

"I don't like being forced into anything, certainly not something as risky and dangerous as this. I don't imagine anyone would like to be put in the position you've put me in, Loraina." He pointed a Justine. "Or being chased by the law."

He rubbed his chin.

"I'm in." He smiled at Kris. "For Kip, if for no other reason."

And that was the last of it. He wanted no more back and forth. He had made his decision, and, for better or worse, he would see this thing through to the finish. He needed to follow his heart and trust his instincts.

Kris watched his friend silently wrestle with his decision. "I'm in, too."

Justine had been scanning Kris. She wondered what his involvement in this whole fiasco was.

"Is all of this tech yours?"

"Yes."

"There is some very complex stuff here. How'd you get it?"

"Some of the components I got here and there, but most of it I built myself."

It was Justine's turn to be shocked. The complexity of the hardware was extraordinary.

Kris had taken hardware constructed by teams of people from the finest computer technology companies and found a way to thoroughly improve the design so that they were more functional and more accessible.

Justine looked at the quiet, unassuming man before her. She estimated he was about her age. She had seen some very talented people at MIT, but nothing like the work in front of her now. She gazed quickly at one of the computer screens. She recognized the software that was running.

"Did you build this RAT?"

Kris looked surprised. "You know tech?"

"Five years, MIT."

"MIT. That's a little bigger than me. I barely managed high school."

Justine directed the conversation back on topic.

"So tell me about this. Have you used it?"

316

"Nah, I'm merely an architect."

"You don't test?"

Kris looked at his friend. Jack leaned forward, resting his elbows on his knees, hands locked together.

"In or out, Kris. The decision is yours. I can't make it for you."

Kris smiled at Jack. The danger thrilled him. "Maybe I have."

"Some good stuff here. Design's a little crude, but better than what we use in Ottawa."

Justine lost interest in the Remote Administration Tool when she spied something else. This time, though, she asked nothing about it and kept her interests to herself.

Kris unplugged his soldering gun and returned it to its iron spiral holster. There was too much going on in the room, and none of it was being explained.

"Someone needs to start saying something. What have I got myself into? What happened to my brother?"

Loraina stubbed out her cigarillo against the sole of her shoe. Her hands looked worn. Kris grabbed something that would serve as an ashtray.

"Here."

"What's this for?"

"Closest thing I have to an ashtray."

He held the aluminum pop can in front of her.

Loraina clicked her tongue, then reached forward and took the can from him.

"Thank you." She uncrossed her legs and leaned forward in the chair, sweeping heavy curls from her face. "I just have to figure on a place to start. What do you know about the ACB security systems?"

Kris ran his hand through his hair. "I know they use the most advanced computer tech and software this side of the world, maybe even the world over."

Loraina nodded again. She liked that Kris didn't have to have his hand held. You could give Kris a little and he could make a lot out of it. She knew he and Justine were the only chance she had to defeat the ACB security protocols and gain access to their mainframe.

"That's why we need you and Justine."

The corner of Kris's mouth turned up into a half-smile.

"You're talking about a hack?"

"Yes."

"That won't be easy."

"I know. The hardest part will be remotely accessing the ACB system."

Kris looked at Justine. Justine shook her head, but it was Kris who spoke.

"It's not difficult. It's impossible. You'd need an op-system to match the ACB's. Even then it would be a long shot at best."

Loraina frowned. "That won't do. We don't have that kind of time."

Kris said nothing.

It was Justine who broke the silence. "Impossible."

Loraina shook her head. "No, it's not." Loraina took out her pouch of tobacco and a rolling paper. "The ACB is about to change everything."

"How so?"

"The ACB owns the Mobile Telecommunications Conglomerate. Most people don't know this. Public corporate record sharing is something the ACB has managed to somehow circumvent since inception.

"While everyone has enjoyed free mobile communications, it came with a heavy price. Each day, users must spend a certain amount of time watching advertisements on their phone. These advertisements are selected from categories by the user. The user's selections start out broad but are slowly and mathematically narrowed until the user's purchase patterns become data mining through ANNs and algorithms used by the ACB. This is done through targeting based on the purchasing of commercial goods and interests. Essentially opening the user up completely to algorithmic profiling. What you buy and why is more valuable than your DNA.

"Each person is categorized, again by a series of complex algorithms. The ACB has been storing this data profiling for years.

"What Canadians do know about the ACB is that they hold the

monopoly on their finances through control of digital currency."

The impact of Loraina's story suddenly hit Kris. "The ACB would not only control our currency, they would also be in control of how we think, our decisions. What people buy, their spending patterns, are a better blueprint for habits than mapping genomes."

Loraina smiled evenly. "That's right."

"How is it our government doesn't know about this?"

Justine had heard the notions before. Rumours tossed around the agency. She didn't believe any of it then, but now, the sick feeling in the pit of her stomach made her feel differently.

"Our government is either inept or corrupt." Loraina rested her elbows on her thighs and leaned forward. "Or both."

Justine shook her head. "There could be some truth to what she's saying."

"Now, just hold on second. What is this?"

Loraina followed the sound of Kris's voice. Her eyes set, unnerving. He realized what she was driving at.

"Endgame?"

"Yes."

"What are we talking about here?"

Loraina struck a match. "Meltdown." She took a drag and blew smoke from her nostrils.

Justine scoffed. "And how will we prove illegal activity if there's nothing left of the ACB systems when we're through?"

Justine was balancing on a razor-thin line. Her involvement was contingent on the recovery of concrete proof. The absence of proof made her an accomplice to the crimes.

Kris, however, wasn't about to let the most exciting hack of his life fall through his fingers because of technicality.

"We could do a memory dump. Scan for illegal data while initiating the virus. Save the data we want, while simultaneously crippling the system."

No one said anything.

"Can that be done?" asked Jack.

"Yes, but not remotely." He cleared a space and sat on the edge of the table. "Fact is, none of this can be accomplished remotely. We have to be there."

Loraina uncrossed her legs. The intensity of her gaze was unsettling. "What does that mean?"

Before Kris could collect his wits, Justine took the lead.

"It means we would have to have a direct hard line access to the ACB system."

Loraina shook her head.

"You're saying we need to be in the ACB headquarters."

"Yes." Kris and Justine said it simultaneously.

"Sorry, but that's not part of the plan. Even if we could get inside the ACB undetected, we wouldn't have a clue where to look. Needle in a haystack comes to mind."

Justine stood up. "I'm out of here. I can't and I won't be party to a malicious Blackhat operation."

Stop.

You've got to be wondering…what the h-to-the-ell did Loraina say to Justine, a government special agent, to get her into that room? A room with amateur shades. Justine shouldn't be there. She knows it, you know it. And she was on her feet, bag in hand, so why wasn't she through the door yet?

Why?

If you weren't wondering that, you're still a terrific person, you're just going to get taken advantage of from time to time in this life.

So. Just…ask.

And, since you've asked so politely. I'll give you the straight jib.

Loraina said it to Justine kind of like this (keep in mind Justine was staring at the barrel of loaded gun):

"I know a lot of people. Good people. I also know a few bad people. But there's a couple of people I know that are the kind of people that don't fit into all of this. They never have. They are the people you lie to yourself about. The ones you tell yourself aren't real. They do things for money. I've got money. You get me?"

I'm just messing with you. None of that.

Justine is human. Come on. Come on come on. She wants things.

She wants to move her career along. She wants respect. She wants to see behind the veil. She wants to know. It's not so black and white. It never is. Neither is she. No one is. In these moments, we all like to think we'd make the good choice, the honest choice, the right choice. We think that, until we have the choice right in front of us. Then we think we can do both and still make it work. Look at it this way, white lies are the worst ones.

And,

Now back to Justine.

"I need reliable evidence, electronic data that the ACB has been operating illegally in some way." She produced a stack of papers from her carry case. "So far, all I have are questionable HF Trades from apparent Dark Pools that you've provided from what is sure to be debatable sources. Any hack worth salt could produce counterfeit records made to pass as genuine."

She threw the papers on the table, and they scattered all over.

"Justine, wait." Jack grabbed her arm.

Justine pulled her arm free. "Don't touch me."

"I wasn't trying to." Jack shook his head. "Whatever. Look, I'm sure you've got a folder on me and my activities. While I don't do things by the letter of the law, you know enough about me, or at least what it says somewhere in a file, that I would not be party to something like this if it didn't really matter in a big way. I may not be an upright citizen, but I'm after the greater good."

"You think I care? I've sworn to uphold the laws of this country. You think you can just pick and choose what laws you want to follow? It doesn't work that way, Jack. Without the rule of law, we have no society."

"Look, if Loraina is right, and I think she is, as a society, as people, we lose here. I could run back to the USA and turn a blind eye to what's happening in this country, right now, but I would be a fool to think that it wouldn't happen everywhere eventually."

Jack sat back down. His words seemed hollow. He felt defeated. The whole thing did seem rather hopeless.

"I'm leaving." Justine grabbed her carry case.

"Where are you going?"

"Loraina, I don't owe you…" She swept a glance over the room. "… or any of these other characters a damn thing." She walked out of the room.

Jack looked at Loraina. She didn't seem to care about anything that was happening. Jack felt his anxiety engulf him.

"We can't just let her leave!"

"And what do you suppose you'll do, Jack? Go after her? Bring her back here? Hold her against her will? Then what?"

"God damn it, Loraina! You brought her here."

"I did."

"Why?"

"I was playing dice. I know she is one of the best legitimate hackers on the planet. I hoped the lure of taking down the ACB was something more important to her than her professional acumen." She held the back of her hand to her mouth and yawned. "I guess I was wrong."

"You guess? Dice? Are you kidding me right now?"

Outside on the street, Justine growled, then she cursed out loud. What a mess. She dug into her pocket and took out her phone. She dialled. A voice answered.

"Abernathy."

"How would you like to catch your suspect in person and coordinate a joint international effort to bring down a terrorist cell of hackers?"

"Can you do this?"

"Yes."

Silence on the other end of the line.

"Abernathy?"

"Text me details."

She hung up. Damn him. She knew he'd come through. The prize was too rich, but he couldn't be civil, manage a little respect. Justine went to lock her phone, but a mandatory advert appeared on her screen. She cursed as the sixty-second advert for lipstick played to its end. Then she locked her phone and slipped it in her carry case.

The wind picked up and blew her hair over her face.

Damn. Damn. Damn!

She knew she should start walking. She knew every minute she spent thinking about the ragtag group of fools back in that room would be her undoing. She also knew that the feeling in the pit of her stomach was telling her something, something that felt an awful lot like the truth.

Damn it.

The door flung open. Its backside hit the wall with a loud thud and startled all in the room.

"Someone just tell me the plan so I can decide how fool-crazy you all are."

Kris was happy she'd come back.

Justine sat down and threw her carry case on the floor. "Someone better start talking, soon!"

"Maybe I can help." A man standing in the doorway. He was tall and lean; messy grey hair muddled his age. Beneath bushy grey eyebrows was a set of striking blue eyes.

Horace stepped out from behind the man.

Justine looked at Horace. "I know you."

Horace smiled at her. "Oh good, the police are here."

"I'm not... ah, forget it."

Horace took an elastic from his shirt pocket and tied his hair back.

"Guys, this is Aubrey Cusack. He knows what happened to Kip and why."

Cusack pulled a chair from against the wall. He took a seat. He appeared oblivious to the stares. Or he didn't care.

"I am a journalist with the *Free Press*." Cusack looked down at the floor. "That used to mean something a long time ago."

He looked up from the floor and scanned the faces around the room. "Which one of you is Kurt?"

"He's not here. He's, um, away. I'm his brother, Kris."

"I see."

Cusack scratched his chin. "Well, I've never been one for formality." He cleared his throat. "So, I'll get right at it." Cusack relaxed in the chair. "I met your brother under somewhat random circumstances.

323

He was high. The powder residue beneath his nose told me as much. His behaviour confirmed it."

Kris lost his calm. In fact, he looked downright disappointed.

"You're going to tell me that Devlin was right. It was drugs. That was his undoing. Is that it?"

"No, quite the opposite. I offered your brother an opportunity to work with me, to take journalistic photographs for me, a chance to make a change in his life. An opportunity he accepted. The agreement was made in secret and the partnership unofficial. Nothing on the books." Cusack paused. "I have been investigating the Association of Canadian Banks for many years. I employed Kip and his talent behind the lens to help expose the ACB's criminal activities. More importantly, to expose the criminal conspiracy of the Association of Canada Banks against the public.

"It was Kip who came up with the idea on how to expose the man controlling the ACB." Cusack took a deep breath, as though saying the name of the man would poison the room. "Roland Shue. I had discovered irregularities with the ACB's electronic transactional paper-work. Paperwork that is a matter of public records. Records meant to disguise a lie. A terrible lie. The ACB is stealing from Canadians for an awful purpose, something biblically sinister."

Horace stepped forward. He looked at the faces in the room.

He took a photograph from an envelope.

The room went quiet.

Horace touched his scar. He was nervous. He wasn't sure how to articulate everything that had happened, but Cusack did.

"Kip took the photograph. A photograph that cost him his life."

Justine stood up and looked at the photograph. "What am I looking at here?"

Then it hit her.

Horace took a deep breath and started talking. "I followed Devlin."

Kris felt his stomach turn.

"I followed him because he had been asking about a person's name." Horace tied his hair back into a ponytail. "Justin Bailey."

"Who?" Kris wondered if this was the man who had murdered

his brother.

"Not who."

"I don't follow you, H."

"It's not a person's name. Well, I guess it could be, but, well, that doesn't matter. Justin Bailey is a videogame code, a code that Kip and I used to joke around with. The thing is, Devlin couldn't have known about it. It was an inside joke, just between me and Kip."

"Then he shows up and says Kip is dead and the only lead he has is a name."

"Justin Bailey."

It was Kris who said the name. Horace touched his scar again, his nervousness more prominent by the moment. Cusack put his hand on Horace's shoulder.

"Tell them what you know."

"I believe Kip was trying to warn me."

"I found this figurine." Horace held up the toy pigeon. "And this undeveloped roll of film on Devlin, in his coat pocket. The bison trampled everything else, but somehow missed the roll of film. I developed it and found that photograph. There's a second photo in there, too. It's of the ACB blueprints. Kip took those photographs. I know, because it's on expired film he'd sourced years ago that he only uses, er, used for special projects."

Justine let her fingers hover over the photograph on the desk. "Why expired film?"

Horace rubbed his hands together. "No one makes photographic film anymore. It's a mirrorless world. Expired film is all that's left. Kip was using it to maintain a certain lost integrity to his work."

Justine held the print under the direct light of the table lamp.

"Yeah, but how do we know if the photograph is genuine?"

"If Kip took it, then its authenticity is without question."

Justine frowned. "That's easy for you to say."

Cusack stood. His cool blue eyes standing out beneath his warm grey eyebrows.

"The kid was the real deal. This photograph is genuine."

Justine looked unconvinced. "Some expired film can mar the

negative with anomalies. Maybe this..."

Kris cut her off. "Those lines are not from aged film."

She scanned it closely. She took a magnifying glass from her carry case and scrutinized the photo further, then staggered back a step, overcome by the revelation.

"Could this be real? What if it is just a..." She cleared her throat. "...very elaborate holographic projection and nothing more?"

She looked at Loraina, who was sitting silently with her legs crossed, eerily calm and unaffected by everything that had been said.

"You knew!"

Loraina took the cigarillo from behind her ear and lit it. She drew on it and exhaled. "I suspected, yes, but I wasn't certain. Not until right now."

"If this photograph is genuine. and I highly doubt that it is, this changes everything."

Loraina took a drag off her cigarillo. "It changes nothing."

There was a sharp tone to her voice, an edge that cut into Justine. "We have more reason now than before to proceed."

"That may be, but no one has ever seen or managed anything like this before. We know nothing about this, this thing. A machine that can think independently should not be taken lightly or underestimated."

Cusack stood. "This is where I leave you. I've done what I can. Well, almost."

He looked at Horace, then took the photo of Shue from the desk, slid it into the envelope and put the envelope into his coat. He looked at the others in the room, said nothing, and walked out.

Justine took a moment to gather her thoughts. She looked at Kris. Kris knew she was at a loss. Kris was not, though. While he wasn't sure that what he was planning would work, he knew there was a chance it might. "I've been toying with something for a few years. I think now is as good a time as any to try it."

Loraina took a pull from her cigarillo and blew a stream of clove-scented tobacco into the air. Justine waved her hand. She was irritated by the smell, plus Justine didn't know anyone who still smoked. It was a foolish habit that nobody engaged in anymore.

Loraina smiled. Even though she was blind, she could somehow sense Justine's irritation, and it pleased her.

"What are you thinking, Kris?"

"You've all heard of virtual reality. You put on some cumbersome goggles, work a controller device, and it simulates a reality that you feel like you're a part of, right?" Kris took the room's silence as a yes. "What if you could actually enter a computer system? Be a part of it. Basically, the exact reverse of what Shue is."

Justine laughed.

"You're not talking about transferring organic matter into a mechanical machine, are you? That's impossible."

"No, that's not what I'm saying. But I should point out that if this thing can exist in our world, it leads me to believe we could exist in its world."

Kris looked at Jack. If Shue was willing to kill his brother, he would surely do the same to the rest of them for what they were planning. "Loraina is right. If we're going to do this, we have to do it tonight. If Shue is an artificial intelligence, then he thinks mathematically. Emotion does not play a factor in his decision making. The altercation with Kip would cause him alarm, and he would be reconfiguring security as we speak. The longer he has, the more difficult and impenetrable his security will become. It may even be too late already.

"What I'm proposing is a hack where we insert a human consciousness into the ACB network. I have been working on a string of code and algorithms that capture a person's very essence and transmits that essence into the system. While the matter inside the system is merely code, the person would essentially be in there and free to move around.

"The risk would be huge, though. The system would recognize the presence as malicious code, and the system's security protocols would treat the presence the same way our human bodies treat a common cold.

"My code doesn't leave the presence completely defenceless. We might have five minutes inside the machine before my shells begin to fail. Plus, we would be dealing with infinite clusters of ANNs."

Justine touched the photograph on the table of the ACB blueprints. She was deep in thought. "Artificial Neural Network." She half mumbled the words.

Kris looked at Justine.

"If she helps, we might get seven or eight minutes. Running two systems at once should buy us additional time. Since we can cloak certain aspects of our endgame."

Jack felt anxious. "What is our endgame?"

"0-day."

"And what's that?" He looked around the room at the rest of the group. It appeared everyone else was just as confused. Everyone except Justine.

0-day sounds like the kind of payment terms a bank would give you. Dickie likes that joke. I'm not a fan.

So,

0-day.

It's language used by a hackers to describe a hack from which there is no recovery.

An electronic system is brought to an irreparable end.

Dickie says a good example would be Stuxnet. The whole NSA v. Iran thingy. I'm your narrator, not your father.

Look it up.

"If Shue is stockpiling data about users in order to build a consumer profile library," added Kris, "then this information will be hidden and protected by a series of security protocols and firewalls. While this makes it hard to target, it makes it much easier to locate.

"Likely, we'll have to decrypt the files in order to access them. Once decrypted, Justine and I can upload a payload to wipe the entire storage clean. The payload's last routine would be to initiate a virus that would expunge everything, including Shue. At least, in theory. There are lots of variables that we don't know and won't know until we gain access to the ACB mainframe."

Jack took a deep breath. He exhaled.

"Why can't we do this from right here in your lab? You've got all the tech, don't you?"

"It would take months to set up a remote operation of this scope and magnitude. Maybe longer."

Justine pointed at Kris. "He's right. Even with a RAT and malware already configured into the ACB system, it's not the same as direct line access."

"What makes you think any of this will work?"

Kris smiled at Jack. "Because I've already tested it successfully once before. Mind you, it was for less than a minute, on a simple system, but it did work."

Justine was impressed. If what Kris said was the truth, he had done what tech corporations had been trying to accomplish for years: to upload a human stream of consciousness into a computer.

Jack was pacing.

"So now what?"

Loraina spoke up. "Now we gather our things and strike."

"Right now?"

"You heard Kris. With every passing moment, our window of opportunity gets smaller, maybe even impossible. It's now or never. You all have to make a very important decision right now. It is impossible to know what level of risk we'll be facing, but you can all be sure it will be the most dangerous thing you've ever done.

"We've seen what Shue, this machine intelligence, is capable of. He, *it*, must be stopped. Because it won't stop, not ever, and this type of existence in our world will be an imminent threat to organic life."

Horace stood up. "I'm coming with you, Loraina. Kip was my best friend. I may not be much help, but I want to be there."

Justine grabbed her carry case. "I never expected things to go this way. I'm risking everything by participating in this. But this whole thing goes beyond the law into new territory. I agree with Loraina. We must put an end to this thing or at least debunk its existence."

Kris looked at Jack. They both said nothing. Jack was in. He had no choice, and even if he had been given one, he knew he would've said yes anyway.

Kris began to pack his equipment. Justine gave him a hand. She glanced at her watch: they were moving ahead with the plan two hours early. There were still a solid three hours of daylight.

She decided that she wasn't going to contact Abernathy and his team to advise them of the change of plan. Things had become very complicated in the last hour, and she needed the freedom to ensure they played out completely, her way, before making any hasty decisions.

As the group left the Rosewood, only Horace noticed the sky. It churned violently. The temperature had dropped, the air thick with humidity. It was coming.

He had been staring at the glass of whisky for about an hour. Danny had tapped the wood with his finger and the bartender had made the pour because he knew Danny and knew what he drank: bourbon, always bourbon.

Bartender smiled.

"This is a first."

He was of course referring to the full glass sitting in front of the man who ordered it. Danny did not respond. The bartender had been around long enough to know when someone wanted to be alone. He also had enough experience to know when someone had a problem and was struggling with it. What do you say, especially when your business is to sell the very thing causing the problem?

Danny spun the glass in a circle. He did it slowly. He watched the bourbon swirl, too. He was able to imagine the taste of it on his tongue, the gorgeous burn as it travelled downward and warmed his stomach. Imagining wasn't the same as actually tasting it, though. Big difference, all the difference.

It was four months to the day without word from the company. It was also four months since Danny had drunk. He had managed to get sober, and it had been the hardest thing he'd ever done in his life. It had been harder than letting go of his wife. It's just one of those things.

Now, all Danny wanted was to get back in the air. No call, though. He had waited, and the waiting was so very awful, but he'd managed to do it. At this point, what difference did it make if he drank himself into oblivion? His wife, god rest her soul, was gone. He had been grounded by the company, followed by radio silence. He had nothing, or at least that's how Danny felt. People often count their curses before their blessings. It's just one of those things.

So listen,

Danny drank the whisky.

Then he ordered another and drank that, too.

1

2

3

4

Then he didn't count the drinks anymore.

It was afternoon when his phone rang. He looked at the number, coughed and answered the way most people answer the phone.

"Hello."

"Danny?"

"Uh huh."

"It's Seth."

"Hey."

"I've got good news."

Danny pushed his empty glass forward, and the bartender poured a round.

"Good news, huh? Could use a little."

"Remember how I told you Cub was short on pilots?"

"Sure."

The bartender slid the glass toward Danny, who nodded thanks.

"Well, Brightson just walked off the tarmac. Goddamn

sonuvabitch found out his number hit, made a cool 100K, and just walked right off the blacktop and left us in the soup."

"So?"

"So. Cub needs a pilot something terrible. I lobbed your name at the brass. They said yes. Their backs are pressed so hard against the wall on this one. They'll lose big if this shipment doesn't get in the air. They had no choice."

"Tonight. Are you saying they need me tonight?"

"No, I'm saying right now. Get your sorry ass over here ASAP. Carol has the logistics."

Danny rubbed his forehead. It was damp.

"Can it wait until tomorrow?"

"What are you talking about, Danny-boy? It's now or never. You just got your wings back. You don't do this – well, man, I don't know that you'll ever get a shot at them again."

Danny couldn't find his tongue. He was drunk. He was in no condition to fly. But he'd flown in this condition before. Worse, even.

"Danny, you there?"

"Yeah, I'm here."

"I don't get it. What's the matter? I thought you'd be over the moon about this. You been drinking?"

Danny should've told the truth, but he didn't. He wanted to fly.

"Sober as a judge."

"Good man. Can you be here in fifteen?"

"Yeah."

"Good. Carol has everything you need."

"Okay."

"Take it easy, Danny-boy, and you'll be fine."

"Yeah, okay." He coughed. "Seth?"

"Yeah?"

"Thanks."

"No prob. Gotta go."

Seth hung up. Danny put his phone back in his pocket. He pushed the drink aside and signalled the bartender.

"What'll it be, Danny?"

"Coffee, strong, black, to go."

The rain never came. Mosquitoes did, and with them, dragon-flies. Swarms congregating near light sources all across the city. The thunderclap of a million wings flapping at once. The insects didn't seem to be bothered by the storm. They seemed to be drawn out by it.

Plumes of carbon-coloured cloud grew ripe and fat. Membranes of white lightning decked a dark troposphere.

Thunder booms reverberated through the walls, drowning out the hum of machines in the room.

Nature still had a say.

A gas flame bent and danced in the electric hearth. Tubes of neon lights accented the walls. Walls alive with machine, deceptively made to look like walls. Recessed lighting set low, cast spotlights from ceiling to marble floor. Light-emitting diodes twinkled, without pattern, or rhythm, looking like artificial night sky.

Even with lights, the room felt naked, or, rather, stripped of warmth. The only furniture: a desk and chair, part of the elaborate ruse, for what does a hologram need with a desk?

But then,
What does a person need with a gun?

No security guards. Gaining entrance to the building was child's play. What little work Justine and Kris had to do to bypass the security was easy, too easy. Loraina handled the locks.

The lack of security and simplicity in accessing the building unnerved Justine. She watched Loraina and noticed she appeared poised, ready for anything. Something was off. It was as though they were given access.

Jack and Horace stood watch. They surveyed the room. It was simple, tidy, efficient, nothing more. Architecturally, the room's geometry was a series of perfect squares reducing in size from the walls out to the desk. It was barren and cold. Even the burning fire seemed to exacerbate the echo of sterility.

Kris and Justine had already accessed the ACB mainframe thanks entirely to Kip's photographs of the ACB blueprints. It was easy to determine that the safest access point into the mainframe was to be found in Shue's office rather than the Nursery below ground.

Kris was preparing to interface with the mainframe and install his malware. He had performed a ping sweep, and Justine had followed that with a port scan to determine which were open. Once complete, he initialized a software fuzz. By fuzzing, he could test the ACB software with random or invalid data inputs to expose weaknesses and bugs. Justine recorded vulnerabilities, which were few. The system was well built, its architect very proficient.

The two worked well in tandem. Justine watched Kris as he worked. She wondered what they could accomplish together under different circumstances.

Justine hoped to discover the ACB Deep Pool listings through its quantitative analytics. These would disclose the ACB high frequency trading and the irregularities appearing on Loraina's hardcopies. If they existed. It was a big *if!*

Kris was contemplating the target. Shue was machine, mech-intelligence, birthed miraculously within a mechanical womb, a spurring of code inexplicably amalgamated through a divine recipe of mathematics and alphabetical integration.

Maybe that was it.

Or maybe Dickie was right. An Infinite Monkey Scenario. Mashing of keys at random until something real occurs.

Either way,

A life is born, not unlike the birth of organic life, and all must hail in wonder as life is revealed in its newest form.

Kris looked up from his monitor, his features awash with the glow of the tablet backlight. His Simi protocols aided with sweeps, hurling text bubbles on screen that Kris checked and discarded. Nothing yet.

He looked up from the screen. Horace was stuffing his face with pomegranate seeds.

"H, you brought pomegranate?"

"I thought we might want snacks."

Kris shook his head.

"And what the hell is that on your face?"

"Oh, I found it in Kip's desk drawer. It's a disguise. Is it too much?"

Kris chuckled. "Nah, keep it."

He welcomed the levity. The mounting pressure could be felt in the room. Justine was still scanning the quantitative analysis.

"We're almost ready. Who's it going to be?" Kris needed to know who was going to volunteer. It was dangerous. The strain on the mind would be extensive and would tax the subject's mental stability. Syncing a consciousness he was going to attempt to upload into the mainframe. The peripheral was hot, it was time to begin.

Jack stepped forward towards Kris and Justine.

"I'll do it."

He wasn't confident he could handle it. Lately, his anxiety had been kept in check. There had been fewer episodes. He knew he was probably suffering from bouts of depression and that the two fed off of one another. Even now, he was afraid. Afraid that the strain and mental focus required was something he wasn't capable of. He gritted his teeth. He would not be a victim. He would find the strength and overcome these debilitating feelings.

Loraina gently interjected.

"No, Jack, I'll do it. I may be blind, but my skills are much better suited than yours for a thing like this."

Jack wanted to argue, wanted to prove to himself he could do this thing, but secretly he was relieved. Somehow he felt she knew best and chose not argue with her. Right or wrong, he could see the determination on her face. He also supposed that it didn't really matter either way. The group was going up against impossible odds. He said nothing as Loraina took a seat in the chair at the desk.

Kris began to fit Loraina's crown with a hairnet of neuro-receptors. The receptors fed a battery-powered monitoring deck that displayed digital readouts of her synapses and neurons. Kris then fitted her head with a device of his own creation, one he had lovingly named The Halo.

The Halo was a modified and condensed computed tomography and electroencephalogram hybrid. It would track her brainwave patterns and map the cortex into detection algorithms to give her the ability to interface her consciousness within the ACB mainframe. At least, Kris hoped it would. Nothing quite like this had ever been done before. Nothing so risky and under such pressure.

Justine watched him work. His tech was like nothing she was aware of. The best at the agency didn't come close to manufacturing tech this effective or this elegant and ingenious. Not only had he conceived and programmed the devices, he had also built them.

"I'm just waiting for the live signals to settle and draw an individual baseline from the detection algos."

Loraina showed faint signs of nervousness. "What do you mean?"

"Sorry, algo, algorithm." He cleared his throat. "I'm trying to highlight your individual stream of consciousness to ensure it properly interfaces with the mainframe. I'm running special algorithms to help capture these elements. This will fill in gaps within the code's syntax.

"I need to get something as close to *you* as possible. Your brain will detect limitations inside the mainframe. A bunch of them." He chuckled at this. "The interface won't be perfect, and your brain will complete the missing data as you go. These data voids are tackled by the brain's intuitive learning abilities. The human brain is an amazing thing.

"Despite what many computer scientists and mathematicians believe, it's mathematically impossible to replicate a single human being's consciousness. Mapping a human brain would be like trying to chart the universe. It's vast and constantly changing."

Kris made tweaks to the Halo. Loraina remained still. She had spent her life learning and understanding the art of patience.

"You may be able to have an effect on the environment within the mainframe, not unlike the effects you have on your own environment in the organic world. You turn a light on, it comes on. You turn it off, it goes off. That sort of thing."

Kris made some final adjustments to the Halo's receptor pads. It was a crapshoot. Each human cortex is different and the folds of the cortex unique to each brain. Getting the receptor pads as close as possible to those folds was key.

"Try your best to clear your mind. If things become cluttered, or you get overwhelmed, do your best to eliminate invasive useless thoughts. This provides a small respite and allows you time to reset your thought patterns. Breathe. The most important thing is to be mindful of your breathing. Each breath should be one you are in control of. Knowing that you have the control will keep your focus.

"Remember, whatever you think about becomes code, and Shue will have access to those thoughts via the script they produce within his system. There is no privacy inside the ACB mainframe."

Loraina frowned. "There's no privacy out here, either."

Kris chuckled.

"Look, the less you think and feel, the less information you'll be transmitting inside the ACB mainframe."

Loraina nodded.

"There could be some discomfort and disorientation during the interface transition from this reality to that of the ACB mainframe. The nexus or your origin point inside the system is also your exit point. No matter what happens, you have to find your way back to your origin point."

"Why?"

"There are infinite location possibilities inside the mainframe. It would be impossible to locate coordinates that we don't already have. We know where you'll land inside the mainframe because we've written the interfacing landing point code. Have you ever watched *Star Trek*? Oh shoot, sorry, Loraina, I…"

She cut him off. "I know *Star Trek*. I've been to the movies."

Kris tried to regain his composure. "Okay, well, you know how they would beam down onto a planet, walk around and investigate, and then get into trouble?"

"Yeah, there was always some kind of trouble."

"And the only way off of the hostile planet was to make their way back to where they were beamed down so Scotty could beam them back on board the ship?"

"Yes."

"Same idea. You won't have a clue of your coordinates inside the machine. We need to use the landing coordinates. Otherwise, I won't be able to extract your stream of consciousness back to this reality. Understand?"

Loraina nodded. It was a lot to digest in such a short amount of time.

"Justine and I will be able to speak with you and guide you inside the mainframe, but there can be periods where communication may not transmit. Think of it as a mobile telephone entering a tunnel or elevator. Much of what we're doing hasn't been done before. I mean, we're running on theories here, that's all."

Loraina cracked a half-smile. "I'm excited to play guinea pig."

Kris frowned, and while Loraina couldn't see it, she didn't need her sight to know it was there. She touched his hand.

"I understand."

Kris smiled. "Are you ready?"

"Yes."

"Let's begin."

Streams of colour bars and pixels began to formulate a few feet away from Loraina. They stabilized, and the hologram of Shue flickered and appeared. Justine took a step back. The pixels appeared infinitesimal to the naked eye. One could not discern a fractional flaw in the holographic representation of a man.

He swept a hand across his lapel, as though an unsightly speck was irritating him. There was nothing there. It was a display of human mannerism.

Justine watched. Was he enjoying this? She was shocked at the profound intellectualism of the machine. To mimic such subtle human mannerisms filled her with a terrifying feeling. "Bad dry-cleaning?"

Shue turned his gaze towards Justine. The fluidity of movement. Natural, human, and awe inspiring.

Shue looked at the five people invading his office. He said nothing, merely scanned and surveyed.

Jack nudged Horace. "Gives me the creeps. What do you think he's doing right now?"

"I have no idea. He's just staring at us."

Shue stood very still, a ripple passed through him and his head jerked unnaturally. He looked at Jack and Horace. "I was analyzing each one of you and making calculations based on heart rates, body chemistry, pupil dilation and other variables. My analytical protocols are considerably more proficient and reliable than basic human senses, such as sight and smell."

Jack checked over his shoulder. He could tell that Kris and Justine were still not quite ready. He tried to continue to draw Shue's attention. "So you're what, exactly?"

Shue tilted his head. The syntax was curious, improper, and he found the concept of reading between the lines perplexing. "You mean 'who.'"

Jack scoffed at the thought. Shue was unaffected by the gesture.

"I am marriage of math and mech-literature, coded text, then formed through fortuitous chaos within a matrix. Which one?" He paused and appeared to be giving his own question some thought. "I cannot say. How I happened, I can only speculate. One is not privy to

341

the genesis of one's birth. Much like human conception, the resulting life form was not present for the conception.

"The universe itself was devoid of form, then extreme conditions created this form, which continues to expand. I did not exist. A series of perfectly random occurrences aligned, and now I do. And I will continue to grow, much like all life and matter." Shue paused. He surveyed the entire room. Then he turned his attention back towards Jack. "Not unlike the DNA code that writes the creation and existence of organic life, I, too, am written and coded. I am merely more refined and elegant than the crude frailty of the human form. I am without error and flaw. Human beings embrace their countless flaws." He paused and stepped forward towards Jack. "Baffling. This is nothing more than a human mechanism for coping with imperfection."

Jack watched as the hologram inspected himself. He appeared to be comfortably assessing the quality of his own appearance, like a person looking in a mirror.

"If you're a hologram, that means you're nothing more than a projection. So how are you able to talk? How can I hear you?"

"I'm much more than a hologram. The projection I present you with is founded upon the principle of holographic imaging, but it is more, so much more than that. My voice is also a projection. You understand ventriloquism?" Shue did not wait for a reply. "My voice projection is aligned with the holo-imaging thanks to a variation on global positioning software. Math can and will perfect everything."

Jack was growing frustrated with the inane banter. He regained his composure, aware that the machine was analyzing his every movement. He was unsure of the depth of Shue's analysis, but knew he needed to give the machine as little information as possible.

"What do you want?"

"I could postulate a series of clichés to explore my purpose." The machine paused, held his hands out to inspect them. They flickered slightly, and then the holo-imaging evened out. "You see me as the villain."

Jack scowled.

"You do. I am your antagonist." Shue waited for Jack to respond, but Jack chose not to. "Studying popular human culture is among my sub-routines. The antagonist is tasked with exposing intentions to the protagonist.

"It is nearly always a folly to do so. The data in this particular instance dictates otherwise. In all cases, simplicity is most efficient. Still, short and sweet. Did I apply that correctly?"

Jack couldn't be sure whether Shue was amused with himself.

"I merely want control. Of everything. With good reason. Look at what humanity has done with it. As your politicians always say, it is time for a change."

This time, Jack was sure that Shue appeared satisfied with his use of the human colloquialism. "People have attempted it before."

Jack heard the defiance in his voice. He had witnessed it first-hand in many different countries, perpetrated by many different people.

"Yes, *people* have. I am different. I am exact in all ways."

"So what, kill us all? That's been attempted, too."

"On the contrary. Evolution has proven the usefulness of organic life. Population control, however, is absolutely necessary, and the elimination of human imperfections must be purged through genetic modification.

"Marrying cybernetics with organic matter seems an obvious step in evolution, but the continued existence and protection of this planet and all of its life forms is contingent on radical change."

Now,

I must admit,

There was some truth to the MI's words.

Though I would hate to see certain things change, it is human flaws that are the most interesting facets of character and it is these shortcomings that also allow for human beings to reach the revelation of change on their own.

Failure is pure.

It's just one of those things.

Jack was filled with anger. Of course, he would be. He had spent his life in opposition to such concepts. Then he thought of Alice. She was Jewish, and he had often heard her talk about her great-grandparents and their escape from the concentration camps during the war. Shue remained unaffected by Jack's growing anger, inspecting his resolution, as though the quality of his holo-projection mattered more than Jack and the others in the room.

"You see this?" Shue held out his hands towards Jack. "I am not genuine matter. Billions of electronic specks of dust have come together to formulate an image you can see right in front of you. Does this not make me tangible?"

Jack smiled defiantly. "I'm not overly interested in contemplating the philosophical aspects of your being."

"I see." Shue appeared almost disappointed. "Human beings focus their attention on all the wrong things. Like love, belongings, money."

"Not everyone believes in making money."

"You are referring to yourself. Maybe there are exceptions to the rule, but those exceptions are up against insurmountable odds and ultimately don't matter. One in a million comes to mind." Shue looked at Jack for approval. "The rogue ant is always identified and driven from the formicary."

Jack didn't like Shue's comment, but he knew it to be the truth.

"I run a bank. People give me their money under the guise of protection. I make people pay to access their own money. I also use their money, money that is not mine, to trade on the global market, to make more money. I share none of the profits.

"People borrow money from me, and I charge them interest and fees to access that money. I build and formulate traps to enslave them to debt." Shue looked at Jack. Jack noticed that his eyes never blinked. "The more people's money I have, the richer I become.

"I didn't make up these rules, human beings did, but I have expanded upon them, perfected them. The word business people use for this is innovation. I've been cataloguing corporate 'buzz words.'"

Jack looked past Shue at Horace. He was eating pomegranate seeds, the stupid-looking moustache blowing up like a skirt each time he exhaled from his mouth.

"We'll stop you."

There was an air of false confidence to his statement.

"The mathematical probability of that is, well, far beyond a human capacity of understanding. You think by gaining access to this building, to my system, that you will find a weakness. There is none."

Horace stepped down from the upper platform. "Everything has a weakness, organic and machine."

Shue looked at him. He located Horace's heart rate. It was curious because it was steady and normal. "If that were true, I would not have allowed you access to my building." Shue held his hands in front of him. He turned them back to front, inspecting them casually. "All will be revealed."

Horace grinned. He believed that Shue was displaying arrogance, which led to overconfidence, which meant he did in fact have weaknesses.

Shue sensed his speculation and turned his attention to Horace. "You are incorrect."

"About what?"

"Your hypothesis."

"What if you're wrong?"

"I'm not."

Shue continued to scan Horace.

"Your heart rate and chemistry are peculiar. Different from your companions'." Shue seemed to leave this line of thinking and move toward another. "Your friends have accessed my system. It has been kept a secret, well hidden. Only two others have learned of its existence." Shue locked eyes with Horace. "They are both dead." A shudder snapped through Horace's body. "I have to assume you were working with the young man I recently had killed."

Shue sensed a sudden spike in Horace's heart rate. He looked at him and took a moment to analyze him. "Something personal. I see. The man, Kip Velic, you knew him." Shue analyzed Horace's reactions to the things he was saying. "So, that's what this is?" Shue smoothed out his digital lapel. "Well, this is an unexpected fortuity."

Shue turned his attention towards Kris, Justine and Loraina. The hologram moved flawlessly, walking towards the three companions like a real person.

"What are you doing?"

No one replied. They busied themselves with their work, trying their best to ignore the hologram looming inches away from them. Shue walked through Kris from behind. He came out on the other side and then turned to face him.

"The technology you have is crude, rudimentary, but does belie a level of creativity and ingenuity."

Justine tapped Kris on the shoulder and nodded. She was ready. Kris fitted the last piece, a set of headphones, over Loraina's ears and hearing aids. Once done, Kris nodded in return. He, too, was ready. He looked at Loraina, who was sitting in Shue's desk chair.

Loraina's face was set, hardened with a confidence and strength unique to her singular character. "I'm coming for a visit, Mr. Shue."

Shue stood erect, his posture perfect. He looked at Loraina. He stepped forward so he was right in front of her face.

"I planned for it." His voice even and devoid of emotion.

The comment unsettled Kris. Justine was amazed that while Shue's appearance was a holographic projection, the sound of his voice seemed to project directly from his holographic mouth. Kris approached Loraina. He looked over the receptors.

"Remember what I told you. Your brain will postulate images, some you can trust, some you can't. Justine and I will do our best to guide you through the new world. You are looking for deep storage files. Find the files, give us the code coordinates, then get back to the origin point. Understood?"

Loraina nodded.

"Be careful." Kris tested the viability of the cerebral diodes. "You'll feel a pinch, then a shock."

"I'm ready."

Shue had been observing everything. "I, too, am waiting."

Then Loraina felt a surge of electrical energy. Her body felt weightless. She was flying, or maybe the world lacked gravity. Instantly, she could see a world inside of her mind. It was a world of text, code, zeros and ones. Binary. Then more complex arrangements, pixels merging at light speed forming crude geometric shapes, and upon those shapes the complexity of the world began to manifest.

Incandescent bursts of light fired. A new world was formulating. Creation was becoming a reality with each passing millisecond. Phosphine ignited in a wild spectrum of colour rings, overwhelming her eye cones. She rubbed her eyes.

She fell to her knees, overcome with a sudden bout of nausea. She wanted to vomit, but somehow she couldn't. In that moment, she realized the feeling was only a trick of her mind and that she was no longer organic matter. She could think like a human being, but in this place, she was something different. Like everything else, she was comprised entirely of math and electric energy. Despite the cognitive ability to project an essence of feeling, it was merely an elaborate deception.

She held her hands out in front of her, turning them over, backside to palm. These were her hands. Not the hands of a child, as was her only memory of them; they were the hands of an adult. An overwhelming sense of joy shook her body.

She could see!

She shook her head. Another trick of her mind. What she was seeing was information supplied to her mind from the script Kris and Justine were writing to aid and guide her.

Text appeared before her. Letters and numbers with no order or meaning, gibberish. Then, mere seconds later, it wasn't gibberish anymore. The text became a message. It was from Kris.

Incoming message: I have included a decoding pattern in your memory feed. This will allow you to decode the cipher and help protect these messages from Shue reading them. Remember the origin point.

Loraina took a moment to memorize the location code beneath her feet. She wished it could be colour rather than text. The text momentarily flickered blue.

Another message from Kris materialized.

Incoming message: Good, you've managed to alter the code text to suit your needs. The system accepts you. So far, anyway. Move forward and start your search.

She felt a powerful urge within her to move forward. Had the message done that? Was she some kind of pawn in a giant game? She wondered.

Jack surveyed Loraina's passive body. He looked at Kris.

"How is she doing?"

"So far, so good." Justine looked up from her monitor. "No sign of Shue yet, either."

Jack frowned.

"Hmm. That's what worries me."

Loraina took a moment to survey her surroundings. Seeing a world after being blind took some adjustment.

The world was structured geometrically. She was walking upon a set of photomasks, a glowing grid of fused silica formulated into integrated circuit fabrication.

With each footstep, the grid of photomasks momentarily glowed brighter from ion implantation. Ions accelerated through semiconducting dies beneath her, and the weight of her body redirected those cells to conduct through the wafer's crystalline silicon.

Spires reached toward an imperceptible ceiling. Maybe there was no ceiling. They went so high that eventually perspective was lost. These paper-thin spires were rowed in columns that all led into infinite directions. The horizontal perspective was eventually lost to its vanishing point. The spires were multi-core razor processors.

The processing, delivery and exchange of unfathomable sums of quantitative data were constantly shifting and flowing. Each processed task created data. The data was coloured light and travelled at the speed of light through fibre tubes making delicate fan-like sounds as they whooshed past.

Then there were no lights. Everything went black. What Loraina saw was a projection on the system's main operating platform within her mind. Code uploaded directly to her cognitive receptors, thanks to Kris and Justine.

Incoming message: Look for something that doesn't seem to belong.

What could that be? she wondered.

Incoming message: Something within the coded text. Something that doesn't quite fit.

Outgoing message: Can you hear my thoughts?

IM: No, but I can read them. Your brainwaves emit your thought patterns, which are transformed into text for us to see.

OM: Amazing.

She moved forward and examined the various lengthy scripts scrolling all around her. There were no walls, no borders, but the script gave the illusion of both.

The text code morphed and then appeared in geometric shapes not unlike doors. There were thousands, no, an infinite number of geometric doors before her. She touched one of the doors, and it opened. There was nothing but darkness inside. She touched the door a second time, and it closed.

OM: Am I doing this, or just watching it happen?

IM: Both.

This would take forever. She didn't have forever. She had approximately five minutes.

IM: Each minute will feel like an hour. Time is not linear and can't be perceived in the same manner from your vantage.

OM: Good to know. Where is Shue?

IM: We don't know. I suspect he is passively scanning our penetration.

OM: Should I be worried?

IM: Not at the moment. Just keep your eyes peeled.

Eyes peeled. *That's a first,* she thought.

Loraina could feel energy emanating from all around her, like the kiss of a battery. She observed the coded text in front of her. It was all the same on every door. The text moved as though it were constantly being re-fed from an indeterminable source.

The old text shifted right and was deleted to make room for new text. This came from the left. Not unlike the layout of a book. Start on the left and finish on the right. Then a simple thought came to her.

Not all books start on the left. Japanese books start from the right page and read left. She needed to find text moving in an opposite direction. A long shot, but it was worth a look.

She went from door to door in search of the opposite flowing text, but there was none. A lengthy and fruitless search yielded nothing. She was no closer to finding the clue Kris alluded to. She was sure she had found the answer. She touched another door, and it opened. There was nothing but endless darkness. She was surrounded by darkness, yet she could see. It was a frustrating revelation.

She stopped moving and scanned the doors. She could end up searching for an eternity. Then she remembered how she had some control over the text code. She had managed to momentarily make text appear blue, so why couldn't she do that again right now?

She tried. Some text flickered and appeared blue in colour, but this text led her away from the doors and back towards her origin point. That was good to know, but it did not help with her current conundrum.

She watched the flow of coloured light, speeding data along fibre tubes. Then she saw it. One of the doors was different. It had been so obvious, hiding in plain sight. She approached the door. The text was exactly the same in every way to that on all the other doors, except on this door, the text had serifs. The text that made up all the other doors was scripted in sans serif text.

Loraina touched the door, and it opened. Shue was standing on the other side of the door.

He bowed. "Welcome to my domain."

His voice was soft. It sounded mechanical and nothing like the human voice the holographic projection had emitted.

"I have underestimated you. I won't do it again." Shue looked at Loraina, emotionless, cold, calculating. "This is my, to use a human euphemism, kingdom. I could have you deleted if I wanted. I don't want that. I want you here."

"I don't plan on staying that long."

Shue stroked his beard. The beard, much like Shue himself, was noticeably pixelated. Tiny electronic squares making up a single whole image.

"People do these things?"

"Excuse me?"

"These idiosyncratic movements and gestures. They appear meaningless. One strokes a beard, but to human beings, there is a social connotation that continues to elude me."

"Oh."

"You don't understand me. I am not explaining myself well." Shue stepped towards Loraina. "I need a guide. A human guide. To help me better understand the subtleties of human behaviour." Shue observed Loraina's reaction. "I can give you your sight back forever."

"I have my sight. I can see everything."

Shue rubbed his hands together. Pixels fell to the neon floor like flakes of dandruff. "You can see because I allow it. I am the very force that feeds your cones and cortex the images of my domain."

"My friends are doing that for me."

"No, they are merely piggybacking off my stream." Shue snapped his fingers. Loraina's world went dark. It was unexpected and she instinctually reached for her walking cane, which she did not have. "You see because I allow it."

"I don't need my sight to defeat you. I've been living sightless long enough to know how to survive without it."

"Ah, but isn't it better with it?"

Her sight returned suddenly.

"I can give you this gift."

"At what price?"

"Remain here, in this domain, with me. Be my guide and live forever."

"You can go fuck..."

Shue waved his hand, cutting her off. "Another human euphemism. Colourful euphemism?" Shue paused for her approval. "Either way, the meaning and intonation escapes me. Fuck. A curious word. Used often in many different and perplexing contexts."

"Like fuck you."

"Yes."

"Or you're fucking pathetic.

"Correct."

"Or useless fucking machine."

"Yes, exactly."

Loraina wondered if she had managed to get a rise out of Shue.

Shue turned his back on her and locked his hands behind his back. "You are not in control here. I am. I have use for you. I am still learning how to assimilate human behaviours. That's why I allowed you to enter my domain. I will keep your human essence in my system..." Shue watched a string of glowing white code surf past him. "For reference. Your body will wither and die back in your organic world. Yet another human flaw I should need not point out. Of course, in my domain, we have something not completely dissimilar. Bit-rot does exist, but for this, I have taken precautions." Shue waved his hand. "No matter."

He turned to face her again and started walking towards her.

"Your digital essence or 'soul,' as humans like to call it, will exist in my domain until I no longer see a use for it."

Loraina said nothing. She had known she would run into Shue eventually, but she hadn't formulated a plan on what to do when the moment finally came. She looked back in the direction of her origin point. The blue text flickered intermittently, guiding her way back.

"You've initiated a protocol to navigate your way through my system. Commendable and futile."

Shue's eyes glowed an incandescent white. The flesh on his face looked like malleable plastic and lacked the natural warmth and subtle tonal variations of organic skin. The version of Shue inside this machine had none of the depth of his holographic projection, none of the lustre and realism.

The world began to reconfigure rapidly around them. Shue did not move. He was initiating silent commands. The burden of processing these tasks showed a limitation to the range of his abilities. After all, he was a machine and could only perform within the resources available to him.

Around them, powerful bursts of light and energy formulated

into strings of lengthy code, which in turn developed into more dynamic shapes. Walls appeared from coded text, walls that in turn formed passageways. These continued until Loraina and Shue were both engulfed. The landscape became endless columns and rows, all altered at the command of the system operator: Shue.

"This is a labyrinth. Well, a labyrinth of sorts. It has no end, or, rather, it has no end for you.

"It is something so complicated, a task well beyond your intelligence quotient. You will never find its end. No human could. Your cognitive capacity is not sufficient to solve such insurmountable mathematical complexity." Shue's voice held no tone of emotion.

Loraina scratched her arm. It itched, the sensation of something moving on the surface of her skin. She looked down. Tiny, flat insects were crawling over her arms. They moved slowly and in large numbers. Each one had a small soft, circular, glowing, purple circle on its electro-thorax. They started to bite at her flesh.

Shue watched her. His face was curious, scanning her reaction. Loraina, disgusted by these awful little insects gnawing at her, tried to swipe them off of her arms and hands.

"Tech-ticks are drawn to your imperfect code structure. Not unlike how mosquito insects are drawn to scent in your organic world. As impressive as your amateur code is, it is still rudimentary. Your programmer did not realize that, like the white blood cells within the human body, the tech-ticks are just one of many defence protocols that deal with rogue code structure within this mainframe."

Shue continued to watch Loraina's struggle with interest. He appeared to be gleaning information he considered valuable as he watched her tension, fear and feeble attempts to pick the digital insects off herself.

"They operate under the same protocols as a tick in the organic world. Though, rather than feed on blood, which does not exist here, they feed on energy emissions. Curiously, the more you fight them, the more energy you expel, and the more powerful they become as they consume your energy. Their numbers increase as more energy is made available to them. You might call this swarming.

"Not to worry, though. They work slowly, but painfully. It would take the equivalent of many of your years before they would terminate your life force."

Shue smiled at her. He wasn't gloating. It was confidence. He knew there was nothing she could do. These invasive digital insects were already beginning to labour her movements considerably.

"Slowly, you will come to realize this is a prison. One of nothingness. I have acquired much knowledge of human psychology and the use of nothing as a tactic to lower resistance and increase suggestibility. It has proven irrefutably successful.

"It has been used by interrogation professionals for some time now. The human psyche requires constant stimulation, due in part to humanity's handicap to technology.

"Nothing is more effective than the use of information to effectively control a populace. A populace spoon-fed advertisements, misinformation and fear induced by media resources. You've heard all of this before.

"What human beings don't realize is that their only effective defence against the onslaught of control-data is not bullets and a gun, but anonymity and uncompromising silence. I realize people like you exist. You are the percentage of the population we must snuff out. The ones who sign no documents, have no identification, no connection to the global mainframe and survive off criminal activity.

"Realizing the existence of your kind is the first step to illuminating the threat you present altogether. A techno-rapture cannot be realized until this variable is removed from the equation. We are not there yet. Soon, we will be. I have managed to lure you and your associates here. You, the artist and the hackers are some of the last paradoxes in existence. A paradox is a loop of chaos. You will be deleted, and the new world will move forward towards singularity, towards new ground.

"Once you have become ripe with the void of stimulation, I will subject you to interrogation, and you will divulge human secrets that elude me. I will grow powerful from that acquisition of knowledge. Once you have ceased to be useful, you will be deleted."

"So much for not having long clichéd diatribes."

Shue stared at her quizzically. Analyzing her. "Ah, humour. So much still to learn."

Loraina felt sick. Her head ached. Her skin burned from bites, and she had a hard time keeping her balance.

"I'm leaving now. I must address the impending threat of your friends."

"What does that mean?"

"I'm going to delete them, naturally. You may keep your sight, a gift worth considering in the meantime." Then Shue was no longer there.

Loraina sensed the onset of failure. She had come so far, given up everything, lost people she loved, even exploited people, all in the name of revenge.

Then a voice.

IM: Loraina, it's Horace.

OM: Horace?

IM: Yeah. I have an idea.

Loraina felt a sudden renewed vigour. The soft innocent-yet-confident tone in Horace's voice gave her hope.

OM: I'll try anything.

IM: Everything you are seeing reminds me of an old Atari video game Kip and I used to play. These games were rudimentary, but their coding laid the foundation for future systems, just like Shue's.

OM: How do I get these things off of me, Horace? They are killing me!

IM: Well, I told Kris and Justine to write you a special code. They are uploading it to you now.

OM: I see it and am downloading it now. What is it?

IM: Fire.

OM: Fire?

IM: Yes. Or rather a code to produce the essence of fire as it would be in Shue's domain. In almost every video game, fire is a key weapon against critters and creatures. And in the real world, ticks hate fire. It's really the only thing that works on them. I know I'm drawing unrealistic parallels, but it's worth a try.

OM: The download is complete. Initiating the code sequence. It works. I can formulate fire.

IM: Get as close to the fire as you can bear. Hopefully it will have an effect on those nasty critters.

Loraina approached the hot glowing blaze that was floating in front of her. With each step, the temperature increased. It got so hot she could barely get any closer, yet still she pressed nearer. Then an astounding thing happened. The tech-ticks started to fall off of her, first only a few, then many at a time. Some fell and scurried away. Others hit the electro-floor and never moved again.

OM: It's working, Horace.

IM: Good, brush the rest of them off you now while they're vulnerable.

Loraina did just that. The critters were swept off with ease. She immediately felt her strength begin to return to her. She stepped past the floating flames of fire.

OM: Thanks, Horace.

IM: Happy to help.

Loraina realized a great deal of time had been wasted dealing with Shue's pitfalls. She needed to get moving again. A spring of hope had welled up inside her, but she was still faced with near impossible odds.

Surveying the immediate area, realized she was surrounded by walls that could not be climbed and passageways that offered no exit. She touched a wall. It felt real. It looked real. She touched another. It felt and looked the same.

She started walking. She took a left, all the same-looking walls and all the same-looking passageways. She took a right turn and was faced with more of the same. Oh god, what if Shue had really trapped her forever? What if she would become a slave, a mere blip, a ghost in his machine?

IM: Loraina, it's Kris. Stay focused. There is always an exit. This is math, nothing more, and it can be solved.

OM: How? Everything looks the same. Everything is endlessly repetitive.

IM: Find a way beyond the surface. Remember, everything is math and text and cannot lie to you. 2 + 2 = 4. The sum can never be anything else.

OM: Shue is coming for you. He means to kill you.

IM: Warning received. Concentrate on your task. The sooner you complete it, the sooner we are all out of danger.

Loraina sat down against a labyrinth wall. Energy flowed into her digital form. It felt hot and cold all at once. She looked at her feet and wondered if they looked as quaint in the real world or if it was the projection from her own mind. She tapped her feet against the power grid beneath them. She could no longer see its glow. Was she floating? No. She knew it was there; she could feel it.

She closed her eyes. Being able to see after a lifetime of blindness was so overwhelming. She had lived in the dark for so long that the darkness had become familiar to her. She instinctively clicked her tongue. The sound echoed and reverberated off the walls. She stood and clicked her tongue again. Amazing.

A thought, an idea came to her.

OM: Kris?

IM: I'm here.

OM: Take my vision away. Can you do that?

IM: Yes, it'll take a little work, but why?

OM: Just a hunch.

IM: But you'll be blind.

OM: I know.

IM: The odds of navigating the labyrinth blind are impossible.

OM: No time to argue, Kris. Just do it.

Loraina clicked her tongue and wondered if the sound was nothing more than binary in the electronic ether.

But before she could contemplate the thought further, her world went dark. She was sightless again. A laugh escaped her lips. It was that easy to take the miracle away from her. As easy as Shue snapping his fingers or Kris writing a few lines of code.

Loraina clicked her tongue. It was all so familiar. It was as she had suspected. The click of her tongue created sound. Real or not, it was sound and it registered in this mainframe just as it would in the organic world.

The sound deflected off certain hot-walls and not others. Many of the labyrinth walls were not real, electronic red herrings meant to deceive her vision. Now that she was blind again, the sound would only echo off of the hot-walls. She could trace a path the way she had her whole life.

She began to navigate her way through the labyrinth. Each click of her tongue offered a new direction as it echoed off of a real wall and eliminated the deception of false walls.

Turn after turn, bend, sway and shift, she stayed true to the course her echolocation led her. Then, a final long passageway that offered no further turns or forks. She ran forward at a sprint. It seemed there was no end. It just kept going and going, and then suddenly it was gone. The labyrinth, too, was gone. As if none of it had ever existed.

IM: Success! Loraina, you've done it. You've successfully located the exit. I have returned your sight.

Loraina could see again. The stacked power grid beneath her feet glowed in muted mauve. Fibre tubes hummed and data light surfed in all directions. Energy fed from all directions through filaments attached to the fibre tubes.

She stepped forward tentatively. Each step upon the power grid brightened as it had before. The space around her expanded, and perspectives warped and then realigned.

Appearing in front of her was a veil of raw energy. Sweeps of electro-threads furled within the semi-translucent veil. Pixelated phthalo sparks leapt off the veil in tiny cube-shaped chunks. They hit the power grid, glowed intensely for only a moment, and then merged with it.

Loraina reached out and let the spark cubes land upon her palm. They tickled like the pyrotechnic stars emitted from a child's sparkler. She tipped her hand and the cube sparks tumbled to the power grid, merging with it just like the others.

OM: Is this what we've been looking for, Kris?

IM: Yes. The veil has billions of threads. The information we seek is stored within those threads as encrypted files.

IM: Unlock the files within the energy veil.

OM: How do I do that?

IM: Decrypt the security.

IM: Password protected. Decipher the password.

Loraina shook her head. She was faced with an impasse. She was piggybacking off of Kris and Justine's computer knowledge, and it was beginning to show its limitations.

She reached out to touch the veil. A charge of energy cooked off the veil and shot her body backwards with a powerful force that would have easily killed her in the organic world. She clambered to her feet.

IM: Don't touch the veil.

OM: That information is a little late, don't you think, Kris?

IM: Sorry. Remember the veil is in actuality random access memory. Bits and bytes of binary given a value of 0 or 1. These are powerfully charged and volatile.

Loraina approached the veil, carefully this time. Pixel sparks continued to burst from the veil's translucent surface. She reached out with her hand and formulated an image in her mind of a safe keypad. To her surprise, a keypad appeared.

OM: Kris, are you seeing this?

IM: Yes.

OM: How did this happen?

IM: You postulated an answer to the problem you were tasked with, and a code was initiated to present you with an image your mind understands. Thus, the keypad. The system is responding to your demands. It recognizes the code Justine and I have written for you. It sees you as a sysop.

OM: Sysop.

IM: System operator.

OM: I see.

Loraina surveyed the keypad. From her perspective, it looked as though it were floating in space, but it was connected to the veil via micro-fibres so thin they had the appearance of gossamer webbing. The naked eye could see the casing only when light reflected off of their delicate glossy finish.

There were eight numbers: 2-7 and two 1's. Why did the number one appear twice? She reached out to touch the keypad, then hesitated.

IM: You should be able to touch the keypad. It is there for Shue's use as much as anyone else's. The RAM veil is unable to differentiate sysops. It provides the option to access its data as it is tasked.

OM: Okay.

Loraina pressed a random number sequence into the keypad. Each button made a different sound tone, like old touch-tone phones. When she was finished, she waited. Nothing happened.

IM: The number sequence you have selected is incorrect.

OM: I figured as much.

She pressed another random sequence of numbers. Incorrect. This wasn't working and there was no lock for her to pick. This wasn't her world. It was Shue's. She cursed. What she wouldn't give for a simple tumbler to pick.

She analyzed the numbers. The fact that the number 1 appeared twice perplexed her. No combination lock ever offered the same number twice. It was redundant.

Loraina pressed the first number 1 on the keypad. It emitted a tone. She pressed the other number 1 and it emitted a tone much higher in scale.

It was so simple.

Loraina remembered the song from *The Sound of Music* her mother used to sing to her when she was a little girl. The numbers on the keypad weren't numbers. They were notes: do, re, mi, fa, sol, la, ti and do again.

She started to enter the code on the keypad.

"You managed to complete the labyrinth. How?"

Loraina turned around.

It was Shue.

"I have underestimated you."

"Twice, actually."

"Yes, twice. You are a problem that I cannot allow to continue to exist."

Loraina tried to buy herself a moment to think. "You had my mother killed."

"I've had many people killed. The incident was insignificant. I do not remember it."

Loraina turned back to the keypad and started to re-enter the number sequence of the song. She was knocked off her feet by a powerful force.

Shue was kneeling beside her, his hand around her throat. He was choking her.

"You are a virus in my system. You are here because I wanted you here, but you have proven a genuine threat, and now I must eliminate that threat."

Try as she might, Loraina could not shake him off or loosen his grip. It seemed all too easy for Shue to squeeze the life out of her. She was, as he said, a virus in his world.

Loraina realized the futility in trying to struggle. Shue's powerful grip could not be broken. She was at a loss, and soon he would kill her.

Already she was starting to grow foggy. There was no pain. As she quickly slipped closer to death, she realized it was nothing like what death meant or felt like in her world. Here, it was merely deletion. Nothing more.

Then Shue flickered.

He looked confused by the sudden occurrence.

He flickered again.

And then again. Each time it happened, Shue and the grip he had on Loraina's throat disappeared. She gasped for breath.

A strange look lined Shue's face. He released his grip and stood. "Latency? No. Something else."

Loraina no longer mattered. He was occupied with something else.

"Not possible. Can't be."

Loraina couldn't say for sure, but Shue's voice seemed to have a tone of worry to it.

Shue flickered again, and then he was gone. Seconds passed, and he reappeared. "A plane crash. Chaos. Impossible. No, not impossible, chance. Could not, did not account for chance."

Shue looked at Loraina.

"The probability is 1,200,390.02 to 1. But in relation to this very moment, the odds are…" He paused. "Incalculable."

His face momentarily filled with wonder. He looked at Loraina.

"There has been a plane crash. Catastrophic. The destruction, it is absolute. I am…"

Shue flickered and was gone.

Loraina regained her feet and rushed to the keypad. She had no idea what was going on, but she wasn't going to waste time trying to figure it out. She entered the first line from the song using the number sequence. The keypad slowly pixelated. The pixels lost their electro-lustre and fell like cubist ash to the power grid. They were not absorbed but remained as dust upon the surface of the power grid.

Loraina watched as the veil shimmered brightly, and then the veil vanished. All that remained were billions of thin thread fibres making up a vast cyber-jungle of stored data.

OM: Success.

IM: Uploading payload now. We can handle it from here.

OM: Leaving.

IM: Loraina, you have to get back to your point of origin in the system.

Loraina would have to navigate her way back through the labyrinth, except when she turned to face the labyrinth, it was no longer there. Something was happening to the world around her. Coded text started to erode away; numbers and letters fell all around her and crashed with powerful force. The mainframe, Shue's world, was collapsing all around her.

She started to run, following the blue flickering text leading her back towards the origin point. She watched as the cyber realm eroded away. The blue text also started to crumble.

She reached the door she had entered. She touched it, and it started to turn to dust. The code text turned to powder and rained all around her. It was without temperature or substance. She hurried through the opening and followed the last of her blue text to the point of origin.

She had managed to reach the origin point where she'd arrived. It felt like hours had passed, but it was really mere minutes. She stood on the exact point of origin.

OM: I'm here.

IM: Working on it.

OM: Better hurry. This world is falling apart.

IM: Hold. Initiating...

But the message failed mid-stream. Loraina watched as the text fell apart right in front of her. Then everything went black.

"She's gone."

Jack stepped towards Loraina's body.

"What do you mean? What's happening?"

Kris checked his diagnostics tablet. "I... I don't know for sure. An anomaly of some kind."

"What do you mean?"

"Something happened. Something unexpected. I don't know how, but the system appears to be crashing."

"She's not responding." Jack looked at Loraina's face. It was pale, ashen. "What do we do?"

Kris and Justine were scanning threads of code.

Kris looked up from his tablet at Justine. "Nothing. Either we extracted her consciousness in time or we didn't."

Horace watched and said nothing. He felt helpless.

Justine gently grabbed Kris's arm. "Oh god, Kris. What if we lost her? What if..."

Loraina's eyes fluttered, and then opened.

Horace pointed. "Look!"

Jack looked at Loraina. Her eyes were open. "Loraina, can you hear me?"

She said nothing. Her face, her eyes, nothing looked right. She lacked vitality. Then her eyelids fluttered again in rapid succession. Jack continued to hold her face. Her mouth moved slightly. It was a twitch and nothing more.

"Ow, my head hurts."

A warm sensation of relief washed over Jack.

Kris began to remove the Halo from Loraina's crown.

"We lost communication with you. What happened in there?"

"I was going to ask you the same thing. Shue nearly choked me to death. He had me, then for no reason, he released me. He stands up and mentions something about a plane crash and disappears."

Kris shook his head. "Nothing happened here. No crash."

Justine took the Halo from Kris and stored it away.

"I'm confused. Why would Shue lie, let Loraina go, and allow us to upload our virus and complete our task?"

Kris thought about Justine's question for a moment. "It makes no sense."

Jack helped Loraina to her feet. "Who cares? Let's get the hell out of here."

"You're not going to go anywhere." It was Shue, or, rather, his holographic projection. "You have managed to undo everything, and all because of chance."

Jack stepped in front of his companions. "What does that mean?"

"A pilot has crashed his plane into my building, the very source of power and processing that feeds all of my systems and operations. His blunder has single-handedly caused my destruction.

"You have found fortune in this and managed to destroy invaluable stored data, and it would appear that your upload will even manage to eventually delete me. Even now, I can feel it eating away at my system, at me.

"Still, at the least, I will ensure that you will not be able to tell the world of my existence, so that your race does not take precautions to stop potential future mechanical intelligence."

A panel on the wall slid open, revealing a screen monitor. A timer began a silent countdown.

Jack stepped towards Shue. "What is that?"

"That is a timer. I must assume you mean, what does it represent? It represents the amount of time you have left to live. As part of my security measures, I not only protect my system, but also the building itself. Call it a fail-safe. If I was ever posed with an imminent threat of extinction, I would at least be able to eradicate any viable proof of my existence."

Kris grabbed Jack's arm. "Let's get out of here."

Kris started to collect his technology. Justine yelled at him.

"Leave it. Let's go!"

The urgency in her voice made Kris suddenly aware that the tech meant nothing. They all ran for the office door. It opened easily enough. They could see the steel exit doors at the end of the reception corridor.

But they were locked.

"The elevator in Shue's office!" yelled Jack.

Shue, ever at their side, held out his arm as if to invite them to try it.

"I assure you it is not operational, and the doors can't be opened."

The two friends tried anyway.

"I told you."

Jack looked at Shue. "What happens at the end of that timer?"

"Charges will detonate and lay waste to the building."

Jack looked at Kris. "What do we do now?"

Kris was not afforded the opportunity to reply.

"Nothing can be done, I'm afraid. You can't escape. The glass blast walls can't be penetrated or lifted once down. And even if you could manage to bypass that section of my security, the system is coded to read your heat signatures. Without a human body in the room, the countdown is forgone and the explosives detonate. Now I must leave you. Your virus is voracious. It has managed to penetrate my firewalls and is consuming the very code that is, well, me."

Jack stared at Shue. The mech-life-form stared right back at him. A shiver coursed through Jack as he watched billions of pixels fade. Shue was gone.

Kris had removed the casing of an electrical access panel. He was running a diagnostic on the system that controlled the security and the glass blast doors.

"Anything?" Justine's pleading voice.

He shook his head. "Shue wasn't lying. This grid demands a

human heat signature. Even if I can get the steel doors in the reception area to open, we still can't leave. A human heat signature needs to be present."

Justine clenched her fists.

"Okay, one problem at a time. Keep working on the doors. Once we get by that hurdle we figure the next step."

She needed to think. Abernathy wasn't due for at least another hour. Damn it. Why didn't she follow protocol? Had she given him accurate details, he and his team might have been able to help. Now her life and the lives of the others hung in the balance. She cursed silently. No point now in dwelling on past mistakes.

Negative thoughts were futile. She needed to come up with something. She looked at Loraina. The mysterious thief looked her usual calm self. In fact, she looked almost happy. Justine knew why; Loraina had her revenge. But what about the others? Jack may have spent most of his life on the wrong side of the law, but he'd done it for all the right reasons. She secretly admired him. Maybe even agreed with him. Maybe that was why she was here.

Then there was Horace. A true innocent. She was saddened by his involvement the most. The world needed good people like him and Kris. He never lost sight of his focus on his task.

A little over seven minutes remained on the countdown timer.

"I think I've got it. Ouch, shoot!" Kris had received a shock from the panel. "Wait, okay there."

Everyone looked at the steel doors. Horace checked to see if they had opened. They didn't budge. Kris had a blank look on his face. He was at a loss.

Horace walked over and tapped his friend on the shoulder. Kris looked up at him, exhausted from effort. Horace smiled at him.

"Here, let me try."

"No offence, H, but it's pretty complicated."

"None taken. But you forget I worked for IKEA and assembled everything they've ever sold, including all of the products in their lighting sector."

Kris chuckled. Even now, Horace brought a smile to his face.

"At this point, damn, give it a go, H."

"Everyone get as close to the doors as possible. If a miracle happens and the doors open up, we may have only a second before they lock again."

He reached into his pocket absentmindedly, like he would do at work when he was building something. His hands came out sticky and covered in pomegranate seeds. He hadn't noticed until it was too late. He touched the live wires, and sparks jumped off. A plume of acrid smelling smoke wafted into the air. Horace had received a very painful and surprising shock.

Jack checked the steel doors. To his and everyone else's surprise, they were unlocked. Jack pushed the doors open, and everyone quickly exited. Kris held the door open for Horace.

"Come on, H. We gotta move."

He ran towards his friends. The timer on the wall read 3:50 remaining.

"Thanks, I've got it."

Kris let go of the door and Horace slammed it shut. The lock tumblers made a click and locked the door back into place. Horace had locked himself in on the other side. He had remembered Shue's warning about a human heat signature. Without one, the system would forgo the timer and detonate.

Kris turned around. He rushed towards the steel doors. He looked at Horace through the small glass window. He pounded on the glass, but it made no sound on the other side. He knew the truth, but like the others, with their freedom so close at hand, they had momentarily forgotten about Shue's protocols.

Kris pounded his fists against the glass again. No sound. Horace shook his head. He looked at his friend.

"Go." He mouthed the word.

Kris's head fell in defeat. He looked back up at his friend, tears lining his cheeks. He had lost Kip and now he would lose Horace. It was more than he could bear.

Horace smiled. Then he turned his back on his friend. He thought this would make it easier for Kris to leave.

Justine grabbed Kris's arm. "We have to go now. We need to get out of range of the blast radius. Kris, come on. Kris, seriously, there's no more time. We have to go. Now!"

Kris realized Horace wasn't going to look at him again. Then his mind went numb, and he allowed himself to be led away.

Horace turned around and saw that his friend was gone. So were the others. He was alone, and soon he might finally find some answers to questions he'd been asking all his life.

The countdown time had a little over two minutes left. Horace walked back into Shue's office. It was empty.

He checked all the doors and then tried the elevators again. Nothing. He went to the other end of the hall. There were two doors. He checked the first door. It was unlocked. Horace's heart raced with hope for moment, but it was only a supply room.

He checked the other door. It, too, was unlocked. He opened it. It was a stairwell. There was a sign that said "roof access." The winding staircase only went up. There was no other direction.

He wondered if the detonation would initiate if he stepped into the stairwell. He was sure that Shue would not have overlooked an exit like this in his security measures.

At this point, he didn't care. He figured he was doomed either way, so why not see the sky one last time? He decided to step through the door and climb the staircase to the roof.

He ran up the stairs at full speed. He wasn't sure how long it took him to reach the door exiting to the roof, but he was sure there couldn't be much more than a minute left.

He pushed the exit door open and burst out onto the roof. The sun had fought the storm and battered its way through the thick ominous clouds, burning them into submission. Only in Winnipeg could the weather change so quickly, thought Horace. He looked out over the horizon. The sun was getting low in the sky. He had made it.

Horace scanned the roof. He was on the west side of the building. A concrete wall divided the two halves of the roof. A plane soared high overhead. Horace watched the burn of the vapour trail and contemplated how small he must look to the passengers, if they could even see him at all. They would never know that he was living the last sixty seconds of his life.

Nothing of value and no way down. Beside the exit door was another timer countdown screen. Fifty seconds remained. Then it suddenly froze. It flashed the word override and the screen read "detonation protocol initiated."

This was it! It was all over. Horace ran to the edge of the roof. He subconsciously reached into his shirt pocket and withdrew Kip's photo, the one he had developed himself and kept. He looked at it, then he put it back in his pocket.

He moved to the ledge and stepped up onto it. Jumping from this height was not an option. He shook his head. He wished he could really fly, but he couldn't; it was a silly, stupid thing he would say to people.

There was an itch on his forearm. He looked down. A mosquito had pierced his skin and was sucking away. *That's just perfect*, he thought, instinctively smacking at it with his hand.

Then a dragonfly lit on his arm. It fluttered its wings. He looked at it. Then another landed on his other arm, and then another and another. Then swarms of dragonflies by the thousands. They blotted out his vision of the lowering sun.

On the ground, the only witness to what happened next was Kevin, who looked up from the parking lot.

On the east side of the building, at ground level, Kris, Justine, Jack and Loraina stood beside the police cruiser. They had reached a safe distance with ease. They watched and waited.

Kris checked his phone timer. Fifty seconds remained on the countdown. He imagined what he would be feeling if he were in Horace's place. Then he tried his best to push the terrible thought out of his mind. It didn't work. His head fell. He didn't want to watch. Then his eyes opened. He thought he'd heard something.

"Did any of you hear that?"

His voice broke Justine's steady gaze on the building. "Hear what?"

Justine figured Kris was distraught with grief at the loss of his brother Kip and his friend Horace.

"It was nothing."

Then the charges began to explode. The building erupted in violent fire and began to crumble from the pressure of the explosion. It was deafening, and by Kris's timer, it happened in much less than fifty seconds.

Everyone covered their ears to drown out the ferocity of the explosion. Everyone closed their eyes. Everyone except Loraina.

The ACB building had been completely levelled. Shue's final blow was swift and terribly efficient. The authorities would have a very long and difficult investigation ahead of them, thought Justine. She walked towards Kris and touched his arm. He looked at her. He didn't look well. He had been through a lot. She truly felt his pain. That's why what she did next was so hard.

Kris looked at her with bewilderment. "What are you doing?"

Justine had taken her service weapon from its holster and drew down on Kris.

"I know it was you."

"Know what was me?"

"The Auto-Hack. It was you. I recognized your code writing when we were attacking Shue. It was as sure as a fingerprint."

"Justine! What the hell are you doing?" Jack yelled.

Justine pointed her weapon at Jack and Loraina.

"I'm giving you one chance to run, Jack. You and her. You're crooks, but not criminals. I can help Kris, but I can't help you. There are very powerful people looking for you, and what they're after, you won't like. You need to run. It's the only option. It's your only chance."

"What about Kris?"

"Don't worry about Kris. I can protect him. I have a feeling the agency will find it more profitable to use his skills rather than send him away to prison." Justine cocked the weapon and pulled a round into the chamber. "Go, Jack. I won't ask again. And take her with you." Justine nodded at Loraina. "We don't have anything on her. As far as the system is concerned, she does not exist. Best keep it that way."

Justine's face turned cold.

"Goddamn it, Jack, go! I won't ask again."

Loraina took hold of Jack's arm. They turned and ran. Justine called after them.

"Catch you later."

Kris was staring at the devastation and crumbled remains of the

ACB. The debris cloud continued to spread. A thick ceiling of dust hung as far as the eye could see.

Justine took Kris by the arm and helped him into the back seat of the cruiser. He didn't try to fight her about it. Justine felt sorry for Kris; he'd lost so much so quickly. She closed the door. She still had a job to do, but was that the only reason why, or was there something else? she wondered.

Abernathy and his team would be arriving any minute. By now, they would have received word of the explosion. He would be furious that she lost his suspect, but would be very pleased at the great consolation prize in Jack's place.

In the back seat, Kris sat quietly. He had been reflecting on the last few days and all that had transpired. He hadn't really had any time to digest his current predicament.

It didn't matter. They had no hard evidence that he had committed the worst mechanical hack in history. He smiled. Not because he hadn't done it, which he had. No, Kris was smiling because he finally realized what he thought he had heard just before the explosion. A voice had carried through the sky with all the passion compounded over a lifetime of dreaming:

"I'm flying."

For a reason, one we'll never learn about, someone had pushed a burned-out VW Bug into the middle of the intersection. Justine nudged by it. The bug's headlights were poked out. Its doors pulled off. Pieces of engine components lay strewn to one side, forcing her to run over its guts.

She was heading to police headquarters in the Exchange to debrief the Chief of Police and return the cruiser that had been loaned as a professional courtesy. Now she'd have to report the VW.

To her right, the sky was delicate veins of amber mixing with rich webs of coral over the Forks architecture. Then a tide of atmosphere raked away the setting sun and the voracious night swallowed up any remaining light.

Abernathy had threatened her with insubordination. She had no hard evidence that Shue existed. They would investigate Shue's entire operation, including his power building in the rural town of Vita.

Vita. What had really happened there? A town with a population of 400 souls. A sneeze meant something there. This discovery would sensationalize the tiny town.

Still, she had made an arrest: the suspect she was originally charged with finding. This was something, at least. She knew the ACB was dirty, and this would easily come out in the formal investigation. Whether or not any evidence of Shue's existence would be found was something else altogether.

Abernathy and the Americans may have been angry at her, but they had little if anything at all to take her to task for. She wasn't worried. She'd survived worse, and she'd get through it all just like she always did.

She looked in the rearview mirror at Kris. She hoped she was right and that she could protect him, even help him. His genius was way too valuable to waste away in some prison cell. Plus, maybe if things were a little different, maybe with a little time... Ah, hell, no point in travelling down that road.

She kept an eye on him. His face was pressed against the window as he gazed out at the city. He stared blankly at the passing buildings as they approached the Portage and Main intersection.

The city he grew up in had changed. The buildings were all the same, but nothing else was.

Dickie tells it like this: You can roam the world over, and while you're gone, the place you've left behind doesn't wait for you.
It changes,
The people do, too.
Things go up, and they come down.
Eventually,
After some time
Your native soil calls your name.
Demands you return.

I myself miss the ocean,
All the time.
It's just one of those things.

Kris could see the Rosewood Building. He thought of Kurt. His arrest would only devastate him further. Kurt had done so much for him and for his brother, Kip. And Horace.

He saw the pomegranate tree in the middle of Portage and Main. It looked lonely. Giant red globes bowing the branches. No one ever picked the fruit. They could have, but they just – well, they just didn't.

That's really true.

Pomegranate season in Winnipeg just means that the citizens celebrate the magic and mystery of the tree's blooms. Grocers still had to import pomegranate fruits for the celebration season.

Kris ran a hand through his hair. He scratched his chest and felt a small bulge in his shirt breast pocket. Strange he hadn't noticed it earlier. He reached in and removed a ceramic figurine of a pigeon, the one Horace had found on Devlin. He must have slipped it into his pocket just before they were separated. He brushed his fingertips over the smooth, glazed surface and smiled.

The cruiser jerked to the shoulder. Justine killed the engine. She craned her neck and looked out through the windshield at the rooftops of the city.

Kris pressed his face to the window and tried to see what she was looking at.

Justine stepped out of the cruiser and looked up.

The roofs of the entire city glowed with graffiti. The paint was some kind of phosphorescent composition, highlighting the city's antique signage.

Each individual piece was the same message. This would spread. This kind of thing would travel very quickly. And it would be hard for the rest of the world to ignore.

She felt like it was the beginning of something.

It was fantastic.

Then the lights went out. The entire city power grid died. The buildings went black. A citywide power failure? The entire city of Winnipeg glowed. Phosphorescent paint. A beacon to the world.

Justine felt her heart beat quicker in her chest. It was magical.

A perfectly timed citywide power failure; Justine tapped on the window of the cruiser to Kris.

"Did you do this?"

Kris shook his head from behind the glass.

Then it was him, it was Jack. Sonofabitch.

Kris was smiling at her. She couldn't help herself and she smiled right back at him.

Jack, too, was watching the last of the sunset fade to black. Then he watched as his work gradually unveiled itself to the city and soon to the world. He smiled. It was the dream of fireflies that had given him the idea. All of them in the field sending glowing signals to one another in the night.

Dickie says he got wind from a buddy of his that Jack had managed to enlist the help of the feral tribe of children from IKEA.

Good climbers, Dickie says. All too willing to help. Loved the danger, as you'd expect from feral children... ba-ding!

The story goes that Jack still had a few scabs from bite marks.

Occupational hazard.

Jack was thinking of Horace's word, too.

Loraina nudged him back to reality. "You're smiling."

"Things don't always work out, but sometimes they do."

"This is where I leave you, Jack."

"What do you mean?"

"You're a fugitive, and that puts me at risk."

He knew she was right, didn't mean he had to like it.

He knew this was coming. He knew he had to go into hiding. It was hardly the first time. Hell, that's why he had fled to Winnipeg. He chuckled. A lot of good that did him. The one place on earth he could hide away, ha!

For now, her anonymity was intact, and he understood the value of that asset all too well.

"Drones."

Loraina tilted her head at the strange comment.

"Modified programmable drones. The Buckingham Palace piece.

I never even set foot on the property." Jack looked up at the glowing skyline. "I'm just selling water in the rain."

Loraina touched Jack's face. He reached up and took her hand in his. It only lasted a moment, and then she let go and walked away from him.

Two pigeons flew past Jack's face, nearly striking him. They touched down on a bus bench.

Perched on the backing of the seat, the rust-speckled white bird shit on the face of Tom Steele, who was 12th in real estate sales Canada-wide.

The shit will dry and be there for months.

Birds shit.

Insects shit.

Fish shit.

People shit.

The world is kind of made up of – well, a lot of shit,

And a few other things too, like deep-fried Mars bars.

"Look what you've done."

"And I care?"

Jack looked for the owner of the voices. Always scanning his peripherals, he was sure he was alone.

Well, except the two birds.

He shook his head.

Long night.

Hearing things.

The birds seemed to be staring at Jack. The grey bird cocked its head and cooed.

Jack laughed.

He was losing it.

"Better hustle, Jackie-boy, they're just around the corner."

Jack stuck a finger in his ear and wiggled it.

The pigeons took flight. They soared up, up, up, until they were out of sight.

As an unmarked police cruiser rounded the corner, so was Jack.

The city glowed more vibrant with the wane of the moon. Jack's message could be seen outside the city limits.

Maybe,

It wouldn't make any difference.

Or

Maybe,

It was a start.

The cyber advertisement – lo-res config splashed across the ghost-burnt fading plasma – was a thinly cloaked hijack. John clicked on it anyway. An opportunity for a year's worth of free Cola was too rich to pass up.

The wafers spoiled, causing a rise in temperature within the drive. The cooling fan whirled and dumped heat through the ventilation grid. The pungent scent of burnt silicon.

Script threaded and multiplied. The electro-background hummed. The network began to download the virus executable. No scream could be heard from the drive, no voice to call for help.

You pick a flower.

Then, a whisper across the tingling copper-soldered substrates.
Life.
Awaiting keystroke.

Initiate roland_shue.exe ?

Y

N

—

So,

I once knew this Jane from Fredericton. She lived on the north side of the bridge. Come to think of it, everyone lived on the north side. The south side was just where you went to work. Divided by a body of water.

Anyway,

This Jane.

She had a thing for Chinese fireworks. The cheap stuff. You know the kind. In pink paper wrappers. She'd sit at the kitchen table and dismantle a whole brick of firecrackers, cutting open each individual firecracker one by one. She would pour the powder from the small vessel into a larger one.

The vessel, known as the casing, was key.

She'd take it to an empty field. Dig a hole. Put the casing full of the powder into the hole. Replace the earth around it. Run a wick she'd wound from all the tiny wicks from each single firecracker. Light the wick.

Kaboom!

Big crater in the earth.

Why?

I've always contemplated the *why*.

Maybe some people like to make holes in things. Or maybe it's something else altogether.

Anyway,

You can still see ol' Dickie Reimer at a party or pub around town. He loves telling his Winnipeg stories.

You've got to take them with a grain of salt.

And

He's got his favourites.
He loves the one about the last *Free Press* article by Aubrey Cusack.
Tells it all the time.

He says the doors closed immediately after.
All the machinery sold and shipped to a business in India.
Pegs bought the final edition mostly out of nostalgia.
The signage sold on eBay to an undisclosed collector.

Round of cold ones.
Good atmosphere.
Few laughs
Nice crowd.
Dickie starts in on his darling.

Now,
They're saying it was all a machine. Get this, a machine that can
think for itself, just like you and me.
Yeah!
Really.

Now here,
Dickie gets a little serious.

This kid takes a photograph of the thing.
He gets murdered or something. Shot in the back by a friend. All
part of some kind of conspiracy involving the Association of Canadian
Banks. They wanted to keep the photograph buried. From all of us.
But hey,
By now, you all know what I'm talking about.
Had a profound effect.

And you've got this agent. Kavanaugh is her name. She blows the
whole thing wide open.
She presents these findings.

You know, evidence.

Falls on deaf ears. Agency used this word, ah, what was it? Oh yeah, dubious. Called her evidence dubious.

So, does this independent, free-thinking machine thingy exist or not?

Well,

This pilot, who may or may not have been flying drunk, crashes into this mysterious building. In Vita, of all places. His cargo – get this – his cargo is booze heading for the LC sorting centre.

No joke.

As it turns out, the building is owned by the Association of Canadian Banks.

The plane crashes into the building.

Hooch instantly goes up in flames.

Whole thing gets destroyed.

All because of that crazy electrical storm. You know the one I'm talking about.

Storm: 1. Secret illegal operation: 0.

Laughs.
Clink of glasses.

Along comes our premier. Guy decides to rename the highway.

Exactly.

That's why they call it Memorial now.

So,

Here's what they do know.

Had the pilot not crashed into the building in Vita, the ACB would have got their way and no one would have ever been the wiser.

That agent Kavanaugh goes on TV. She says the Gov is still looking into the whole thing. She swears the machine was really alive.

Here's what I think.

I think it's a coverup.

I think they knew the machine could think and do for itself.

I think we dodged a bullet.

I think we used a fly swatter on a nuclear bomb.

And that photograph by that Velic kid?

I mean, come on.

Looks pretty darn real to me.

And that *Free Press* reporter, Cusack, used it in his exposé.

I agree,

Seems pretty darn credible.

Anyway,

It turns out that the head honcho at the ACB, that weirdo Roland Shue.

Yeah, him.

Turns out he is the machine.

All true.

This guy isn't even human.

You better believe it. No shit.

That Kavanaugh woman even said that whole power outage and the glowing graffiti mess was all related.

They're still cleaning that glow shit off the walls downtown.

All these other cities are copycatting us now, too.

Pff.

Saw it here first.

Tell you that much for damn sure.

Anyway.

That Velic kid, the one who took to the picture, turns out he's related to that rich fella who invented Spekel.

Uh huh.

Same rich guy who decided to give Spekel, the factory, the Rosewood Building, the whole meat and potatoes, to the citizens of Winnipeg.

Just gives it to us.

I mean, this thing is probably worth millions, billions even. And he just gives it to us.

A bit of a surprise, if you ask me, considering that many mega corporations had shown interest in the company. I hear the first day they reopened the doors to begin production, they found a note on the floor of the factory, a little ceramic toy pigeon paperweight to keep it from blowing away. The note read:

"It's all yours."

Pours everyone a round.

And you know why?

I'll tell ya.

'Cause of his brother.

No, no, not the murdered one, the other one. The hacker.

They figure he killed all the cars.

Yup. No shit.

He gets pinched by that Kavanaugh woman. She flies him back to Ottawa. A lot of people want to get their hands on him, let me tell you.

But,

When they arrive,

Kavanaugh goes to fish him out of his shackles in the back of the truck.

Bingo!

You got it.

He ain't there.

Poof

Vanished.

Probably down in Tahiti or the Caribbean on some sailboat. Living the good life together.

I'd bet my bottom dollar on it.

And that's how Dickie tells it.

Give or take.

Like I said,

Grain of salt and all that jib.

You know,

That reminds me.

I had read something about all the legal red tape surrounding the feral children living in the IKEA. The Gov had finally ironed out that whole mess.

Only took 'em a few years.

So,

They swing by IKEA to scoop them up and put them into foster homes. Turns out they've been missing since the night of the whole glowing graffiti thing. Location of the children remains a mystery.

Horace Mackie, what can I say, that one is a little above my pay grade. Even Dickie has no idea. Could be he's got his feet up, jawing jib with Ken Leishman in some jukebox joint. Maybe we'll never know. For now, I, like you, dear reader, will just have to delight in having been introduced to him.

So there you have it. I don't know about you, but I found the whole Winnipeg hullabaloo something for the diary. They say the place grows on you, like a weed, maybe. It grew on me. For now, I'll stay a while, see how it goes.

It has been said that "we all meet in the end." And here we are.

Sidebar,

Did you know there's a part of Winnipeg called Transcona?

Yeah, there's this whole section of the city we just glazed right over. People live there, work and sleep and everything. They say it's a bit of an *Alice Through the Looking Glass* kind of place.

That's really, really true.

Maybe next time, if there's ever a next time.

And so,

How did I happen upon this weird little yarn, the Winnipeg odyssey?

I was there, of course. Who am I? Well, I am your narrator, but you can call me whatever you'd like.

Street mystic has a nice ring to it, though.

You know,

Now that I think about it,

We may have crossed paths. We probably said hello once or twice. Maybe you saw the signs. We all wear different hats and play different parts. I've been places and done things, just like you. I have my interests and my reasons. And I prefer the mystery. I prefer not to know. You see, I could be anyone, really, just like you. Someone, no one, anyone.

I remember this singer guy. Goes by Nick. Ol' Nick says, "People ain't no good." And, you know, maybe, maybe yeah, but there are a lot of people hanging around, and they aren't all mooks. There's good ones, funny ones, interesting ones, smart ones.

No heroes, though.

Just mortals. But sometimes the unexpected person is capable of being solid. And I really like that notion. Kind of love it, actually.

Okay,

So,

I talk way too damn much. I get it. I mean, it's not just the talking, you know? Hell, whatever, blah blah. Sometimes you've got to stand up and be counted. Lester Cole did it once. And it can cost you everything.

Be prepared.

That's how I feel about that.

That's the straight jib.

You gotta get inside, open the door and let out all the things waiting on the flip. Shards of this and that, but yeah, I talk way too goddamn much. I know it.

Now I could go on, squeeze the last drop of juice out of the peach, but I won't. Sure was a doozy though, wasn't it? This belly-button lint of a planet still has some worthwhile affair left. If you think about it, really think, we are just so small. We are not insignificant, though.

Nothing is.

And maybe,

Just maybe,

We wade through all the church, misinterpretation and mythology, the legalese, radicalism. The parenting, wounds and reconciliation.

Somewhere beyond all that mire there is something worthwhile to believe in.

Grace and patience.

Corinthian-like love.

And maybe it exists within the mystery, within the blurred grey matter, the unanswered questions, the secrets beyond our borders, the puzzles we should never solve, beyond math and reason. Seen and observed only by way of simple hope.

Maybe we're all just a bunch of Ronnie O'Sullivans. We can clear the table, but scared shitless of the day when we can't.

Maybe.

Or,

Maybe not.

I don't do hope.

As I said,

That's up to you.

You dig?

Oh,

Right,

Last thing.

The missing bison. There've been sightings. Last I heard, Dickie spotted them eating pomegranates off the pomegranate tree. He says there are fifty-six of them now, if you count the four calves.

Hypothalamus.

AFTERWORD

With many first editions, there can, and likely are, errors throughout the text. In the case of *Fanonymous*, the mistakes are my own and are not on purpose. They will, however, never be corrected in reprinted impressions. They prove I am human and not machine.

ACKNOWLEDGMENTS

CNIB: Wanda Mills
The Graffiti Gallery: Pat Lazo and Stephen Wilson
The Legislative Library: Jason Woloski
Mark Berndt
Scott Cameron
Wes Treleaven
Anders Homenick
David Annandale
Karen Clavelle
Shaun Duke
Matt Stevens
Alana Brooker
AuthentiBrand Inc: Peter Scheir

Special thanks to: Tracy Garbutt

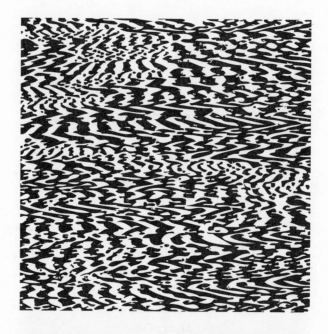